LIVING IN AFRICA

Book III

MARIE PIERCE WEBER

OF THE TRILOGY:

Marooned/Missing in Africa

Surviving in Africa

Living in Africa

iUniverse, Inc.
Bloomington

Living in Africa

This is a work of fiction. All of the characters, names, incidents, organizations, and dialogue in this novel are either the products of the author's imagination or are used fictitiously.

iUniverse books may be ordered through booksellers or by contacting:

iUniverse
1663 Liberty Drive
Bloomington, IN 47403
www.iuniverse.com
1-800-Authors (1-800-288-4677)

Because of the dynamic nature of the Internet, any web addresses or links contained in this book may have changed since publication and may no longer be valid. The views expressed in this work are solely those of the author and do not necessarily reflect the views of the publisher, and the publisher hereby disclaims any responsibility for them.

Any people depicted in stock imagery provided by Thinkstock are models, and such images are being used for illustrative purposes only.
Certain stock imagery © Thinkstock.

ISBN: 978-1-4620-8444-9 (sc)
ISBN: 978-1-4620-8445-6 (hc)
ISBN: 978-1-4620-8446-3 (ebk)

Library of Congress Control Number: 2011962929

Printed in the United States of America

iUniverse rev. date: 01/05/2012

*To my husband, Jack, who supports me
unfailingly in my endeavors.*

*To Carolyn Weber Lewis, Ph.D., who gave
most generously of her time and editing expertise.*

*To the computer gurus who found my lost manuscripts.
Without them, you wouldn't be reading this story.*

For My Horse Friends

"That is a good book which is opened with expectation and closed with delight and profit."

A. B. Alcott

Contents

Prologue

A sea of rainbow colored flowers covered the treetops below – the rarely seen grandeur of the rainforest. From the arid plains to the tall grasses of the savannas with their island clumps of woodlands – past vast stretches of sucking bogs to the snow-capped mountains with secluded valleys of dense vegetation – the helicopter revealed the beauty and fascination that is Africa.

The story of my journey will astonish the Zuri Watu, Thomas thought, for I have traveled almost forty thousand miles on three continents in the last moon … before that, if I wanted to go anywhere, I walked.

The sweeping vistas passing below flaunted one spectacular sight after another, providing a bird's eye view of the wildlife fleeing from the concussive thumps of the ominous black shadow. The view was unlimited, with visibility clear to the horizon, and it held Thomas spellbound; until, glancing at Paula, he noticed she looked tired.

Our month-long travels and the busy days with the kimmea plants have taken a toll on her reserves. Her only diversion was riding Sunshine, the palomino mare my mother gave her as a wedding gift … as Windy, my foundling Afghan hound puppy, was my respite. Paula and I are both addicted to our work … but we will have a good rest in the lands of the Zuri Watu.

Manutu and Sashono will be pleased that I have a bride, and yet disappointed, for they will now see that I will never follow in their footsteps, either as medicine chief after Manutu or as tribal chief after Sashono. Nanoka would be delighted with Paula, were she alive … although, if Nanoka was alive, she would not have sent me to find my birth family. Only by leaving the Zuri Watu did Paula come into my life.

He remembered his first glimpse of Paula as she came into the forest clearing – traveling through the trees as easily as he walked on the ground. *Her agility amazed me, as did her reckless abandon when she crawled under the toxic kamikiza plant. Totally fascinated and incredibly curious, I hid in the dense foliage high in an oak tree – intending to follow this unusual woman to see what else she might do.*

I had no way of knowing that a tsunami had storm-tossed her and the Expedition yacht into a vast volcanic tidal pool – separating her from her scientific group. Or that, days later, natives abducted her to be a trophy wife for their Chief; or that, when I first saw her coming through the trees, she was fleeing from her captors.

I wondered then if all white women could travel through the trees so easily. Watching her fascinated me from the first moment I saw her, and shadowing her delighted me. When the forest thinned, she came to ground, and wandered into an area of lion dens. The females soon picked up her scent, stalked her and trapped her, making it necessary for me to show myself to save her – and nothing in my life has been the same since.

Thomas thought of all the subtle changes in his life since saving Paula, each change seemingly insignificant in itself, until nothing of his former life remained. *I have come to a hard place. Now I must choose, or have I already chosen – and do not yet see the path?*

I was ten years old when our plane crashed in the jungle river, and the only one to survive. Roving scouts of the Zuri Watu found me and carried me back to their village where Nanoka, wife of Chief Sashono, cared for me through a long illness. They called me Tamubu, for they felt I was a sweet gift from God; and having no children of their own, they raised me as their son.

Manutu, the Medicine Chief of the Zuri Watu, took me for an acolyte when I was twelve. I loved the years of learning with him, and the long days spent doing unusual things.

Windy, a four month old Afghan hound puppy put his head in Thomas's lap – looking for a bit of reassurance. Thomas stroked the dog to comfort him in the noisy, often tilting chopper – wondering if dogs get air sick.

Petting the puppy, Thomas marveled at the incredible events of the last moon: his wedding to Paula in the States, his honeymoon cruise in Hawaii and circumnavigating the earth; the family reunion in England, and seeing his twin sisters again, no longer the little five-year-old girls of his memories. They were now lovely young women graduating from The Croft School.

Paula and I repeated our wedding vows in the school chapel, and Aunt Marga'ret and Uncle James hosted a wedding and graduation reception combined at Woleston Hall. Seeking a bit of quiet from all the to-do, I took a walk in the woods, where I found Windy, abandoned at three months old, with broken toes and a torn ear.

Our travels delighted Paula as did all the gay and lively social events; she was happy through it all. It pleased me to see her so happy ... that's it! If Paula is happy, I will be happy too. His sudden insight diminished the anxiety Thomas felt at taking Paula to visit to the primitive Zuri Watu – the natives with whom he lived for fourteen years, since he was ten.

Buoyed, his thoughts became optimistic: if growing the kimmea is a success, I will be able to set up first-aid clinics in the bush all over Kenya ... but I'm getting ahead of myself, which is not like me ... but then he remembered the anticipation of his youth for the events of tomorrow; and smiled at his return to the boyish habit he thought he had put aside.

I must take life one day at a time, for that is the only way life can be well-lived.

Family Tree of Peter Thomas Caulfield – a.k.a. Tamubu
Anno Domini 1960

Elizabeth Anne Hudson – m. 1882 – Lord William Edward Clark
b. 1860 |————————————————| b.1855

Dame Edith Anne Clarke   Dame Rebecca Alice Clarke (Lived at Woleston Hall)
b. 1884 | b. 1887 |
   m. 1906   m. 1910

Edward LeClaire Woleston ~ Sir Phillip John LeClaire Woleston   Alfred William Cecil (2nd son)
| b. 1884   b. 1880 | b. 1880 |
Daughter, Elspeth   No Issue
m.
|
No Issue

Lord Edward George Greystone ~ John LeClaire Woleston ~ Marga'ret Clarke Woleston ~ Mary Edith Sommes Woleston
b.1910 ~ d.1943   b.1915 ~ m. 1936   b. 1913

m. 1936   James George Sotheby ~ b. 1910

James ~ George ~ Alice ~ Edith
b. 1939 ~ b. 1941 ~ b.1942 ~ b.1944

Jane Elizabeth Nelson
b.1913 |————————————|

Emily Jane b. 1937 ~ John LeClaire,Jr. b 1939 ~ Elizabeth Anne b.1941

Sir Peter Thomas Caulfield, Capt. R.A.F.
B. 1911 |
   m. 1934

Peter Thomas Caulfield, II ~ Jonathan Edward Caulfield ~ Hanna & Sara (twins)
b. 1937   b. 1939   b. 1942

1 ~ Jon

Jon watched the Boeing 707 accelerate down the runway. The thrill of watching a 707 take-off never diminished for him. From full throttle to wheels off the ground took less than 40 seconds, depending on air temperature and load; but the 45 degree ascent was always spectacular. Jon liked to imagine the incredulity of the Wright Brothers, had they been standing next to him, watching the plane take-off too; the idea made the experience even more thrilling. When the 707 was out of sight, Jon sighed and went to find Captain Jones.

Well, Thomas and Paula are off to Hawaii. I wish I could have gone with them, but if ever there was a fifth wheel – it's a brother on your honeymoon. I will have to console myself with the interesting day Captain Jones has planned for us: sculling races on the Schuylkill River; a visit to the Philadelphia Art Museum; lunch, and a walking tour of Colonial Philadelphia; then dinner with Jonas and his mother at Bookbinders on 15th Street to celebrate her seventieth birthday, after which, we have seats at the Orchestra for Peter Nero and the Philly Pops.

What a surprise it was that Captain Jones and Jonas, his ship's cook, planned their annual visit from Africa to coincide with Paula's and Thomas's wedding. Jonas's mother conveniently lives in Philadelphia, but Captain Jones's brother lives in St. Augustine, Florida … so Philly's not exactly on the good Captain's way.

Now, where did he go? I know I left him right here.

I can still see Paula's astonishment when she saw Captain Jones and Jonas waiting near the finish line at the Fair Hill Competitive Trail Ride. Paula's sister, Sallee Ann, had made the local arrangements for them, keeping their arrival a secret for a surprise … and what a thrill it was! Thomas, who is deadpan most of the time, looked so very incredulous – his mouth was gaping when he saw Captain Jones and Jonas walking across the field at Fair Hill. It was a jolly good show all 'round!

Fourteen years ago, everyone thought Thomas was dead after his plane disappeared, and massive searches turned up nothing. My heart and my instincts told me differently. Thomas is a survivor; he has a sixth sense that seems to protect him, no matter what happens.

In my certainty, I joined up with Max Mason's trading safari to go deep into the wilderness to search for Thomas amongst the remote tribes in the area surrounding the Benue River in Nigeria. Massive flooding had carried a wing of the lost plane down river, sparking another search four years after Thomas had gone missing. They found the fuselage of the plane smashed into a tree trunk fallen across the river ... with its grisly contents ... but no sign of Thomas.

If I could find both Thomas and Paula in the African wilderness, I should be able to find Captain Jones in this airport! Where did he go? I know I left him right here ... standing next to this lounge!

If we don't get off soon, there will be no sense in going at all, for we will be back here again late this evening: me to go to London on the Red-Eye, and Captain Jones to leave for St. Augustine in the morning.

Captain Jones – where the deuce is he – is great company if you can find him! He's been a jolly good friend to all of us, the best ever. He rescued us twice in Africa, putting his luxury yacht and crew at our disposal for nothing more than wanting to help people in a tight spot. He must have deep feelings for Paula coming to the States for her wedding – but so do we all.

After Paula resigned from the Expedition, she went on a cruise up-river with Captain Jones and Anna Chumley to deliver missionaries to study with Dr. Albert Schweitzer at Lambaréné.

Captain Jones also picked Paula for his watch mate on our escape cruise south to Angola. I wonder if he confided in her during those long night watches. I, myself, found Paula to be a font of practical wisdom in our confidential little chats. However, Captain Jones's reason for doing the things that he does remains an enigma to me. The man is truly a puzzle.

"Aha! There you are, Captain. I'm looking forward to the great day you've planned for us."

"Well, we'd better be about it, laddie ... or we'll no see the races."

2 ~ Jon & Anna Louise

Mid-afternoon is a good time to arrive at Heathrow Airport. London traffic is horrendous most of the time, but eases a bit after mid-day. Rumpled, hungry and stiff, Jon scanned the waiting crowds, looking for Anna Louise.

He heard a *toodle-oo*, and turned to see Anna and her mother waving at him. He smiled happily, and made his way out of the crush leaving passport control.

"How was your flight, Jon?" Anna Louise asked.

"Good! I slept most of the way. We had a good breakfast, but just a light snack for lunch; I'm starved for some greasy old fish & chips!"

"We pass a nice tea shop on the motorway. Can you wait an hour?" Julia asked.

"Of course," Jon replied. "Now that I'm here, I have nothing but time, so don't let me interfere with your plans or schedules."

"We are starting final exams at school," Julia said. "Today is *turn in notebooks day*. Tomorrow, we administer the first exams, so I will be gone all day. You will have to make-do with Anna Lou for company."

"I think I can deal with that, if I brace myself," Jon retorted.

"You two are a disgrace!" Anna said, amid the cheerful chuckles.

"I'd like to have a go at Woleston Hall tomorrow – you know – report in to the family, and borrow a car for the duration," Jon said. "Should I hire a ride?"

"Not necessary," Julia replied. "Anna can take me to school in the morning, and use my car for the day. I'll catch a ride home with Georgina; I'm not far off for her."

"What time do we need to be off in the morning?" Jon asked.

"Anna Lou will take me; you may want to sleep-in from jet lag."

"It will be better if Jon goes with us, Mother. Then I won't have to double back to pick him up."

"What time should we get cracking?" Jon asked warily.

"We should be off at 6:30 a.m. – I hope that's not too early."

Jon groaned inwardly. He would have to be up at 5:30 a.m. to be off in good time. "I'm not putting you out, am I?" he asked hopefully.

"Not at all – unfortunately, Harold goes southeast to Newbury and doesn't leave until 8:00 a.m., so he's of no help to us. However, it's just for tomorrow. Do you have anything else on the schedule – besides going to Woleston Hall?" Julia asked.

"No. I have been on schedules for weeks now; I could use a spot of not-much-to-do, or just doing whatever comes along – unless Anna Louise has something in mind."

"I hoped we could travel around the countryside a bit. There are many places I have only heard about, and would like to see. I thought we might also go up to Oxford after we left Lyford," Anna replied.

"Oh! Here we are! I was thinking about your sight-seeing schedule, and almost missed the tea shop; a bite now should keep us to dinner."

Early the following morning, Julia stopped her Mini-Cooper in front of a lovely Georgian manor, formerly the Bedercroft Estate, and now The Croft School. The pleasingly proportioned brick building had lead mullioned casement windows and granite trimmed windows and doors. Unlike most English manor houses, neatly trimmed boxwood hedges lined the front below the windows. Set back on each side was a long single storey addition sporting a crenellated roof of granite notches filled with decorative concrete planters of trimmed boxwoods. Above the three storey façade of the main building were three dormer peaks, leading to a ridgeline dotted with groups of chimney pots. The dormers were sided in decorative cut slate to accentuate the slate roof. The ambiance was one of elegant simplicity.

"What a grand and charming structure," Jon said, as he walked around to take up driving the Mini-Cooper. "I can see why the school has a waiting list – if the interior and the curriculum are as pleasing as the façade."

Julia never tired of hearing praise about anything concerning The Croft School, which had achieved international accreditation under her auspices.

"Thank you, Jon. We are very proud of the women who graduate from The Croft School. Most of them excel in other fields as well as the home and hearth. Our graduates have excellent minds and do not limit themselves, but apply their abilities in many areas. After examinations, I'd be glad to give you a tour, if you like."

"Yes, indeed, I'd like that very much!"

"Well, run along now and have a nice day – dinner is at seven-thirty."

Jon squeezed behind the wheel of the Mini-Cooper, turned to Anna Louise, and said in his best chauffeur's voice, "Where to Miss?"

"Woleston Hall, Jeeves," Anna replied, with grand dame hauteur. Jon then bounced the car around the circular courtyard to the tree-lined drive, provoking gales of laughter from Anna, as he also ground the gears with his poor clutch work.

"It's good you intend to borrow a car from your uncle today," Anna laughed. "After that departure, I don't think Mother will ever let you borrow her car again."

"I'm sitting too close! My knee hits the wheel and I can't engage the clutch!" Jon said, frustrated as well as embarrassed. Side-splitting gaiety followed when Jon tried to adjust the seat, which slid so far back, that now, he could not disengage the clutch. It seemed the seat was either all the way forward, or all the way backward, with no stops in between. When they finally controlled their gales of laughter, Anna Louise offered to drive the Mini-Cooper.

Jon asked, "Do you know how to get to Woleston Hall?"

"No, but I'm sure you will tell me. Just, do not tell me how to drive! If you do, I will stop driving and let you bruise up your knees." While Jon chuckled at her warning, he also felt surprised: I think I'm going to see a different Anna Louise here in England, not the shy and timid creature I met in Africa. It's quite possible I will like this Anna Lou even better.

When Anna turned into Clarke Lane, Aunt Marga'ret and Uncle James came trotting across the lower field on a morning ride. Anna

Louise stopped the car, and Jon rolled down his window, saying, "Hi, I'm afraid we're a bit early. Are you coming or going?"

"We're coming back. We only picked up the trot when we saw the car come into our lane. Go on up to the house. We will be up directly. Ask Victoria to serve coffee and tea in the library, will you?"

"Righto," Jon replied, and Anna drove on to the Hall.

Jon asked, "Anna, do you ride?"

"Yes. Mother insists that all the students of The Croft School be accomplished equestriennes. I have known her to sift out applicants by those that have never ridden, and those that have no interest in learning to ride. For Mother, riding is de rigueur."

"Do you like to ride?"

"Smart you! For me, riding is like driving a car. I do it, and do it well, but it is not something I seek out to do – how about you?"

"Likewise, we had a pony cart when Thomas and I were boys. I liked driving better than riding. We had great fun dashing all over the farm in our pony cart. Mother prefers Haflingers for driving, rather than the big draft breeds. They are quite strong and agile, much easier to tack up, and, I dare say, easier on the feed bag."

"I remember seeing a palomino pony, a stocky horse at Dela-Aden, was that the Haflinger?"

"Yup, but not the one we had as boys."

"I felt drawn to him. He seemed to like me."

"Finn prefers women and children. He only tolerates men."

"That's odd. Why is that?"

"Finn came to Mother as a rogue, and untrainable. After Mother had finished his training, the owner came back for him. Finn attacked the man with teeth and hooves, and meant him serious harm. Mother had never seen anything like it. She offered to buy Finn on the spot – and did. Finn has behaved well in our barn. He is obedient for father and me, although aloof. With mother, he is like a big puppy."

"I never knew horses could have that kind of discernment."

"Haflingers do, and they are as loyal as a dog. They are even courageous."

"Whatever do you mean?"

"In World War II, there are recorded instances of Haflingers saving injured soldiers, or bringing stranded women and children to safety."

"Is that really true?"

"'Tis indeed, if you don't believe me, ask my mother."

"Here come your aunt and uncle, and we haven't even knocked on the door yet!"

Uncle James came up, opened the driver's door and asked, "Need me to fetch a crowbar?"

Chuckling at his uncle's wit, Jon got out and came around the car while Uncle James handed Anna Louise onto the drive.

"We were talking about Haflingers, and the time just passed in a flash. Did you have a good ride?" Jon asked.

"Great day for a ride, not too cool, not too humid – hated to come back, but I have clients waiting for their house plans," James replied.

"Uncle James, Aunt Marga'ret, let me present to you Miss Anna Louise Holmesby from Swindon. Anna, this is my mother's sister and her husband: Marga'ret and James Sotheby. Anna Louise visited Dela-Aden when she and her parents were in Africa on tour this past winter."

"We are delighted to meet you, dear. Mary Edith wrote to me about your visit to Dela-Aden. Please come in, I'm dying for a cup of tea."

"Marga'ret, while you are waiting for the tea, I'll take Jon down to the garages and get him a vehicle to use while he's here."

"Don't be too long, James, I know how you like to show off your cars," Marga'ret called as they walked away.

"Come, Dear, who knows when they will be back. You can come upstairs with me while I change, or, you can look about the place, if you prefer. Jon already knows every nook and cranny. My sister told me you went to The Croft School with the twins, Hanna and Sara. Were you ahead of them?"

"No, we're in the same forme." Seeing the quizzical look on Marga'ret's face, Anna continued. "Mother is the Principal of The Croft School. She took a sabbatical for our trip to Africa, so I sat my examinations in January. I was one of five day-girls who did not board at the school, which worked well for me. I was still in on all the fun, but not looked on as a possible snitch."

"Did you enjoy Africa?"

"Yes and no. It was so beautiful, especially at Dela-Aden, but it was also wild and dangerous. Seeing the bars on the windows and doors at Dela-Aden, and glass shards atop the walls surrounding the hotel, with the armed guards patrolling the grounds, frightened me."

"The precautions at Dela-Aden are left over from the Mau-Mau uprising. In Nairobi, there are a great many displaced natives, who would be better off back in the bush, where there is a natural dignity in their ancestral way of life. In the city, there are not enough jobs, so there is nothing there but degradation for them.

"Most of the older generation cannot read or write, and are unsuited to any work except as laborers, and the men are apathetic workers. It is these gangs of displaced people that make the armed guards necessary. If you think of these natives as they once were, warriors, hunters and gatherers and goat herders, with the Masai being cattle herdsmen, you will see that their natural, self-sufficient dignity is lost to them in the city. Now, they are no longer welcome in the villages, for others have taken their places. Native populations have increased, diminishing the land for each family, and natural game is either scarce or protected.

"The government needs to find a solution; education being one, but until the generation of the educated grows up into the working place, the uneducated and unemployed will remain a problem."

"It makes a bit more sense to me now, after your explanation. I wish I had understood those things in January," Anna said.

"I'm afraid, though, there is another, and worse, underlying reason. The Englishman in Africa looks on the native as an inferior human being. My sister and her husband have shown us that they are not inferior, they are just different. The way they think and reason is a product of thousands of years of survival in tribal Africa, where superstition affects everything, even to what hand they use to eat certain foods. We can see the faults of such reasoning, but they do not.

"Even more unfortunate are the attitudes of the natives who adapt themselves to the white man's ways; for they scorn their unenlightened brothers, and treat them much worse than ever a white man did.

"However, Peter and Mary have made great strides in improving the lot of the native in their small world, and some of their neighbors have also adopted the same progressive ways. In time, they hope their examples will improve the lot of all the natives, eventually producing a healthy and prosperous Kenya."

"Isn't it a no-win situation; if the black man that learns, treats badly the black man who has not?" Anna asked.

"Are you ladies going to join us before the tea gets cold?" James called up.

"We're coming," Marga'ret called back.

"We ought to go down," Anna said. "Thank you for giving me the benefit of your opinions. You've helped me a great deal."

"You are very perceptive, my dear. Talk to Jon – he understands the native like no one else I know. He studied all the tribes of Africa while in college, hiring his own tutors to learn to speak the languages. He is most exceptional."

★   ★   ★

"What were you and Aunt Marga'ret talking about this morning?"

"Mostly about Africa … "

"How did you get on that subject?"

"She asked me how I liked touring Africa. I told her I loved Dela-Aden, but the rest of it frightened me. She told me her views on the native's predicament and told me to discuss her opinions with you. However, that will have to wait. Right now, I want to talk about you."

"Me? Why do you want to talk about me?"

"Because, Jon, I'm at a point where I can still go either way … and I want to know the best way to go, for both of us."

"That sounds serious."

"Yes, it is serious. Are you up to serious?"

"How about we climb that hill over there, and discuss serious from the top?"

"Yes, let's do!" Anna cried, leaping out of the car, parked at an overlook, and bolting for the path up the hill. Thirty minutes later, huffing and puffing, they sat with their backs against a boulder, and saw below them a vast green valley dotted with villages along the banks of a stream, which meandered under little humpback bridges. Fields of all shapes and colors, like a patchwork quilt, were bordered by rock walls, hedges, tree lines or stands of woods. The panoramic beauty of the landscape, from such a high view, captivated them, and thrilled by the bucolic vistas they sat in awed silence.

After long minutes, Jon asked, "Now what is it that you want to talk to me about?" He reached over and gently took Anna's hand in his.

"Your future, Jon; what are your plans?"

"Shall I be completely honest?"

"But, of course."

"I don't have any plans ... other than getting to know you better, and having you get to know me. We have ten days before Hanna and Sara graduate. I want to spend every one of them with you, doing everything and anything you like. I have strong feelings for you, Anna ... and I think you like me too, but you are worried about getting involved with me only to find you would have to live in Africa."

"Yes, that's it – although your aunt did give me a new outlook on Africa; one that I will reconcile with you later, but first, I need to know how you will earn your living?"

"Do you always beat about the bush this way?"

Anna laughed happily and replied, "Always, I find it hard to be direct!"

"I have prospects only. Thomas and Paula have asked me to be the Chairman of the Board of a new corporation they are forming to build first aid clinics in Africa, but I told you that in Nairobi. Until they know the viability of the kimmea – that it will grow in hot houses – and that the hot-house plants will contain the pharmacologically-active principle – I won't know if there will even be a corporation. That decision is a few months down the road, late fall, I expect."

Jon saw the confused look on Anna's face. "Problem?" he asked.

"I heard what you said ... and it sounded like English ... but I have no idea what you were talking about!"

Jon laughed. "Paula said that to me – I have no idea what it means either!"

They laughed until they cried, with Anna saying, "How did you even remember her words?"

"It's a fault of mine … I can parrot anyone, no matter what they say!"

They laughed again until, from improper breathing, Anna began to hiccup … then, with great determination to speak normally, she returned to her agenda.

"If the corporation goes through, where will you live?" she asked.

"I suppose in Africa, at least most of the time."

"Where in Africa, exactly?"

"My parents have asked me to live at Dela-Aden, if possible. They too, will be on the Board of Directors of the new corporation. It's been suggested that I build a separate domicile on the farm … if I marry."

"Where will Paula and Thomas live?"

"At Dela-Aden; they both love it there. Mother gave Paula a palomino mare for a wedding present. However, they are not making any firm plans until the results are in on the kimmea plants. They might build, or stay in the manor house – there's certainly plenty of room."

"You don't know how pleased I am by your answers. With Paula at Dela-Aden, I would not yearn for the company of my peers. In attending a ladies academy and finishing school, you get accustomed to associating with intelligent women who share and appreciate your interests in life."

"I don't think you and Paula have much in common, other than being women."

"Silly boy, she is intelligent, educated, and only a few years older than me, that is the bond. Without someone who is able to share my ideas and feelings, living in Africa would be like going on a diet of bread and water."

"I've been called many things … but never a diet of bread and water!"

Anna laughed. "You would be my feast. However, you are a man and men never fully understand the needs of a woman, or even how a woman thinks; so lack of female companionship would be my famine."

"What about mother?"

"What about her? She is not my peer. She could be a good friend, but age separates our drives, desires and perspectives. I have another question: What if the kimmea is not viable when grown in a hothouse. What will you do then?"

"I'm not sure. I spent my college years learning African languages, so I could go and find Thomas. Now that Thomas is found, I don't have much of a use for speaking a hundred dialects, unless it is to deal with the locals when setting up first aid clinics."

"How would you support yourself?"

"Father wants me to help him with the farm. I would like that. I have been helping father since I was a boy — after Thomas was lost. It was what I intended to do all along, and will still do even if I am Chairman of the Corporation. Do you see yourself happy at Dela–Aden?"

"Yes, except for the issue we previously discussed," Anna replied.

"I broached that subject with Paula. I was surprised to find that she, too, plans to leave Africa to birth her children in America. Her decision stunned Thomas, but she was adamant on the subject. It's a bit different for us. Our children, if born in Kenya, would be British citizens because we both are British. For Paula's children to obtain British citizenship, she would have to give up her American citizenship, or have her children born in England, neither of which is she willing to do. Thomas and I have accepted that our children will not be born in Africa … unless we marry natives." Anna poked Jon in the arm at his facetious comment.

"Ouch! Am I to expect a pummeling every time I state my opinions?"

"Yes, if you are flippant with me."

"Who is to decide my respectfulness?"

"Yours truly, of course!"

Jon turned to Anna. "I'd like to seal that pact with a kiss; may I?"

Anna's heart thumped; a tingly feeling rose and fluttered. "Yes."

Smiling with his eyes, Jon took Anna's chin softly in his right hand. He put his left hand on her shoulder and with fingertip pressure moved her towards him. He kissed her tenderly and chastely. She moved her left hand up to put her fingertips on his right hand, and moved into his embrace. The kiss deepened and lingered until Anna needed air, and reluctantly withdrew.

"I think we will have to make a great many pacts," Jon whispered.

"Shall we make a pact on our pact?" Anna asked.

"Indubitably!" Jon replied.

★   ★   ★

"Well, what did you do, and where did you go today?" Julia asked when Jon and Anna Louise came in the front door, laughing. "You have apparently had a good time."

"Oh Mother, I didn't know there was so much beauty in England. We climbed Walberry Hill today and had a grand view of the valley. We had fish and chips at an old pub with a lintel so low, we had to duck to get through the door. We just drove and drove, stopping at every overlook."

Harold came into the parlor door, exclaiming, "I say, whose Aston Martin is out front?"

"It is my uncle's car, Sir; he collects them. It is the least of his treasures, so he let me borrow it while I'm in town," Jon answered.

"I hope the neighbors don't get the wrong idea! If that car is out front for ten days, they'll want me to up my subscription at chapel."

"Shall I park it down the lane?" Jon asked.

"That's a good idea. You could ask Pete Fields if you can park it in his garage lot. Be safer there anyway!"

"Now – or tomorrow, sir?"

"He's shut up now. Tomorrow will have to do. I don't think one night will damage our local image too much."

Over dessert Harold asked, "Jon do you play bridge?"

"Yes, Sir, bridge, dominoes, chess, checkers and Scrabble. We often play games at home in the evenings."

"How about you, Anna, feel like a rubber of bridge?"

"Yes, I do. Do you want to draw for partners?"

"No, I will partner with your mother. I only play round-robins at the club."

"What bridge method do you prefer, sir?"

"I used to play Elwell, but I moved on to Goren a few years ago. How about you; does Goren suit you?"

"Most certainly, sir."

★   ★   ★

Saturday afternoon, Julia took Jon on a tour of The Croft School. "We have an exceptional program here. We accept only the best applicants after aptitude tests, I.Q. tests and a personality profile, for the regimen is challenging. We are looking for versatility and adaptability as well as intelligence and common sense in our students. We accept girls at age fourteen or fifteen. Our program is a six year program combining advanced high school and junior college, and all our programs include finishing school techniques. Our studies and texts are adapted for our program. We are fully certified, and The Croft School is a leader in high test scores, by age, and is the leader for private academies. The Croft School is multinational, with preference given to British students who qualify.

The original endowment came from the Bedercroft estate, which began the school. Over time the school has received other endowments as well. Still, tuition is high, for we engage only the best teachers, who must have personally high ethics to meet our standards. We are not stuffy here – we are diversified and socially correct. Our aim is to turn out girls who will have the confidence and knowledge to go anywhere, and do anything – with anyone – from natives in Africa to the Queen of England, to an Arabian emir."

"Did Anna Louise have to take all the tests too?"

"Yes, she did, and I'm pleased to say, I did not have to show her preference."

"How many girls do you have a term?"

"Our capacity is one hundred and twenty students – twenty for each year, but one year I took in twenty extra new students. We do experience some beginner drop-outs, but that year, no one dropped out! However, with creativity and diligence, we did manage."

"Where do you house so many students?"

"There is a newer building at the rear of the manor house, across the courtyard arcade. There are three floors of dormitories above the gymnasium, housing forty students per floor, Each student has a room

14

and bath, not dissimilar to a cruise ship, but with a twin size bed, dresser, desk and chair, lounge chair and ottoman with reading lamp, bookcase, large closet, a small refrigerator, a snack cabinet, an electric tea pot and a shower bath. Each floor has a laundry room, sewing room and a community room with ping-pong tables and card tables for the bridge or hearts players, with game/project tables and a movie screen. It is a comfortable and enjoyable life. We treat all the students like responsible adults. We do not have a discipline problem, for that is grounds for immediate expulsion, and this has been done only twice."

"Only twice ... in twenty years ... how is that?"

"The only *down* time is when the girls are asleep. The rest of the time, they are so busy with classes, sports, studies, projects or games, that they don't have the time to make trouble. The two expulsions, I'm sorry to say, were for *sticky* fingers.

"The girls wear uniforms, skirts, blouses, jackets and knee socks, for classes. They wear Bermuda shorts for recreation or dress suitable to each sport. We have an indoor complex with two tennis courts, two badminton courts and four shuffleboard lanes, all surrounded by an indoor track with a banked skating ring; we also have four indoor bowling lanes and an Olympic size swimming pool in the gymnasium basement. We use the grass courtyard for croquet, horseshoes and bocci bowling. Horseback riding and lessons in horsemanship are at the barn, or on our trails. There are also two outdoor tennis courts and a track for running sports or competitions."

"I'm suitably impressed. You have more facilities than Oxford!"

"Not really, just different ones."

"Do the girls ever bring their own horses?"

"Only those in the British Isles are allowed to bring their own horses. We keep a full stable of twelve horses, but can accommodate twenty four horses."

"What do you do with the horses in the summer?"

"They are turned-out, and brought in each morning when they are grained, groomed – or have their hooves trimmed. One of our former students runs a riding camp here in August, which conditions our horses for the fall term. She has use of the facilities – in return for looking after the horses in June and July."

"I can see why you have a waiting list a mile long. Makes me wish I were a girl!"

15

Julia laughed. "It is the best and most rounded education available today."

"Do the teachers commute?"

"No – only a few. We have two lovely apartments on each dormitory floor for the teachers who wish to live-in. They act as floor proctors as well. We prefer couples who work at the school, either as teachers or sports coaches or in the office. In the summer they supervise repairs, redecorating, improvements, and the garden staff. They also keep the library and supplies up-to-date. We have a long waiting list for teaching staff too."

"I'm simply stunned … this school makes Oxford look positively antediluvian."

Julia smiled. "That was my intention!"

★   ★   ★

Alice and Edith with their cousins Hanna and Sara arrived at Woleston Hall with Marga'ret in time for lunch on Saturday. Jamie and George came down from Oxford at teatime. Jon and Anna Louise, Harold and Julia came for cocktails at seven, making a party of twelve for dinner with round robin bridge afterwards. The Holmesbys were to stay the night and join the picnic ride to the castle ruins on Sunday after chapel.

Jon began going through his voluminous mail on Saturday morning and finished up on Sunday, after the picnic. Harold, not a horseback rider, walked in the gardens and spent some time with George, viewing his father's auto collection. After tea, James took Harold for a countryside ride in the Aston-Martin DB3, the same model of sports car used in the James Bond movies, without all the armored hardware, of course.

"Julia, what does all this mean to you?"

"What does what mean, dear?"

"You know – all this mixing in with Jon's family?"

"I'd say they are preparing for any eventuality with good grace."

"Yes, they have been pleasant; I've enjoyed being with them – how about you?"

16

"Silly man, need you ask? I enjoy associating with people who are above the one-ups-man-ship level. They concentrate on being pleasant. They know not everyone has money or a title, so they judge others on merit. In that aspect, we hold our own, so they are behaving quite well. I know Anna Lou is in love with Jon. If I have to let my only child go to Africa for most of the year, I'm glad it will be with Jon Caulfield."

"Yes, of course. He's a fine lad," Harold replied.

"Did Anna Lou ask you about going to Africa this summer?"

"Yes, she did. I think it is a good idea. She should make sure that living in Africa nine or ten months of the year will agree with her. Did she tell you she wanted to go after graduation and the wedding reception for Thomas and Paula?"

"Yes, she asked me if she could start packing," Julia replied. "I don't know what I'm going to do with myself all summer with her gone."

"I'll tell you what you are going to be doing!"

"Whatever do you mean, Harold?"

"When not touring Europe, you're going to be riding every day! I heard Marga'ret ask you to bring your horse to Woleston Hall for the summer."

"Yes, wasn't that nice of her?"

"It's just as well. The Horticultural Society has asked me to head up a research grant at Inkpen this summer. They want to know why it is the lilies there have been blooming since the Knights Templar brought them to Inkpen from Asia. They wonder if Le Nôtre did something special when he planned and planted the rectory gardens. It's quite unusual to have flowers growing and blooming continuously for hundreds of years."

"Oh, Harold, how wonderful for you – when did they ask you?"

"A month or so ago, but I had to make sure I would have my current project completed before I could accept."

"Did you tell Anna Lou?"

"Yes, she was just as pleased as you are. It was nice to be asked."

"Never a door closes, that a window doesn't open … "

"What did you say, dear?"

"I said, 'It's a feather in your cap', love."

3 ~ Hanna & Sara

The hall bell rang. Exams were over. Hanna felt depleted, yet free. The senior's finals were difficult; the rumors had not been an exaggeration. A few days of relaxation at Woleston Hall would put her straight. She waited for Sara, surprised that no one had come barging out of the exam room door yet. She crossed the hall, glanced in, and saw that everyone still had their heads down over papers. I wonder why?

Mrs. Holmesby came out of her classroom carrying a sheaf of exam books. Hanna asked, "Mrs. Holmesby, why are they still sitting the examination?"

"Hanna, dear, they were given the wrong exam books, and were half an hour late starting. Why don't you go to the cafeteria and wait for Sara there? They are serving ice cream sodas today. Sara will be along in a bit."

"Thank you, Mrs. Holmesby. I'll do that."

Sara came rushing into the cafeteria, straight towards Hanna, saying, "Did you hear what happened?"

"Yes, Mrs. Holmesby told me. You were given the wrong exams."

"Yes and no; they were the right exams … but some of them had the answers on them."

"What! Who filled them in?"

"I don't know, but it was Hillary Enright with her whiny voice that said, 'Mrs. Raft, one of these answers is wrong. What should I do?"

"Erase it dear."

"But it is written in ink and I can't erase it."

"What! Bring your exam here please!" Hillary walked up the aisle looking so smug.

"Oh, my goodness!" Mrs. Raft exclaimed. "Girls, pencils down!"

"We had to sit there for twenty minutes in total silence while they made copies of a master exam for us. You know the rules, no reading or talking in the exam rooms, ever. I was too keyed up to take a nap, so I just sat there, bored out of my mind!"

"Why didn't you speak up?"

"My test didn't have any answers on it … at least I hadn't gotten that far."

"I'm glad for that; but if prissy missy Enright had not spoken up, you all might have been failed, or had to sit a new exam later."

"I didn't think of that."

"You never do, Sara, how often do I have to remind you to think!"

"I know you like school, Hanna, but I can't wait to get out of here … for good!"

"Someday, Sara, you may look back and say to yourself: 'I didn't know just how good I had it in my school days'!"

"Right! I'd have to be looking at a jail sentence to think that."

"Well, don't give up just yet, you still have time!"

"Time for what?"

"Time to get a jail sentence!"

"Just because you are twenty seven minutes older than I, does not give you the right to bully me."

"You are my best friend, Sara, but you are wound much too tight. You think with your emotions, not your head. If you don't change your ways, your unruly emotions will get you into trouble, and a jail sentence is not at all out of the realm of possibility."

"You make me sound like a juvenile delinquent, when all I want to do is have some fun; rules are so tiresome."

"Rules keep us out of trouble; that is why they have them. I can think of several situations where you broke the rules and needed rescuing, by me, or others. Soon, you'll be making your own decisions – with no rules to restrain you – and it's possible that no one will be there to help you out of an impulsive decision that's gone wrong."

"Yes. There were a few sticky-wickets, weren't there? But I'm more curious than you, and I like excitement; it is my nature."

"True, but you need to control your nature with your mind. There are times when you are positively brilliant, so I know you have the ability to think! Remember: 'Fools rush in where angels fear to tread.' That is you, Sara – always rushing in before you think. Think what an *F* on your final report would have done to Mummy and Daddy!"

Sara dropped her head, and Hanna felt remorse for getting on her case; but Sara never seemed to learn. Hanna loved Sara more than anyone else, but feared her quick and impulsive nature would get her into serious trouble one day.

"Are you finished packing yet?" Hanna asked.

"Almost, I need to go through my papers. Are you tossing any school stuff?"

"I'm getting rid of all the work papers, but I made a binder for my essays and I'm keeping my evaluation reports. We are limited to forty pounds of luggage with our airfare, so I have to ship a box, even if I throw the stuff away later."

"Aunt Marga'ret is picking us up tomorrow at eleven. We might be able to leave a box or two at Woleston Hall."

"Yes, but to what purpose? Your stuff would be here, but you'd in Africa!"

"That's true; I might as well sort it here. What a nuisance!"

"What time did Mrs. Rice say she wants us onstage, at the pianos?"

"By a quarter to seven," Sara replied.

"What I would really like now is a nice long nap!" Hanna sighed.

"No time, dear sister, we have to finish our packing." Sara frowned.

4 ~ Marga'ret & James

"Well James, it looks like Jon has found himself a gal and a very nice one too, which pleases me. As a boy, he took so little time out to play, he was always reading or studying, not at all rambunctious like our boys."

"Well, thank heavens for that! Two like ours is all this earth ever needs!"

"Oh, James! Why would you say such a thing about your own sons?"

"Because living with those pranksters was hell on earth! If we had not been able to send them off to boarding school, I would have left you and gone into a monastery."

"James! How can you say such outlandish things to me?"

"When Brompton retired, I asked him if there was anything I could do for him. He replied, 'you've done so much already that I am loathe to ask for anything more; but, if it is at all possible, I would like my cottage to be off limits to your boys, sir.'"

"He didn't say that to you. You are just being absurd."

"Why then, did Brompton choose the old gate house at the other end of the property, which was quite run down? Then Mrs. Cleary retired, and went to the old gate house as well, under the pretext of wanting to keep an eye on old Brompton. Did it not surprise you at all when Andrews joined them, making it a full house?"

"Now that you mention it, I was surprised when Andrews went to live there. He could have stayed in his old quarters, since he had just stepped down from being head gardener to summer beds gardener."

"Also, Tomison declined to move onto the estate when he was promoted to head gardener, saying he preferred to stay in the village with his wife and daughter."

"Are you saying Andrews went to the old gate house as a haven from our boys?"

"I didn't say that, you did; but I agree, it was a definite possibility."

"They are not bad boys, just boys with high spirits. I can't imagine that people don't like them."

"Imagination was never your strong suit, Marga'ret. You were always so much better at planning social events and being charming."

"James, are you saying that I coddled the boys?"

"What I am saying is that they were mischief makers of the worst kind, but they were careful never to incur your ire. On the other hand, I was not so fortunate, for they knew I would not carry tales that might upset you."

"Oh, James, I'm so sorry. You should have told me. Now that they are grown – are Jamie and George nice boys – to others?"

"The change in them was miraculous after they were sent off to school. Apparently, they were pikers in the mischief-making department compared to their peers at school, which is a very scary thought! However, their puerile pranks here at home were a source of unpleasantness for the staff. I can't tell you how many bonuses I paid out for extra work because of the boys."

"Our girls, do you have secrets about them too?"

James gently lifted Marga'ret from her dressing table bench, and turned her to fit in his arms. He held her close, resting his chin on her head while saying, "Alice and Edith have always been just like their mother, perfect in every way."

Marga'ret pulled back a bit to see the look on his face, and saw only love and pride. "Yes, our girls have always pleased me too."

"Let's not stay too late tonight. We'll call it a night if a rubber ends after ten thirty … okay?" James smiled with a twinkle in his eyes.

"I'd like that. I have a busy morning tomorrow even before I go to school to pick up the girls." Marga'ret reached up and gave him a peck on the cheek, but James seized the advantage and pulled her close as he softly, but searchingly, kissed her – lingering to enjoy the mutual pleasure they felt in his ardor.

Still holding her close, James asked, "What time are you picking the girls up tomorrow? Will we have time for morning ride?"

"Only if we are out early; I told the girls to be ready at eleven; that way we will be back in time for lunch, and I can still get to my book club meeting on time."

"It will be nice to have Hanna and Sara here until graduation, we really didn't get to see enough of them, and soon they'll be off to Africa permanently. Do they know that Thomas and Paula will be here next Thursday?" James asked.

"I think so … it is going to be so wonderful to see Thomas again. I wonder what he is like as a man? I wonder if the twins remember him at all? They were only five when he was lost," Marga'ret mused.

"I'll bet Alice and Edith are pleased the twins will be here for the week, although they do get to see them at school."

"Yes, everyone will be here next week. What a wonderful time we will have – it will be like the war years, when we all lived here together, waiting for you and Peter to come home on leave."

"What have Mary and Peter been doing since the wedding?"

"Going west touring America; then taking the Trans–Canada railway coming back east."

"Yes, you did tell me that; it sounds like an interesting trip. Would you ever want to do something like that?"

"I'd really like to do the Alaska cruise tour. I've heard that the land portion of the tour is a step back in time. How about you, could you get away for two or three weeks at a time?"

"Let's plan on it! In late August, when the children are back in school – the weather should still be tolerable in Alaska then." He smiled at his wife who swung around in a circle and danced with herself. "The thought makes you happy, does it?"

"Yes, it makes me very happy – happy at the thought of having you all to myself for two or three weeks."

"Silly puss, I'm here every day, all day, since I went into business for myself."

"Not the same – not the same at all!"

James walked to his dressing room for his sports jacket.

Marga'ret waited for him at the door. "Let's not tell anyone of our plans. I want it to be our secret, okay?"

"Mum's the word," James replied, thinking: she is more like a new bride than a wife of twenty-four years. How fortunate I am.

5 ~ Alice & Edith

"You said I could sit in the back seat with Hanna and Sara. Why are you being so mean to me?" Edith asked.

"What difference does it make where you sit? Mother wants us both to sit up front to make room for hand luggage in the back seat. We have too many suitcases. The back of the Rover is stuffed. The custodians had to put my cases on the roof rack. I just hope the tires are fully inflated!" Alice huffed. She then put her little sister out of mind, as she always did when in the company of others. Her mother insisted that she treat Edith as an equal, like adults … and Mother was prone to disappointing her, as punishment for being disagreeable to Edith. If she wanted to go shopping in London for new clothes for summer fêtes and visits, she had better be nice to the little nuisance for a few days.

When Marga'ret saw the luggage on the roof rack, she said, "If I had known you gals had so much baggage, I would have brought a horse-box to cart you home!"

Edith idolized Hanna and Sara, thinking: they are so beautiful with their shining blonde pageboys, blue-green eyes, broad smiles, white even teeth and rose petal complexions, and they are nice, especially Sara, who is great fun and laughs a lot.

Edith was at an age where she felt awkward. She and her sister resembled their father, with reddish brown hair, hazel eyes flecked with green, slender noses on oval faces with ruddy skin. Edith had morphed from a girl to a young woman this past year; she would be sixteen on July 31st. She had just completed her sophomore year at The Croft School.

She and Alice boarded at school during the week, but went home to Woleston Hall for the weekends. Alice, two years and two months older, was often dictatorial towards Edith, an unpleasant attitude Alice had picked up at school towards lower forme students. Alice had been her friend before going to The Croft School, but peer influence had wooed Alice away from her. Alice was better on weekends – unless she brought a classmate home; then her deliberate snub of Edith was hurtful.

Edith began inviting Lena O'Daire home on weekends. Lena came from Shannon, Ireland, and was great fun: she was witty, loved to ride, played tennis and was skillful at all board games. Lena had no qualms or reservations about her status – anywhere. She was as sure of herself as a twenty-one year old, and completely ignored Alice and her friends.

This was a great boon for Edith. It gave her the confidence she needed to like herself in the midst of her sister's often hurtful disregard. Edith had a free and open nature, and was kind and considerate. She expected kind treatment from others … even Alice, although that happened only when Mother was present.

Alice was constantly concerned with what other people thought of her, once she began at The Croft School, where the international elite of young women attended. Alice now disdained anything that did not actively improve her image. Conceited, you might say.

Marga'ret paid little attention to their discord, remembering her youth and the difficulties of her teenage years with her older sister Mary. Edith was more like Mary as a teen. Alice was more like herself. It would work itself out eventually. In the meantime, she treated both girls and their friends as adults. Marga'ret's attitude made them toe the mark at home, for Marga'ret could be severe for lapses.

Alice and Edith both liked The Croft School. They found their teachers pleasant, as well as stimulating. The classes were interesting, for the curriculum at Croft was more like college than upper forme. Along with algebra and geometry, math classes included mechanical drawing and bookkeeping. The school was heavy on English-type classes, especially composition.

They learned languages in usage segments: simple sentences, questions and answers later applied to travel idiom, bits of history and geography specific to the area of travel. Being able to speak the language and make oneself understood was more important than conjugating verbs. History included art appreciation of the era under study, and geography contained the social mores specific to the area of study. Deportment and public speaking included Parliamentary Rules of Order.

The Croft School used a club system for language study, wherein the students spoke only the language under study. Using new words, with the proper translation and usage and spelling, earned the user a study group chit. It made learning languages fun and slightly competitive. Chits were redeemable in the school store.

Each year, Mrs. Holmesby and her assistant, Georgina Raft, would take eight of the graduates on a tour of Europe for the month of July. Hanna and Sara were going this year, and Alice hoped to go next year. Edith still had four years of school, and looked forward to Alice not being there for the last three years.

Overall, Edith liked being at school better than being at home. At home, she had to defer to Alice — Mother's rules — eldest first. She also had to put up with her brothers, who, while not overtly unpleasant, snickered a great deal. The only good things at home were her horse: a nine year-old half Arabian and half Saddlebred Pinto gelding, The Cisco Kid, and her father, who took her side whenever he could without upsetting his wife. Were it not for her horse, she would never go home! She hated being the youngest of four siblings.

"Edith, what is Lena doing for the summer?" Marga'ret asked.

"Lena is going to start flying lessons this summer. It is part of her father's plans for her to become a commercial pilot. It's a youth program he started after he became Director of Shannon Airport."

"Oh, my! Is Lena sixteen yet?"

"Lena will be sixteen on August 4th."

"That reminds me, did you gals know that Jon is in England?"

Surprised, they all chorused, "No!"

"He has been quite busy with Anna Louise. They have been touring the countryside in one of Daddy's Aston Martins. Jon has been staying with the Holmesbys, so we have seen little of him. Jon and Anna with Julia and Harold Holmesby are coming to dinner this evening. After Chapel tomorrow, they are going to join us for our Sunday ride. We are going to the old castle ruins for a picnic. Harold has agreed to drive the cart with our picnic lunch. I thought you gals would enjoy that."

The girls were pleased, for Marga'ret made things so delightful.

Alice asked, "Mother, what about our shopping? You didn't forget, did you?"

"Of course not, Alice, I have reserved Monday, Tuesday and Wednesday for shopping. Just this morning, Lady Greystone called and invited us to stay with them while we are in London. It seems your father has business to discuss with Lord Greystone, as well."

"Why would Lady Greystone invite us to stay, Mother?" Alice asked.

"Elspeth is my first cousin. They have been out in India for the last fifteen years. She has opened her house to the lot of us, for the week. Elspeth is very family oriented, since her uncle, by marriage, was Alfred William Cecil of family infamy.

"I hope Jon and Anna will be able to join us in London too. Hanna, Sara, do you think you would enjoy a few days in London as the guests of Lady and Lord Greystone – just until your parents arrive?"

"Oh, yes," the twins replied, delighted, for they enjoyed meeting new relatives.

Alice, as usual, spoke for everyone. "Mother, you make the best plans of any mother in our school. I don't know anyone else who could turn an ordinary shopping outing into a social event."

"Thank you, dear. Your father seems to think it is my forte. He will be pleased that you agree with him."

"Aunt Marga'ret, you mentioned that Alfred William Cecil was infamous; would you tell us why?" Sara asked.

"Of course, dear, it is family lore. Elizabeth Anne Hudson married Lord William Edward Clarke in 1882. He built Woleston Hall for her as a wedding present, naming it Clarke Hall. They had two daughters, Edith Anne and Rebecca Alice.

"Edith Anne, my mother, married Sir Phillip John LeClaire Woleston, my father, and lived in London. Rebecca Alice, my mother's sister, married a second son, Alfred William Cecil, who had no inheritance, but a small military income. It soon became obvious that Alfred had married Rebecca for her money, which was considerable.

"Rebecca had married for love. After they married, it devastated her to find out that Alfred was not in love with her, for he left her, and went to live in London at his club. Rebecca gave him an allowance, and remained alone on the estate until she died.

"She renamed the estate Woleston Hall to honor my father, who was a pillar of stability for her through her years of emotional suffering. She had great respect and love for my father, who was there for her whenever she needed help or advice.

"Rebecca, a beautiful woman, became ever melancholy. The humiliation of a philandering husband turned her into a recluse. She could not bear to go anywhere, for she never recovered from the shame and dishonor of Alfred's deceitful and nefarious treatment.

"The Hall went to my older brother, John, when Rebecca died, and then to my sister, Mary, when John died in the war.

"This story is usually told when our daughters start to have beaus, to remind them that they must be certain their beaus want them for themselves, not just their money."

"How then, is Lady Greystone related?" Sara asked.

"Her father and my father are brothers. Elspeth's father, Edward, is my uncle, and a Woleston second son, who had a legacy from his mother, Dame Edith Anne Clarke. Elspeth is my first cousin, and is married to Lord Edward Greystone. They have no children."

"Is Alfred somehow related to us?" Hanna asked.

"Yes dear, but only by marriage. Rebecca was your great aunt and Alfred your great uncle, and without issue, so no tainted blood has entered our line."

"What happened to Alfred?" Hanna persisted.

"He became a drunk and wastrel. People avoided him for his callous treatment of Rebecca. His only brother, my father, refused to see him, and Rebecca would not consider reconciliation. "Eventually, Alfred immigrated to Australia. No one knows what became of him, for his allowance did not follow him to Australia."

"I wonder why Mother has never told us this story," Sara said.

"I'm sure she will, when you have chosen beaus … or start dating young men with intentions of marriage."

Edith listened to the chatter thinking: while they are all out shopping, I might be able to corner Dad for a bit. Lena has asked me to go to Ireland in August for her birthday. If we wait until Jon goes to Africa with Hanna and Sara, and George has gone off on his tournament, then Daddy can ask Mummy to let me go to Ireland. She tends to put me off when there is a house full. Alice will be partying all summer and I will only be gone for two weeks. The big unknown is whether or not Mummy will let me travel to Ireland by myself. Lena thinks her father will let her travel back with me before school begins … however, before I can come back, I first have to get permission to go!

6 ~ Jamie & George

Jamie sat in the sunny bleachers at Oxford watching his younger brother play Cricket. George is top batsman on the team, and Jamie sat admiring his skillful play. I have no talent for sports. I'm always in the wrong place at the wrong time. My forte is music, which comes naturally to me, as does playing most instruments, although I prefer the challenge of the violin, as well as the versatility of the piano. George has musical talent too, for he has a very nice baritone voice, and is a member of the chorus; however, if you find him inside, he will usually be reading or writing. He's a good tennis player too and likes golf; he's a natural at any sport, except riding; I don't know why, but he's absolutely ungainly on a horse, whereas riding is my only outdoor accomplishment. I love riding and horses, and I especially enjoy playing polo.

Why we are so different? We have the same parents, the same upbringing and go to the same schools. The only traits we share are our looks, our love of one another, and our delight in pranks. I'm shy with girls, and George attracts them like flies to honey. I have walked many avenues here at school, but I am only attracted to the music, yet I do not have the touch of genius needed to be a concert soloist, nor the temperament to strive constantly for perfection. Maybe, I could get a spot with the London Philharmonic Orchestra … yeah, in my dreams!

"Ooh, Rah! Rah! Go, George, go!"

I'm not interested in architecture like Dad and George. I do so feel at odd ends, as if I have no place in the world. George will be involved with the cricket tournament this summer, and I will spend mine in Africa, which should be a joy, for Hanna and Sara are very accomplished pianists. I have but one year of school to find myself; not only do I feel clueless … I feel a bit of panic.

Jamie stood and cheered loudly for the winning team. "Jolly good show! Great game, George!"

George turned to Jamie, waved and hollered, "I'll meet you on the tarmac!"

"Don't dawdle; we don't want to be late and upset Mums," Jamie called back.

"I'll be along directly," George shouted, and sprinted towards the lockers, thinking: I can't wait to see Hanna and Sara again. It's too bad Sara is my first cousin, she's hot! Hanna is just as pretty, but a bit stiff, where Sara is easy-going and tons of fun. Hanna and Jamie hit it off well … so we do have fun together.

Mums, as usual, will have all our time organized until I leave for the tournament games. This will be the first summer that Jamie and I have gone different ways, but this is the first year our cricket team has been in the national playoffs. I'm a bit concerned about Jamie, for he only has one year left of school, and he's clueless. He doesn't want to teach music, for he has no patience with disinterested children – and he's too young to teach upper forme. Oh well, something will come along, it always does. Dad told me if I did well in school, he'd invite me to join him in his architect's business. I did well in my draftsmanship class this year; however, three years is a long time, and the classes will get harder.

"Don't drive so fast, Jamie. We won't be late."

"Sorry old chap, I was thinking about seeing the twins again and lost track of my speed."

"I suppose they've changed. I hope they haven't become superior, like so many ladies' school graduates."

"How many ladies' school graduates do you know?" Jamie asked.

George laughed, "None but Alice – who's become quite hoity-toity."

"We can't judge anyone by Alice. Number one: she's our sister; number two: she's become a snob; number three: we never liked her to begin with!"

The boys laughed, and George added, "You know who I really like?"

"No, who?"

"I like Lena O'Daire. She has the courage of a lion and, like the lion, makes you respect her for what she is, not what she would do if provoked; and she *is* a looker."

"Yes, that's for sure, Lena does sparkle. Even better though, she's a good friend to Edith. Edith needs to emulate someone with courage. She is far too timid."

"Comes from being the youngest of four, I think."

"Are you looking forward to seeing the twins again?" Jamie asked.

"Yes, we always have a good time together. Are you looking forward to going to Africa?"

"Yes, very much so. You will go in the summer before your senior year too. I think it is a good idea for us to see other cultures and different continents. Travel broadens our perspectives and our choices for our futures ... or, at least, that is what it is supposed to do."

"I already know what I want to do. I want to work for Dad."

"Lucky you! I love music, but I haven't a clue about what I will be doing."

"We never know what's around the next corner, so don't worry about it, old chap. There is always the unexpected, don't you know?"

"Did I tell you I had a letter from Mother?" Jamie asked.

"No, what letter?"

"Here, it is just a short note, read it yourself."

Woleston Hall – May 20, 1960

Dear Jamie,

I have learned about some of your past 'difficulties'. I expect that you and George will be on your best behavior on your return from school. I am counting on you to treat Alice and Edith like young ladies, as gentlemen should, and to treat your cousins likewise.

With a house full of guests, I will need your full support and cooperation in all aspects. Your father also expects your cheerful, adult assistance.

With all my love to you both, Mother

"When did you receive this?"

"Yesterday."

"I wonder if she found out by accident."

"Makes no difference how she found out. That she knows about some of our past *difficulties*, as she puts it, makes it imperative that we toe the mark while we are at home. She can put the kibosh on my trip to Africa and on your tournament too."

"Mother wouldn't do that!"

"Do you want to bet the summer on it?"

George sat thinking. I would be the most hated boy in school if I did not show up for the tournament. Mother would not do that to me! However – and then again – Alice did not have a sweet sixteen party after all the months of planning for it, because she left Edith stranded after a local birthday party, and … she has warned us!

"You are right, James. We are going to have to toe the mark carefully; agreed?"

"Agreed."

7 ~ *Woleston Hall*

Marga'ret zipped around the Hall: asking Victoria, the housekeeper, if she had any questions; glad to see that Suzie and Mabel, the housemaids were helping Victoria with the fresh flower arrangements. They had cleaned on Monday and made up the bedrooms and baths on Thursday, their regular days. Tilly, glad for the extra time on a Saturday, was washing up the extra bed linens, and pressing the table linens for dinner.

Elizabeth always had the kitchen under control; she was incredibly efficient, as well as a marvelous cook. She had the daily help of a kitchen maid, Betsy, and if needed, her husband Albert would lend a hand. Albert also served as butler, and occasionally as chauffeur for the 1934 Rolls-Royce Silver Ghost, a legacy from Aunt Rebecca, and the first acquisition in James's *unusual* automobiles collection.

Marga'ret went over the details as she drove to The Croft School, mentally thanking her lucky stars for Victoria, who manages the day staff. She knows what needs doing, and gets things done – especially the extra little touches when guests are expected; she is a treasure. My only job is to answer questions or to make decisions, which, of course, I like to do.

Elizabeth and Albert are autonomous, for they deal with James and me directly. What plums they are, both in their ability and dedication. I'm so pleased they adore the little summerhouse cottage at the end of the formal gardens. Elizabeth calls it, "A charming and cozy little doll house for people. I love the goldfish pond and the wonderful herbs and flowers. I hope I never have to live anywhere else."

The cottage, which would fit in our dining room, is two rooms, divided down the ridgeline: one half is the parlor, and the other half is the kitchen and dining area. A screened porch abuts the peaked end on the south side of the cottage, accessed from the living room and the kitchen. A closet stairway in the front inside corner of the kitchen leads to a dormered garret bedroom. James enlarged the water closet under the stairway, to include a shower bath by removing a bulky china cabinet, which left enough space for a coat and boot closet too. It is small, snug, and quite cozy, since James put in a wood stove, making the little summerhouse suitable for year-round use.

Marga'ret segued mentally to her guest accommodations: the boys had doubled up to give Jon a bedroom, and they would share a bathroom. The girls had done the same for Hanna and Sara, and the four of them would share a bathroom, which I hope will not be a disaster. Mary and Peter are in the east guest room, which has a separate bath, as does the west guest room where Paula's parents, Charles and Lisa will stay. Paula and Thomas are in the third floor west guest room, with Julia, Harold and Anna Louise in the third floor east guest room, which was the old nursery, and has a small nanny's room off the bathroom for Anna Louise. We still have the upstairs afternoon reading room, with the two sofa beds and another bathroom – if the girls end up needing more space. A pleasantly full house – and we still have the bachelor's quarters over the new barn addition: two bunkrooms with shower baths.

Jamie and George arrived at four in time for tea. There was much ado as Hanna and Sara greeted the boys, whom they liked and had not seen since Easter. Alice and Edith gave Jamie and George dutiful pecks and hugs – after all, they were their brothers. James and Marga'ret were happy to see the boys looking so robust and grown up; just a few months makes a big difference at this age. At five-thirty, Jon and Anna Louise arrived. The girls, of course, knew Anna Louise from school, but Jamie and George had not yet met Anna Louise, and could not help envying good old Jon for his curvaceous friend. Alice, Edith, Hanna and Sara had not seen Jon since his graduation from Oxford last summer, so they all had a lot of catching up to do.

Marga'ret rang for fresh tea as the six young people crowded 'round Jon and Anna Louise with greetings and questions. Marga'ret took James's hand and made a beeline for the door, with Marga'ret pausing briefly to say, "Jackets and ties for dinner; cocktails in the library at seven."

"I wanted to stay," James said when they were well away from morning room.

"Me too, but they will do better without us right now. There may be things said that parents do not want to hear, and I need a nap. I've been on the go since six o'clock this morning, and it is going to be a late night."

"Now that I think on it, I'm bushed too!" James smiled slyly.

8 ~ Castle Ruins

James and Marga'ret led the pack on the Sunday picnic ride, while Harold drove the surrey with the Haflingers in harness. George sat groom, with Jon and Anna sitting second seat, with the picnic baskets filling the cargo space behind them. Spirits were high, for the day was bright and crisp, a perfect day for both a horseback ride and a picnic.

The castle ruins sat on a high bluff above an endless field, now used to make hay. On a wide shoulder below the bluff, a natural spring formed a pond flanked by willow trees to the north. In a clearing, there sat a large round flat stone table, with not so flat stone seats around it − relics of a far distant past. The view was ancient, unchanged by time, except that the castle was now mostly ruins. The woods had grown thick from a lack of timbering for fire wood, and a delightful updraft breeze rose up the hill to the pond. The horses, tethered among the willows, sharing hay nets, munched contentedly. The surrey rested beside the ancient stone table, with chocked wheels to serve as a pantry. The young adults headed off to the ruins.

The wooden parts of the castle had burned away long ago, leaving only the jagged outside walls of the ruins. Inside the fragmented walls, the remnants of stone steps made a daunting climb up to the fallen ramparts. Jamie and George rushed to climb the steps, but Jon, who didn't even climb trees, declined. The girls wanted no part of the crumbling steps either, and wandered through the maze of fallen stone walls, to peer down holes left by disintegrated stairs, that led to the nether regions of the castle. Trees had grown up through cracks in the stone floor and wild shrubs had fixed themselves in the sandy mortar of the crumbling walls. Piles of stone debris blocked some of the old passages, while others, that retained an arch or two, remained open.

Restrained from their usual pranks, Jamie and George suggested a game of hide and seek. George, easily bored, wanted to explore. "Outside, there is an entrance that leads to the bowels of the castle — and the dungeons. Light comes in the passages from the entrance, cracks in the floors and holes left by long gone doors … anybody game?"

"Absolutely not," Jon said. "We are not prepared for exploration; nor have we told the parents what we planned to do. Just because this castle has been standing for hundreds of years, does not mean it's reliable. Any one stone moved accidentally could have far reaching and fatal consequences."

"Well, I've had enough," Edith said. "Let's explore outside of the castle. We might find an old arrowhead or something."

"I don't think we should walk around in that tall grass. There could be holes, and I'm not up to a sprained ankle!" Hanna replied.

"Plus, there could be snakes and ticks," Alice added.

Sara, usually game for adventure said, "Why don't we find a nice place to sit, and let Jon tell us how he found Thomas and Paula in Africa?"

Diverted, they chorused agreement. Only George, who was hoping for the opportunity to scare the girls, felt thwarted.

They sat on the crumbled and rounded rampart steps where Jon said, "The whole story is too long to tell now, so I'll just give you the highlights."

'I was with Max Mason on a trading safari for several months before we went to the Ndezi Village. The Chief there bade us talk to a captive before we traded; the captive was Paula. We were unable to free her — so Max made our prices so high the trading was soon over. The Chief, suspecting a ruse, sent a warrior escort with us to our base camp, delaying our arrival until dark.

'Long ago, Max had put antennas up high in the trees, for the radio at the base camps. When we could no longer hear the warriors chanting, or the walinka hitting spear noises to ward off predators, Max contacted Enugu Station in Nigeria, and arranged for Paula's rescue.

'When the troops arrived the next morning, Paula was gone, and no one knew how she had escaped, for the Ndezi had found no spoor. With no alternative, Max and I continued on with our trading safari. I felt awf'ly discouraged by Paula's disappearance.

'Days later, when I could no longer stand the guilt of doing nothing to help her, I asked Max to let me take some men to retrace the trail that Paula had traveled from the beach to the Ndezi village. She had no other way to go on her escape. She had no maps, she did not know the wilderness; if she knew anything, it would have to be that trail, if she could find it, which was a stretch of supposition, and of her ability to survive in a wilderness full of carnivores, lethal plants and poisonous critters.

'However, at that time, I did not know of Paula's vast hiking experience, or of her unusual athletic ability. The six of us were out four days before we reached the ridge that the natives had traveled back to the village. We found no recent spoor, only a few ricochet marks on stones and a spent bullet cartridge. However, we knew that Paula was unarmed. Finding her trail seemed hopeless, considering how long ago she had escaped.

'On the second day on the ridge, while Motozo was making dinner, Kimbo and I scouted down the trail. We had seen some unusual footprints the day before – those of a very heavy man – and I wanted to look for other prints before it rained again that night. We had gone a mile or so when we came to a native traveling hut surrounded by a thorn boma. Inside the boma, leaning against the wall of the hut sat Miss Thornton, sound asleep.

'Overcome with relief, and thrilled by our incredibly good luck, I hardly knew what to say. We soon found that she had injured her ankle in an encounter with a bull ape, and Tamubu, her guide, had carried her piggyback, hence the prints of a very heavy man. 'When we arrived, Tamubu was inside the traveling hut smoking a piglet.

'I did not recognize Tamubu as Thomas, due to his native appearance: he wore a loin cloth and a cloak about his shoulders, with a dulband around his head, and amulets hanging from his neck with sandals on his feet ... but every now and then, he would do something that reminded me of Thomas. I put it down to wanting to find Thomas so badly, that I was inventing similarities.

'The eight of us traveled back to the beach together. We made a litter to carry Paula, or Thomas carried her on the steep downhills. Other small things happened, which made me wonder even more about Tamubu ... his laughter, a certain lilt in his voice and his smile, which stunned me. Oh, how I hoped ... but I was wary of disappointment. I told myself I was imagining similarities so ... I went slowly, looking for positive proof.

'On the third day, we arrived at the cove where the yacht was stranded, only to find it gone. The Expedition leader had left a tarpaulin-covered ball hanging in the trees containing supplies and a note for Paula, saying they had taken the yacht south to Port Gentil. Paula felt devastated to see it gone.

'The next day, I went far out on the crumbled remnants of a sunken volcano wall that formed the northern side of the immense crater that was now a vast tidal pool, to radio Max; to let him know that we had reached the beach safely. I had radioed him from the ridge, while I still had a signal to let him know that we had found Paula with an injured ankle, and an African escort. 'Tamubu went with me, fascinated by the idea of talking to people we could not see with a box, and that we would also hear them talking back to us.

'Afterwards, we went fishing. Walking up the beach, I had a thought – what are we going to use to fish with? Surprised that I had not thought of this sooner, I turned and said, "Thomas, what are we going to use to fish with?"

'He turned to me and asked, "Why did you call me Thomas?"

'I asked him if he would answer some questions, by way of an answer. His answers to my questions left me no doubt that Tamubu was indeed Thomas. The Zuri Watu scouts had found Thomas, wandering and sick after the plane crash and took him home with them. He suffered from malaria for two years until a missionary doctor came to the village and gave him quinine. He had almost total amnesia from the disease. He did not remember us, except in his dreams.

'When Nanoka was on her deathbed, she told Tamubu to go and find his birth family, so he could know his true destiny. Thomas was on walk-about to Kenya when he saw Paula coming through the trees to hide under a toxic plant. His curiosity about this amazing white woman made him wait for her to emerge, so he could follow her.'

"The rest of the story is for Thomas to tell," Jon smiled.

"Oh, what a marvelous story, Jon," Anna Louise said with tears sparkling in her eyes. Jon's sisters, Hanna and Sara, were so proud of him, they could find nothing to say, and ran to hug him. Alice and Edith had always admired Jon, but now, they felt him to be a hero, and felt honored he was their cousin. Jamie and George wondered if they would ever do anything as courageous, and looked up to Jon as never before.

"What sayeth you? Shall yon lads fetch the damsels back to their Lords and Mistresses?" Jon spoketh.

Not to be outdone, Jamie said, "My Lord, would thee doeth thy humble servants a boon, and showeth us the way?"

Amid gay laughter, the group returned to the stone table.

The adults heard them coming, and Harold said, "If I didn't know better, I'd think they been to the pictures and had seen 'Some like it Hot', which I understand is quite a boisterous comedy."

"It pleases me so, to see them all together, and having such a good time," Marga'ret said.

Julia thought, yes, this family is all I could ever want for Anna.

After lunch, the six riders went for a ride on the miles of trails through the woods, while Harold, George, Jon and Ann Louise headed the surrey back to the Hall. The men tended to the horses and put the surrey away, and then helped Anna Louise carry the picnic baskets back to the kitchen, where they thanked Elizabeth for the marvelous picnic lunch. She had sent her special chicken salad, with pecans and crushed pineapple; a potato salad with sunflower seeds, grated carrots and parsley; succulent fresh strawberries and brownies, with iced sun tea and lemonade. Lunch had been a feast.

Elizabeth was setting out the tea things before retiring for the day. Unless Marga'ret and James decided to go to the Club for dinner, they would fix a late meal for themselves of soup, sandwiches and fruit tarts with ice cream. Most of the time, when there was a crowd, it boiled down to just fruit tarts and ice cream and coffee with a liqueur.

Harold and Anna took a stroll through the gardens at Woleston Hall. Anna loved flowers and plants too. Jon went to his desk, where he did a rough sketch of the ideas he and Anna had talked about for a house in Africa. He wanted to get his Uncle's opinion about their ideas when James returned from the ride.

9 ~ Jon & James

The riders returned about three and saw to their mounts. Jon gave Uncle James a hand, and asked if he had a few moments to talk a bit of business with him.

"Of course Jon, come up to my office." Jon liked his new office with its walls of framed projects done in photographic montages, with two corner tables displaying intricate cut-away models of estate homes that James had designed. The ambiance in the office exuded talent, good taste and success.

"Now then, what can I do for you, Jon?"

"I'd like to commission you to design a house for Anna and me to be built in Africa. We would like it all on one level with guest quarters upstairs, or bedrooms for children, whichever comes first." He smiled.

"I'd be delighted, Jon, but shouldn't we have Anna's input too?"

"Anna has told me what I am telling you. She would like the kitchen on the southwest with a screened porch off the kitchen on the south; the entrance hall on the north with the living room on the northwest. The dining room is on the southwest with a solarium bordering both living room and dining room. The morning room, library and master bedroom are on the east with a screened porch on the south of the master bedroom. The butler's pantry is between the kitchen and dining room. I did a sketch of the floor-plan. Being on the equator as we are, the direction of the sun is almost the same each day.

"Shall I wait for the wedding before I begin?"

"No, start as soon as you are able; I intend to build a home in any case. Thomas and Paula can use it until I marry. I like Anna's ideas, how about you?"

"From an architect's point of view, she has made sensible choices, but a home should never be square to the compass. It must be set off just a bit."

"That is why I am hiring an architect! One last thing — I insist on paying the going fee, whatever it is for the working plans; how do you charge?"

James did not want to charge Jon — he was living in his house, as the Hall would pass to Jon when he was twenty-five — but the tone of his voice told him he would go elsewhere if he did not charge him a reasonable fee. Doing this for them will pleasure me. I will tell him my hourly fee, and only charge him for half the hours. "I'm afraid I am expensive. I charge thirty quid an hour for building plans, with three copies."

"We want all the conveniences of a well-planned working kitchen with both an old-fashioned woodstove and a modern gas stove, refrigerator, freezer, dishwasher and stainless steel sinks (two 25" bowls) and plenty of room for a big round dining table. An adjoining pantry, scullery and laundry are on the far west wall of the kitchen, here," Jon pointed to his drawing, "where we can pipe waste water to the solarium or gardens.

The estate houses have raised footers, and feature peaked terra-cotta roofs that run over the porches. We catch all the rainwater in cisterns to water the plants in the dry season, and to flush the toilets to septic tanks. The cisterns are boxy structures built on the corners of the porches, with the water piped to the toilets or stored in tanks under the house for the dry season. That way we use gravity for pressure. Cistern overflow is piped to a small pond in the pasture, which overflows into a stream that waters the tea bushes, or it can be diverted for the gardens."

"How do you obtain water for the kitchen and baths?" James asked.

"We have a water tower filled from a good-sized spring fed lake. A gas pump starts the siphon to fill the tower, which is below the intake in the lake reservoir. It fills at night and supplies filtered water to all the farm buildings, except for the native village, where Dad has installed hand pumps on wells. This improves the quality of the water supply, while maintaining the communal spirit of water-gathering for the native women.

"The front porch is an open porch across the front of the house, leading to the center hall with stairs to the less spacious second floor. To the rear and south of the house is a large screened porch divided into three sections: the west section off the kitchen is for the help;

the narrower center section is a solid walled mud room leading to the entrance hall; the east corner is the master bedroom screened porch. We have decorative iron grillwork on all openings, windows doors and screened porches. Off the center hall to the west is the living room, and beyond it, the conservatory, aired with upper and lower grilled jalousie windows and venting skylights. South of the living room is the dining room, with the butler's pantry between dining room and kitchen. Off the center hall to the right, as you enter, is the morning room, the library and the master suite, with an adjoining nursery and nanny nook, which can double as a sick room or sewing room until there are children. Did I mention a linen room and sewing room next to the laundry, and that the waste water is used to water the solarium or vegetable gardens in the dry season?"

"Yes, you certainly make good use of your water supply and know what you want. I wish all my clients were so sure of their needs."

"I am basing our home on what I like best in the estate house, but not quite so grand. Anna wants no live-in accommodations for help, only day workers, which is just fine with me."

"I will do up some sketches. You can make any changes you might like on them before I do the finished plans. One last question, what size rooms do you prefer?" James asked, looking at his notes.

"Generous rooms, but not opulent – spacious but not grand, with good light and ventilation. African nights are cool, so there should be fireplaces in the master suite, the sitting rooms and the dining room, which should easily seat twelve and will double as a breakfast room. We have generators for the lights and refrigerators. We use copper lined black iron grates in the back of the fireplaces to make hot water, which circulates to a central storage tank."

"I'm glad you mentioned that," James noted.

"Do you have a time frame in mind?" Jon asked.

"I could have floor plan sketches done by the end of next week. Would that do?"

"That would be smashing! Thanks, Uncle James. I'm glad you took the job."

"I'm delighted you asked me! Come along, it's time we cleaned up for tea."

10 ~ *Sir Peter & Lady Mary ~ June*

Seated in the dining room of the Vancouver Hotel in British Columbia, Peter remarked to Mary, "This has been a delightful trip, has it not? I wonder why doing something so enjoyable, is so very tiring. We've hardly had a chance to chat. I fall asleep as soon as my head hits the pillow."

"I know, it is quite unusual for us, we always chat. I think it must be the air ... it seems a bit more humid, possibly denser and harder to breathe than African air. Does that make any sense to you?" Mary asked.

"It's possible that you're right. Las Vegas was the only place where I didn't feel so tired at night. However, thick air or thin air, I'm glad we decided to tour America west to Vancouver, and go east on the scenic railway tour in Canada. I just wish we had the time to go on to Alaska."

Mary smiled. Here sat a man who never had time for vacations ... and now, he wishes he could do more.

"Yes, I too, wish we had the time to go to Alaska. However, I still feel the enchantment and profound tranquility of the redwood and sequoia forests; those majestic trees made the whole trip worthwhile for me. Yet, the truly spectacular and towering magnificence of the Rocky Mountains filled my soul with awe – such a contrast to the vast lonely spaces of the prairies – just as the Sierra Nevada Mountains redeemed the heat and despairing emptiness of the Nevada deserts with its cool shade, and the serene tranquility of the redwood and sequoia trees. The vistas of the Pacific coastline were also stunning and panoramic. I wonder if the Canada Scenic Explorer railway trip east will offer anything to compare with what we have already seen."

Their northwest salmon dinner arrived. Peter took a bite and smiled. "The food has been excellent too. I'm glad Charles helped us plan our itinerary; he certainly knew what he was doing. Paula was right when she said, 'between Daddy and Keystone Automobile Club, you will have the best tour ever'. We have managed to see exactly what we wanted to see without the tedium of an escorted tour.

"Flying to Kansas to see a rodeo was my favorite experience," Peter continued. "Seeing the cowboys, the prairies and the old western town brought the Louis L'Amour stories to life for me; for even with his vivid written descriptions, it was impossible to imagine the epic proportions of life in the west."

"I liked the train trip through the Rocky Mountain gorges to Glenwood Springs," Mary added. "I'm glad we rented a car to go to Aspen. Those soaring mountains were spectacular, and felt unchanged through the eons ... like a step back in time. Riding in a car made those passes feel personal – a part of me – less like a tour. I only wish Independence Pass had not been closed with winter snow."

"I enjoyed the lower flight altitudes of the shuttle flights from Aspen to Grand Junction, to Salt Lake City and Las Vegas. They certainly illustrated the vast and drastic changes in scenery; from spectacular mountain beauty and greenery to seemingly flat and empty deserts with high forlorn mesas to unbelievable man–made glitz."

"I thought you liked Las Vegas," Mary said.

"I did, but not because it was arcadian; the casinos were fabulous! Charles's suggestion to fly to Reno and hire a car and driver to go through the Sierra Nevada Mountains to Sacramento made the trip outstanding."

"That was my favorite part of the trip," Mary replied. "Our driver knew the quiet and remote places to stop, so we avoided the crowds of tourists ... one can't commune with nature in a crowd. Walking among those giant redwoods and sequoias was an antediluvian feeling for me. I felt reborn and at one with the world. Those magnificent trees filled me body and soul with peace; it was an exalting and euphoric experience.

"Paula and Thomas are going to Muir Woods, in Marin County across the bay from San Francisco. Thomas will enjoy the Park's redwood trees, for he loves the podocarpus tree, Africa's equivalent of the redwoods."

"I thought the highlight of the trip for you would have been The Butchart Gardens in Victoria, before we came to Vancouver," Peter said.

"They are fabulous, vast and incredible man-made gardens, while the other is the epic and lavish beauty of spectacular feats of nature. Touching trees that were standing when Christ walked the earth was an indescribable experience for me, for centuries of time flashed through my mind. I didn't want to leave those trees. I would have been happy to stay there forever."

"Well, I'm certainly glad you tore yourself away! Losing you to a bunch of trees would certainly have ruined the trip for me!"

Mary smiled. "Did you not feel the serenity of the trees?"

"I liked the pine smell in the air. It was so fresh, clean and soothing."

"Yes, it was that," Mary replied.

"I'm looking forward to just relaxing on the railway excursion. I could use a bit of quiet time before the doings in England." Peter smiled.

"Tomorrow, the Scenic Explorer train to Winnipeg, Ontario, then a 707 to London. That long rest should recharge your batteries, dear."

"I intend to drop Keystone Automobile Club a letter telling them how much we enjoyed their trip-tiks and the tour books, with a thank you note to Charles for expediting our tour – passport out in Philadelphia, to passport out in Vancouver, B.C., to passport out to board the 707 to Chicago, New York and London."

"Not at all like traveling in Europe," Mary remarked.

"You mean you didn't miss standing in long lines to get arrival and departure stamps in your passport?" Peter smiled at her.

Mary chuckled, "I'm surprised you even asked ... if the States were like Europe, we'd have stood in long lines twelve times, and lost a full day of sightseeing – so no – I don't miss the little stamps at all. As a matter of fact, I felt a marvelous thrill of freedom from bureaucracy, especially when the Canadian border agents came aboard the ferry to check our passports, like conductors on a train, and we remained seated! That was a first for me!"

"Speaking of freedom, I wanted to get your thoughts on making changes to our wills, now that Thomas has come back to us. I'm not sure what to do. He hasn't shown the least interest in the farm. On his first tour the evening they arrived, all he asked was, 'When did you add the vineyard?' Jon, on the other hand, has always been very involved in the running of the farm. As the first born, Thomas should inherit, but I think his interests lay elsewhere. What do you think?"

"I think we should leave things as they are, with Jon inheriting the farm. If the kimmea is as lucrative as Cyril Latham has led us to believe, Thomas will have no economic worries. Until we know, we could add a codicil saying that Thomas and Paula and their heirs have the right to live at Dela-Aden, if they desire to do so."

"Have you decided how you are going to handle Woleston Hall?"

"It is mine until Jon reaches his 25th birthday. Then, it is Jon's legacy. I thought I would talk to Jon. See if he has given any thought to Woleston Hall, for James has put a good deal into the property on his own."

"Yes, they certainly have a vested interest in Woleston Hall. Any feelings about what Jon might do?"

"No, but I'm sure he would never turn Marga'ret and James out."

"Well, it will be wonderful for all of us to be together again at the Hall for a few days. Are you looking forward to the festivities?"

"Of course, I'm certain Marga'ret has a marvelous time planned," Mary replied.

"I'm glad our girls will be coming home until their Grand Tour in July. I missed them when they were away at school, but I enjoyed their letters so much, that I feel I know them better for being away. It lessened the ache of not hearing their cheerful noise in the house, especially their piano playing. I kept telling myself that they were better off in England for schooling. It worked out well with Marga'ret and James just an hour's drive away. The girls still had family for week-ends and school breaks, and our jaunt to the Hall for a long Boxing Day visit, between harvests in Africa, worked out quite nicely too."

"Yes, it did. I thought you'd be missing the farm by now and anxious to get back."

"I'm surprised at myself. I hardly think about the farm at all!"

"What have you been thinking about then?"

"You, mostly."

"Me, whatever for?"

"I'd forgotten what fun it is to do things with you. Everything is much more interesting from your point of view. I'm so dull. You see so many things that I would have missed, and you enjoy everything."

"You cut yourself short. You are just focused, but I'm so glad you are enjoying yourself; maybe we can get away more often."

"Do you dislike being tied to the farm?"

"Good heavens, Peter! You may not miss your tea leaves or grapes, but I am at odd ends without my horses!"

"Glad to hear you say it. You had me worried for a minute. I thought you might want to become a jet set-er."

Smiling, Mary took his hand and said, "I am a jet set-er, dear; I certainly didn't walk here!"

Grinning at her humor, he replied, "The night has grown late, Mary. We are the only ones still in the restaurant. Are you ready to go up?"

"Yes, let's go up," Mary agreed, with a coquettish smile.

11 ~ Thomas

Thomas sat in the aisle seat of the Boeing 707 jet airplane. Paula was asleep, nestled on a pillow against the window. Why is air travel so tiring? You don't do anything but sit – and eat. I've felt restless ever since we changed planes in Cairo from Shanghai. If we had not been committed to going to England for Hanna & Sara's graduation, we could have just gone home. Paula told me that we had circumnavigated the earth when we landed in Cairo; I was stunned. I can't imagine what the Zuri Watu will think when I tell them that I have gone completely around the world!

To relieve his boredom, Thomas closed his eyes and happily thought about the fascination of his honeymoon – which began with the opening of wedding presents to one another in their elegant room at the Fairmount Hotel in San Francisco. Inside his present, which was a new suitcase full of vacation clothes, were the boarding passes for a five-day cruise of the Hawaiian Islands aboard the U.S.S. Independence. I did not know about the wedding gift ritual – but as usual, Jon was prepared. Before the wedding, he gave me a nicely wrapped package, saying, "This is your wedding present for Paula; it can be a surprise for both of you."

Paula's delighted reaction to her present pleased me. She was thrilled with the book of house plans and designs. However, I soon regretted giving her the book. She spent hours poring over the designs when we could have been doing something else!

The Hawaiian Islands are like an enchanting story. They fascinate and delight with their spectacular beauty, and are truly the gems in all of creation. Each island is different, not only from the others, but from itself. Each island has a windward and leeward side. Some parts of the islands are as wild and free as Africa, lacking only the herds of

50

animals and the feral essence that is Africa. The rugged windward sides of the islands are rainy and full of the lush tropical beauty of rainforests, with high bluffs and fantastic waterfalls. The leeward side of the same island, on the same day, is sunny with sandy beaches, delightful breezes, palm trees, sedges and palmetto bushes. The air in the Hawaiian Islands is different too: dense, sweet and fresh, smelling often of the sea or flowers – it surrounds you and holds you close, while allowing your spirit to soar. The air in Africa is evanescent, always with you, but vast and free, and a bit lonely.

Each day we had a different adventure. We disembarked at island ports for land excursions. Two ports were not deep enough to dock a cruise ship, so we loaded onto tenders from the loading bay. In the choppy Pacific seas, it required nerve to leap from a perfectly good ship onto a ramp that rose and fell wildly, as the tender also rose and fell in the swells. Paula leapt out, as if she were on dry land … I had no other choice.

Another day, our excursion took us to the top of a volcano, now extinct, where exists a huge barren dust crater – miles wide – that is used in movies to simulate the surfaces of other planets. We rode bicycles, equipped with drum brakes front and rear, down from the 9,000 foot summit. This was extremely exciting, for the bicycles quickly reached speeds in excess of 35 miles per hour on the straight-a-ways, all of which led to hairpin turns – and I hadn't been on a bicycle since I was ten years old. At the start, we were a thousand feet or more above the clouds, and rode down through the clouds where it was wet and freezing cold, with limited visibility. The tour provided us with warm rain suits, helmets and heavy gloves, as well as a nice roadside picnic lunch once we were below the really steep slopes.

During a day at sea, the Captain sighted a migrating whale pod, and hove-to while the pod passed. The whales were majestic in their size as they surfaced to blow and breathe. Some breached and dove into the water, slapping their huge tail fins as they submerged; it seemed as if they were putting on a show for us; another amazing story for the campfire.

Thomas opened his eyes and glanced around. The man across the aisle had his reading light on, which made an eerie glow on his features as he read a book. I liked to read when I was a boy. Dad read *Moby Dick* and *Twenty Thousand Leagues under the Sea* and the *Tarzan* stories to us. Mother liked to read us fairy tales at bedtime; she liked the morals of the stories. Paula chose *A Connecticut Yankee in King Arthur's Court* for me to read at Dela-Aden, saying I would like it; but once I sat down, I usually fell asleep.

I love traveling with Paula; she is so enthusiastic about everything and enjoys doing almost anything … but I yearn for Africa and Dela-Aden. I remember Woleston Hall and playing with my cousins, who were awful mischief-makers. I wonder if they are still pranksters, or if manhood has tamed the rascal in them. As much as I long to return to Africa, I do look forward to revisiting the Hall and remembering more of my childhood memories there.

The end of this long flight can't come soon enough. I need to move about; maybe take a long walk in the woods at Woleston Hall. Although, remembering Aunt Marga'ret's propensity for organization, she might have my time fully committed. She does so like to arrange things … and people. However, I now remember how to escape her machinations … as I often did as a boy.

The walk across the tarmac to passport control felt good. Even standing in line felt good. I caught sight of my parents waiting for us in the crowd on the other side of the barrier. My heart took a little leap of joy; I had missed them since our wedding. We lost so many years – so many milestones had passed while we were apart – so many little joys went unshared. I might be happier in England than I expected.

After hugs and kisses, his father helped with the luggage, saying, "James has the Land-Rover in the car park. Our bags are on roof rack, so he stayed with it. How was your flight?"

Paula and I both said, "Long!" at the same time, and laughed.

Walking to the Land Rover, Lady Mary said, "Your Aunt Marga'ret has a surprise for you. We are staying the night in London at Greystone

Place with cousin Elspeth – as will your parents, Paula – when they arrive later today."

Once on the road, Lady Mary continued, "Hanna and Sara, Alice, Edith and Jamie, with Jon and Anna Louise are all in London too. They have been touring the sights, while Marga'ret and Edith have been shopping. Cousin Elspeth is much like Marga'ret in that she loves a full house. Lord Edward and Lady Elspeth are hosting a champagne tea this evening in honor of the girl's coming graduation, and to celebrate your marriage last May."

Paula looked at Thomas, who just shrugged his shoulders. "Have I ever met Elspeth?" Thomas asked.

"I don't think so dear. Lord Greystone was out in India for the last twenty years. Just remember, Elspeth is family just like Alice and Edith are family – with an age difference, of course!" Mary smiled at her pun.

"It is just for overnight," James added. "Marga'ret wants to toddle off to Woleston Hall early, so we can all go riding tomorrow after lunch."

12 ~ Greystone Place

A footman escorted Paula and Thomas to their room, on the third floor of Greystone Place. The suite was as lavish as what they had seen so far of the rest of the house, with India pervading the décor.

"This place is simply fantastic. I feel like I'm in a Maharajah's palace in India," Paula said, taking Thomas's hand. Together they explored their accommodations. They had entered into a sitting room, with a sofa, two club chairs, end and coffee tables with lamps, nicely grouped on the right with all sorts of objet d' art on every flat surface including the walls. On the left were double doors. To the left of the double doors stood an ornate bookcase stuffed with ancient looking tomes, and a huge frond plant. On the right of the doors sat a lady's desk with a lamp and chairs on either side, with a smaller box table nearby with ice bucket, water jug, glasses, a bowl of fruit and a box of chocolates.

Straight ahead, in the bay window nook, sat a small round dining table with four chairs. The double doors, on the left, led to a bedroom at the end of a short, wide hall. Off the hall were dressing rooms, his and hers on the left, each with a marble basin vanity. On the right opposite the dressing rooms was a full bath of marble with a whirlpool tub, a large etched glass shower, toilet and bidet.

"What's the funny-looking toilet for?" Thomas asked.

Paula smiled with a twinkle in her eyes, and said, "I'll show you later."

The bedroom had two twin beds pushed together to make a king size bed, with night tables and foot bench. Lounge chairs and ottomans, with a table and lamp between them, sat in another bay window. Everywhere there were artifacts from India. Their bags sat on luggage racks in the dressing rooms. The back of each dressing room door held a full-length mirror, as well as large mirrors above each vanity and basin with make-up and shaving lights, and a full complement of personal accouterments.

"I've never seen anything like this in my life, have you?" Thomas asked.

"Only in the movies!" Paula replied. "I think an overnight stay here will not be long enough … oh my, what luxury!"

"There are many guests staying here. Do you think all the rooms are this spacious?" Thomas asked.

"I don't know. But you're right, there are twelve guests that I know of, which would mean at least seven guest rooms." Paula opened the door to the hallway and looked around. "It looks like there are four suites on this floor, and if there are four suites on the second floor, that makes eight guest suites – that is, if they are all laid out like this one – which means, this incredible mansion was built for the purpose of accommodating many guests in extreme luxury. When your mother said we had a surprise coming, she definitely understated herself! Shall we tidy ourselves up a bit? Lady Elspeth said, 'lunch would be served at one', and I'm for a quick shower, how about you?" Paula asked.

Thomas replied with a sly smile, "Yes, a shower would be quite nice!"

"Paula, I don't have a thing in common with the Greystones; and I haven't seen any of my English cousins for more than fourteen years. Everyone and everything is going to be so different … I feel a bit daunted."

"We have been over this before, Thomas. You must be you, for you can be no one else! What you don't realize is just how marvelous you are, being you. Just be yourself, don't worry about the social mores. Trust me in this – no one will apply them to you. Your story has preceded you and everyone will make allowances and not think the less of you for doing so. A very great lady once said, 'No one can make you feel inferior without your permission.' Have I ever steered you wrong? Just be you! Just enjoy yourself. Pretend this is just a different tribe!" Paula laughed. "You know, this tribe is so different, I'm not sure of what to do either!"

Her words and laughter relieved his anxiety. She always knew what to say to put him at his ease. I'm such a fortunate man, he thought.

Everyone gathered in the huge parlor before going into lunch. Paula and Thomas were the last to arrive. Sir Peter and Lady Mary came over to them with Lady Mary saying, "Let me take you around to say hello. Some of the faces may have changed a good bit." She first took them over to their hosts.

"Lord Edward Greystone and Lady Elspeth, I would like to introduce our son Thomas and his new wife, Paula, nee Thornton."

"We are pleased to meet you. Congratulations to both of you on your marriage. Edward and I have yet to go to Hawaii. Did you enjoy it?" Lady Greystone asked.

Thomas answered, "Yes, It was a bit like Africa without all the animals, and the air was marvelous."

"Ah, the air, that is so good to know," Lord Edward remarked.

"Our home is your home, enjoy yourselves. If you need anything, just ring. I'm sure we have it," Elspeth smiled.

"Thank you for inviting us into your home," Paula said. "I feel like I'm in a Maharaja's palace. It's simply delightful."

"I'm glad you like it, my dear; we simply had to bring our home in India back with us. We spent so many years collecting all these interesting pieces." Lady Mary inclined her head saying, "Lord Edward, Lady Elspeth."

She then escorted Thomas and Paula around the room, stating first names with a mini-bio:

"This is your Uncle James and Aunt Marga'ret, my sister and her husband, the keepers of Woleston Hall. Here are Jamie and George, their sons, down from Oxford. They have changed a bit, haven't they? These are your cousins, Alice and Edith, who attend The Croft School with your sisters and Anna Louise. And, your sisters, Hanna and Sara ... " The sound of Lady Mary's voice trailed off ... for Thomas had not been prepared to see Hanna and Sara all grown up.

He knew they were not going to be five years old anymore, but he had pictured them more or less as gangly girls. It took every ounce of his self-control to keep the tears from his eyes. I have missed all their growing up! The loss made a terrible ache in his chest, with a tightening in his throat. The five-year-old princesses that had so delighted him as a boy, wearing pink organdy dresses with white satin sashes and shiny white shoes with pink bows in their hair, had matured into lovely young women.

They seem shy of me, Thomas thought. Do they even remember me as a boy? The man I am is a stranger to them. Well, I will have none of it. Thomas smiled and, in turn, hugged each of his sisters, whispering, "I never forgot you. I carried a picture of sweet little girls dressed in pink in my heart. For a long time, I thought you were only a dream, but it was a happy dream." The girls still seemed reluctant, for Thomas had guessed right: they did not remember him at all. His soft, kind words and gentle hugs made the tears brim in Lady Mary's eyes.

A glance at the emotions so evident in their parent's faces removed the girl's reserve. They hugged him back and kissed Paula on the cheek, their shyness put aside.

Lady Elspeth came over and took Thomas's arm saying, "We have the afternoon to chat and catch up. We don't want the soup to get cold." She walked Thomas to the dining room. Lord Edward smiled and offered his arm to Paula. She smiled back, thinking: Mother is going to love this place.

The afternoon flew by. Jon, Anna and Edith left for the airport to fetch Charles and Lisa. Sir Peter and Lady Mary, along with Thomas and Paula, pled jet lag and went up to nap. James and Lord Greystone went into the library to talk business. Marga'ret and Elspeth sat in the breakfast room, chatting and folding napkins for the champagne tea. Hanna, Sara and Jamie ended up in the music room playing Gilbert and Sullivan, while George and Alice sang duets together, all having a time of rare good fun.

Paula set the clock as Thomas climbed in bed, saying, "I was dismayed to hear that Hanna and Sara are going on a Grand Tour of Europe in July. They will only be home during June. I know we had planned to go and visit the Zuri Watu after we inspected the kimmea plants. Would you mind if we delay going until after Hanna and Sara leave?"

"Not at all, I will be delighted to spend some time riding Sunshine. We can leave whenever you like, as long as we are back to harvest the kimmea at the right time."

"It went nicely today, don't you think?"

"Yes, it did. Everyone loved you, as I knew they would. I'm not the only one taken in by your charm."

"You can't flatter me into attentions – I'm much too tired."

Paula snuggled up anyway, but Thomas was already asleep.

13 ~ Charles & Lisa

Lisa looked out the window at the clouds below her and thought about their impending visit to England. Neither she nor Charles had ever been to England, and she had little idea what to expect. Certainly Charles Dickens was of no help, nor was Wilkie Collins. Lisa eschewed espionage and spy thrillers, and her reading of the Plantagenets would not help her either. She thought of Sir Peter and Lady Mary when they came to the States for Paula's and Thomas's wedding. They were just themselves, or at least, so they seemed. I have a habit of putting my foot in it when I'm just myself. I will have to take my cue from others.

No matter, I'm happy to get away. Tax season seemed never-ending this year with the late filings. I should drop some of the clients who, year after year, can't seem to get their act together, and end up requesting a late filing. It ruins our Spring Competition Season. What's the sense of having horses if you can't do what you want with them? I think I will send out a notice that I will not accept tax returns after March 31st. I have too many clients anyway. Although I do like the money, which we don't really need now that everyone is out of college and on their own, but it does help to build up our retirement fund.

I hope I have brought the right clothes; I have no idea what they wear here. We wear riding clothes most of the time, at home, with shorts and knit tops for sailing. The college functions are usually casual business attire. Marga'ret said to bring riding clothes, but mentioned nothing else. I brought my emerald green shantung sheath with a bolero jacket for the wedding/graduation ceremonies; it's a bit dressy, but as Mother of the bride, I felt it would be appropriate. The timing worked out well, with the New Jersey 3-day 100 mile Competitive Trail Ride held on the 26th to the 29th of May. It is usually our last competition until fall unless we do the 50 mile Endurance ride in Leesburg, Virginia. As I get older, I find that I cannot tolerate the heat as I once did, and the second weekend in June is often a scorcher in Virginia, two thousand feet closer to the sun. We have not entered the endurance ride these last two years; instead, we have gone down to help out, taking the horses along for a bit of pleasure riding.

I wish Sallee Anne had been able to come with us, but she had a benefit concert scheduled for The Children's Hospital, and so offered to take care of the horses for us; although Eric would have been more than willing to do so while we were gone. It would please me to see Sallee Anne get out more. Since Julian died in that freak auto accident, she has become a recluse. It has been more than a year now, although getting over a lost love does take time. I thought she perked up for Paula's wedding, but once it was over, she fell back into her routine of painting and practicing. She has not sketched any clothing designs since the tragedy either. She once said to me, when I thought she was trying to do too much ... 'Designing clothing is happy work, Mom.' Charles thinks I should let her be ... but he doesn't understand apathy. I don't think men do. It's the testosterone; it keeps them charged up most of the time.

Sallee Anne did say she would love to go to Africa when she talked to Lady Mary and Sir Peter at the wedding. They made a point of inviting her — and all of us — saying, 'It would be our pleasure to have you come and visit us ... anytime. There's plenty of room.'

I would love to see their farm in Africa. I can't even comprehend a farm of a thousand acres. We have twenty-three acres, and I think that's a lot of land!

However, I do comprehend jet lag, so I'd better try to get some sleep. Charles was asleep the minute we were at cruising altitude. I'm so wound up, I'll have to read, or I'll never drop off.

Charles spotted Jon when they were in line at passport control. He looked for Paula and Thomas, but he did not see them. Jon was talking to a pretty girl; I wonder if she is the Anna Louise whom Paula mentioned. Jon waved and came towards them once they were through the stiles.

"Hullo! Glad to see you made it okay. How was the flight?"

"Long, but good," Charles replied.

"I'd like to introduce you to Anna Louise Holmesby. We met when Anna and her parents were touring in Africa earlier this year. Anna, meet Lisa and Charles Thornton, Paula's parents."

Anna Louise shook hands and said, "We're so glad you were able to come over to attend the festivities." Jon led the way to the car park and the Land Rover, saying, "It's not too far; we are staying with our cousins at Greystone Place in London this evening. We will be going up to Woleston Hall in the morning."

Lisa asked, "Where are Paula and Thomas?"

"Sleeping," Anna replied. "They only arrived this morning. Lady Elspeth, Marga'ret's first cousin, has a do planned for this evening."

Lisa felt a qualm. "What kind of do?"

"It's a champagne tea to celebrate Thomas's and Paula's marriage, and Hanna's and Sara's graduation on Saturday."

"What is a champagne tea?" Lisa asked, now feeling worried.

"A sort of a cocktail party with a champagne punch served in cut glass tea cups, with tons of marvelous hors d'oeuvres, which I call petit farine (small meal), and a table of fruits, cheeses and shrimps, and of course petits fours.

"Lord Edward and Lady Elspeth will head a receiving line at five with our guests of honor. Afterward, Marga'ret and James will each take a daughter to talk to people who have similar interests. Sir Peter and Lady Mary will do the same for Thomas and Paula. Jon and I will do the same for you. I think you will enjoy yourselves. It's a very nice party with friendly people, polite questions and interesting answers, all with sumptuous food."

Seems like a lot of trouble for just a few people, Lisa thought and then asked, "How many people do you think will attend the tea?"

"Lady Elspeth has invited some of her close friends, so there should be about fifty at the tea."

Oh, my! Lisa thought. Am I ever glad that I brought my shantung dress. I thought it might be a bit dressy for Saturday, but I will wear the shantung this evening and my powder blue linen suit on Saturday.

"I should also mention," Jon added, "that Aunt Marga'ret wants to leave early tomorrow morning, so she can get a ride in before lunch. She hopes you will join her, astride, so get your riding duds

out to wear in the morning. After the ride, you can settle in before
tea; Marga'ret has authorized me to give you a tour of the Hall and
grounds before dressing for cocktails and dinner. I'm afraid we dress
for dinner, jackets and ties, at the Hall. It is a tradition, started by
Rebecca Alice Clarke, though she dined mostly alone. Marga'ret
does it to honor her memory," Jon said.

"Why did she mostly dine alone?" Lisa asked.

"Her husband, the blighter, said he didn't care for country living
shortly after they were married. He said he had not much in common
with grubby farmers, and moved to London. Rebecca then began
to dress for dinner, requiring dinner jackets for male guests. Until
shortly before her death, she dressed for dinner every evening. We
honor her memory by following her tradition."

"Why didn't Rebecca go to London with her husband?"

"It seems the cad intended to stay at his club."

"Oh, how sad, and how awful that must have been for Rebecca."

"Yes. She became a recluse, except for occasional dinner guests."

"Jon," Charles said, "I did not bring formal clothes. Do we need
to stop so I can rent a dinner jacket?"

Jon smiled. "No, we honor her memory with jackets and ties
for the men and dresses, no slacks, for the ladies. Aunt Marga'ret
most often wears floor length skirts, but she is the chatelaine and
wears whatever she likes. Aunt Marga'ret dresses in riding clothes
each morning, changing to a skirt and sweater set for lunch and the
afternoon, with a frilly blouse and long skirt for dinner. We all enjoy
the tradition. Me, I love to wear outrageous ties, and the girls get
extra use of their party frocks. It's not stuffy, just a family tradition."

"That is the one thing we seem to have lost in the States —
tradition. People have become so casual, that many eat dinner while
watching TV."

"I hope you don't go into denial. We don't have TV at the
Hall. After dinner, we usually play bridge, or hearts, or word games,
depending on the number of people involved. Aunt Marga'ret prefers
round-robin bridge, but, when she has new guests, she lets them
choose their poison."

"What about this evening? Will a suit do?" Charles asked.

"Yes, of course, or a blazer, ascot and white slacks. It is not a
formal evening, just a tea to celebrate a graduation and a marriage

and introduce members of Elspeth's family in Africa to her friends in London. Elspeth jumps on any excuse at all to entertain."

"It all sounds a bit formal; do you ever just sit and chat?"

"We chat over cocktails and during dinner. Aunt Marga'ret prefers a bit of mental stimulus during the evenings. She also believes that too much chatting leads to boring conversation, such as gall bladder surgery."

"Do you ever play poker?" Charles asked.

"No. What a noveau idea ... gambling!" Jon replied.

"I'm talking about penny-ante gambling, actually, nickels, dimes and quarters, with a ten dollar limit, about five pounds to you." Charles said.

"Women usually don't gamble unless they go to a casino, but the men often gamble at their clubs. It is a novel thought."

Anna Louise sat and listened, but thought: leave it to the Colonials to want to whack up our traditions, but they are going to run into a brick wall with Marga'ret – a brick wall covered with velvet.

★   ★   ★

"I'm never going to forget this evening," Lisa said to Charles when they were preparing for bed.

"Me either, I enjoyed every minute. Every conversation was about something interesting, with much of it about world travel. It took me a few minutes to get over the shock of this house. I felt like a time traveler when I walked in the door – transported to India on the spot."

Lisa laughed, "I know what you mean. I had a feeling of jamais vu; like I had stepped into the unknown and ... I'm still walking around in it!"

They both chuckled with Lisa commenting, "I think I'm going to like knowing fabulously wealthy people, what about you?"

"Yes, they are certainly a cut above the rest of us. Do you know not one of the persons I talked to asked me what I did for a living. I think they assumed I had a living without working for it."

"I know what you mean. Never once did I even think of my tax business. Most everyone wanted to talk horses. They don't have any competitive riding over here, but I think there was enough interest tonight to get a group started. I promised to send Julia an ECTRA Rule and Conditioning book. Did you like her?" Lisa asked.

"Julia? Yes, very much so. Her deportment is impressive. I'm looking forward to a tour of The Croft School on Saturday. I enjoyed all the horse vignettes, and I would have enjoyed more details; however, I soon realized that in depth conversations are inappropriate at a tea."

"Charles, have you ever been in such a splendid home, with such interesting people?"

"No, I have to admit not, except for the Biltmore House, in Asheville, which is more a relic of the 1920's than a fabulous home of the 1960's. I can see why George Vanderbilt, his wife and daughter spent so much time in England. Ambiance here is the gauge of status, and I daresay, there are probably more nabobs here too."

"I brought my camera, but Anna mentioned that Lady Elspeth engaged a photographer to take shots of the casual groupings, which she would mail to us. I could get used to living like this all the time."

"Please don't. If we cashed in everything, I don't think we'd last a month!"

Lisa laughed and then sighed. "You're right, this is way over our heads, but for an evening, it is simply delightful."

"Are you going to be able to go to sleep, or would you like a sleeping pill?" Charles asked.

"I don't think a sleeping pill is a good idea after all the champagne punch."

"Good thinking, but I've thought of something else that's guaranteed to make me drowsy."

"Yes?" Lisa smiled knowingly, "Whatever could that be?"

14 ~ Marga'ret

Marga'ret snuggled under the summer comforter and nestled her head on the pillow. "I feel like I could sleep for the next week! This past week has been grand with all the children together – but they're not really children any more, are they? Did you notice the change in Hanna and Sara when Mary and Peter arrived? I found their sudden dependence amusing. Our children don't cling, do they?

"Thank God in His mercy for returning Thomas to us – and what a glorious man he has become: so strong and masterful. I have been trying to remember him as a ten-year-old boy. Even then, he was reserved and quiet, usually off somewhere drawing something. I do remember him as being cheerful and agreeable in adult company though. Jon was always in tow, like a shadow, when they were here on visits, Find one boy, and you found them both. They had a little secret world that only they shared. Losing Thomas must have been especially awful for Jon. However, God has returned Thomas to us with a wonderful way about him, quiet, masterful and self-confident."

Marga'ret continued: "And Paula is delightful. Not only is she intelligent, she is a skilled horseman. Yesterday, she chose to ride The Sultan, the only rank horse we have – you know how unpredictable he is. I would have sold him long ago, if it were not for his marvelous conformation and size.

"Paula skipped lunch and spent forty-five minutes in the round ring with him. I did not see her working him, just the results. The Sultan stood quietly while being tacked up, and was just as calm at the mounting block; now you know that getting on him has always been a three-man affair. I asked Jamie to lead the group, so I could observe The Sultan on the trail. He responded with alacrity to her every command; it was simply amazing! I wish you had been there to see it."

"I had *work* to do – too many days off lately. It is enough that you saw it. I like The Sultan too – remember, I bought him," James replied.

"Yes, you did. Well, you will have to make the time to watch her work him in the round ring. The change in him is simply amazing."

"I plan on doing just that, on Monday. I want to witness this miracle for myself."

"Our boys have made us proud this past week," Marga'ret went on. "Alice has been a nicer person towards Edith. I hope it becomes a habit with her. Alice can be so sweet if she doesn't worry about what people are thinking of her!"

"Maybe you should have a chat with her."

"I would if I could, and will, if she doesn't grow out of it soon. How do you like Julia and Harold?"

"They are a breath of fresh air," James said.

"Yes, that's a good way to put it."

"You are wound pretty tight tonight. I thought you said you were tired," James snuggled closer.

"I am tired, but my mind is going full tilt. I admire Julia; she is fast becoming a dear friend. We have many interests in common, and talking to her is a delight. Anna Louise is a carbon copy of her mother. She, too, is her own person. Listen to me nattering on. I must shut down. How do you put up with me?"

"It's quite easy, actually. It's like listening to someone read a newspaper to you, pleasant in that you don't have to do it yourself."

"You always say the nicest things, James; don't ever stop. They sustain me body, mind and soul."

James snuggled closer. "Would you like me to turn out the light?"

Marga'ret wriggled a bit, saying, "James, you are amazing!"

"You, my dear, are the marvel. This house has been bursting at the seams and it has been one of the most pleasant weeks of my life."

"I know. It has been grand, hasn't it? Everything went like clockwork. We sailed from one event to another almost effortlessly, and each one was a success. I'm almost sorry it's all over. Julia had everything beautifully organized at The Croft School for the graduation and luncheon tea afterwards. It surprised me how many of the students and their parents stayed to attend the wedding ceremony; for the little Chapel was filled to overflowing. We even managed to arrive home in plenty of time to change for the receiving line of our relatives, friends and neighbors, for the reception here at the Hall."

"You must be tired, Marga'ret."

"I'm exhausted!"

"Are your defenses down?"

"My defenses are so low, they're not even there."

"That's good. Are you too tired to say no to me?"

"I'm too tired to open my eyes."

"Then don't open them, just say, yes."

"Yes."

"Now go to sleep. Tomorrow we ride to the lake to see the cygnets."

Surprised, Marga'ret drifted; what did I say yes to? Since it was not what I thought it would be … is he mucking about in my bailiwick? … Well, it must be important … and he does puts up with my rambling, ever so sweetly.

I must think of something nice to do for Elizabeth. She has been on her feet since last Saturday with this full house, and has refused to have any extra help in the kitchen, especially not the caterers for the wedding reception this evening.

She promised me, if I relented, that she would keep everything simple and what did she do? A magnificent buffet of cheeses, fruits, little Swedish finger sandwiches, crackers and shrimps; plus three of our largest chafing dishes: with one a chicken, noodle with peas and celery, another: a beef burgundy with new potatoes, carrots and mushrooms, and a lobster and crab in cheese sauce over rice, all with an enormous green salad.

I do think Elizabeth hits her stride when we have company, but, I'm ever so glad I ignored her protests and ordered the wedding/graduation cake from the bakery.

Albert always tends the punch bowl – everyone likes his sangria, and Betsy kept the buffet tables neat and organized. She is such a dear girl, so loyal to Elizabeth.

Actually, I think Elizabeth has emotionally adopted Betsy as a daughter since she is an orphan, living with a spinster aunt … but Elizabeth needs a good vacation. She won't admit it, but … yes, that's it! A vacation! A grand vacation! We can send them all on a cruise back to Sweden – Betsy going with them, for she has certainly earned a special treat too. I believe Norwegian Cruise Line sails from Portsmouth to the Baltic with several ports in Sweden.

Smiling happily, Marga'ret finally fell asleep.

15 ~ Thomas at Woleston Hall

I long for the peace and serenity of Africa. I have had enough social activity in the last five weeks to last me for a lifetime. Even as a child, I used to seek serenity here at Woleston Hall by finding new places to hide in the multitude of nooks, crannies and cupboards, especially when I played hide and seek with my cousins, who were terrible mischief-makers. Even now, they seem just over the edge into manhood, almost as if they could slip out and be rascals again – if the opportunity arose ... although Jon seems to have them well under control. It surprised me that they seemed so shy and reticent with me at first, until Edith told me that Jon had told them a story about finding us in Africa, and how I had carried Paula piggyback after she injured her ankle. It seems they were duly impressed once they saw Paula's height.

We were a family of fourteen for dinner on Friday evening, which included Anna Louise. Elizabeth served roast beef and Yorkshire pudding with a vegetable medley, a salad, popovers and spotted Dick for dessert; the traditional English celebration dinner. It was just as delicious as I remembered as a boy.

We gathered by the fireplace after dinner, where Aunt Marga'ret asked me to tell a story saying, 'Jon has often mentioned the stories that are told around the campfires; would you share one with us.' I suppose she realized I didn't play bridge!

"I would like to tell you the best part of our story, which is how Paula and I met in the wilderness of Cameroon ... if Paula has no objection."

"I have no objection, if you will allow me to ad-lib, if necessary."

Everyone chuckled and I began.

My story took them to the wilds of Africa: to the ever-present dangers of hungry carnivores, and to the vast, incredible beauty of this sparsely populated land. Telling the story made the evening special for me as well, for who knows when, or if, we will all ever gather together again? I felt a deep nostalgia for my lost years, so these special moments with all of us together made the extra twelve hours of flight time worthwhile.

The togetherness ended after my story. Paula went up to write in her diary. Marga'ret, James, Julia and Harold headed for the bridge table, with Peter and George headed for the chess table. Hanna, Sara, Jamie and Alice headed for the music room.

I lingered by the fire with Edith, the youngest of my cousins, who was but a toddler when I was lost. She is the one in whom I see the most potential. She has a mind like a steel trap and quickly grasped the deeper meanings of parts of my story, asking discerning questions that surprised me. Mother went to help Edith bed down her horse, The Cisco Kid.

I sat looking into the fire embers, thinking: I like the Anna I met here in England much better than the Anna I met in Africa – where she was frightened of her own shadow. I hope Anna is able to accept and adapt to life in Africa on her summer visit – especially for Jon's sake. He is so smitten.

Anna might just find the support she needs with Jamie there. He has a shy, retiring temperament like hers, so their perceptions of Africa might be the same. While Jamie is reticent, he has courage, so Anna could gain some confidence from him. Jon – dear, dear Jon, he does not see how Africa, in itself and by itself can affect others. Jon enjoys whatever he is doing – whenever he is doing it – wherever he does it – which is usually of little importance to him. I must have a little chat with him. He needs to be aware of, and consider Anna's fragile emotional nature.

Of the four cousins, I think Edith has the most promise. She is amazingly like Mother. I often hear Mother in her voice. Edith is going to surprise this family one day; I sense greatness in her that is yet unknown.

It delighted me to observe Hanna and Sara – surreptitiously of course – noting the little differences between them. Their voices sound the same, but the timbre differs slightly. Sara uses hand and facial gestures when she is speaking; Hanna is more composed. The pages of my life that I regret losing the most are those of my little sisters growing up. I will always be curious about their childhood.

Saturday was one of those days, where you are there, but so many things are happening at once, like a juggler keeping five balls in the air all the time, that it takes all the self-composure and concentration one can muster to keep a clear mind and take each surprising moment in its stride.

We crowded into the two Land Rovers at nine-thirty to be at The Croft School by ten-thirty, for graduation ceremonies at eleven, with the graduation tea-luncheon from twelve to one-thirty. Paula and I reaffirmed our wedding vows in a ceremony held in the Croft School Chapel at two-thirty, followed by champagne and hors d'oeuvres. We left at four to be back at Woleston Hall by five – to change for the receiving line at six – and the buffet dinner and wedding reception at eight. We cut the cake at nine-thirty, and the guests began to leave at ten. Paula sparkled through it all; only her pleasure in the event kept me going.

Aunt Marga'ret asked me to continue my story after the picnic lunch at the lake on Sunday. I had ended on Friday evening with Paula leaving the cove with Captain Jones and her parents. While I had not witnessed it, I decided to tell the short story about Paula and the Wahutu boys; which happened before we began our trek across Africa to Kenya, which story Julia and Harold had not yet heard. I also knew that Aunt Marga'ret wanted enough time for a nice ride after the picnic lunch.

Once I finished the tale, everyone asked Paula to demonstrate what she had done to awe the Wahutu boys who had jeered at her when she offered to show them how to do a handstand. Without ado, Paula stood up and began stretching exercises. One moment, she seemed to be reaching for the sky to limber her back muscles, and the next, she stepped into a cartwheel – into an aerial – into a perfect handstand – to a leg split on one hand – back to a perfect handstand – dropping into a dive-roll to end up standing on her feet – to take a bow.

The delighted cheers and clapping frightened the horses, which limited the enthusiasm to verbals of 'jolly good!' and 'simply marvelous!' with a few remarks of 'extraordinary' and 'unbelievable' added as well.

"You did that as easily as I walk!" Uncle James said. "It's no wonder that those native boys were astonished. I, for one, am simply astounded." Smiling, everyone agreed with him. I had forgotten how pleasant Uncle James and Aunt Marga'ret are to be with; there is never any obvious parenting or condescension; just adults enjoying other adults … even when we were young, we all behaved in Aunt Marga'ret's presence; much like the Zuri Watu, who parent by example. The main difference being, in Africa, if you do the wrong thing, at the wrong time, it can cost you your life.

Mom and Dad are leaving tonight on the red-eye, taking Hanna and Sara with them. Dad is starting to worry about the farm, and Mom is anxious to get the young horses back in training. They have been gone three weeks, a first for them, and twice as long as any other vacation.

Also, the girls are anxious to get started on their sewing for the European Tour. I will be sorry to see them go. I found their conversation and points of view interesting. I thought an exclusive girls' school education would make snobs of them, but it proved to be just the opposite. They have a broader knowledge of the world, which provides a greater interest in other cultures, as well as a better tolerance of them.

They even expressed a desire to go and visit the Zuri Watu when they return from the Continent. I told them the village is very primitive, which only seemed to increase their interest.

Nothing I said deterred them, for Hanna replied, "Those are the very reasons why we want to go and visit them. This primitive village turned you out, did it not? There must be a premise of life, a basis of argument for their way of life, in this primitive order, which could be the basis of a thesis I am going to write about Africa. The Sara Lawrence Writing Program has accepted me as a non-matriculated

71

undergraduate in September; I will have two years to finish my work."

Hanna's statement astonished Paula, who asked, "When did you apply?"

"Soon after I learned that Thomas had been found alive and well, and, according to Jon, a superior person to boot. Will you mind being my guinea pig, Thomas?"

"No, not at all; in fact, I think I will enjoy it."

Paula persisted with her line of thought, "That was only early April!"

"April 15th. Mrs. Holmesby helped me with the presentation. I received a reply on April 27th saying they would be delighted to have an undergraduate in Africa based on the premise I submitted."

"I'm ever so impressed. I would love to see your presentation. Would you consider letting me read it?"

"Actually, I was hoping you would help me! I based my preliminary proposition on your point of view. Mrs. Holmesby felt certain you would share your experiences with me."

"You can't imagine how you have roused my interest, Hanna. I always intended to finish my degree, but I lacked the instrumentation to do so. Your project has inspired me. With the work Thomas and I are doing with the kimmea, I would have a most excellent basis for an entirely new thesis."

Paula's animation and excitement pleased Thomas, for he remembered hearing Paula tell her father, "I have chosen love over my degree right now, but I will finish it one day, you will see."

Her assured manner that day had planted the seed of a small nagging worry that Paula might, one day, be unhappy with the simplicity of Africa. If Paula could work on her degree, she would be content in Africa – as I am content in my work.

Paula would have Hanna and Sara. Hanna would have Sara and Paula. Thomas did not see Anna Louise in his picture, but felt no concern, for Jon was not in his mental picture either.

As Thomas listened to their chatter, an unexpected thought occurred to him; were Hanna and Sara also gifted? Was that the reason why they looked at me so oddly when they first saw me? Of course! They were not being shy – they saw something unusual – why did I not sense that before?

In his thoughts, Thomas said, *'Hanna, look at me.'* With a slow turn of her head, and a questioning look in her eyes, Hanna faced me. Our eyes locked. *'What did you see when you first met me last Thursday?'*

'I saw your aura. I had never seen an aura before.'

'Did Sara see it too?'

'Yes.'

'Did it frighten you?'

'Not exactly; it was just seeing an aura that startled us.'

'How long have you been able to communicate mentally?'

'Sara and I? For years, but never with anyone else — until now.'

'Does anyone else know you can do this?'

'No, Sara and I have made a pact never to tell anyone.'

'Do you use your ability for anything?'

'Yes, we use it when we play the piano together. Will you tell?'

'Absolutely not! Your secret is safe with me. Paula asked you a question; answer her, we will talk again later.'

"Do you think Mrs. Holmesby would counsel me?" Paula asked Hanna.

"I can't speak for her. You can ask her at tea this afternoon. Paula, why did you ride back with the cart, and not go out with the others?"

"The Sultan has not had much work. A long vigorous ride would have overtired him ... and possibly soured him for trail work."

"You are really marvelous with horses," Hanna said. "Even Aunt Marga'ret is impressed, and she does not impress easily when it comes to horses."

"I have been around horses all my life. They are second nature to me. When I first saw The Sultan, he avoided me in a way that said, 'I don't like people, go away.' I knew then that his life had been one of forced submission, and he didn't like those who had forced him ... for he had never said to any man, 'Okay, you can be the boss.' After a bit of round ring work, The Sultan said to me, 'Okay, you can be my boss.' Once he said that to me, he was a different animal, it was as simple as that."

"Why do you say it is simple? What makes it so simple?" Hanna asked.

"It is their herd instinct. Every horse has a place in the herd. First, there is the Stallion, then the Lead Mare and her daughters – the stallion will chase off the two-year-old colts. Every horse says one of two things to obtain a place in the hierarchy – either: 'I'm the boss of you,' or 'okay, you can be the boss of me.'

"Now, all The Sultan needs is schooling: to learn the aids (rider signals) that tell him what the rider wants him to do, all of which must be learned from the ground."

"Why from the ground?"

"Because a horse learns from the ground: from his dam, from the other horses in the herd and from his experiences. From the ground, the horse learns the subtle body language of his trainer that goes with a command, even as he learns the words that go with that command. He will learn more from watching you than you will want to teach him; so you must always keep the lesson simple, not for the horse, for yourself, so you can duplicate it the same way each time."

"The Sultan seemed to do well on the trail," Hanna remarked.

"Yes, he did, but I asked little of him but to start, stop or turn. He is a marvelous animal, with tons of versatility. He just needs the proper attention and training. Why did you come back with the cart, Hanna?"

"Frankly? I'm tired. It's been a very busy week and I wanted some quiet time; something that Aunt Marga'ret cannot understand. I also hoped to talk to you, just as we have done."

Thomas heard the riders returning, and went out to help with the horses. His spirits soared, for Paula, Mother, and now Hanna got along famously. Everything is shaping up nicely. Now, we just have to work on Anna. She has the makings of an excellent African wife – she just doesn't know it yet.

16 ~ Paula

After breakfast on Monday, James and Paula took The Sultan into the round ring, where she groomed him.

James remarked, "He always dances around when I groom him in the cross-ties. Why is he so obedient this morning?"

"He submitted to me on Friday. He might dance around for someone else."

"Is this training good only for you – no one else?"

"Once his basic training is finished, you will go through the steps with him and obtain his submission. Eventually, the training will become a part of him; although exceptionally smart horses have been known to pick and choose among people."

"Is grooming a part of the submitting process?"

"Yes and no. It has no effect on his mind-set, but it does affect his attitude, for he likes it."

"He never seemed to like it before."

"That's because it was a prelude to being forced to submit, and he knew what was coming. I'm going to do some basic lead-line work until Marga'ret comes out. She wanted to talk to Elizabeth this morning. The Sultan already knows about leading; now what he has to learn is my space versus his space. We will do the leading basics, all with his head just forward of my shoulder, and then back three steps."

"He does not back."

"You mean he has not backed before today."

"Yes, that's right." James felt a little put out. She is talking to me as if I am a pupil. Thank goodness, here's Marga'ret … now, we will see how Paula talks to us."

At that precise moment, Paula had come to the point in the leading exercises where she wanted The Sultan to back up. Placing the butt end of the short tip buggy whip on the point of his shoulder, she said, "Back!" and stepped into his space. The Sultan immediately backed up three steps, whereupon Paula stepped back, out of his space. She then reached up and patted him high on the neck saying, "Good boy!"

Paula turned to look at me and saw Marga'ret. She said, "He did that nicely, don't you think?"

Neither one of us could respond – we were in shock. He had done it nicely, and he had never done it before – at all. Marga'ret was the first one to recover her speech.

"We are here to learn from you. Would you please show us what you did with him on Friday in the round ring?"

Paula removed the halter and sent The Sultan out on the rail. She took up a spot in the center of the circle, and using her arms to hold him in a frame – with the whip held low in the hand at his rear – she walked a circle of about ten feet in the center of the ring. Paula kept him moving in a nice strong trot until The Sultan started moving his mouth. Several laps later, he dropped his head halfway to the ground. After a few more laps, she lowered her arms and backed up a few steps. The Sultan stopped, and turned in to face her.

Stepping to his left, she said, "Reverse!" raised her arms and sent him out on the rail in the opposite direction. She repeated the same process in the opposite direction. When he had again turned to face her, she dropped the whip in the center of the ring and walked up to him, turning just before she reached him and walked away … The Sultan followed her. The whole process had taken less than fifteen minutes.

She put his halter and lead line on, and went through the leading exercises again. "Always begin and end with leading exercises, it is important that responding to the pressure of the lead line becomes automatic in a horse. I would normally call it a day, since he has done well. A trainer always wants to end on a positive note, when the horse has been willing and responsive. Short lessons are more effective than long lessons. However, I did all this with him on Friday, so today we can add a new lesson. She took the lead line and laid it across his back. Walking around past his head, she took up the lead line which she had tossed over his back, and applied a bit of pressure. The Sultan thought a moment and then followed the lead away from

Paula, turning until he was standing in front of her once again. She did the same thing again from the other side. This being his *off* side, he thought a moment longer before he complied to follow the pull of the lead to stand before her once more. She reached up, and patted him on his neck and said, "Good boy!"

She repeated the follow the lead line exercise twice more, and asked him to back again. She again patted his neck and said, "Good boy!" Paula led The Sultan over to us, where she dropped the lead line to ground-tie him. She began a system of hand massage, saying, "The Sultan is a marvelous horse. He is very smart. He thinks, which is not unusual in a horse, but he comes up with the answer you want, which is unique."

As she hand-massaged him, she told us what she had done and why. "I did not want to talk to you while I was working him," Paula said. "I did not want to confuse him. He would have tried to connect my words with his actions, and not being able to do so would have frustrated him. You have a horse in a million here. Not only is he gorgeous, he is very intelligent. Best of all though, and most surprising – he is kind, and kindness is all he asks in return for his obedience."

James felt vindicated. Marga'ret had never said so, but she had always thought he had purchased a gorgeous horse without a mind. He also felt a bit ashamed of his earlier attitude towards Paula. I am the pupil. I could not have achieved the same results in a month – or maybe even six months – which she has accomplished in a half-hour.

Marga'ret wondered if she could tempt Paula into staying over for a few days, thinking: I have so much to learn from her.

"My dear, you are simply marvelous. Where did you learn your technique?"

"From my mother; she has been training horses all her life. She started out West with the mustangs and progressed to problem horses."

"From whom did she learn, may I ask?"

"From her father; he broke mustangs in the usual way until he went to Australia, where he met a man named Jaffrey, who also broke wild horses – brombies – but with an entirely different approach. What you saw today is a combination of the best of several techniques, fused into a system that any caring horseman can do."

"I wish you could stay a few more days. I would clear my calendar, and we could just work the horses."

"I will talk to Thomas. I would like to stay a bit longer too … to complete The Sultan's basic ground work; he has so much promise."

James left to show Paula's father, Charles, his auto collection – totally impressed with his niece-in-law. Marga'ret asked Paula to work one of the Haflingers who would go in double harness, but not as a single. Paula had never heard of such a problem, but started in the usual manner. She immediately noticed Willie Le La's reluctance to go in a counter clockwise circle, or to the left. She asked Marga'ret, "Will he only hitch to the right of the team?"

"Why, yes, how did you know?" Marga'ret asked astonished.

Paula finished the right circle, obtaining mouth movement, and a lowered head with a face center. She went up to him, passed him, and he followed her. When she stopped and turned, she took off her cap and held it over his left eye. She moved her left hand quickly towards his right eye and he blinked. She reversed the procedure, but Willie did not blink his left eye. "I think he has vision problems; your Vet should see him."

They worked horses until lunchtime, before going in to shower, and change to street clothes. Marga'ret and Paula were taking Charles and Lisa to the airport after lunch.

Paula did not see Thomas before she went up to shower and change, and wondered where he'd gone. She knew that he felt saddened when his sisters and parents left for Africa last night … but we will soon see them again at Dela-Aden.

Lisa had gone with Jon and Anna to the village that morning; she wanted to get some local trinkets for gifts. George had to pack up for the tournament; he could be gone a week, or three … if they made it to the final play-offs. Alice had gone off to visit a friend for the day. Edith and Jamie went out riding; the youngest and the oldest siblings had found a mutual passion – horses.

Thomas stood in the entrance hall surrounded by the others when Paula went down for lunch. He was holding something in his arms, and turned at her step. Surprised, Paula saw he held a big puppy.

"Where did you get the puppy?" she asked.

"In the woods; I heard a whimpering, looked over, and he hopped towards me. He has two broken toes in his right front paw and a torn left ear."

"I wonder where he came from." Paula asked.

"I know where he came from," Marga'ret interjected, "we often find injured or sick dogs in the woods. We just take them to the Shelter. People don't want to pay the Vet bills or the Shelter donation, so they just drop them off in the woods. They drop off cats too, but the cats go feral so fast, we can't get close enough to catch them. However, the cats do keep the rodent population down, and once a month we put out meat that has medicine in it to keep them sterile and wormed.

"This little fellow looks like some sort of sight-hound, but his coat and color are unusual. That is excellent splint-work, Thomas. Can he walk on it?"

"Yes, he can stand on his foot, now that his toes don't touch the ground. How old do you think he might be?" Thomas asked.

"I'm not sure," Marga'ret replied, "maybe four months, he's going to be a big dog – look at those paws. Well, Jamie can drive him to the Shelter after lunch. Paula and I are driving Charles and Lisa to the airport."

The family gathered for tuna salad sandwiches, home fried potatoes a'la Elizabeth, and a fruit and nut jello salad.

Jamie had promised Edith a tennis game in the afternoon; so Jon, Anna and Thomas took the puppy to the Vet.

"What have we here?" Dr. Hank Springer asked Jon.

"I think it is another drop-off in the woods," Jon replied. "Anyone report a puppy missing?"

"I don't know. Florence, call 'round, see if anyone is missing a male puppy, sort of light palomino in color, about four months old, possibly a sight hound. He looks in good shape, except for the broken toes and torn ear. Your splint work is better than my splint work, so we shall leave it be, and give this guy a shot to make sure he doesn't get an infection. If you like, I can keep him today and transfer him to the Shelter tomorrow."

"That would be good, thanks." Jon settled the bill and they left for Inkpen. Talk of the old monastery gardens had piqued Thomas's interest.

Paula found Thomas sitting on the chaise lounge in their bedroom. "That is a most comfortable chair, isn't it?"

"Yes, I sat down and found I didn't want to get up. Actually, I dozed a bit. How was your day?"

"Marvelous, I love working horses. These horses go fox hunting, so they are somewhat bull headed – but the two we worked today are no longer obstinate. Marga'ret and I skipped tea and worked horses all afternoon. She is a quick study. She watched me work the first horse, and did the second one by herself, with very few suggestions, which brings me to a question."

"I don't know a thing about horses, so what kind of question do you have for me?"

"If we can get another flight, would you mind staying on for a few days?"

"Was that Aunt Marga'ret's idea?"

"Yes, but I would love to stay and help her, if I can."

"Coincidentally, I was sitting here figuring out how much time we have before we have to be back for the kimmea, and if we will still have time to visit the Zuri Watu. I wanted to work in the time to talk to Jon. He needs to understand Anna's fears, for Jon has almost no fear himself. Anna needs to realize that her fear is crippling her emotionally. Of course, there are things to fear: lions, elephants, earthquakes, wars and pestilence, but not until they are real possibilities."

"Oh Thomas, that's exactly what they need: Jon is too carefree and Anna is too worrisome. Why don't we all take a hike together, and split up – with you talking to Jon and me talking to Anna. What do you think?"

"I think you had better keep your distance, or I won't be able to stop myself from giving you a big kiss for being so clever … and you know what happens when I give you a big kiss."

Paula finished her toilette as they talked. She put on a fluffy terry robe and strolled over to the chaise lounge. "Is this enough distance?" she asked, smiling.

"It is exactly the right distance, even if it is not enough distance … " He reached out and took her hand, tugging her gently down next to him, where he held her for the promised kiss. As he tiptoed around her face with little kisses, he whispered in her ear. "When you call the airlines, see how much it would cost to transport a puppy to Africa," he whispered between the little kisses.

"Liked him, did you?"

"Yes, but more than that – I know he is meant to be mine."

"Then I will call the Vet too, and get the puppy up-to-date on his shots, and get the necessary travel papers for him too."

"This is a problem?" he asked.

"No, but we will have to stay a few more days, which is just what I wanted."

"Me too, I had forgotten how much I liked this big old house with all its cozy alcoves and hidden cupboards … and I love the woods. I spent many happy hours playing Robin Hood there, rescuing an imaginary damsel in distress."

"What about Alice? Didn't she want to play?"

"No, she didn't like the woods … or getting dirty."

"She hasn't changed much, has she?" Paula said chuckling.

"No, I don't think Alice will ever change." Thomas smiled back.

Thomas showered and dressed for dinner, while Paula called the Vet Clinic to say they wanted to keep the puppy. She asked them to prepare the papers and the needed shots for the puppy to go to Africa. Paula called the airlines: changed their departure date and reserved a crate for the puppy. Now, we have three more days at Woleston Hall before we leave for Africa on Friday.

17 ~ *Walberry Hill*

Paula found Marga'ret in the library and told her about the revised travel plans. Marga'ret smiled her pleasure saying, "You changed your flight to leave on Friday? How marvelous, you will be traveling back to Africa with Jamie, Jon, Anna Louise ... and a puppy."

"Yes." Paula smiled. "If we work two horses in the morning and three in the afternoon, we could finish the barn before I leave. Thomas wants to take a morning to go hiking with Jon and Anna Louise. Even so, we will have a bit of time for second rounds, if any of the horses are inordinately slow or difficult."

"I would like you to go through all the training on one horse, if that is possible, so I can watch you. Will any of the horses do?" Marga'ret asked.

"We can try with The Sultan. If we start with him each morning and end with him each afternoon, it might be possible. He is the only one, so far, with the willing temperament and intelligence needed to enjoy the extra work."

"He does seem to like the training; even I can see that ... it just amazes me to apply the adjective *willing* to him. He has been anything but that, for two years!"

"You shouldn't belittle yourself just because you didn't know about the miracle of round pen training. You have a wonderful way with horses, and they show you the same attention they show me, and I have been training horses for years!"

"Thank you, dear. It is kind of you to say so. I find the work fascinating − for the results are astonishing! Oh, here come Julia, Harold, Anna and Jon. Where have you been all day? We missed you at lunch!"

"We took a drive to Inkpen to see where Daddy will be working this summer," Anna replied. "It is a step back in time down there."

After dinner, while James, Marga'ret, Julia and Harold, Alice, Edith, Jamie and George played party bridge, Thomas and Paula took Jon and Anna Louise aside to ask them if they would guide them on a hike of Walberry Hill. "We have heard you talk of it, and it sounds quite nice."

"Righto," Jon said, "We'd like that, wouldn't we, Anna?"

"Yes, it is a great spot for a picnic."

"Would Wednesday suit you?" Thomas asked.

Anna nodded her head happily, and Jon said, "Wednesday it is!"

Jon, Anna, Thomas and Paula stopped at the Veterinary Clinic on Wednesday after the hike and picnic to pick up the puppy.

Florence said, "I found the owner. Someone stole the dog from his crate at a dog show. When I told the owner that the dog had a torn ear and broken toes on a front paw, he said the dog would no longer be suitable for showing, which is what he does with his Afghan hounds.

"I told him how nicely you had splinted his paw, and the man was so pleased that the puppy will have a good home, that he asks only his out-of-pocket costs for papers, which is twenty five pounds. The dog's registered name is Son of the Wind, called Windy. I didn't think the price would be a problem for you; these dogs usually cost hundreds of pounds. He will send us the papers after we send him the funds."

Jon wrote a check on the spot for the puppy, and a check to cover the shots and travel papers, with a donation to the Veterinary Clinic for their help in finding the owner.

Dr. Springer went and fetched the puppy. Windy walked with a little limp, but he was bright and eager. "He is a fine animal. He now weighs thirty-two pounds, and he will top out at ninety or so. You do know that this breed is the fastest of the large breeds; he will be able to run sixty-five miles an hour for short bursts when he is grown. It is imperative that you train him to come with a silent whistle or you might lose him to a chase. He has been our darling during his short stay here. He is quite affectionate. Good Luck to you with him."

Thomas knelt down and the puppy came to him and licked his face. "We are going to be good friends, you and I. You will like

Africa." On his new training lead, with collar and tags, Windy walked beside Thomas as if he had always walked there.

On arriving back at Woleston Hall, Paula went out to help Marga'ret with the horses. Marga'ret had worked two on her own before lunch and said, "I think this is the most marvelous thing I have ever learned. Even Dingbat came alive this morning! She actually seemed to see me for the first time."

"I think you should change her name," Paula suggested. "Horses know when you call them derogatory names and it affects their attitudes. How about calling her Ding-a-Ling? It's similar, but not disparaging."

"I must say, why do you think horses are that smart? How do they know what their names mean?"

"It is in the tone of your voice. Horses learn those tones like they learn the meaning of other horse's ears."

"If you say so, but I'm skeptical; although I'm willing to try whatever you suggest."

"Trust me, calling her Ding-a-Ling instead of Dingbat, will change her attitude in a positive way."

Jon had brought Anna Louise's packed bags to Woleston Hall. Marga'ret had trailered Spice to the Hall for Julia, who was taking time away from her year-end reports to be with Anna Lou and Jon before they left for Africa ... as well as enjoying the morning rides with Marga'ret, James and Paula. Edith and Jamie rode later, not wanting to get up at the crack of dawn to ride with them. Harold commuted to Inkpen from Woleston Hall, but he anticipated feeling lonely: "What will I do with myself when Julia is on the Continent and Anna Lou is in Africa? I will be lost!"

Thomas took Windy for a walk in the woods to practice with the silent whistle Jon had bought on the way home. Watching Windy limp along, Thomas suddenly remembered Foxy, the perky little fox terrier he had as a boy at Dela-Aden. Foxy had a hurt paw too ... he was my first patient. That happy little dog went everywhere with me. He always followed me if Jon and I split up. Why had I forgotten him? I had loved him so. When I saw Windy limping, I felt a connection with him instantly … feeling he would make up for my lost years with Foxy.

Thomas read the directions on the whistle package and lightly blew on it, but heard nothing. Windy cocked his head to the side and looked at him expectantly. Thomas gave Windy the palm-out hand sign, while saying *stay*, and stepped behind a tree, where he lightly blew on the whistle. In a moment, Windy stood looking at him, happily wagging his long tail. Thomas told him he was a *good dog* and rubbed him all over. They played the game a dozen times or more. Each time, Thomas hid a bit better, or went further afield; he even climbed a tree. Each time, Windy found him within moments, and stood wagging his long tail, where Thomas ruffled his silky coat and told him he was a *good boy!* The game was so much fun, that Thomas hated to stop; but Windy did have a sore paw; though he didn't favor it at all, but Thomas stopped anyway.

Thomas sat in the woods with his arm around the dog, feeling as happy as ever he had at being alone … before Paula came into his life. Being alone, after he met Paula, had become a trial that was increasingly harder to bear. He rubbed Windy's head and said to him, "You and I have a destiny to share; I don't know yet what it is – however, we will find it together, won't we?"

It was a glorious morning. Marga'ret, James, Julia, Edith and Jamie all went for a morning ride on the retrained horses. Edith worked the Cisco Kid with Paula's guidance; she, like her mother, had a natural flair for horses.

Elizabeth packed peanut butter and jelly sandwiches, cookies, apples and lemonade for the hike to Walberry Hill. Jon hiked happily – it felt like old times in Africa. Anna Lou enjoyed the old camaraderie between Jon, Thomas and Paula.

Halfway up the hill, Thomas said to Paula, "You go on. Jon and I will be along in a moment."

Paula whispered to Anna, "potty stop." The girls walked on with Paula adding, "You seem to enjoy hiking, Anna. Have you done much of it?"

"Yes and no. Daddy has walked me through half the gardens of England, but that is not really hiking, is it? Jon, however, loves to hike and we have done that almost every day. I never really knew England until we started our daily tours."

"Did you do much walking in Africa?"

"Only in the bazaars; everywhere else, we rode – mostly in mule-drawn carts, with a few cabs or tour buses."

"Are you looking forward to returning to Africa with Jon?"

"Oh, yes. Jon and Marga'ret told me a bit about Africa. On our winter tour, I was not prepared to see glass-topped walls, armed sentries and bars on the windows – the need for them frightened me. Once Marga'ret explained why the bars were there, I realized I had over-reacted."

"You do know that no matter where you go there will always be an element of danger – even London or New York."

"Yes, until Jon got back, I went to school every day with Mother and studied the different cultures in Africa. I read about Morocco too, for I was just as frightened there as I was in Nairobi, but for different reasons. The opportunity for Mother's sabbatical came up suddenly, so there was little time to read up about the peoples we would meet. Well, I'm better prepared now. I still have a lot to learn, but I think I will be able to meet new situations without trepidation."

"Jon, hold up a moment longer."

"What's up old man?"

"I'm going to come right to the point, is that okay?"

"Seems everyone wants to stop beating around the bush with me; am I in the soup?"

"No, of course not … at least, I don't think so. Is there something you have done that I should know about?"

"Egads! Don't be a frightful bore! Just get on with it, will you?"

"All right, I just want to say that I don't think you are as sensitive to Anna's feelings about new places or unusual situations as you should be. You base everything on how you feel, not on what Anna might feel. You need to think of her first."

"Did someone put you up to this, Thomas?"

"No, it is my idea, but Paula agreed with me."

Jon sighed. "As usual, you are right. I don't see what she sees, the way she sees it. I found that out in our ten days junketing about the countryside. Anna is really quite brave, you know. It is just situations where she has no information that balk her. She knows so much that when faced with something unknown, she falters."

"I'm glad to see that you're becoming considerate of her feelings. That is all I wanted to ask you to do. Anna Louise will come to love Africa if we present it to her properly ... and slowly, so she can acclimatize to it."

"That's a bit much! Have you been reading dictionaries?"

Thomas laughed, "No, just talking to Paula. She likes eleven letter words."

"Well, if you've had your say, let's get cracking. Anna will think I have stones!"

Thursday dinner arrived in a blink of the eye. Marga'ret and Paula finished working the horses to a point where Marga'ret could carry on alone, or with Edith's help for the mounted work. Paula saw that Edith had a natural flair with horses when she watched her working The Cisco Kid. The horse did as he was asked, responding willingly; he had already decided to let Edith be the boss of him – horses will do that when they are treated with consistent kindness. The problem being ... without submitting under pressure, the horse feels free to withdraw his cooperation at any time, which is usually at the worst possible moment, like when crossing a scary wooden bridge or fording a river.

Marga'ret sipped her tea as she made mental plans: James will take Harold and Julia, Anna Louise and Jon and luggage to the airport tomorrow, while I will take Jamie, Paula, Thomas and the dog, and their baggage. That way Harold can ride back with James, and Julia can ride back with me.

This house is going to seem so empty when everyone is gone. I will feel woebegone. Marga'ret said, "Harold, you must continue to stay with us while Julia is on the continent. We can play hearts or fool's bridge and bid for the dummy."

Harold was non-plused at the invitation and stammered, "How kind of you Marga'ret, but I couldn't possibly put you out!"

"Nonsense, if it would have put us out, I wouldn't have invited you."

James, who usually stayed out of the social stuff, added, "I want to take the new Aston Martin out for a long spin, Harold; you could go along with me. Marga'ret doesn't like me to go over hill and dale alone; and I can't get her away from the horses long enough to go very far. It would be awf'ly convenient, if you were already here, old man."

"Yes, it would be fun to help out," Harold replied. He loved running about the countryside in the Aston Martins. "Let me think on it."

"Harold," Julia said, "you could look in on Spice; he so likes you to groom him."

"Yes, I could do that too, couldn't I?" Harold also loved horses. He just could not ride very well. Julia had decided long ago, that if she wanted a live husband, he had better go to driving, which he did … and does, and likes very well.

It took Harold only a moment to realize how lonely home would feel all alone. He said, "Thanks awf'ly, it would be nice to stay here while Julia and Anna are away."

James looked pleased at having an ally. Julia felt delighted that Harold could look after Spice, and Marga'ret was happy that James could dash about the countryside taking Harold with him. For the near future, she and James would be attending George's Tournament games, which would give Harold and Julia a bit of togetherness time before she left for the Continent.

Marga'ret walked out on the patio, ostensibly to look at the newly planted flower beds. James had asked her if Edith could go to Ireland in August. It was the sleepy *yes* he had elicited from her the night before graduation. "Edith may go whenever she likes, but she may not travel alone." James had approached George, who said, "I would love to help out, but I've signed up for a tennis tourney the last two weeks in July."

James had called Lena's father, Captain O'Daire, to tell him of the problem: Marga'ret would not allow Edith to travel alone, and George had a conflict.

Lena was counting on Edith being there for the Air Show the last week in July. It was a stalemate, until Captain O'Daire called and said, "I have a friend, Commander Evans, who is leaving from Bristol on the 22nd of July for the Air Show. If you can get Edith to Bristol Airport by ten a.m., he will give her a lift. His wife, Rita, and sons, Rob and Sean, will be traveling up with him. Edith was ecstatic, George was relieved, and James was delighted. He and Marga'ret would make a day of it, and take Edith to Bristol in the Rolls. Edith's cup runeth over: she was going to Bristol in the Rolls Royce Silver Ghost; she was going to Ireland; and she was having her first aeroplane ride.

Marga'ret booked the Alaska Cruise Tour on Holland American Cruise Lines for Friday, the 26th of August. She looked forward to celebrating their 24th wedding anniversary, on the 27^{th,} aboard the ship. The boys will be back in school, and Alice will stay with Cousin Elspeth in London. Edith will be in Ireland with Lena, and will travel to England together when school starts. Elizabeth and Albert were going on a cruise of the Baltic, taking Betsy with them; and would disembark in Copenhagen to visit family in Sweden before flying home.

"You are smiling so sweetly, my pet; a penny for your thoughts," James said.

"I was thinking about what a nice summer we are having," Marga'ret replied.

"The summer has barely begun, my dear."

"True, however, so far, it is going swimmingly, isn't it?"

18 ~ Dela-Aden

Jamie settled in his aisle seat at the back of the first class section of the Boeing 707. He was so excited about going to Africa, that he never once gave a thought to the actuality of saying good-bye to Mom, Dad and Edith. Leaving them there at the gangway had made an awful tightness in his chest, which he had not expected. Saying good-bye to Alice, when she went off to the beach, had not fazed him at all.

With George away for his Tournament, I found a friend in my little sister. Edith is a super gal, which I never suspected while Alice dominated the scene. I will miss her, for not only is she clever, she's interesting and very nice ... so different from our self-absorbed Alice.

Edith is a grand horseman, and The Cisco Kid is one heck of a good horse. The only other horse in the barn that compares to Cisco is The Sultan, and he was off-limits until Paula finished his training. Now there is a most marvelous horseman. Paula is the most gifted person I have ever known. I wonder if she is typical of American women. Thomas can count his blessings – and I think he does – for women like Paula don't come along very often.

I learned patience by observing Thomas and Paula and the way they approach life. Yes, I am still undecided, but I no longer feel at loose ends. I now realize that no one knows what tomorrow may bring. Each of us goes along each day, doing the needs of the moment, when the coming of tomorrow could change everything.

'Man plans but God commands,' now where did I hear that? If that is so, why do we make plans ... to have a sense of the future, or for our convenience? If we just got in the car and started out on a trip, all sorts of annoying things could happen: we could run out of gas; miss the rest stop and restaurant; have a flat tire and a flat spare and no place to phone for help. Well, I'm going to plan for my convenience, to know as well as I can what to expect, and I will deal with the unexpected when it happens. I'm going to see and do as much as I can while I'm in Africa – and that is plan enough for now.

Sir Peter and Lady Mary were on the porch to greet the weary travelers. The bags were hustled to their rooms with Sir Peter directing the traffic. Lady Mary had white wine, salt crackers, strawberries and brie waiting for their refreshment. Even though they had been doing nothing but sitting, it was somehow much better to be sitting at their destination, rather than sitting while traveling to it.

"It's a long flight," Mary said. "Rest here a bit – then go for a nice walk before you freshen up for tea. I planned a dinner tea, so you can just go to bed afterwards. It is what we did when we arrived back."

"We slept around the clock," Peter added.

"I want to have a look at the kimmea," Thomas said. "I don't think I could sleep until I do."

"Your plants look healthy and are growing well," Peter said. "Samuel has done a fine job of taking care of them."

"We felt Samuel could be relied on to do as we asked. He seems quite interested in horticulture," Paula replied,

"Yes, the man has a green thumb," Peter added.

Thomas was gone when Paula awoke. She smiled inwardly thinking, I knew I would never have to worry about another woman, but it never occurred to me that I might have a puppy as competition. However, puppies grow up quickly, so I should not languish for long. After a good stretch and a mental plan of the day, Paula went down for breakfast. It was almost ten o'clock, but a cold breakfast was still on the buffet. Elizabeth heard her in the dining room and poked her head in the door. "Do you want anything else, miss?"

"No, this is just fine. It's my usual breakfast, unless Thomas is cooking, then I have oatmeal," Paula replied.

"Mr. Thomas told me to tell you he has taken the puppy for a walk, and then he will be in the garden shed with the plants."

"At least he is predictable." She smiled at Elizabeth who smiled back in a knowing way, and returned to her kitchen.

Paula had dressed in riding clothes, anxious to take Sunshine out for a ride; but first, a stop at the garden shed greenhouse. Thomas had pulled up a plant and was taking it apart leaf by leaf. Windy lay beside him, smiling – if dogs smile, he was doing it!

"Is there a problem?" she asked.

Thomas turned and smiled at her. "No, sleepyhead, but I wanted to make sure we hadn't acquired some bugs ... bugs that would normally be eaten by guinea fowl and other free-ranging birds."

"Oh, Thomas, look! There are birds in here."

"I know! Samuel keeps canaries at home, but they are seed eaters. So, he went out and found some bug eaters for us. Somehow, Samuel caught a pair of tits and brought them and their nest into the greenhouse ... actually he brought the whole tree! He put it in the back, where it is quiet, so the birds are still coming back to their nest. If we have bugs, I hope they will eat them."

"Are they locked in here?"

"No, the male comes back because the hen is sitting on her eggs. If we don't bother them, they will finish the cycle. Since we are only in here for a few hours each day, they might get used to us."

"Do you think they will come back for another nesting?"

"I have no idea, but we shall see, for they usually nest twice a year."

"I'm going to go for a ride before lunch; not for long, I'm so out of shape."

"You look in pretty good shape to me," he said, while eyeing her up and down.

"Silly boy, you know what I mean – my muscles are out of shape!"

"Don't worry about it, dearest, it doesn't show at all."

When Thomas was in a bantering mood, he always bested her. She gave him a quick peck on the cheek, but gave Windy a big hug and smooch.

Feeling a bit jealous, he said, "If you manhandle my dog, he might bite you!"

Paula laughed merrily, and dashed away, saying, "But then again, he just might like it ... like someone else I know!"

Lady Mary thought Paula might want to go for a ride, and had kept Sunshine in the barn with a flake of hay after her morning feed. She was busy working a youngster in long lines when Paula came down to the barn, tacked up Sunshine and went out for an easy ride, mostly walking. Over the years, Paula had had other hiatuses from the saddle, and knew that slow and easy starts after time off, was not only good for the horse, but spared her the discomfort of sore calf muscles.

When she returned, Lady Mary asked, "How did she go?"

"Oh, this mare is the sweetest horse I have ever ridden … she is absolutely game for anything, and has the most marvelous gaits, and transitions."

"Yes, that's why I kept her. With her Saddlebred characteristics, a longer back a longer neck, and longer canon bones, she would make beautiful foals. Although most people want purebreds, or Sport Horses, not show horses. But, I agree, she is the sweetest riding horse ever."

"Thank you again for giving her to me. Nothing else you could have done would have made me feel so much at home here."

"I had my reasons, don't you know? Selfish reasons – I wanted someone here that loved horses as much as I do, and understands horses the way I do – and you fulfilled my dreams as much as you fulfilled Thomas' dreams. I should thank you! Well, now that we have my motives out in the open, I'd like to talk to you about the round ring training you did for Marga'ret. She sent me a letter filled with your, as she said – 'absolutely amazing abilities'. I would like to see what you did that – 'transformed her mindless hacks into delightful mounts'."

"I think Marga'ret exaggerates, but we did turn some of them around. Is there any particular horse that's a problem for you?"

"I don't really have problems, but every now and again, for no reason that I can perceive, a horse will fall out … that is, not do what I expect of him."

"Under saddle?" Paula asked.

"Sometimes, or like hosing off Diablo the other day when he leapt away without warning. Fortunately, no one was in his way to get hurt."

"Sounds like he took a nap and the hose woke him up by surprise. Horses do fall asleep with their eyes half open, especially when they like what you are doing, like grooming them. When do you work Diablo-Airé ... in the morning?"

"No, I usually work the youngsters in the morning and work him in the afternoon, after lunch."

"Good – why don't I come back with you after lunch and show you the round ring training method, using Diablo?"

Mary took Paula in her arms for a hug, saying, "I am so pleased you are here. I hope you will be very happy here."

Diablo settled to work in the round ring right away, but he took a long time to drop his head. In fact, Paula thought he might be her first failure, for it took forty minutes in one direction before his head dipped to his knees. Paula then realized that this horse was so well-conditioned, he was toying with her – well buddy – you picked the wrong lady to play games with ...

"Have you ever thought Diablo might have a stubborn streak in him?" she asked Lady Mary, who watched from the stands.

"I always thought of him as being tough, as in durable, but you may be right, he might be a bit stubborn too."

Paula reversed Diablo and had a big surprise when he dropped his head while licking and chewing in only three laps. So, you were playing with me; well, I think I will now play with you. She kept him circling for fifteen minutes, letting him slow several times as if to stop, but pushing him on again before he did. She could see, by his body language, that he was regretting his earlier mistake. He wanted to stop, he had lost his edge, but, just to make sure he was truly repentant, she pushed him on until his gait lost its sharp, precise action. She stopped, he stopped – she stepped towards him with the whip reversed, and ten steps out, (usually much too far out for join-up) she turned and without hesitation, he followed.

Paula haltered Diablo, and went through her leading routine, obtaining a beautiful four step reverse, before she led him to the rail, where she dropped the lead and began to massage him.

"This is a very smart horse. Has he ever tested you the way he tested me today?"

"Many times, I'm sorry to say. How did you know he was testing you?"

"Horses usually take the same amount of time in both directions, unless they have physical problems. When he submitted in three laps, I knew he was testing me, and made him work until he regretted having done so."

"Marga'ret, I'm sorry to say, was not munificent enough in her praise of your abilities: she fell far short with simply marvelous. I'd say you are absolutely incredible in your understanding of horses."

"Thank you. I love round pen training because I love horses, and I know how much happier they are when they have agreed to be your partner."

"Do you really think it makes the horse happier?"

"I'm 100% positive of it. Horses are herd animals – when you make them part of your herd, you fulfill their deepest innate desire."

While Thomas tended the kimmea plants and trained his dog, Paula spent her time in the barn with Lady Mary. Jon spent a great deal of his time helping his father with major projects that required a constant eye to get the job done right. Both the overseer and the farm manager were natives, and while they were excellent workers and bosses, they lacked the technical education needed for involved projects. Jon's duties threw Anna Louise and Jamie together during the day, for Hanna and Sara were busy sewing, day and night, for their European tour.

"Thomas drew a small copy of the trails from the farm map in Uncle Peter's office for us to use when out riding, Jamie told Anna. Now, we can explore without getting lost. A thousand acres is half the size of England!" Jamie exaggerated.

"It may not be half the size of England, but I agree, it is an incredible amount of land!" Anna said, laughing. "Where are we going today? I'd like to see that road (she pointed to the map) – it goes all the way around the property. What do you think?"

"Looks good to me – from here (he pointed to a spot on the map) we can take this trail around the reservoir and end up on the boundary road. It doesn't look as if there are any intersecting trails to confuse us, and then come back on this trail." (Again, he pointed at the map.)

"I'm game, if you are."

Jamie led off on a walking path, which led to the reservoir. Going single style, Anna thought about her days riding with Jamie. He had an excellent seat, and had thrilled her when he posted the canter, which she had never seen done before. She was, for the first time, enjoying riding just for itself. It felt so different to ride out and explore new places, than it did to ride in a ring or the same trails over and over. This is the way riding should be … and probably is … on the competitive trail rides that Paula enjoys so much.

At dinner, Thomas asked Anna, "How did the map work out for you today?"

"It was great. We had to clear some fallen branches, but nothing major."

"If you give me your map, I'll mark the trails that I know are open," Jon suggested. "I'd rather you told me where you want to go, so I can send someone out to make sure the trails are clear for you."

"Oh, we don't want to be a bother to you, Jon. We don't mind clearing a bit of brush, do we Jamie?"

"I don't mind, but I'm a guest here, and will do as my hosts ask."

He's right, Anna thought. I'm acting proprietarily – I wonder if that means I have accepted the idea of living in Africa. It's too soon to know, but it's a good omen.

Jon smiled, thinking: for a girl that said she didn't seek out riding, I would say Anna has changed her opinion. Jamie has been a different lad here too. Is it Africa? Or is it something else?

Lady Mary spoke up, "Our Sunday ride with the neighbors is coming up, I'll show you the trails I thought we'd use on the map; you can send a crew out to make sure they're clear for the ride."

"While we are on the subject of trails," Sir Peter said, "I would prefer that you use the boundary road as little as possible. We have found squatters out there, and they can be belligerent. You don't need that kind of hassle when you are out for a pleasure ride; however, if you do see squatters, make sure to note the place on the map, so I can send men out to move them off."

"What is the harm of a few squatters?" Paula asked.

"Basically, a few squatters are not a problem, anymore than a few weeds in a garden are a problem. But both weeds and squatters, if not removed early, expand exponentially, so like weeds, you must keep after them." Sir Peter smiled at Paula; she was a kind person and considerate of everyone.

Evenings at Dela–Aden were not structured as they were at Woleston Hall. Lady Mary did not feel the need to organize everyone as did Marga'ret. Thomas and Paula often took long walks with Windy, and sometimes Anna and Jon went along with them. A bond was building between the four of them, as couples, a different type of relationship than the one between Thomas and Jon, giving them a feeling of contentment, home and stability.

Jamie found a great chess opponent in Sir Peter, and they went at it most evenings. Hanna and Sara did hand sewing by the fire, with Lady Mary helping, while chatting and listening to classical music. On rainy evenings, Thomas, Paula, Jon and Anna liked to play hearts, with Anna unable to figure out why she was the one most often stuck with the queen!

Dinner was at eight, so the evenings were not long. Most everyone was up at first light or a little before, at six, to be ready to go at first light. Peter and Mary preferred cereal or oatmeal, fruit and toast for breakfast. Elizabeth had sausages or bacon and eggs to order, at seven.

Hanna and Sara usually practiced first thing in the mornings after breakfast, leaving the sewing for the heat of the day.

19 ~ Mr. Athos and Max

"A great deal of time is passing; I am starting to lose confidence in the legitimacy of these delays. I think Cyril Latham has them looking around for a better deal, which is not a smart thing for them to do. I thought we had made enough of an impression on them before you met them in Luanda to eliminate any funny business. Maybe they need a reminder!"

Max studied Mr. Athos, who was a choleric man, easily upset by delays of any kind. That he had been patient this long was unusual for him. Max needed to plan his words carefully: "You have, indeed, been patient, and so far, the delays have made sense. They wanted to be sure that the plant would grow from seed in a hothouse. Then, an African plant specialist said that changing the growth medium of the plant could change the properties of the seed. They are now growing plants from hothouse seed, to test its viability. In all, the process will take six months from the beginning, which was about the middle of April."

"We have the word of their attorney that this is what is actually happening, and nothing more. I'm beginning to feel the fool, believing them without proof!"

"What kind of proof can they possibly give you?"

"You seem to accept their reasons. Why?"

"I have met these people. I have dealt with them. They had us captured, knew everything about us, and could have turned us into the authorities, but they did not. For this reason, I trust them and I trust their word. They say they are trying to protect your interests, and I believe that to be true."

"Yes, I too, have wondered why they did not turn you in; I don't believe that such good and tolerant people really exist. I want proof. I no longer believe in their good intentions. I think they are playing me for a fool."

"What do you have in mind?" Max quaked inside, thinking: I should have quit when I had the chance, but fifty thousand dollars is a big bonus if the deal goes through.

"I want you to get me a hostage."

"You want to get involved in kidnapping?"

"I want irrefutable insurance, what else is there?"

"How about if we got a spy into the compound; if we were certain that they're doing what they say they're doing ... would that work for you?"

Mr. Athos thought, tapping a letter opener on the metal of the ring on the inside of his hand. Max hated the sound; it was like a funeral dirge. "You have forty-eight hours to come up with a plan. This is the biggest deal of my life, and I don't intend to lose it by stupidity ... and trusting someone's word has always been stupid business."

Max obtained a map of the original land grant in Nairobi, locating the boundary road of Dela-Aden. He also found the grouped mail boxes, where he waited, hoping a neighbor might provide some useful information. Mid-morning, Jon arrived and opened the mail box to take the outgoing mail to Nairobi. Max ducked down in his seat; the last person he wanted to see, or be seen by, was Jon.

When Jon was gone, Max followed the boundary road until he came upon a group of squatters who blocked his passage. Going in the opposite direction, he came to a tree fallen across the road. The land grant map also covered a bit of the adjacent properties. Max thought he might find access to the Dela-Aden boundary road from a contiguous farm. He looked up from his map to see a huge Nigerian approaching his Land Rover. Max waved and smiled, whereupon the Nigerian asked if he could help him. Somehow, the man seemed familiar to Max ... but all Nigerians looked alike to him.

"I'm looking for a vineyard here-about. I seem to have gotten lost," Max said to the Nigerian.

"Go back to the junction, take the second left turn. That will take you to the vineyard."

"Thanks for your help." Max drove off, but he had a nagging feeling. After getting the lay-of-the-land, Max again staked out the mailboxes. It was afternoon when Jon returned and deposited the mail in the boxes for each farm. On an impulse, Max followed Jon at a goodly distance. Coming to the top of a rise in the dirt road, he saw Jon approaching a large house with a red terra-cotta tile roof in the distance. Not far ahead he also saw a sign with an arrow to the vineyard. Max decided to go to the winery to purchase a case of wine; it would be his cover story.

The winery was a stucco building with tile floors and a terra-cotta tile roof in the southwest ranch style of the States. It was an open and airy room with vats along one side and a long bar along the other backed up by shelves of assorted vintages with trays of tiny glasses for wine tasting. The room had groups of potted ferns around the pillars with rattan stools in front of the long bar. In a discreet corner, fronted by ferns, was the cash register.

I wonder how much business they get way out here. Maybe they're set up for winery tours, like in California. Max had not long to wonder when a middle-aged woman asked, "May I help you, sir?"

"Yes, I wonder if you have a light and slightly sweet white wine."

"We have a white wine that might suit you; taste it, see if it seems sweet to you."

The wine was delightful. Light, slightly sweet, not tangy with just a hint of fizz. The bouquet was soft and light. "This is indeed a delicious wine, what do you call it?"

"It is our Chateau Chardonnay; would you care to taste the red wine?"

"I don't care for red wines, nor does my wife. I would like a case of your Chateau Chardonnay, please."

"Would you like a full case, twelve bottles, or a half-case, six bottles?"

"I think I will take two half-cases."

"May I show you around the winery while your order is being packaged?"

"Yes, I'd like that."

Max was more than pleased with his tour. The vintner and his wife were obviously transplanted Californians, and like most Americans, were open and friendly. The brochure listed the wines available, as well as a map of the winery showing the vineyards, the vats, the processing area and the reception area, all of which were a boon to his machinations.

"Did I see tea leaves in the distance?"

"Yes, tea is the basic product of the farm. The winery is only ten years old."

"Does the farm produce anything else?"

"Lady Mary breeds and trains horses."

"For what discipline?"

"Dressage, 3-day Eventing and Driving; she also trains pleasure horses, mostly Arabians."

"Well, I must go. Thank you for the tour."

"Do come again, and bring your wife."

On his way out, Max again passed the huge Nigerian in native garb. Max waved to him and smiled.

Kybo had followed Max. He had recognized him immediately, for Max Smith's burn-scarred face was unforgettable. Even though Kybo seemed familiar, Max did not connect him to West Africa or the flight on the DC-3 where Kybo was dressed in khakis like a white hunter. Nigerians, because of their size and skills, were favored watchmen by Kenyan land owners. Kybo, in native dress, did not at all resemble the Nigerian he had seen on the plane. Kybo followed Max to the main road and watched him head towards Nairobi. Then, he jogged back to the big house and Thomas.

"What do you think he was doing here? I don't believe it is a coincidence, do you?" Thomas asked Jon.

"Hardly, Max is a mercenary – if he does something, it's because he has been paid to do it – that's the part that worries me most. What has he been hired to do? I'm going to call Cyril Latham and tell him of Max's visit. See what he has to say about it."

Cyril was rightly upset. "This is grounds for cancelling the agreement. We do have a better offer from APCO, but I knew how you felt about keeping your word ... well, when you deal with ruffians, there is no such thing as integrity.

"I'll call Mr. Athos right now and confront him with the breach of contract, and then get back to you."

"Mr. Athos, I understand your man, Max Smith, was at Dela-Aden today. You do realize that this is in direct contravention to our agreement."

"Max went out to buy a case of wine for me. I had heard that Dela-Aden has a marvelous Chardonnay."

"And so it does, but our agreement states that Max Smith is not to get any closer to Dela-Aden than Nairobi; so, as far as we are concerned, you have contravened our agreement. Bids for the kimmea are now open to all comers. I will return your contract today, voided for cause."

"Mr. Latham, please reconsider, it was a careless, but honest mistake."

"Mr. Athos, in my opinion, you have never made an honest mistake, careless or otherwise, in your life. I'm glad to get my clients out from under this deal. You see, while they abhor dealing with you, they are people to whom their word is their bond, and you were too disingenuous to realize it. A word of caution to you: should anything untoward happen, anything at all, the blame will fall at your feet. It's not too late to prosecute you and your minions for kidnapping and extortion. Good day!"

Petrides Athos sat in his big executive chair, watching Lake Victoria sparkle in the late afternoon sunlight – he was seething. The vast lake, as big as all of Ireland, soothed him, not only for its immense size, but for its uselessness: the water held bacteria that killed man from within; while the air above the water was thick with biting insects that caused blindness. He liked the image: beautiful to look at, but deadly.

Athos Petrides first reaction was to blame Max, but he realized that Max did not know about the *no-fly zone* of the agreement, and he had not put any restrictions on him. Athos never blamed himself when things went awry – his minions were always at fault – but Max had always been successful in the past. Just the sight of him, with his facial scar, was enough to bring people around to his way of thinking.

Now the unbelievably lucrative deal was lost, and he would have to compete with other bidders – not his usual way of doing business. Petrides mulled over the problem. He had an idea, a long shot, but if it worked, no one could blame him. In fact, he might end up being a hero.

Since Max came to work for me directly, things have not gone as well as when Bob Hunter was in charge, but Bob annoyed me with his scruples. However, I sense a not dissimilar reluctance in Max in this instance, and I'm not sure why.

20 ~ *Jamie & Anna Louise*

The African equatorial sun had begun its slow decline; the intense light of day diminished to a soft golden haze. For many people, the twilight hours after tea, were the most enjoyable part of the day. The imperceptible fading of the daylight began about four in the afternoon, and lasted until nine each clear day. With the lowering sun, the air cooled; making it the best time of day to take a walk, play tennis, garden, or go for a pleasure ride, with dinner eaten after eight.

Hanna and Sara left for their European tour on the twenty-ninth of June, with Thomas, Paula and Windy also leaving to go and visit the Zuri Watu.

Jon worked for his father each day, supervising projects, which left his father free to keep an eye on the tea or grape harvests.

Lady Mary worked with the horses, or rode the three year-olds along with Sir Peter on his slow daily inspection tour of the estate, where Sir Peter noted the progress of ongoing projects, and made notations of things he wanted to discuss the next day with Mr. Hanley, his overseer who directed the workers.

Jamie and Anna had each other for company during the day, usually riding in the cool of the morning, and playing games or duets, during the hot afternoons, after lunch and a nap. In the early gloaming after tea, Jon often joined Jamie and Anna Lou for a game of tennis. Playing two against him evened up the odds, for Jon had been captain of the tennis team at Oxford.

Jamie often rode with Lady Mary to work the young horses under saddle on the daily inspection tour. Anna usually declined and spent the time reading. Mary found that Peter's horse, Midnight Rider, a twelve-year-old gelding, gave the young horses confidence on the outings. They accepted new things and places with equanimity.

Before dinner, Jon and Anna Louise strolled along the garden paths edged with Thumbelina zinnias and dwarf marigolds, savoring the cooler daylight.

"Anna, are you feeling lonely now that Hanna, Sara and Paula are gone?" Jon asked. "I miss Thomas. However, you still have Jamie. He's good company, isn't he?"

"Yes, Jamie is delightful company, and I do miss the girls and Paula, but I'm happy for some quiet time. As an only child, I had quite a bit of it, and I sometimes find myself longing for a respite from all the bally-hoo."

"But, isn't it just like school? Having gobs of gals everywhere?"

"Not at all; school was structured, which allowed for quiet time at specific periods, so you could count on it. I have had some days here, when I didn't even have the time to enter notes in my diary."

"Do you keep a journal too? I started keeping one on safari with Max Mason. I wanted to keep track of weeding through the tribes looking for Thomas, but it ended up being more than that. It became a journal of events too."

"Mother thinks keeping a diary is important, so it is a habit with me. I feel the day is unfinished if I don't note it in my journal. While so much is different here, I have yet to note anything that would be interesting fodder for a story, except for trying to catch the toad in my bedroom."

"What toad? You didn't tell me about that!"

"My riding boot had fallen over, while in the mud room, and a toad went in before I brought them upstairs. I kept hearing this *croak-croak* just as I was nodding off. I had a devil of a time finding him. He made nary a sound when I moved about but waited until I was quietly in bed."

Jon laughed. He could imagine the odd croaks in the dark of the night. "Good thing you didn't try to put your boot on with him in it!"

"Remember, you told me never to put on a shoe before banging it a few times. It was quite a shock when the toad fell out!"

Jon and Anna laughed merrily. She enjoyed his sense of the ridiculous, which made it seem as if such inane things could not possibly happen to him.

"Do you like flowers, Jon?"

"Of course, doesn't everyone? I don't know if I have a preference, I just like to see gardens of any kind. I like all greenery, especially the wild woods here at Dela-Aden."

"You sound like my Dad; if it's green and it grows, he likes it! I couldn't imagine a life without flowers. We have always had lovely gardens. My Dad is a wonder at growing things. It's one of the reasons I like Dela-Aden so much. Besides the flowers and herbs, there are the tea leaves and the grapes, and now the kimmea. Everything is so verdant here. It makes me feel good. We'd better go in for dinner, it's getting late. African twilights are so deceiving."

"Where do you plan to ride tomorrow?" Jon asked. "I have marked all the cleared trails on your map."

"I'd like to go on the perimeter trail – see what's adjacent to Dela-Aden. Have the squatters been moved?"

"I don't know, we can ask Dad at dinner."

"Jon, would you help me with this map?" Jamie asked. "Anna and I are going to ride the perimeter tomorrow, and we'd like to find a good place for a picnic lunch."

"Well, Dad says the squatters are still here … and there is a big tree down here. Jon marked the map accordingly. By next week, that trail should be cleared. You can go this way along the perimeter, and then cut back to the barn here." Jon drew a line, and stood thinking – it will be about ten miles – are you up to that, Anna?"

"I think I'll be fine, since we are stopping for a picnic lunch. Where do you think would be a good spot?"

"There is a nice little clearing here, with a spring pond to water the horses," Jon replied.

Lady Mary came over and looked at the map. Pointing, she said, "I use this trail and this trail, but I haven't been on this part of the perimeter for a long time, have you Peter?"

Sir Peter heard his wife's question and peered over her shoulder at the map. "I was on that trail last week. We had squatters there last year and I checked to make sure they had not come back. That loop is the one that's closest to the winery, so I check it more often than the others. You should be just fine riding there."

"What about this part of the trail, Peter?" Mary asked.

"That's the part that crosses the lime pit; not much grows there but sedge grass; it's always open – even the squatters avoid it."

21 ~ The Zuri Watu ~ July

Paula compared her second and infinitely more enjoyable, ride in a helicopter to her first – when abductors had drugged her and wrapped her in a musty rug, for interrogation by a man with his face covered by a bandana and reflective sunglasses below a bush hat pulled low on his forehead. This parody of a western bandit wanted my diary for the medicinal plant drawings that Thomas had sketched and described on the back pages. I was unable to give him what he wanted, for Cyril Latham had taken my diary to Nairobi for safe-keeping. They drugged me again and returned me to the airport, leaving me in an abandoned crop duster. The encounter scared me badly, and to keep the artist, Thomas, out of the clutches of the mercenary, we escaped into the wilderness with Jon and Kybo ... hard to believe that was only four months ago.

The helicopter, flying just above the trees, gave a delightful view of the wildlife below. The elephants running with ears flared resembled a bunch of gray rocks with huge gray butterflies peering up at them. The wildebeest scattered like fingers on a hand; the gazelles leapt away in golden waves and the small herds of bongo, sitatunga, kob, and duiker, bunched up and fled in zigzag escape patterns. The lions scrambled awkwardly for cover. The monkeys scampered through the trees in all directions, while the baboons mostly sat and scolded the noisy intruder. Giraffe, usually camouflaged among the acacia trees, galloped across the grassy plains with long undulating strides. Water buffalo, feeding in the marshes, stampeded into the open where they stopped and faced out with heads lowered, prepared to deal with the enemy.

They crossed pockets of rainforest where the flowering vines turned the tops of the treetops into stupendous flower gardens. Here and there, great flocks of gaily colored parrots, or flocks of hundreds of

106

smaller birds flew in billowing swells, desperate to escape the shadow of the noisy monster.

The whirlybird flew across island clumps of woodlands dotting the bush – home to the leopard, the squirrel, the monkey, and other tree dwellers including the tree hyrax, a small nocturnal animal with a mating call that sounds like a woman being axed to death as the scream escalates to a fearful end.

The helicopter climbed rugged ridges to cross secluded alpine valleys filled with dense montane forests, home to the western or lowland gorilla.

The fascinating scenery riveted Paula's attention, the deep forests and the grassy valleys tucked away at three or four thousand feet, the shimmering lakes, the winding rivers and the spectacular waterfalls – all were seen at once, giving her a feeling of omniscience. How different was the topography of Cameroon from Kenya.

Thomas tapped Paula's arm and pointed to the village in the distance. She smiled at him and nodded her head. The Zuri Watu village lay two hundred miles, in a straight line, from Yaoundé, but the trail on foot was tortuous. They watched as people came out of their homes to point at the helicopter, flying low and heading towards them. Thomas saw Manutu and Sashono come and stand quietly in front of the gathered villagers. They knew who this must be, coming to the village in such grand style. Pride and pleasure shone in their eyes as they watched the whirlybird land.

Thomas's right hand clasped Paula's left hand, with Windy on lead to his left as they walked over to greet Manutu and Sashono, who smiled their pleasure.

After the initial greeting of ritual arm clasping, with smiles and nods in Paula's direction, they strolled to the village. Thomas squeezed Paula's hand reassuringly.

The formal introductions would take place after they had refreshed themselves from their travels. While the need to wash up did not exist, the need to talk privately did. Thomas said, "For just a bit, sit quietly and say nothing; Manutu will be impressed if you do. When it is time for you to speak, I will squeeze your hand. I do not know what Manutu or Sashono will say – or do – when they find

107

we are married, but I'm sure they will be pleased. If you need me to translate, squeeze my hand. Ready?" Paula nodded. She could hardly wait to meet the legendary Manutu.

Chief Sashono spoke to the crowd that followed them. "This is a great day for us. My son has returned to visit us, and has brought with him his new bride."

A roar of cheers greeted the announcement, and smiles lit every face.

They did know we were coming! Thomas thought. If Manutu has been with me, why was I not aware of it?

Chief Sashono waited for silence, and then continued: "We will have a family gathering now, but later, we will have a celebration feast when Tamubu will tell us about his travels. Everyone is invited to attend the feast and to listen to the stories."

There were murmurs of approval and happy grins as the villagers turned to go about their business; with the women planning who would make what for the feast, and the men looking forward to Manutu sharing his palm wine, which he did on special occasions.

On days that Sashono declared a feast, most of the women abandoned the stew pot and made specialty dishes in their big black iron skillets. They made biscuits, and the flat pancakes used for roll-ups for the pot-roasted meats. The women would offer their specialties to Sashono, then to Manutu and then to the guests, and their husbands. The women and children ate whatever was leftover, or a serving of stew.

A sebula (roofed porch) now stood adjacent to the opening of Chief Sashono's hut. The addition surprised Thomas, but amusement trickled into his thoughts. Had Manutu been keeping track of him? They did know that Paula was his wife.

They sat on deer and antelope pelts around a new long low table. Mohboa placed pitchers of lemon water and platters of the honey cakes called tamutunda on the table. Coconut husk bowls of minted water sat before each person with a small fuzzy leaf for wiping the fingers – tamutunda are sticky. Most of the natives just lick their fingers clean, but Manutu does not approve of this … for he knows of germs.

Chief Sashono sat at one end of the table; Manutu sat at the other end. On the long side Thomas sat with Sashono to his left with Paula beside him next to Manutu's wife, Mohboa. Their sons, Benima and Kenga sat opposite to them.

Chief Sashono said, "Mohboa has made fingirisha (roll–ups) and tamutunda (sweet cakes) for our mid-day meal. Manutu will now offer the words."

Manutu arose, looked at each person, and then spoke, "Each one of us is truly blessed. The One God, Who is always with us, has showered us with His love, and we thank Him for His bounty." Manutu sat, took up the platter of roll-ups, served himself and passed the wooden plate to Tamubu while saying, "We are pleased for you; your bride is not only lovely, she is your equal."

Paula smiled and glanced at Thomas, who said, "I hope you are right, for it sometimes seems to me that I am much less than her equal."

After the surprised chuckles, Manutu replied, "Humility is a main ingredient in a happy marriage."

Mohboa covered her face with her hands, but her shaking shoulders gave her away. Her sons made no effort to cover their delighted grins.

Thomas squeezed Paula's leg, for her hands held a roll-up. She smiled at his permission to speak saying, "I think the main ingredient of a happy marriage is respect, one for the other."

Manutu looked at Paula sharply, for he was startled. Those were his exact thoughts even as he bantered with words for amusement.

Thomas recognized Manutu's sharp look ... a look that said something had surprised him ... a look Thomas had occasionally seen during his lesson years. He thought, aha, Manutu does not know everything – he is in for a surprise!

Sashono saw, as well as felt, his twin brother's wonder. He smiled to himself. His son had always been a source of boundless joy for him, and yet, of sorrow too, for he knew that Tamubu would never follow him as the leader of the Zuri Watu. His nephew, Benima, seemed the logical choice, for Benima did not have the skills of a medicine man, as did Kenga.

Sashono could not let the joy in his son go unspoken and said, "My son is a special person. He came to us in a special way, and suffered from a long and severe illness. He grew to manhood being special in many ways. Now, he has found a special woman to share his life. It is no more than we expected. It just happened sooner than we expected."

The pleased smiles of his audience were comforting, for Sashono's humor was always subtle, usually just a play on words.

Paula's reply had peaked Manutu's curiosity, so he said to her, "Paula, come and take a walk with me. Would you like to see the place where Tamubu had his lessons as a boy?"

Tamubu was startled. No one but acolytes ever went there. *Why is he taking her to our special place?*

"Yes, I would like that, and I would like Tamubu and Chief Sashono to go with us – if that meets with your approval."

Now what is going on here? Tamubu looked at Manutu whose face gave away nothing as he replied, "That is up to you, Mkebibi." (lady wife)

Manutu looked deeply into Paula's eyes, he held her gaze and scanned her thoughts seeing only love; but a thrill went through his bones to his heart, which took his breath away when only he heard her words, *'The spirits of love still watch over Tamubu. They are not gone; they are there when he needs them.'*

It took every bit of the self-control Manutu possessed to keep the tears from his eyes. She was kuzimu akili. (a spirit talker) She had spoken to him with her thoughts and she had done it without the use of inhalants or stimulants. He broke off his gaze and said aloud, "We could not possibly go alone."

Tamubu sensed Paula going to a higher plane. When he saw the joy in Manutu's face, he knew she had communed with him – and him alone, which caused a great feeling of peace to flow through him – like strength through Samson.

They crossed the savanna in the dappled shade at the edge of the woods. "See that tree over there," Manutu said, "that is a good tree to climb if elephants are in the area. They come to the grove to eat the tall grass and the tender shoots of the vines growing up the trees. If you are hiding in the high branches, you can hear the soft rumbling noises they make to reassure one another. Female elephants stay in the herd in which they are born all their lives; the bulls leave when they have matured."

110

Paula looked at Tamubu with a question in her eyes. He gave a brief nod of his head, which said, yes, that is the tree I told you about.

"Across this tall grass, at the base of those distant hills, are lion dens," Sashono said. "It is best to stay out of the tall grass in Africa." He gave Thomas a knowing smile.

They came to the learning circle, huge stones with aligna trees growing between them. Manutu used his spear to deftly move aside the thorn bushes that closed the entrance to the circle. "Come and sit; Tamubu will make a small fire for us, while we refresh ourselves with a drink of lemon water."

"Why do we need a fire? The day is warm and dry," Paula asked.

"Yes, it is. Tamubu, we will talk without a fire," Manutu said.

We always had a fire – I never gave it any thought, it was just part of the learning ritual, Tamubu thought.

"Paula, come and sit in front of me. Tamubu, sit beside Paula. Brother, please come and sit beside me."

Sashono sat beside Manutu saying, "It will seem odd to talk without a fire, but I am willing to give it a try."

Paula felt chagrined. Her thoughtless question had changed the ritual; she must take more care with her words in the future.

Tamubu, sensing Paula's discomfort, spoke up. "This is Manutu's special place, if he is willing to do without a fire, I am willing also."

Sashono nodded his head in agreement.

"We are going to sit quietly for a while," Manutu said. "We are going to be very still. We are going to clear our minds and think only of the sky or the breeze. When it is time, I will speak."

Paula cleared her mind, feeling a tremendous sense of peace. She looked at the sky … it was a soft baby blue, with not a cloud in sight. The slight breeze she felt moved only the tips of the draping fern-like leaves of the aligna trees. She began to feel sleepy and closed her eyes. She began to float – lighter than a feather. Up she rose into the sky with Manutu on one side of her and Tamubu on the other, with Sashono beside Manutu. They floated like clouds, higher and higher. Her view was fantastic, for she could see 360 degrees – everywhere! She could also feel the sun on her face and the breeze in her hair. She felt truly happy and serene. She cared for nothing but the joy of the moment, and the incredible feeling of floating weightless. She was free – totally and utterly free!

'Mkebibi, open your eyes.'

'I have my eyes open ... I can see the land beneath me, the trees and grasses and the lovely blue sky.'

'What else do you see?'

'I see you, Tamubu and Chief Sashono. We are here together in the sky.'

'Do you see anyone else?'

'No. Oh, wait! There is Lady Mary with Jon nearby.'

'What are they doing?'

'Lady Mary is working her horse, Diablo-Airé, under saddle in the arena. Jon is smoking his pipe and watching them.'

'Mkebibi, I want you to go back to the learning circle now. Listen for my voice.'

In an instant, Paula heard, "Mkebibi, open your eyes!"

Paula opened her eyes and smiled at the men watching her.

"I'm so sorry, I fell asleep ... but I had a wonderful dream."

Sashono came over to Paula and said, "Come, walk with me. I get stiff if I sit too long. I will show you the elephant wallow."

When they were out of sight, Manutu asked, "Do you know about her abilities?"

"Yes, a bit. I looked into her eyes one evening and it just happened."

"She is stronger than I am ... do you realize that?"

"No. How can that be?"

"She needs no guide, no intermediary, and no psychoactive herbs. She can go where she wishes without aid. She is the one who took us with her. You were there."

"Yes, but I thought you took us."

"No, Mkebibi took us with her."

"I am stunned. Only once did she become esoteric on her own that I know of ... we communed by thought, but we did not travel."

"I sensed a strong presence in her. That is why I brought her here. I'm glad I did; she needs training. She could go off and never come back. She was euphoric today. When did she see the spirits that watch over you?"

"The time we communed by thought. I was amazed for she saw all five of them, then three and then none. She didn't even know what she had done."

"What are your plans? How long do you intend to stay with us?"

"We are growing the kimmea plant to sell as a business, and will have to return to harvest to the plants in a moon's time."

"Will you stay ... so I can train your Mkebibi?"

"I will be delighted to stay. Windy will be delighted to stay too, won't you, boy? We will have to ask Paula if she wishes to stay. I have to tell her why, now before we go back. We must be very open with her. She will resent any other treatment."

"It never occurred to me to do otherwise. After all, I will be able to train her, but she will be teaching me."

"You were serious about her being stronger than you?"

"Yes, quite serious. I'm just surprised that she doesn't know it herself."

"She may not know it, but I think she feels it. She has almost no fear, and there is nothing she can't do and do well if she sets her mind to it. After I fired a shot, and chased off the lions that had her cornered ... I sent her to the other side of boulders to climb a tree. The lions then had me flanked. I startled them with an attack, and used my spear to pole vault to the top of a boulder next to the same oak tree. I almost didn't make it into the tree in time – Paula pulled me up, right out of the lion's reach. Not a usual thing for a woman to do ... and she can climb a sheer cliff wall like a fly ... and travel through the trees like a monkey."

"Why am I not surprised? Is that how you met?"

"Yes, we talked while sitting in an oak tree with lions raging below."

"Ah, here they come. I am going to let you tell your Mkebibi ... or ask her. She should hear it from you."

Sashono waved and said, "Manutu, I must return to the village."

"I will go with you, I have patients to tend," Manutu replied.

"Thank you, Chief Sashono, for showing me the elephant wallow. I've seen elephants covered with mud and wondered how they did it. Now I know. Thank you too, Manutu, for bringing me to the learning circle; Tamubu has told me a bit about the happy days he spent here with you."

Paula, with Tamubu's arm around her waist, watched them walk away. She turned in his arms saying, "I can see why you are so placid and kind. You had wonderful teachers."

"Would you like it if Manutu taught you too?"

"Me! Why would he want to teach me?"

"Because you are the most interesting person he has ever met."

"And just what, may I ask, makes me so interesting?" Paula laughed.

"You are kuzimu akili. (Spirit talker) Manutu says you are stronger than he, but that you need training. Without training, you could go away and never come back. Do you remember what happened in your dream today?"

"Yes, I remember. Why do you ask?"

"Because I'm going to tell you what happened in your dream."

"I saw you there, but I did not know you knew my thoughts."

"Yes, we all did. Manutu said you were euphoric. Is that true?"

"Yes, I wanted to go on floating and dreaming forever."

"That is why you need training. You know how to leave ... but you don't know how to come back. Without training, you might leave on your own one day ... and not be able to come back."

"Well then, I just won't leave anymore, if it's that dangerous."

"Something could happen to force you to leave. Do you want to take the chance that you might leave by accident and never come back?"

"Of course not ... I do understand what you are implying ... I didn't want to come back today. Did Manutu take control? Did he sense my danger?"

"Yes. You know, it would destroy me to lose you. Your body would be here, but your mind would be gone – forever. It would be a great tragedy for everyone. You don't really have a choice ... if you want to have children."

His words felt like a physical blow; a wake-up call of ice water! What if they had children and, for some inexplicable reason, she went away and couldn't come back? Yes, she had to stay and learn.

"How long will it take to learn how to come back?"

"I'm not sure. Manutu thinks you might learn control before we have to leave to harvest the kimmea. Would you mind staying so long?"

"I don't seem to have a choice … do I? You know, I've never before had an out-of-body experience like I did today. We talked in our thoughts once, and you showed me the dead apes, but you were the first person to do that with me. Why is that?"

"Very few people have our abilities. Only another skilled kujua akili (transcendentalist) could show you the way. Mother and Jon have some psychic abilities too, that is why you saw them today. Manutu thinks you are in danger until you learn to control your gift and can return."

"I'd say it's a curse … not a gift!"

"When you save a life, possibly of someone you love, by using your gift, you will no longer think it to be a curse."

Paula leaned into Tamubu and snuggled – he held her close. "I will learn to control my gift, as you call it, because I love you, and I want to bear your children."

Sashono gave Tamubu and Paula ground adjacent to the sebula as a wedding present. Manutu chose the area for the structure's foot-plan. The women began building the hut, with Manutu directing the placing of the windows – lattice openings in the walls covered by tightly woven roll-up mats. Paula told Manutu of her desire to plaster the floor. It was unheard of to plaster the floors, but Manutu immediately saw the wisdom of the idea and spoke to the women. "Mkebibi has the knowledge of the world, we will learn from her."

Day one, the framework and roof thatched; day two, plastering of the floor; day three, floor dries; day four, plastering of the walls; day five, the receiving of wedding gifts from all the villagers.

Manutu gave them a sleeping bench, much like the rope beds of the American pioneers. Mohboa and the other women each gave them a utensil: a cooking pot or hardened gourds, coconut shells, wooden spoons and bowls, woven mats for the floors and windows, woven blankets and cooking herbs. The men gave pelts, stools, knives, weapons and stacks of wood for fires. Who was giving what, and what the couple needed, had been a topic of conversation, ever since Tamubu had arrived home with his bride.

Manutu and Sashono inspected the domicile, making sure they had everything they needed for their comfort. Sashono spoke to the villagers saying, "Thank you, we are all well-pleased with your generosity. Tonight, Tamubu will tell us a story; all are welcome at my fire. Manutu will share his palm wine to thank you for your efforts."

Tamubu looked at the sea of eager faces, each one held a look of expectation, which pleased him. He remembered his formative years, and the love and respect that had nurtured him as he grew to manhood; it felt good to be home again.

'Before Nanoka died, she said to me, "After I am gone, go and find your birth family — so you will know yourself fully."

'I did not want to leave the Zuri Watu, but Nanoka bade me do so, and I had to respect her dying wishes.'

He then told of his trek to the rainforest foothills bordering Mt. Cameroon, and of watching Paula hide under a kamikiza plant; and of having to save her from the lions. He told of the eagle attacking Paula; and of the murderous bull ape and how she had injured her ankle; of how he had carried her piggy-back through the heavy rain to a traveling shelter; and of her falling down the mountainside. He told of his brother, Jon, finding them, and of their trek to the beach together. He told how they found the yacht gone, but found a net full of supplies in a tree for Paula.

There, Chief Sashono stopped the story for the night had grown late. "Tamubu will continue his story when the moon is full."

Two nights later, as the full moon rose, Sashono stood before his people. "My son has had a great journey – he has found a good wife – not always an easy thing to do." When the laughter ebbed, Sashono continued, "Tonight we will hear more of his travels in the lands beyond."

"You see me sitting here; I look the same to you as I have always looked, but now, I'm really another person. One cannot go out into the world without changing … it is the price we pay for leaving the womb … the womb of the Great Nations of the Zuri Watu … the womb that formed my character and my soul. One good thing about the soul is that only the owner knows it, and what lies deep inside.

"Some of the things I am going to tell you will be difficult to believe. The knowledge will not change you, and that will be a blessing, but it may open your mind; in only hearing about the wonders, you will still be who and what you are ... only if these things touch your life, might you change, as I have done."

'My life as Tamubu ended when my brother called me Thomas — even Manutu wept, for he knew my heart sang with joy. My recurring dreams of a small happy voice had become a reality. The owner of that voice was my brother, and his love for me was undiminished by the passage of time. I crossed over then, but I did not yet know it.

'While roaming the beach, I found a Fulani boy with a deep, infected cut under his ankle, and took him to our camp. He and three friends were out on their manhood trials.

'Paula's parents arrived a few days later on a luxury yacht, but could not remain at the cove until Kasuku was healed. Paula left on the yacht to go to Port Gentil to resign from the Expedition, for she felt that Dr. Miles had willfully abandoned her — once she was kidnapped by the Ndezi.

'Jon and I stayed behind until Kasuku was able to travel home. We then left for Douala to meet up with Paula, as we had planned.

'Paula did not arrive in Douala or send word, as agreed. We radioed to Arthur aboard the Just Cause in Port Gentil; he told us, "Missy Paula went home to the States." We were mystified. Why would she go home without telling us that she was leaving ... we had made plans to meet again in Douala.

'Unable to obtain further information, Jon and I left Douala for the Wahutu village, where Kybo, now my afisa (aide), was visiting his cousin and her family. We were a day and a half into our trek to Kenya when a runner caught up to us and told us that Paula had arrived at the Wahutu village. Jon and I left our gear with Kybo, and hastily returned to the village — and Paula.

'Together again, we found that Paula had left two messages, which we did not receive, with Paula saying, "I would have been better off using drums." (Tamubu paused for the hearty laughter.) 'During our talks, we decided that Paula's ankle needed more time to heal before embarking on a long trek. We made plans to meet in Yaoundé in ten days. Paula would go back to Douala and travel by train to Yaoundé. Jon and I went to visit the Gielli Pygmies, before returning to Douala to tell Captain Jones of our plans, and flying to Yaoundé.

'In Yaoundé, we learned that Paula had come out to the airport to greet us, but had gone missing. The spoor indicated abduction with a helicopter, but we could not fathom a reason for it.

'*The following afternoon, Paula awoke in an abandoned plane at the Yaoundé airport. The mercenary that had abducted and questioned her had wanted her diary for my plant drawings, but Paula had already sent her diary to Nairobi with her attorney.* (At this point, Tamubu passed a plant drawing to a listener with a gesture to pass it on.)

'It then occurred to us that the mercenary might now go after the artist – me – so we fled east to Lomie. The mercenary placed watchers in various towns, and so arrived at Lomie before us. We then enlisted the aid of the tribesmen to travel through the deep forest. The Gielli Pygmies, the Umpiti, Machozi, Duibo and the Djoumani all helped us in our escape.

'*On the Kom River, the Pymtu replenished our staple supplies and sent porters with us for the portage around the waterfalls and rapids. Hoping to elude the mercenary, we now traveled west, back to the ocean to meet Captain Jones who, with his yacht, was once again going to help us.*

'*Jon had arranged to meet Captain Jones using the wireless radio. It never crossed our minds that the mercenary would monitor the airwaves, and thereby hear our plans.*

'*We sailed halfway to South Africa on Captain Jones' yacht,* The Wind Drift, *to escape the mercenary. However, the mercenary continued to shadow us on another ocean-going yacht.*

'*In order to stop the mercenary's relentless pursuit, we forced a meeting with him in Luanda, where we agreed to sell to his boss the information they desired about the kimmea, if it proved viable under cultivation.*

'*A tape of the meeting and our agreement was sent to Paula's attorney in Nairobi.*

'*Once freed from the dread of pursuit, we went sight-seeing across Africa: from Luanda we flew to Kinshasha, then to Kisangani, and then to Kampala. I will tell you many stories about the marvelous places we saw while we traveled.*

'*With his stories, my brother helped me remember our childhood on a tea farm in the Ngong hills of Kenya ... my life before the plane crash, which brought me to the Zuri Watu.*

'*In Kampala, I had a wonderful reunion with my parents, after which, we all flew to Nairobi.*

'I cannot express the incredible joy I felt at meeting my parents again. We recognized each other at once. I remembered my mother's lavender fragrance and my father's manly bear hugs; I also remembered their voices. They recognized the boy in the man I had become and remembered the ways of my personality.

'Paula and I were drawing closer all the time. We had spent as much time together, as if I had courted her for two years. We went to America to meet Paula's family and married there. So, you see, I am not the same person I was when I left here … I am now a married man.'

★   ★   ★

There was a slight pause, and then hearty laughter. Sashono arose and said, "We will have many evenings of stories. It has grown late. Many have worked long today and need their rest."

Manutu came and spoke to Paula. "We will meet in the morning after we break our fast and return to the ring of stones. You must wear simple clothing, no adornment or jewelry but your wedding band; bring nothing else with you." He turned and left.

Paula looked at Thomas who beckoned her into their new abode. "What was that all about?" she asked.

"The spirits can be jealous. If you have something they want, but of course, they cannot have – it makes them unpredictable. It is a problem you do not need."

"Should I be worried?"

"Good heavens, no! I would not let you go if there were any danger. But spirits are quirky, and it is best if your clothing is plain. You could wear your safari shorts and the shirt with the chest pockets, your socks and soft shoes. Do not wear your whistle, sunglasses or pin up your hair. Wear only your cap for shade."

He drew Paula in his arms gently, and, feeling her nestle close to him, began his courtship of little kisses as he murmured of his love for her. The little kisses were the beginning of their journey of love. Paula was predictable, for she could not resist the tattoo of little kisses on her face, neck and ears. It gave him a thrill every time she succumbed to his amorous approach. Only the path did not always lead to the same place. There were byways he had not yet explored. His curiosity and craving to know all of her intimate secrets led him on.

119

22 ~ *The Learning Circle*

Manutu came at first light. He had a bowl of gruel for Paula. "It will purify your blood," he said. "Drink only water today. I have food for our mid-day meal. We will be gone until mid-afternoon. Come to my kibanda (hut) when you are ready to go."

Paula looked at Thomas, "Did you have to eat this stuff? What is it?"

"I don't know," Thomas said, as he sniffed at her bowl. "But, whatever it is, it will not harm you. More than likely, it will protect you. You must trust Manutu completely – just as much as you trust me."

Paula was ready with a riposte, but Thomas looked so serious she could not make light of his sincerity. She knew she was going into the unknown and suddenly craved his support, saying, "We will make a pact. If you perceive a problem, you will talk to my mind, saying: 'Sunshine! Sunshine come home.' I will always heed your call."

Paula carried the water jug, while Manutu carried a sack on the end of his spear, which rested on his shoulder. She felt naked without her backpack. Manutu did not speak until they were half a league away from the village, when he said, "You are a very brave woman, but this is not a time to be brave – it is a time to be obedient. Will you obey my every word and command?"

"I will try."

"That is not good enough. You must do more than try, you must succeed."

"Would you please tell me what I am to expect?"

"I do not know what to expect – that is why you must obey my every command without hesitation."

"Tamubu and I have a secret command, should he perceive a problem. Do you want to know what it is?"

"Yes. It is good that you have established a link with him."

"He will call out, 'Sunshine! Sunshine come home.' I have promised to heed his call."

"I do not think we are near the time of return commands, but Tamubu is very gifted, and he knows you better than I do. If he thinks this is wise, we too will have a command. I will say, 'Mkebibi! Return now.' You have a great gift and your aura is very strong. We will go slowly, but we go into the unknown. You must first learn control. Once you can control your abilities, we can then explore."

They entered the learning circle, and Manutu closed the thorn-bush gate. He made a small fire while Paula prepared the sitting pallets. She was glad for the shade of the aligna trees, for Manutu had asked her to remove her hat.

"May I ask questions?"

"Yes, of course."

"Why do we need a fire?"

"For the smoke – the spirits dwell in this place. If they come near the smoke, we will be able to see them … that is, if they want us to see them."

"Are the spirits here, the same spirits that watch over Tamubu?"

"No, the spirits that watch over Tamubu are spirits of love. I once thought them to be his ancestors, for I only saw them when he was very ill. He came close to death once – then the five spirits hovered until the crisis was past. I knew then that Tamubu was a *chosen* one. When he was well, I took him to be an acolyte. Teaching him made my heart sing. He has great powers, but he does not rely on them. He relies on himself, which makes him a truly great man."

"Yes, his intelligence is impressive. I'm glad you speak Swahili. My Bantu is limited … my Swahili is not that good either, for Tamubu wants to speak English most of the time. The tribes we met on our travels also spoke Swahili – but those men did not speak to a woman."

Manutu smiled. "The tribal world is a man's world outwardly, but we listen to our wives in secret, for they have a natural wisdom given them by God. He made them the vessels of new life to remind man that he is nothing without a woman."

"Well, put like that, a woman is nothing special without a man."

Manutu chuckled, "Women rarely get carried away by the driving force that exists in men, for their glands are different."

"Do you know the name of the secretion that makes the male driving force?"

"No, does it have a name?"

"Yes, it is called testosterone. There is no Swahili for it. It comes from the pumba." (Testicle)

Manutu laughed. "That is fitting. That is where most of a man's trouble comes from," he chuckled happily. "How did you know that?"

"It is common knowledge in America, it is taught in our schools."

"They teach you about the secretions of testicles in your schools?"

"Yes, it is a study called biology. It covers all life: human, animal and vegetable."

"I think I would like this biology."

"Yes, I think you would ... actually, you are a biologist without knowing that you are one. Tamubu has told me a bit of the things you taught him as a boy, about bones and teeth and the habits of birds and wildlife and the plants and trees. You know more than many biologists, in as much as you know what caused an animal to die. You know which plants to use for medicinal purposes, remedies not even guessed at by the rest of the world. Take the kimmea, a plant with a property that relieves anxiety and aids sleep, but has no side effects. This is a truly remarkable plant. There is nothing like it anywhere else – if it exists elsewhere, no one is talking about it."

"We do not talk about it here either. How do you know this plant?"

"Tamubu drew some of the helpful and healing plants in the back of my diary while on our trek back to the cove."

"Ah, yes. The paper he sent around when telling us his story. It looked exactly like the kimmea plant, remarkable; although, I did not understand the tiny shapes marked above the plant."

"You remember the little shapes at the top of the paper? They said, 'The Kimmea Plant' in Swahili." While she spoke, Paula wrote the alphabet in the dirt with a stick. "There are twenty-six shapes, which are called letters and make up the basis for all the words we write in English or Swahili. If we use these letters, ANT, they mean ant in English, and these letters, SISIMIZI, mean ant in Swahili – and these letters mean TREE in English, which is MTI in Swahili." She smiled at Manutu, "Am I boring you with my explanations?"

"No, Mkebibi, I find it interesting. We have heard of this writing, but our village is so remote that few missionaries come here. Each year, we go back to our old lands by the sea to trade and barter for goods, so we have learned to count and know the value of goods. But we have not yet this writing – or drawing."

"I don't know that the Zuri Watu really need writing or drawing. You live a good life without them. But, if civilization comes closer, you will need to be able to read and write to deal with it. I have enough paper and pencils with me to make a start, if you and Chief Sashono are inclined to learn."

"I thank you for your offer … I will think on it. If you are ready, we will again sit quietly and empty our minds. You must use your voice to talk to me. Do not speak to me with your thoughts."

Paula sat quietly and gazed at the blue sky. A paradise flycatcher flew into view, with a long silvery tail that was three times the length of his sapphire blue body and head. The flycatcher alit on a low branch of an aligna tree above the learning circle. His rasping *chwe* sounded almost lilting.

Manutu said aloud, but softly, "Do you know this bird?"

"Yes, he is a flycatcher. Are they abundant here?"

"Not at all; sparse woodlands are their preferred habitat. We are a bit high in these mountains, but we sometimes see them near the rainy season. Can you follow him with your mind?"

"I don't know how to do that."

"When he leaves, close your eyes and think of him. See if you can see him in your mind, and then follow him."

The paradise flycatcher seemed content on his perch while Paula watched him preen his feathers. His long tail must cause a lot of drag; I wonder what can be the use of such a long tail? The bird suddenly let out a loud rasping *chwe* and flew off. Paula closed her eyes, but did not see the flycatcher in flight; instead she saw a kestrel diving from the sky. She looked in the direction of the kestrel's dive and now saw the flycatcher, and the use of his long tail, for the flycatcher dropped into a dive just as the kestrel zoomed near with talons extended; but only the long ribbon-like tail remained where the kestrel expected bulk. The missed strike tumbled the kestrel, forcing him to flap his wings for revised momentum. The flycatcher landed on a low sheltered branch of another aligna tree, pausing only momentarily before heading off into the woods. Paula began to follow the kestrel.

Manutu said aloud, "Mkebibi, return now."

Paula opened her eyes instantly. She smiled at Manutu and asked, "did you go with me?'

"Yes, I went with you. Did you not see me?"

"No, I did not."

"Are you sure? Did you not see the kestrel?"

"You were the kestrel? How did you do that?"

"One day you will know, but today we will talk about all you experienced with the flycatcher. This is how we begin to learn control."

Paula felt pleased to see Tamubu coming out to greet her. She had missed him today. It was their first all-day separation since they had married. Short though it was, it seemed odd to be doing something without him.

"I have made a roast pork dinner for you and Sashono. I hit a piglet with my walinka, though I was aiming at a fox," he laughed. "I wanted a pelt, not a meal. I didn't even see the pigs. I'm teaching Windy to hunt, although he just wants to run and chase, not hunt, for he is still a puppy, but he is beginning to pay attention to me."

"Speaking of Windy, where is he? He didn't come to greet me."

"He is tied on the other side of the bed. I made a little place for him there. He went off coursing twice today, and I didn't see him go. He came back to the silent whistle each time, but I began to worry – what if I hadn't noticed he was gone? So I made a place for him when I am busy."

Tamubu opened his arms and Paula snuggled close to him. He rested his chin on her head and asked, "What did you and Manutu do today?"

"Mostly talk, we talked about everything: you, me, writing and drawing. I offered to teach Manutu and Chief Sashono to read, if they wanted to learn. Manutu said he would think on it."

"What did Manutu teach you?"

"He shared his wisdom about the nether world. He took me on a short trip, and with signal words made me use my willpower to return. It was a new feeling, this feeling of decision. So, I think, we have begun."

Tamubu smiled to himself. He knew Paula would enjoy being with Manutu. He longed to join them himself, but Manutu preferred to teach one-on-one, for he adjusted his approach to the student.

"Hold me close, I will sleep better if you do … I feel the need for deep sleep," Paula murmured. Thomas never tired of holding her. It was the one thing that pleased him more than anything else. He felt utterly complete with her in his arms.

The following days mirrored the first day. Paula and Manutu were gone all day, returning as the sun slipped into the long dusk. Tamubu took over Manutu's duties with the sick; gathered plants to dry for medicines, and cooked the meals for them – all the while training Windy. The dog was brilliant, and a delight to work with, even with his puppy foibles.

An elderly widow, Cenye, who had begun caring for Chief Sashono after Nanoka's death, now helped Tamubu, for Sashono, by invitation, ate most of his meals with them.

In the evenings, Tamubu told stories around the fire: of his travels, of the unusual sights he had seen, of the different customs he had encountered – especially table manners – which he mimed, sending his audience into paroxysms of laughter. He told vignettes about amusing individuals and the little happenings: like finding Windy, or Paula stunning his family with her gymnastics … wherein Paula, once again, gave a demonstration, causing ooohs and aaahs, laughter and high pitched warbling (a signal of approval) from the audience. It was a pleasant and productive time. It made him wonder about his future, which he felt would be productive, but would it be as pleasant? There was a feeling of peace in the village that he had found nowhere else … a predictability and order, which filled him, mind and soul, with satisfaction and comfort.

The weeks passed in this easy way. One evening Tamubu walked with Manutu, who said, "I would like you to come with us tomorrow. Is there anyone who needs your ministrations just now?"

"No one is sick at this time. Loufa is expecting her first child any day now, but the midwives will be there for her if I am gone. I can be back quickly if we are at the learning circle."

"Good. You must see your Mkebibi's progress for yourself. She will astonish you."

"It is enough that she has amazed you," Tamubu replied.

"This is only the second time I have been amazed."

"Am I aware of the first?"

"You were the first."

Tamubu built a small fire to which he added a few green leaves for a bit of smoke. Manutu and Paula sat at the fire silently watching him until he finished, when he sat back to join their silence. Tamubu did not know what to expect today. He knew only of his experiences in the past ... and dwelling on the unknown possibilities caused him to drift. He was going to shake himself free when Manutu said in his thoughts, *'Go with the flow ... now open your eyes.'*

Tamubu opened his eyes to see Paula flowing upward, with Manutu not far behind her. Suddenly, he was pulled along with them; he was not in control, he was like an arm that had to go where the body went. Floating high, he saw his father as a young man, handsome and virile, with his arm around his beautiful and smiling mother, the man and woman of his malarial dreams. Nearby, he saw himself and Jon as boys ... before I was lost. Oh, here come Hanna and Sara all dressed to go visiting. I remember this Sunday. It was our last day together as a family before I went to the Science Fair.

Just as quickly, Thomas saw Nanoka tending to him as a sick boy. Then he saw himself in the learning circle with Manutu for the first time. He closed his eyes to dwell on the moment and found himself sitting in the circle with Manutu smiling, and Paula fast asleep.

Manutu raised a finger to his lips for silence and rose, leading Thomas out of the circle. When they were out of earshot Manutu asked, "What did you see?"

"I saw myself as a boy with my family the day before I was lost. I saw Nanoka tending to me when I was sick."

"Amazing, yes?"

"Very, it was quite unexpected, for we used no psychical plants."

"Not only that, it was Mkebibi who took us with her. On our first day, I thought you took us, Tamubu. I can join others, but I cannot take anyone with me. Can you do that?"

"Not like she did today, although she did go with me to see the dead apes. Did she also bring us back?"

"Yes, your Mkebibi is no longer in danger of going and not coming back. But now, she must learn when to use her powers, since she does not need psychical plants to travel. Let us return to be there for her when she awakens."

"Why is she asleep?'

"Because I wanted to talk to you. I planted a command before we traveled. I did not want her to awaken until I called to her."

Tamubu lay awake, thinking of Paula's esoteric abilities, which amazed him. She seemed unchanged by the knowledge of her special talents. Actually, she seemed to ignore them. Paula snuggled closer to him, encouraging him to begin his litany of little kisses. She sighed and wiggled closer, where she succumbed to the pleasure of his embrace. Amongst the little kisses, he whispered in her ear, "I love you more than life ... each day with you is a day in paradise. Are you happy here?"

"Mm-huh."

"Not bored?"

"Uh-uh."

"Shall we stay here always?"

"Mmm-huh, until it is time to harvest the kimmea."

She was bewitching and beguiling, Tamubu puller her closer and moved into second gear, Paula smiled inwardly and led him on ... and on ...

There came a tapping on the entrance post. "Who is it?" Tamubu asked.

"It is me, Aku. Loufa's time has come. The mid-wives need you."

Paula chuckled, "I will keep the bed warm for you." Thomas gave her one last kiss, dressed and was gone. As she dozed, she wondered why Aku had come for Thomas when Manutu was here. Hmmm, I wonder, which one would I choose if I were birthing my first child ... experience or empathy? I think I too would go for empathy, since empathy is also capable – and good looking!

Thomas returned later with Manutu. Paula offered them tea, scones and oatmeal. The small talk over the meal was about the birthing of Loufa's big baby boy, well over eight pounds. The discussion centered on the problems of birthing such a large baby in an older woman. Loufa was eighteen and several years beyond optimal age for the birth of a first child.

Paula, surprised by the comments, said, "White women rarely bear a child before eighteen. Most are born to women who are in their early twenties to thirties, with some being born to women who are almost forty. Why do you consider eighteen to be old for a first child?"

"A woman's bones," Manutu replied, "may still be a bit pliable at eighteen, but as a woman ages, her pelvic bones harden. Birth in an older woman places stress on the baby who has to pass these bones, and even more stress on the mother, whose bones are moved during labor for the baby's passage. Since we do not see first births in women of the ages you mentioned, it may be that once the bones are set, the difficulties do not increase. However, Loufa was in labor many hours longer than most of the women bearing children at a younger age."

Paula went out to get more water, thinking: There is no way I'm going to birth a child in Africa. Here, it is all up to God ... with no aseptic help available. She remembered her discussion with Jon, who said that Anna Louise insisted on going to England to birth their children if they married. I think I stunned Jon when I told him I wanted to birth our children in America. If we are successful at growing the kimmea in hothouses, we could add maternity clinics to the first aid clinics ... although Manutu has a good point about the age difference between a white woman and a black woman when birthing a first child.

Manutu was gone when she returned, and Tamubu was asleep.

Paula took her diary out to the sebula and began to write:
We will leave soon. Manutu and Sashono come every day, in the early dusk, to learn to read and write, and to see the plant drawings that Thomas did that day. His artistic skill and the life-like plant pictures fascinate them. Manutu immediately saw the advantages of the drawings for teaching acolytes.

Thomas works on his drawings each day, when he is not out training Windy. I'm not sure which he loves more, training the dog or doing the drawings. She smiled, feeling contentment in his happiness.

I regret the need to leave, for life here is peaceful. The only stress comes from outside sources: the wild animals, unfriendly tribes, and nomadic travelers – mostly white hunters. Life here is also productive and just. Chief Sashono settles grievances fairly and Manutu keeps everyone clean and healthy. Their lives are uncomplicated, basic and serene … I find there is much to say for serene.

"I watched you writing in your diary," Manutu said. "What is it that you write with such concentration?"

"I am writing my impressions of your village. What I think and feel now, so I will remember it all later. Do you never say, 'I wish I could remember how I felt that day when Tamubu arrived in our village?' Or do you remember every day as if it just happened?"

"I remember that which I need to remember – that which is important."

"Did you never forget where you found a helpful plant, and wished you had a way to remember where you had found it, or what season you harvested it?"

Manutu thought a moment, "The plants I remember well. It is the communing with the spirits that fades in my memory. It is their wisdom and advice that becomes indistinct. I can see where learning to write could be useful. I know the letters, but the spelling frustrates me."

"I will tell you a secret. Spelling is not important; just put down the word as it sounds to you, for even if you spell it wrong, you will understand it when you read it, like: tamootonda, spelled with o's instead of u's, will still mean tamutunda to you. If the first letter of a word and the last letter are correct, you will most likely know the meaning of the word."

"We are going to miss you and Tamubu. Your being here has added joy to our lives. Nanoka, who we felt had second sight, sent Tamubu to find his heritage. Sashona and I often wonder if she saw you."

"It was Tamubu's leaving that saved my life. I would have been a meal for lions without his coming to my rescue."

"Tomorrow will be a different day. Make sure to get a good night's sleep."

23 ~ Spirit Travel

Paula sat in the learning circle wearing the shift Manutu had left for her, without undergarments. By now, she was used to his machinations; although not evil, they were secret. Each day he reminded her that she was not to tell anyone but Tamubu of the day's events, which caused Paula to smile inwardly – like whom am I going to tell? The villagers all smile and greet me, but the women panic if I speak to them.

"Today, I want you to take a pinch of these herbs, rub them to powder in your palm; then sniff them up, clearing your mind of everything but the thought of where you want to go – which is to your kibanda in the village, to see what Tamubu is doing, and then return to me. Speak to no one, touch nothing until you return."

Paula rubbed the herbs to powder and sniffed. They smelled sweet like lavender and sharp like spearmint. She pictured Tamubu at the fire making one of his tasty stews. Suddenly she was by his side – watching him cook at the fire. "I can see and hear all that is going on – yet Tamubu ignores me, even though I'm standing right in front of him. I'm not sure I like this ... "

"Mkebibi, wake up!"

Paula opened her eyes to find herself sitting nude. Manutu stood with his back to her. "Dress yourself, and then we will talk."

"What just happened?"

"Your corporeal self became invisible and you traveled back to the village. What is Tamubu making for dinner?'

"Stew, from the leftover guinea fowl. I did not like spirit travel. I felt cold and all alone – as if I was no longer of this earth. I am still cold. May I add a few sticks to the fire?'

"Certainly, but you will soon be warm again. It is our last lesson. You may never need to use spirit travel, but your training would not be complete without it. This knowledge will allow you to travel vast distances in moments, and return to where you were only minutes before. When you leave, only your clothes will remain. If you come back to a different place, you will be naked. Without the herbs, you may not be able to return to your clothes; so before you *roam*, you must set both your destination, as well as the place of your return, in your mind."

"I did not do that today; why not?"

"Because I was with you, and acted as your host."

"I can't imagine that it will ever be necessary for me to *roam*. I have no reason to use spirit travel, but I thank you for all that you have taught me – although I feel a bit befuddled by it all. I used to be an ordinary woman who had learned to do unusual things. Now I find I'm an unusual woman who will have to work hard to be ordinary."

"You have never been ordinary, Mkebibi. You have always been special. This knowledge and ability do not change who you are. You are still who you were – just as you were. Only you will know there is a different and specially gifted you. It is like being able to do gymnastics, which is quite special too. You don't do gymnastics until you need to do it; and like gymnastics, your gift will be there for you if you ever need it. Gymnastics did not change who you are and your esoteric gifts do not change who you are … they add to and complement who you are"

"Well, putting it like that makes me feel better. I didn't want to become some weird, eerie woman. I just want to be me."

"Tamubu would never forgive me if I turned you into some weird, eerie woman," Manutu said smiling. "You, like Tamubu, have a strong nature. You will be able to carry the additional knowledge with ease, once you have accepted it. Nothing has changed; yet, everything has changed; it is like being born again, stronger … better … wiser."

"Is this our last day in the learning circle?"

"Yes. We can use the time we have left together to explore. Would you enjoy that?"

"Oh, yes! Can Thomas go with us?"

"But, of course. It will be a busman's holiday."

"How do you know about a busman's holiday?"

"We had three British hunters stop at the village, one of whom had a bad infection in a deep cut. I healed it for him. He used the expression – I liked it, and adopted it."

"I see you had a good day," Tamubu said. "You seem happy and gay."

"We did have a great day. It was our last day in the learning circle. We are now going to explore! I can hardly wait!"

"Who is we?"

"You, me and Manutu."

"He told you this?"

"Yes. Is there a problem?"

I wonder what he has up his sleeve now. "No, no problem. Did he say where we might go exploring?"

"No, but we begin the day after tomorrow."

"I will prepare for wilderness travel. Did he say how long we would be gone?"

"Nope, I think you should go and talk to him; I know nothing."

Tamubu approached Manutu's large and airy hut. He rapped on the entrance post saying, "Manutu, it is Tamubu."

"Come in, Tamubu. I suppose Paula told you we are going to explore, and you want to know how best to prepare for the journey?"

"Yes, that is so."

"We have four days. I thought we would go to the Valley of the Sun Spirits. What say you?"

"It is a dangerous place for clairvoyant people – why go there?"

"It will be Mkebibi's final test. She is strong, so strong I don't know the limit of her abilities."

"Why do you feel you must know, or test, her limits?"

"I want to learn from her. I want you to learn from her."

"I do not want you to put her in harm's way!" Tamubu spoke firmly. Then, in a kinder voice, he asked, "Is there nothing else you can do to test her mettle?"

"I will think on it. In the meantime, prepare for a journey of four days. We will take dried meat with us to avoid the need to hunt."

"Who will tend the sick while we are gone?"

132

"Kenga. While he's not yet finished his training, he has a great deal of ability with good intuition and judgment; he will be able to tend to anyone that might need help while we are gone. I have great confidence in him – he has a caring heart."

Manutu watched Tamubu leave with mixed emotions. I do not want Tamubu to be angry with me, but I must find Paula's limit. So far, she has shown me no limits at all ... and as such, she is the most unusual person I have ever known. It could be that she has powers of which I have never even dreamed ... she might be able to travel back in time ... or even be able to travel forward in time; her aura is so elastic; it is fascinating. I, myself, can only travel on the same plane in the same time frame.

24 ~ Valley of the Sun Spirits

They left the grasslands and climbed a craggy hill almost two thousand feet high. At the top, they overlooked an arid rocky plain, a desert, but not of sand – a desert of rocks and clay. Down the center of the plain ran a ragged streambed filled with reeds and dried sedge.

"In the rainy season, this whole place is a quagmire," Manutu said.

"Why have we come here? This place makes me feel lost and bereft; it's a scary, helpless feeling and I don't like it," Paula said to Manutu.

Manutu pointed, and said, "We will spend just the one night by that circle of rocks near the pool of water. In the morning, we will go to the crested butte." Manutu stood gazing at the angular tor, his thoughts far away.

"Why go to the crested butte … and for what?" Tamubu asked.

"I wish to climb it, but cannot. Mkebibi will climb it for me."

"Manutu," Tamubu said in a rigid tone, "I do not want Paula to climb that crested butte or go anywhere alone, while we are in this valley. We must be with her at all times."

Manutu sighed. "It will be as you wish, Tamubu. She will never be alone."

"You know my meaning. We must always be with her!"

"Yes, I know your meaning and respect your wishes."

Paula, who loved rock climbing, had gone on ahead and did not hear their exchange. She had put aside her intuitive dislike of the place, to occupy herself with the challenging descent into the valley. The men followed her trail, as she led them along skinny ledges and past jutting rocks. She found the descent, which had looked impossible, to be a maze of narrow little paths, ledges and crevice-like tunnels. In the shade of one such tunnel, they sat to rest and ate lunch.

Inside the circle of rocks, near the fire pit, stood a meager supply of woody bushes, left by someone who had camped there before. Tamubu made a fire and began to make broth, a stew and biscuits. Manutu went out looking for more tinder.

"This is an awful place; why did Manutu bring us here?" Paula asked.

"This awful place is called the *Valley of the Spirits*. Manutu comes here to commune with the Ancients. He comes here to seek their help when all else has failed. He has brought you here to see if you too, can commune with the Ancients, for through the ages, there have only been a handful of people able to do so."

"I don't care about communing with the Ancients. I'm not going to spend my life with mysticism – I don't even like it very much. I thought we were going on an adventure!"

"It is an adventure – an adventure of the mind. We will only be here for one night. I will be with you at all times. Remember our signal, *Sunshine, come home*. It will bring you back to me ... always heed my call!"

"Should I be worried?"

"No. I will hold your left hand, the hand closest to your heart, so I will always be with you – even if you don't see me."

In the ensuing silence, Manutu returned with a dried bush, which he set about turning into kindling. He felt the atmosphere of unrest and to lighten the mood said, "Mkebibi, you are most fortunate to have married such a good cook. I could smell the stew for half a league; it kept me from going further in my search for tinder."

"If I'm a good cook, Manutu, it is because you were my teacher."

"I readily accept that; but the pupil has surpassed the teacher with his skill."

"Tamubu makes better meals in the wilderness than I have ever eaten anywhere," Paula added. "He has amazed even his family, with his cooking ability."

"That may be," Tamubu replied, "but I have the Pymtu to thank for that fish recipe. It was the best fish I have ever eaten in my life – ever!" He smiled at Paula.

"I agree," Paula smiled back, "it was the best fish ever – as good as yours!"

Sipping broth after the meal, Paula realized she could never go back to bouillon cubes. She closed her eyes, feeling a weariness that had nothing to do with physical stamina. Her mind was blank, and her body felt in Limbo; replete from her meal, she began to doze. With her eyes closed, she saw the five spirits of love surrounding Tamubu. This startled her and in her mind's eye she glanced at Manutu, there she saw other emanations, wispy ones, long, thin and willowy; not the softly rounded shapes that surrounded Tamubu.

I wonder if Tamubu spiked my broth with something. Why are the spirits floating around Manutu shaped differently from the spirits floating around Tamubu? I wonder if I have spirits floating around me.

Manutu answered her question: '*You have no spirits, you have an aura. It is like a blessed light. I take this to mean that it is not earthly spirits, but angels that look over you. The emanations you see about me are the spirits of the past; those that helped me before and have come to help again, if needed.*'

'*Do you need help? Is that why we are here?*'

'*No, we are here so that Tamubu and I can learn the source of your exceptional power. Do you have any questions for the spirits?*'

'*No ... well maybe ... just one.*'

'*Speak it.*'

'*Is there something special I'm supposed to do in my life?*'

'**Yes.**' An eerie sound like the moaning of a high wind on the corner of a house.

'*What is it?*'

'**Follow the path that is before you.**'

'*What does that mean?*'

'*It means just what it says. You will attain your purpose if you but follow the path that is set out before you,*' Manutu replied.

'*Go to sleep now, Mkebibi. All is well.*'

"Tamubu, were you with us?" Manutu asked.

"Yes," he replied.

"It is more than I expected. What do you think?"

"I don't know what to think, so I'm not going to think about it at all."

"Hiding your head in the sand is no answer," Manutu chided.

"I don't want answers. I want us to live ordinary lives, and not think about our destinies. I want to go on, just as we were, following our natural instincts, doing what seems right for the moment."

"That is what she was told to do: "Follow the path that is before you."

"And that's what we will do. Will Paula remember any of this night?"

"Yes, I think so, if not as an active happening, then as a feeling she must follow."

"Good! She is perfect just the way she is; she doesn't need mysticism in her life."

"You are angry. Why?"

"I don't want her changed. I don't want her on a quest. I want us to go on doing things together. I missed her the days she was with you. I told myself it was for her safety, and I put up with it. We now know all we need to know. We will go on as if none of this has ever happened. I want no mention of it ever again!"

"I don't think I have ever seen you so upset and belligerent. We will do as you ask. I have overstepped my bounds and interfered with your life; I apologize."

Tamubu felt guilty. He had never been so outspoken with Manutu, nor had he ever told him what to do. His guilt turned to remorse. "No, I lost control. It is I who should apologize. I meant what I said, but I should have said it in a kinder, more tolerant way. You taught me that. You taught me to be diplomatic, not dictatorial."

"Your meaning came through loud and clear. It was only the loud that was unnecessary. We will speak no more of this. It is forgotten."

They arrived at the base of the crested butte, by mid-morning. It was an unusual rock formation, with the forbidding look of endless time about it.

"This will not be hard to climb … but why am I climbing it?" Paula asked.

"Up there, where the ledge forms a crest, are said to be remnants of a time before time began. I would like a small rock to take home with me," Manutu replied.

"I will go with you," Tamubu said firmly.

Paula looked at him and said, "Don't be silly. This is a climb for an expert. You have no skill with ropes and pitons."

"I will be with you none the less."

"Suit yourself, but I will not be able to help you. It would be best if you waited on the ground and belayed the jump line for me."

"Manutu can do that. I will be with you."

She turned to him, looked him in the eyes and said softly, "I love you too!"

Paula attained the ledge, which was higher than it looked. A strong breeze gusted – warm then cold. She did not like the place … it smelled feral and dead. She spotted a small rock; one that did not resemble the others, for it was pointy on all sides. The other rocks were just angular.

Paula picked it up, and in a flash, she saw the lush forests of prehistoric times, and in the distance, a volcano spewed lava; the smoke choked her breath. She felt helpless, as if she was in a coma: she could hear and see, but she could not speak or move. The millennia flashed by in fast-forward scenes of the Triassic to Cretaceous periods, changing as the ages had changed. Paula found it hard to breathe … grew faint, fell and dropped the rock.

Instantly, she was herself again and back on the ledge – with a naked Tamubu holding her in his arms. "Are you alright?" he asked.

"I don't know, I think so," she replied. "Something incredible happened when I picked up that pointy rock for Manutu. I won't pick it up again. I'm going to hit it off the ledge with my hammer. Go tell him not to touch it until I have talked with him. Thomas, please go – I want to leave this place now!"

Paula rappelled off the cliff face as fast as she could safely go. She felt a desperate need to reach the valley floor … to be off and away from the butte.

Manutu and Tamubu stabilized the line for her return. In minutes, she stood beside them.

"I have seen many things in my time, but never anyone who can climb, or descend, like you can – you are indeed an expert!" Manutu praised. "Tell me what happened to you up there. I saw you go rigid ... frozen and unmoving for long minutes ... why?"

"Let's go and sit, I could use a drink, I feel parched."

"Of course, what is the matter with me? Here is some broth. It's not hot anymore, but it will restore you," Manutu said.

"I felt like the first person in all of time to be on that ledge. The air felt thick and moist, warm yet cold, full of oxygen, sickly sweet, but dead. I saw an odd, pointy rock. I picked it up, and in an instant I was back in prehistoric times, in the lands of erupting volcanoes, dinosaurs and land reformation. I could not breathe for all the ash in the air; I felt weak and then faint, and must have dropped the rock. Instantly, I was back in the present with Tamubu holding me. Where is that rock now?"

"It's over there next to my pack," Tamubu replied.

"Is that why you wanted a rock? Because it can carry you back in time?" Paula asked of Manutu.

"I did not know of its properties. I only suspected the unusual. I would not have allowed you to touch one had I known. I would have told you just to knock one off the ledge down to me."

"Well, how do you expect to get it home?"

"I do not yet know. I will have to think on it." Manutu replied.

"I have a suggestion," she said. "We can push it into my film bag with my hammer; the bag is lined with thick black plastic."

"We will try that, and then leave this place. Do you feel strong enough to climb out of here today?" Tamubu asked.

"Yes, I'm fine now. Your broth always makes me feel better."

That night they camped on a ledge just below the mountaintop savanna. "Paula and I spent the first night of our wilderness trek on a ledge similar to this one," Tamubu said to Manutu. "Paula demonstrated her rappelling skills with the grapnel and line there. You think you were surprised today, well, I was totally stunned then." He smiled at Paula, and continued, "And I have been stunned and amazed ever since!"

Paula smiled back, saying, "And that's just the way I like it. I want all my men to be stunned and amazed by me."

As Manutu listened to their bantering words and saw their smiling eyes, he suspected that they did this often. He laughed with Tamubu, saying, "I think you have met your match, Tamubu, Paula is quite clever."

"Possibly, but she's not as good a cook as me – even if she is so clever."

"I'll settle for good cooking; clever doesn't taste nearly as good," she replied. "Is there any more broth?"

They settled for the night. Paula sipped the last of her broth thinking: No one will ever believe the things that have happened to me since the tsunami set the *Just Cause* and me adrift.

I feel like Dorothy – swept away to OZ – where everything around me is outlandish. Tamubu was one, Manutu is two, who or what will be the third in the trilogy? Who will be my Tin Man? Or will it be a when, a what, or a where? I feel as if there is something more in my future – but I don't know: who, what, when, where – or even why.

25 ~ Dilemma at Dela-Aden

Thomas and Paula arrived back at Dela-Aden in mid-afternoon. They did not expect a welcoming committee, but they did hope there would be a cart waiting for their luggage. Paula grabbed Thomas's forearm – he glanced at her and saw concern. "I know," he said. "I'm surprised that no one is here to greet us too."

"It's not that, Thomas; I have a dreadful feeling that something is very wrong!"

"Let's leave the luggage and go to the house; I too, feel a foreboding."

They found Elizabeth sitting in her kitchen rocking chair. She looked up as they came through the door and burst into tears. "Oh master Thomas! They're gone – just disappeared!"

"Who's gone? Who's disappeared?" Thomas asked.

"Master James and Miss Anna Louise; they found the horses tied to a tree, but there's no trace of them. They are just gone!"

"When did this happen?"

"The day before yesterday; they took a picnic lunch, but didn't return for tea."

"Where is everyone?"

"They are all out searching – looking for them – it's as if they vanished. They searched all day yesterday too; they even had Mr. Phillip's bloodhounds with them … they found nothing. Everyone is out looking for them again today. I'm so glad you're back – you'll know what to do."

Thomas patted Elizabeth saying, "Fix us a cup of tea … and compose yourself; you need to tell us everything you know – all of it."

When Elizabeth finished her tale, Thomas asked, "Who is still here?"

"Just the lads, Abumi and Suffo, in the barn; Hanley, the overseer, and the women who work in the fields; and Mr. Simmons the estate manager, who is coordinating the men who are out searching. Lady Mary took Pompito with her. They went riding over to the neighbors. I was told to have sandwiches and drinks ready for anyone that came to the house."

"Well, I could use a sandwich, how about you, Paula?"

"Yes, but I need my luggage."

"Have a bite; I'll call down to the barn, and ask Abumi and Suffo to go and fetch our gear. Then we can talk while we change."

Paula listened with half-an-ear while Elizabeth told about events at Dela-Aden for the past thirty-two days. It seems Jamie and Anna went out riding most days, often taking picnic lunches. Anna rode Finn, the Haflinger, and Jamie rode Sunshine. Since the horses were found tied to a tree, no one suspected an accident. That Jamie and Anna were just gone made everyone suspect foul play.

Paula went up to their third floor bedroom, the old schoolroom and playroom, now a guest room, to take a shower and wash her hair. Showering is what she missed most while visiting the Zuri Watu, for dipping water with a gourd to wash her hair and sink bathing were not as satisfying as a nice hot shower. She also wanted to be alone to think. Why would anyone abduct Jamie and Anna? Who would have anything to gain from such treachery? I can't even think of a reason for it.

Thomas was supine in the chaise lounge when Paula stepped out of the bathroom. Without preamble, he said, "Cyril cancelled our deal with Mr. Athos because Max came out to the farm – ostensibly to buy wine. However, it was in clear contravention to the terms of our agreement. Kybo saw him and told Jon, who told Cyril. Athos, with his twisted mind, is the only swine who would do something like kidnap Jamie and Anna. I can't imagine what he thinks he will gain. Surely he knows that he and Max would be the prime suspects ... even if they can prove they were elsewhere at the time. It is time for me to pay Mr. Athos a visit; what do you say?"

"When you say a visit, do you mean *roam*?"

"Yes, if I knew where Athos and Max were, I would go this moment. I know Manutu says that distance makes no difference, but I did not find it so when I went to the *Gallant Lady* to leave that note for Max – it depleted me."

"That frightens me. I never expected to have to *roam* again."

"Nor did I ever expect I would need your help. But, we are going back in time – something I have never done before – but you have, and you have the ability to bring us back," Thomas replied.

"Now I'm really scared. How do you know I can do these things?" Paula asked.

"Manutu told me. That rock, the one that took you back in time, well, it did nothing when Manutu touched it, he felt nothing. I have just had an idea, a much better idea than going to visit Athos or Max. I'll be right back!"

Thomas soon returned and held out his hand: he held Anna's locket, and Jamie's school ring. He handed them to her saying, "Take one in each hand and concentrate. If you can see where they are, then we can go there; and if we can go there, we can bring them back. Are you willing to try?"

Paula sat on the bed, still in her robe. She had a peculiar feeling of déjà vu. No sense in getting dressed if I'm going *to roam*. I can't let Thomas know how scared I am of doing this; but if it will help to find Anna and Jamie – then I don't have much of a choice.

Thomas went and told Elizabeth that they were not to be disturbed for the next hour – **for any reason** – and for the boys to leave their luggage in the entrance hall.

Thomas put out the Do Not Disturb sign and locked the bedroom door. Paula picked up the ring and the locket, one in each hand. Thomas took a pinch of roaming herbs and ground them in his palms, holding his hands close to their noses while they sniffed.

Paula closed her eyes. She freed her mind and thought of Jamie and Anna. She pictured them riding on the farm trails, then pictured the horses tethered near the grassy pond for a picnic lunch.

Almost at once, Paula saw the lime pit with its eerie mist floating above the surface. Littering the area and spiking the mist were the pearlescent gray remains of fallen trees that had petrified into grotesque shapes. The low swirling fog shifted and glowed in the lowering sun, giving the eerie shapes life, or the impression of ghosts evanescing.

Without warning, Paula was standing on a small littered patch of dry land surrounded by bogs and deep impenetrable forest. Three shabby lean-tos and a dismal little fire with two men hunched over the meager flame, also occupied the patch of dry land.

'Is this a squatter's hunting camp. Why am I here? What has this to do with Jamie and Anna?' She communed with Thomas, who, in holding her hands had *roamed* with her. 'Do you know this place?'

'No, but we are here for a reason. We should look inside the lean-tos, unpleasant as that might be.'

Joy consumed them both, when in the last ragged lean-to they found Jamie and Anna, bound and tied to posts, sitting on the ground. Anna was pale; her eyes were wide and glazed with fear. Jamie looked dazed, as if he wasn't totally conscious.

'Stay here with Anna and Jamie; I want to explore a bit and find out where this camp is located. I won't be gone long.'

In moments, Thomas returned. 'This camp is on a neighbor's land, where he has let it go wild because the ground is full of boggy sink holes. This is a little dry island surrounded by sucking bogs. The only way in or out is over that fallen oak tree. You go back and get the pony trap; I will meet you on the boundary road, and guide you to a meeting place not far from here.'

In an instant, Paula was back in their bedroom; glad to don jeans, flannel shirt, thick socks and her boots, for she was cold, very cold. The pervading dampness of the bogs had chilled her to the bone. Her concern and empathy went out to Jamie and Anna who had endured three days in that dreadful place.

Paula grabbed some blankets and towels, with Thomas's kitu-kina, loin cloth and sandals. Downstairs, she called out to Elizabeth to put a dozen sandwiches in a bag with a flask of hot lemon-honey tea and a canteen of hot water. She then called down to the barn and told the boys to harness Finn to the pony trap, and bring him up to the house as quickly as possible. She needed him right away.

Minutes later, Elizabeth handed her the bag of sandwiches, the flask and the canteen, "Have they been found?" She asked hopefully.

"I don't know ... Thomas told me to be prepared," Paula replied.

"I see Sombuto – I see Minba – I see you suffering a horrible death!" Thomas intoned in a ghostly voice. "You must return God's children to the place from which you took them, and do it at once, or the skin will begin to rot off your flesh, and your eyes will fall out and your manhood will shrivel up."

The men sat completely awestruck and terrified, unable to move.

"I will take no pity on men who steal innocents – MOVE!"

Instantly, the men at the fire became almost hysterical. They leapt up, jabbering in panic. One doused the fire while the other freed the prisoners.

"Handle my children gently, or you will lose the use of your hands, and others will feed you only offal."

The men, terrified as never before, quaked with eyes so wide and white that their irises seemed but dots; their movements were haphazard and frenzied, for they constantly glanced about in trembling fear, expecting a horrible retribution, at any instant.

Thomas watched as they lifted Jamie and Anna to their feet. They were both stiff from the pervasive cold, dazed from shock, and faltered from weakness. Thomas ached for them as he watched the natives guide them across the log bridge. Once he was satisfied the natives would continue to obey his orders, he went to show Paula the rendezvous point, for Jamie and Anna were much too weak and dazed to walk very far.

The drive out to the boundary road, to the grassy area near the pond, where the horses were tethered, seemed to take forever … even though Finn maintained a strong, steady twelve mile an hour trot, covering the ground rapidly.

Paula smiled with great relief when Thomas appeared sitting next to her naked, saying, "Stop, so I can put my clothes on. If we happen to pass a native, who sees me sitting here naked, with you driving as if devils were on your tail, it will start a legend that will have no end, and everything we ever do will be fodder for the tale!"

Paula chuckled as she pictured his words, "That will never do, now will it?"

Thomas related the events at the squalid camp, and Paula, while horrified, could not help smiling at the terror he had wreaked upon the abductors. But her heart ached for Anna. Why did this have to happen to her – of all people?

Nearing the pond, they saw Jon on the other side, looking in the soft earth for tracks. He had tethered Sunshine in the shade nearby.

"Jon!" Paula called.

Jon looked up and waved wildly, running back to the road. "Did you just get back? Did you hear the awful news? I'm beside myself. Anna is going to hate Africa! I don't know what to do!"

"Mount up, Jon; we have a way to go yet. You can tell us your version of what happened on the way," Thomas said.

Jon was so distracted and worried, that he didn't pick up on Thomas's words, or even wonder where they were going in such a hurry.

"We can't imagine why anyone would abduct Anna and Jamie," Jon began. "However, everything does point to abduction. Why would anyone do such a terrible thing? What have they to gain from it? I'm out of my mind worrying about them."

"I don't know yet, Jon, but you can be sure I will find out, and when I do, they will suffer." Thomas replied in a menacing voice.

"Doesn't seem right to me, making others suffer, but what else is there to do when they have made you suffer? If you do nothing to retaliate, then there is no reason for them to ever stop making you suffer. Yes, Thomas, we must find out who did this and obtain retribution. Where are we going anyway? You seem in an awf'ly big hurry."

Paula, at a touch of her arm from Thomas, pulled Finn gently to a halt. She alit from the cart and tethered Finn's lead line to a tree. Thomas joined her and Jon dismounted, tying Sunshine to the rear of cart. Paula took Jon in her arms to comfort him. She thought she felt him sob as she held on tight.

Long moments later, when the lump in her throat had gone, and she could speak, she said softly, "Don't turn around just yet Jon, but prepare yourself … Anna and Jamie are coming through the trees. She is quite bedraggled, but she is now smiling, and tears of joy stream down her face, for she sees us standing here."

With a wild look at Paula, Jon turned, faltered, and then raced towards Anna, with Paula and Thomas not far behind him. The natives melted into the underbrush, as only natives, at one with Africa, can do. Jamie and Anna clung to each other as they avoided the dead branches and ubiquitous thorn bushes. Then Jon swept Anna off her feet and carried her to the cart, hugging her and kissing her teary face. Thomas helped Jamie who had apparently put up a fight, for he was all bruised and swollen. He was probably weak from hunger too. Jamie tried to be manly, but his tears of inexpressible relief had a mind of their own.

Paula took some of the hot water and wet a towel and passed it to Anna, who gave her a weak smile as she wiped her face. "How did you know we were going to be here? You seem so prepared."

"How would you like a sip of hot tea and a bite of one of Elizabeth's special tuna fish sandwiches?" Paula asked.

"Oh, would I. We've not eaten in days. Those men only gave us bananas and some water. I'm just so thankful to be away from them, and rid of that awful place. Who were they? What did they want with us? I've never been so terrified – my mind ran amuck! I'm glad to see Finn and Sunshine are okay. Ohhh … I'm so glad you're back; I missed both of you awf'ly," Anna said through her sobbing tears.

Jon tried to comfort Anna, to set her mind at ease by answering her questions. "We think those natives may have been the squatters Dad evicted last year. It's also possible that someone paid them to abduct you; we're not sure about that – yet. The horses were tied to a tree a long way from here – on the day you went missing."

"Yes, they drug us through the woods for a long time," Jamie replied.

Jon drove the pony trap back to the farm, while Thomas dispensed first aid to cuts and bruises. Paula mounted Sunshine, and went to spread the good news at the tea sheds and the winery.

Once home, both Anna and Jamie wanted to bathe and dress in clean clothes. Thomas sent the stable boys out to tell the neighbors the good news. Paula arrived back at the barn while Jon and Thomas were hosing Finn down, for he had worked up quite a sweat, from speed out and a heavy load on his return.

Sir Peter and Lady Mary heard the news from Paula and rushed back to the barn, only to find that Jamie and Anna were already up at the house. The stable lads were still out delivering the good news to the neighbors, so Peter and Mary put up the horses themselves. It was just as well. It gave them time to talk, and to get their emotions under control, for the dreadful events had once again shaken their confidence in their personal safety at Dela-Aden. Something would have to change!

By tea time, those involved in the search knew that Jamie and Anna were back home, alive, but much the worse for the encounter, although recovering from their dreadful experience. Even so, the consensus of opinion among the neighbors was that the situation needed immediate reprisal.

The native police in Kenya have a reputation among their own people as being brutal. A reputation that is well-deserved, for it is true. When called in to deal with recalcitrant squatters, they have been known to brutally beat the men, rape and maim the women and mature girls, sell the children to Arabs, and kill the babies. It is for this reason that squatters move when asked, and do not usually return. So, it was of great concern to the land grant farmers, that squatters had had the audacity to kidnap Jamie and Anna Louise.

At a meeting two days later, when Jamie and Anna had recovered a bit, and felt well enough to answer questions from the land owners, they decided, by a consensus of opinion, that the land owners would no longer deal with the squatters by asking them to leave. They would call in the Kenya police to move the squatters. It was a severe measure, one that none of them liked doing, but the abduction was such an outrage that they felt it was the only effective avenue open to them. The squatters had done the unforgivable: they had abducted white people.

Lady Mary and Sir Peter were dismayed at the decision and asked that posters, with a drawing of a squatters camp with an 'X' through it showing the Kenya Police Patrol logo, be put up along the perimeter lines, giving advance notice to warn away any would-be squatters. The land owners agreed to the stipulation; even so, the decision frustrated Peter and Mary in their efforts for humane treatment of the natives. However, drastic and stern measures became the order-of-the-day after the Mau Mau uprising with its brutal and senseless murders of white women and children.

Sir Peter and the neighboring farmer, on whose land the kidnappers had hidden Anna and Jamie, volunteered to go into Nairobi to talk to the police chief. It was already known that neither Jamie nor Anna could identify their captors, whose faces had been covered with mud and feathers, whose clothes had been rags; and they had not heard them speaking amongst themselves. The only clue had been Jamie's drawing of their handmade spears.

The word went out: the Kenya Police Patrol will move off all squatters on land grant properties. The Kenya Police were to make spot checks of the boundary roads, beginning immediately. The farmers wanted retribution.

Even so, it was felt that the squatters would not have abducted Anna and Jamie on their own – it served them no purpose. The culprit had to be Mr. Athos, who did have an axe to grind. Cyril Latham had corroborated the evidence given to the Kenya Police, including the previous abduction of Paula and the attempted abduction of Thomas. Max Smith and Petrides Athos became wanted men in Kenya.

A week had passed in which Jamie and Anna had not gone out for more than a walk in the gardens. Physically the damage was superficial, but psychologically, the damage was deep. Anna had trouble sleeping, even with the kimmea, for she had nightmares of her ordeal, where horrible things happened to her. In the mornings, she was as tired as when she went to bed, and would have gladly gone back to England had her mother been at home to comfort her.

She still loved Jon, who was supremely attentive to her. In fact, she loved him even more for his utterly kind and unfailing devotion.

Anna had long talks with herself, reasoning with her fears, demanding that she put the episode aside. It had always worked before, but this time she could not convince herself – this time the fragile fabric of her new confidence was badly torn. She did know that if she went away now, she would never return. I'm too frightened to even leave the house, and I almost jump out of my skin if someone appears without notice. She longed for England and home.

Jon watched Anna for a week. She seemed lost – wrapped tightly in a cocoon. Jamie had taken to playing the piano for long hours and

Anna had taken to reading while he played. Neither one had much cheer. Jon decided to change the situation. Enough time had passed; both of them had healed physically; they just needed a mental change and a physical stimulus. Jon discussed his idea with Thomas, who had been treating Anna with kimmea. While she no longer jumped at every sound, she slept too much, and had no interest in the life about her. She definitely needed a change.

Thomas suggested that Jon and Paula take Jamie and Anna on a vacation to visit the Zuri Watu. Paula agreed, it was just what Anna needed. To live among friendly, caring black people. To understand village life, and the ways of the native African, to see them for the people most of them were: ordinary families working hard for peaceful living in Africa.

Manutu's wisdom and abilities could help restore Anna's peace of mind, and give her back her confidence in herself. It could rid her of her abject fear of the native. They had only a passing association with them at Dela-Aden. A white man had instigated their horrible abduction

Jamie was delighted at the prospect. Anna thought not long before she agreed to go, which pleased Jon immensely. He did not know that her real reason for going was that she felt safe when she was with Paula.

The day of her rescue, it was Paula who given her strength; it was Paula who had reached inside her and brought her mind back from the edge of disaster. Anna had wanted to retreat into a never-never land, and was half-way there when Paula had calmed her fears It was Paula that brought her out of herself, by making her aware of poor Jamie, who was badly beaten. . It was Paula's kind understanding that kept Anna from a deep regression. Paula had saved her mind as well as her body.

Jon and Thomas had shown her love and tender care. Jon had wrapped her in a soft warm blanket, and held her close to him all the way home. Anna did so love Jon. She had not much experience with men, but instinctively, she knew that Jon was singular among them.

"Yes, I would like to go to visit the Zuri Watu," Anna said. "It will be wonderful to see some of Africa from a helicopter, and to meet Manutu as well."

Jamie echoed her opinion, adding, "I've never been in a helicopter."

"Well, you're both in for a special delight," Paula said. "I found the experience incredible. We will take a DC-3 to Yaoundé, then a helicopter to the Zuri Watu village."

In the bustle of preparations, a semblance of joy returned to the household. Peter and Mary had been beside themselves with Anna's blue funk, and Jamie's lack of enthusiasm for the out-of-doors. Thomas had told them that time was their ally when healing, especially for the psyche, saying, "One day, they will just be recovered, and then they will want to get on with their lives, just give them time."

A complete change will aid in their recovery, Thomas thought, and Manutu will be pleased to help. I might just go and join them in the lands of the Zuri Watu when I'm finished here. They are two very different worlds: the world of the white man in Kenya, and the world of the African native in his own lands. Thomas understood the way of the British, who loved to colonize; although, for all their vast experience, they were not very good at it.

26 ~ European Tour ~ July

"Are you having fun, Hanna?" Sara asked.

"Yes, of course ... aren't you having a good time?" Hanna replied.

"Well, we are going lots of different places, but it's sort of boring ... looking at old buildings in decrepit towns."

"What did you expect? New towns and new buildings!"

"You know what I mean. It's all so repetitious. If you've seen one old building and one old town, doing it over and over becomes boring."

"I don't find it boring at all. Each town has its own personality, its own charm and interesting sights. The people are different too."

"Yes, they are all different, but they are all different the same!"

"I don't know what to say to you, Sara. If you are going to be malcontented, then you will have an awful time, and we have only just begun."

"We spent so much time making pretty dresses, but no one ever sees them. We are on tour buses all day, or walking around these ghastly towns. We never meet anyone interesting."

"You seemed happy enough on the cruise ship."

"I was happy on the cruise ship. We had time to do as we pleased and we met those nice boys at the pool."

"Is that what this is all about? Boys!"

"Well, at least they were interesting. They feel the same as we do ... "

"Don't include me in your feelings. I like what we are doing. I like seeing old towns and old buildings. I like looking at the past. It makes me feel as if my life could count for something, when I finally decide what that something will be."

"I think the main difference is that you are looking for something to do, and I'm looking for something to be," Sara replied. "I'm tired of learning today, to be prepared for some distant and unknown tomorrow. I want to live for today! Who knows how many todays we have left!"

"None of us knows how many days we have left. You are foolish to dwell on such a thing, using up today by longing for an unknown tomorrow."

"I can't help it. Today bores me."

"Sara, only you can make today interesting. If you wait for outside influences to come along that interest you, you waste today waiting for tomorrow. One day, you might wake up to find the best years of your life gone – wasted by longing for tomorrow!"

"Don't you ever feel bored?"

"Of course I do! I hate standing in lines; it bores me to tears. Flying also bores me, so I use the time to read, which I enjoy. Waiting for someone to call or show up bores me – and annoys me – so I use the time doing things I need to do. If you can't avoid something, make the best of it!"

"Why are we so different? We're twins!"

"We are two different people who happen to look alike; you should know that by now."

"I can't take three more weeks of this, I'll go gaga!"

"Talk to Mrs. Holmesby. Is there anything on the itinerary that interests you?"

"Only the recital in Vienna; I do so love to play the piano."

"Well, the Vienna recital will be on Monday, then the river cruise to Budapest. Don't you look forward to seeing the Lipizzaners in Vienna?"

"Of course, silly; you know I love horses, but again we will just be watching, not involved. I want to be involved in something."

"We are involved in a European tour, Sara. Who knows what waits for us around the next corner? I'm quite happy looking forward to each new day."

"I know that, and some days I envy your complacency."

27 ~ Julia and Georgina

"So far, so good; what do you think Georgina?"

"This tour is the best ever. None of the gals were ever on a cruise ship before, and the day excursions in the Baltic countries were interesting for them … and me too. A different port and a different culture each day. I enjoyed Stockholm the most; so clean and well-kept. What about you, do you like the new itinerary?"

"Yes," Julia agreed. "I enjoyed the park-like feeling of Stockholm too. It's too bad that the decorative plaster work on the old buildings in St. Petersburg is falling into disrepair … and the number of street urchins there was distressing. The docent's explanation – that apartments are shared by two or even three families, making those that can, go outside – stunned me. Yet enough of the past beauty still remains. I think the girls are enjoying our new itinerary; I know I am. I like the control and the freedom of the cruise ship for the gals. The land tours are less active, and a bit more restrictive with having to return to the cruise ship before it departs.

"Have you told the gals about the formal reception after the recital in Vienna?"

"No, not yet; I think Sunday morning will be soon enough."

"You might want to tell them sooner. Give them some time to primp."

"You're right, Georgina. I forgot about primping; I don't do it much anymore."

Georgina smiled, "You're a natural beauty, I doubt if you've ever had to primp."

"What a nice thing to say; no wonder I like you so much!"

28 ~ Vienna ~July

The Lipizzaner Hall was adjacent to the Schönbrunn Palace on one side of an enormous arcaded square. The limousine arrived at a stone porte-cochere set onto the end of the Lipizzaner Hall, guarded by beefeater-type sentries with halberds. The narrow winding steps led up to an aisle behind the top tier of the loge below the Emperor's balcony. The upper balcony and the loge below it are at the far end of the arena, opposite the portals where the Lipizzaners enter.

In the loge, three walkways lead down the rows of tiered upholstered seats, with the first row being on a level with the arena floor, separated only by a hip high wall. The seats in the loge are reserved for the crème de la crème, and invited guests. The guests in the loge have an unobstructed view of the Lipizzaner performance.

The upper and lower spectator's galleries – above and outboard of the arena on both of its long sides – are backed up by two storey Palladian windows. At intervals inside the stone balustrades, massive Corinthian pillars support the upper gallery and the arched and vaulted roof. Only in a small corner standing space above the horse portals is there an unimpeded view of the arena from the spectator's galleries.

From the arena floor to the five story ceiling, the space is open above the arena, with the massive crystal chandeliers hanging down the centerline.

"I had no idea we would be treated like royalty," Sara said to Hanna. "I'm overwhelmed!"

"I wonder why," Hanna replied. "I was suitably impressed when the limo arrived. Now, I'm a bit worried."

"Why are you worried?"

"If we are treated like royalty for the Lipizzaner performance, what will the reception be like after the recital?"

Even Mrs. Holmesby, Mrs. Raft and the other girls sat completely awed and speechless … as well as simply delighted.

A uniformed usher gave each guest a small booklet as they entered the loge. Seated, Sara read in a low excited voice, " … each rider must ride for two years, before he is allowed reins … "

"Can you imagine that, Hanna? Two years of riding without reins?"

"No, I wonder why?"

"It says, 'to develop seat and leg aids in a proper position at all times'."

"Oh my, did you read that ' … Archduke Charles founded the Royal and Imperial Court Stud of Lipizza on the Karst in 1580'? This tradition is almost four hundred years old – incredible!" Hanna said, awed.

Neither Sara or Hanna had time to speculate on the rest of the booklet's interesting information, as the overture to Rodetzsky's March Militaire began and the wide Palladian doors, on either side of the gallery at the far end of the vast arena opened, and out came the most beautiful and talented stallions in the world.

The riders rode the horses at a slow collected trot down the long side walls of the arena, crossing in the center in a pas de deux to form two lines facing the Emperor's box above them.

Hanna and Sara were so close to the riders that Hanna could see the wrinkles under the eyes of the lead rider, and Sara could smell the polished hooves, while they both listened to the snorting of the Lipizzaner stallions.

The music stopped. In a synchronized movement, the riders doffed their hats and bowed their heads in a Memorial salute to a nobility that no longer ruled. The last Emperor, Franz Joseph, died in 1916. In 1918, the palace and hall became the property of the new republic. The music resumed, and the horses moved off in two lines, one line to the left and one line to the right to begin the quadrille.

The quadrille was simply perfect: each horse placed the same hoof on the ground at the same time as its counterpart, the spacing remained exact through all the movements performed. The riders maintained perfect positions; they never moved – only the horses moved, and the riders moved with them. The aids were unseen.

156

It was a precision ballet of horses and riders; a magnificent and incredible display of skill astride superbly trained horses.

During the training segment of the exhibition, when the horse and driver passed in front of the loge, Hanna and Sara could hear the soft encouraging sounds of the walking driver and the regulated breathing of the horse, as they strode past – not six feet away from them. An unforgettable thrill – unfortunately, cameras were verboten.

The music ended with the horses and riders once again lined up, spot-on, to salute to a memory. The horses turned as before, moving in a slow collected trot, again crossing in the center of the arena – below the sparkling crystal chandeliers suspended for two stories down the center of the arena – to pass through the portals to the stables.

The Croft School group followed their fellow guests from the loge across the square to the arcade attached to the palace entrance, where they presented their engraved invitations to a tall young man in a magnificent uniform flanked by beefeater-type guards. In taking Hanna's and Sara's invitations, the young man looked at them, and then smiled, saying in excellent English, "Welcome to Schönbrunn Palace, Miss Hanna, Miss Sara; we are quite pleased to have you with us this evening. Thank you for coming." As they gathered with Mrs. Raft and Mrs. Holmesby, Hanna heard the uniformed greeter speak German to the guests behind them, saying only, 'Willkommen zu Schönbrunn'. She felt a little thrill. They had been welcomed personally.

They followed the guests across the huge and pillared hall to the curving granite steps with their wide red runners, which ascended to the first floor from either side of the hall. At the top of the long staircase, another magnificently uniformed man stepped forward saying, "Will the Misses Caulfield, and Madam Holmesby please follow me?" Another young man, not so elaborately uniformed, also stepped forward, bowed and said to Mrs. Raft and the other girls, "Ladies, this way, if you please." He escorted them to of the concert hall vestibule for refreshments.

The elegantly uniformed young man said, "My name is Wolfgang. I will escort you to the stage ante-chamber where you can rehearse before the recital. It is a sound proof room. No one will hear you unless they are in the room. Later, when it is time for the performance, I will return for you and escort you to the stage. When you enter the stage, move to the front of the pianos; there you will curtsey deeply, bowing your heads towards the Emperor's balcony, the front rows of which will be empty. The Archduke and Duchess will be sitting in the second seats, as they did at the Lipizzaner Hall. Most likely, he will nod his head at you. Then arise and go to the pianos. At the end of the recital, you will again repeat the curtsey in front of the pianos. You may rise, but please wait for the Archduke and Duchess to leave the balcony before you leave the stage. Do you have any questions?

Hanna smiled saying, "Where is the nearest Ladies room?"

Wolfgang snapped his fingers. A tall skinny young man, in almost plain livery, promptly came to Wolfgang's side. "Damen," Wolfgang said. To Hanna and Sara, he then said, "Please follow Kurt, he will show you the way. I will be here when you return."

Sara wanted to talk to Hanna when they were alone in the ladies room, but they were not alone; an older woman in a black dress with a white lace collar and apron shadowed their every move, offering them a fresh bar of soap, then folded linen towels and expensive perfume.

Kurt waited outside in the hall, a discreet distance away. As soon as they appeared, he came over, nodded to them and once again led them back to the rehearsal room.

Wolfgang awaited them and said, "If you require anything – anything at all – just ask."

They started, as always, with scales and Cherney exercises for timing, which nimbled the fingers and concentrated the mind, before moving on to the pieces they had prepared for the recital – practicing for the first time in ten days. It took a few minutes to settle down, before the concentration and the joy of playing together closed out everything else. They played in such perfect unison that it sounded like only one piano amplified. They played parts of each piece: the Gershwin, the Mozart and the Chopin, mostly the fast passages, as well as the adaptation to the introduction to Strauss' Blue Danube Waltz. The girls had scored all the selections with improvisations possible only with two pianos.

Polite applause greeted them when they appeared onstage, where they followed Wolfgang's instructions. Thank goodness, Mrs. Holmesby had purchased long dusters for them to wear to the Lipizzaner Hall, to keep their recital attire spotless. She had also taught them how to curtsey deeply, which they had practiced often in a laughing parody, never ever expecting that someday the skill would be needed.

The girls wore long full black taffeta skirts and long sleeve white silk blouses with a discreet bit of black taffeta at the collar. They wore their shoulder-length golden hair with the sides pulled back behind their heads and fastened with a small black taffeta bow, which looked absolutely charming. When the footlights dimmed, they looked one another in the eye, mentally counted to three ... and began.

The music flowed from their fingers, ebbing and flowing like a waterfall of enchanted notes. Each selection received thundering applause; they rose and stood beside the pianos to head bow. When the applause died away, they resumed playing. They had chosen a series of shorter pieces, rather than one long piece, in case any one of the pieces did not suit the Viennese ear. They never expected the standing ovation they received, or the ringing cries of 'encore'. Vienna is the city of music, and the appreciation of their talents was lusty, enthusiastic and stimulating.

When they began to play the variations on the prelude to the Blue Danube Waltz, the audience went wild, for Strauss is the musical king in Vienna. He is loved and adored. The final applause lasted for five minutes, with Hanna and Sara smiling and curtsying in front of the pianos.

Back in the soundproof room, Wolfgang said, "You were a tremendous hit. The Archduke and Duchess never sit through five minutes of applause. Ending up with the Strauss was perfect!

"It will now be my pleasure to escort you to the reception. Would you like Kurt to take you to the ladies room first?"

"Yes," Hanna replied, "thank you."

Hoping the ladies room attendant did not speak English, which she did – but not well enough to follow their rapid conversation – Sara said, "I think we were a success!"

"Yes, I think so too. Were you nervous?" Hanna asked.

"I was scared witless until we started to play. Once we began to count together, everything else went away, but you and the music; then I felt at ease," Sara said.

"That's what happened to me too. It's what always happens to me when we play for a public audience."

"I'm happier playing the piano than doing anything else," Sara said.

"Me too, I hope we will always play the piano together. I wonder what will happen next. Do you think we will meet the Archduke and Duchess?"

"Oh, my gosh! A receiving line! I won't know what to say!"

"Let's ask Wolfgang," Hanna suggested.

"Yes, that's a good idea … oh my gosh! Meeting the Archduke and Duchess! I'm not sure I won't faint dead away!"

Hanna laughed, "If you do, go first, so I can fall on top of you!"

The openness of these talented young ladies fascinated Wolfgang as much as their extreme talent. The recital had been a huge success, delighting everyone.

"After you are introduced by the Major Domo, who will say, 'the young misses: Hanna and Sara Caulfield,' you will again curtsey, but not so deeply, whereupon the Archduke will extend gloved hands to signal you to rise. He will probably say something like: 'We enjoyed your talent and listening to your music. Thank you for coming this evening.'

"You will respond by saying, 'Thank you, your highness, for inviting us. It was our pleasure to play for the music-loving and discerning Viennese.'

"It is possible the Duchess will have something to say. She might ask a question, like: 'How long have you been playing duets?'

"You will reply: 'Since we were seven years old, your highness.'

"If she does detain you a moment with a question, again curtsey, not as deeply, before you depart. You must never introduce anything into the exchange. Then follow the other guests into the ballroom. I will join you there, and take you around and introduce you to other guests. Again, it is best if you only answer questions, and do so as briefly as you can. If you are asked a question that is difficult to answer, just say, 'Why do you ask?' That should put an end to the subject. If I see you are getting into deep water, I will clear my throat, and possibly intervene."

"Where are Mrs. Holmesby and Mrs. Raft?" Sara asked.

"And the other girls?" Hanna added.

"Mrs. Holmesby will join you later. Mrs. Raft and the other young ladies are in the reception hall lobby. Friedrich is introducing them to other guests as they approach. He is their escort and translator, if such is needed."

Sara asked, "Wolfgang, would it be possible for Mrs. Holmesby to join us now?"

"Of course, if that is your pleasure." He signaled to Kurt who had been hovering in the background, who said, "Sir?"

"Locate Mrs. Holmesby, and ask her to please join us. Would you ladies care for a cup of punch?"

"I'd really like a glass of water, if that's possible."

"Of course, and you Sara, would you also like water?"

"Yes, Wolfgang, that would be nice."

"Before I go to get your water, let me introduce you to our Maestro at the Strauss Concert Hall. They play to a full house six days a week."

Hanna and Sara had no opportunity to say anything before Wolfgang returned, for the maestro gushed on about how delighted he was with their performance ... and what a wonderful introduction to the Strauss Blue Danube Waltz, finally asking, "Who wrote the score?"

"We did," Hanna and Sara replied together. The Maestro laughed a hearty laugh, saying, "I did not expect you to also speak in unison, how delightful!"

At that moment Kurt arrived with Mrs. Holmesby, and took the opportunity, in Wolfgang's absence, to introduce her to the Maestro.

"Are you the young ladies' music teacher? The Maestro asked.

"No, I am the Headmistress of the Croft School"

"Aha, I know of this school. My niece went there a few years ago."

"What is her name?" asked Mrs. Holmesby.

"Louisa Marie Adolfson."

"Of course, why did I not connect Wiener-Neustadt with Vienna? She was a delightful student, one of our very best!"

Wolfgang returned, gave the girls their water in crystal goblets and said, "I have been asked to escort the young ladies to Lady Vandercleve. Would you kindly excuse us, Maestro?"

"But, of course," the Maestro replied, seeming reluctant.

"Lady Vandercleve is sister to the Duchess. She is also a harpsichord player of some repute."

"Do we curtsey to her? Hanna asked."

"Yes, a small curtsey will do after I make the introductions – only because of your ages. Mrs. Holmesby is not required to curtsey."

Lady Vandercleve had a small gathering around her, but, at their approach, the other guests melted away. Hanna and Sara both sucked in their breath. The woman was possibly the most beautiful woman they had ever seen. She had silver blonde hair artfully arranged on top of her head, with a sapphire necklace threaded in amongst the curls. She had luminous sapphire blue eyes and lovely arched eyebrows, with a perfect nose and full lips, and a smile displaying white, even teeth – and dimples, which were charming.

Her whole persona said charm, grace, good manners, and somehow, she exuded an air of intrigue.

"My dears, how simply delightful you were tonight. I have never enjoyed a concert so much. You were absolutely marvelous! How long have you been playing the piano together?"

Hanna replied, "Since we were little girls. We have always played together."

"Have you always used two pianos?"

"No," Sara replied, "not until Father put an addition on the parlor to make a place for them."

"And, how old were you then?"

Sara looked at Hanna, "I think we were ten."

Hanna nodded her head in agreement.

"Do you often perform for an audience?"

"Yes," Hanna replied, with Sara adding, "We often play for charity."

"How delightful! Have you ever played the harpsichord?"

"No," they said in unison, with Sara adding, "We don't know anyone who has a harpsichord. Is it very different from a piano?"

"The sound is different. The keys when pressed do not strike the strings, but instead pluck them, much like plucking a harp, hence the name; but the sound is a tinkling sound, not a harp-like sound. I find the sound charming and quaint."

"I read that the harpsichord has had a revival in the twentieth century. Is your instrument a new one, or an antique?" Hanna asked.

"I'm happy to say, it is an antique. Wolfgang wants me to stop monopolizing you, so off you go."

The names and faces fell into a blur. Everyone was kind and complimentary. Mrs. Holmesby said very little, answering only questions directed to her. Two hours later, Wolfgang escorted them back to the waiting limousine – long before the evening had ended, saying, "It is not expected that you will stay for the late supper. It is known that you are leaving on Der Mozart for Budapest in the morning."

Standing beside the car, Hanna, Sara and Mrs. Holmesby all thanked Wolfgang for making the evening so memorable for them. "Without you, we would not have known the proper protocol," Sara said.

"And we would not have had such a nice time," Hanna added. "I'm certain this evening will be the highlight of our tour … one never to be forgotten!"

Back at the hotel, the girls were too excited to sleep, and gathered together in the drawing room of the suite. Julia and Georgina reveled in the girl's excited chatter while they nibbled from the trays of tea sandwiches, pastries, assorted fruits and cheeses sent to the suite by the hotel manager, who was simply delighted that honored guests of the Schönbrunn Castle were staying in his establishment.

"Well, that went very well. I'm so pleased with the girls. None of them appeared at all out of place. It gives me great satisfaction to know that they have the self-assurance to carry on in such unusual situations." Julia sighed. "It is a satisfying culmination to The Croft School's long regimen."

"The girls have sent some very positive postcards home. It was a good idea, Julia, to tailor the tour to fit the girls who would be on it. Not only is it different from past years, but I think it's exciting too – at least for me," Georgina sighed.

"Yes, it's not every day we're in the same room with nobility," Julia added. "I hope the rest of the tour is just as pleasant. I was on pins and needles this evening. The Minister of Tourism outdid himself after my note. I think Vienna will become a permanent addition on our tour. I find there is more true culture and refinement here than in Paris, and certainly far better manners. Well, let's get the gals to bed, we have an early departure in the morning."

"Give them a few more minutes, let them wind down a bit; they're so excited, they won't sleep anyway."

"All right. Would you hold the fort while I shower and change into my robe?"

"Of course," Georgina agreed. "I want to write to Robert about our evening."

29 ~ On the Danube River

The girls settled into their cabins aboard the Danube River cruise ship, *Der Mozart*, the next day. The ship was a startling change from the ocean cruise ship, with only two decks. In the girl's cabins on the lower deck, the windows are only inches above the water line. The Danube River is a fast flowing river over 1700 miles long, which flows into the Black Sea. There are fourteen locks controlling the flow of the water between Vienna and Budapest, which was at one time, considered a suburb of Vienna.

Two double beds and a single bed, line one wall from the windows to the closet wall, with a shower bath, vanity with two sinks, toilet and bidet off the small entry hall. Along the wall at the foot of the beds, stood a long bureau, flanked by writing desks with mirrors and benches to serve double duty as vanity tables, and two straight chairs. It was obvious that the rooms were only places to sleep, bathe, dress and write a few postcards.

There was a built-in clock, announcement speaker and music center above the end desk. During the cruise, they would come to hate this piece of equipment, for it was impossible to shut off the overly frequent announcements! Guests were paged over this device, meal sittings were announced, disembarking times were announced, on board events were announced, sailing departure countdowns were announced, lost and found items were announced, the departures of postal packets were announced, as well as messages from the Captain and crew, or, as they sailed, endless comments about the riverside sights they were passing. Derogatory comments to the staff about the annoying device were to no avail.

The Captain's reception began at four on the first afternoon, followed by a dinner buffet at six and a dance at eight. The shore excursions would begin tomorrow morning with Bratislava.

The Purser took the proffered invitation at the Captain's reception and said to the Captain, "Miss Hanna Caulfield and Miss Sara Caulfield." Captain Schuch took their gloved hands in his gloved hands saying, "Good evening ladies; we are delighted to have you on board *Der Mozart*! I understand that you were a grand success in Vienna! Would it be an imposition to ask you to play a tune or two for us this evening? I'm certain it would please the other passengers, as well."

Hanna glanced at Sara, and then said, "We would be pleased to enliven your party; would Strauss do?"

"My dear girl, are you jesting with me?"

"I beg your pardon, sir. What is the jest?"

"In Austria, Strauss does not *do*, Strauss is *paramount!*"

Hanna smiled, "But, of course! What time would be convenient?"

"Shall we say at five? After the receiving line, I give a little welcoming speech. I will then announce your impromptu recital." Which he did with, " … straight from the Schönbrunn Palace and an invitational recital yesterday evening, I would like to present the twin sisters, Hanna and Sara Caulfield from Kenya, Africa who have agreed to play a tune or two for us!"

Once through the receiving line, Mrs. Holmesby cornered Hanna and said, "Were you being pert with the Captain?"

"No ma'am, I wanted to know what kind of a recital he expected without a formal request, or preparation."

"You're right, it does seem cheeky, but the Germanic way is blunt. It would behoove you to always practice your good manners, no matter what the situation."

"We will play the Mozart Allegro, which is appropriate, the Gershwin, and follow up with the Strauss Blue Danube, if asked for an encore. Do you agree?"

"Yes, those are excellent choices, dear."

After the recital, Captain Schuch stood by the spinet pianos, glowing and pleased. He accepted the wholehearted applause, as if he had played the selections himself. He then thanked Hanna and Sara grandly for the recital, which garnered another rousing response from the surprised, but delighted, passengers.

While the reception guests departed for the buffet, the Captain detained Hanna and Sara, saying, "It would please me greatly if you ladies and Mrs. Holmesby would join me and my four guests from Vienna, for dinner. I cannot seat everyone in your group, for I only have a table for eight in my little dining room. I do hope you will join us – I look forward to hearing a bit about Kenya."

Julia Holmesby never faltered socially. She decided on the spot that this Captain was first and foremost a sailor and a gentleman second. He was accustomed to command, and apparently, command did not require social polish.

"We accept, and thank you for your kind offer, although I was looking forward to the Kaiser Schmarren and Tafelspitz listed on the menu posted for this evening."

The Captain, surprised by her familiarity with the local cuisine, found a smile and replied. "If it is on this ship, and the chefs know how to cook it, you may order whatever pleases you."

"Then it is settled," Julia replied. "What time should we arrive?"

On the way back to their room, Mrs. Holmesby said, "I hope you understand why I accepted the dinner invitation for you gals, without asking your pleasure; I did so, to let the Captain know that I, not he, am in charge of your socializing, and will brook no interference from him."

"You were marvelous, Mrs. Holmesby. Captain Schuch does have a bit of an autocratic manner," Hanna said.

"But what are Tafelspitz and Kaiser Schmarren?" Sara asked.

"Tafelspitz is Hungarian beef pot roast, a dish to die for. The Kaiser Schmarren is also a Hungarian dish, like a soufflé, made in a pot with eggs, butter, farina and sour cream. Calorically deadly, but scrumptious! My grandmother always made it for us when we visited her. It's a master chef's feat. I tried to make it a few times, and never managed to achieve her results."

The Captain of the Der Mozart hosts a reception at the cocktail hour the evening of departure from Vienna; a buffet dinner dance follows in the dining hall. The other evenings there are two dinner seatings, one at seven and one at eight-thirty, where the wait-staff acts out skits while the dinner orders are in the works – for incredibly,

167

each person is served dinner at the same time. The skits are a bit zany, but pass the time, thereby avoiding awkwardness between the diners, for it is possible, even probable, that diners at the same table would speak different languages, and not be able to understand one another enough for casual conversation.

Most travelers understand English, but are shy about speaking it with a foreign accent, not realizing that it is only Parisians who are so disdainful and rude to foreign travelers trying to converse in their language.

However, Mrs. Holmesby has the unique ability to speak English with the local dialect inflection of most languages, and finds nearly everyone speaks to her. English is the lingua franca of the United Nations, and is required in every European school.

Captain Nicholas von Schuch had but one dinner seating at 8:00 p.m. with his guests in his private dining room.

As the captain of a river cruise vessel, Captain Schuch did not have the vagaries of wind and tide; however, the fast flowing Danube made the ship a constant challenge and responsibility, especially at the locks. The travelers though, savored the smooth, land-like stability the Danube River provided the cruise ship and its passengers.

At ten minutes to eight, a steward knocked on their door, saying, "The Captain has asked me to escort you to his dining room."

Lisette passed a little camera with a battery operated flash to Sara, saying, "Take some pictures for us."

The captain was effusive in his greetings. Standing by the windows near a small bar, and chatting in German were four men dressed in dinner jackets, who turned at their arrival.

The Captain said, "Let me introduce you to my other guests: Hans Bruenner – my nephew; Carl Lutz – his roommate in Saarbrücken; Wolfgang von Hauptsborg and Friedrich von Hauptsborg, cousins, who are emissaries to the politburo in Budapest."

Wolfgang took Hanna's hand and air kissed it, saying with a pleased smile, "So, we meet again, how delightful!"

Friedrich had taken Sara's hand, and he too had air kissed it, but unlike his cousin, he said, "I only came on this trip because I knew you were going to be here!"

Sara blushed, as Friedrich turned to Mrs. Holmesby saying, "I hope you will forgive me for being blunt, I'm not at all suited to courtly conversation. I promised Wolfgang to keep my mouth closed when we reached Budapest, but he placed no restrictions on me before then." He then laughed gaily, as if he had pulled the wool over Wolfgang's eyes.

Wolfgang's eyes went skyward, as if pleading for help from the Almighty. However, never at a loss socially, Wolfgang smiled at Mrs. Holmesby saying, "Friedrich is outrageous, but he's also a good deal of fun, and I don't see much of that attached to service at Schönbrunn Palace."

"We British understand royal service … it's a dull job, but someone must do it." The men laughed heartily, delighted by Julia's wit.

The steward took their drink orders: wine for Julia, cider for Hanna and Sara; the men ordered cocktails.

Wolfgang turned to Hanna and Sara. "I'm sorry I skipped the reception this evening. I hear Captain Schuch asked for an impromptu recital, probably my fault, for I was extolling your virtuosity earlier, while telling him how much you had charmed your Viennese audience. The newspaper reports were glowing."

"Why didn't you mention that you, too, would be on the cruise?" Hanna asked. "You mentioned *Der Mozart* when you bid us an early good-bye."

"Normally, I'm not a courier. Maybe that's why I'm here – confusion to the enemy and all that!"

Hanna laughed at his laisse-faire attitude, certain he was being facetious about his reasons, although a strong air of intrigue lingered.

Friedrich took Sara to look at a large painting on the wall above the buffet. He pointed out his home, perched on a hillside above a marina filled with sailing craft of all sizes, saying, "Here is the boyhood home of Captain Schuch and here, at the top of the hill is where Wolfgang was born. It is where he goes in the summers. Hans painted the picture. He is quite good, is he not?"

"Yes, but what an unusual perspective."

"Hans!" Friedrich called, "I think Sara has guessed your ploy!"

Hans joined them, asking, "Why do you think the perspective unusual?"

"Well, were you on a large ship when you painted this? Somehow, you were high and out to sea, for the view is towards the land, with the water in the foreground."

The others joined them, with Captain Schuch saying, "I think she has you, Hans. You might as well confess."

"Not yet. If I was not on a ship, how else might I have done it?" He asked, smiling.

"Well, I can only think of one way. Did you take a picture from a plane and use it as a guide?" Sara asked.

"You have half of it right."

"Which half?"

"There was no ship and no plane."

"Well then, how did you take the picture?"

Smiling and pleased, Hans pointed to the painting and said, "I took two pictures from here." Pointing to a balcony on Captain Schuch's boyhood home."

Sara cried, "I know what you did! Your pictures were slides, and when you printed them, you reversed the images!"

Hans cried, "Bravo!" And all around the others clapped.

Captain Schuch said, "You are very clever Miss Sara, and the first to ever figure it out. Everyone else had to be told!" Smiling happily, the Captain continued, "It is time to sit and order dinner, I'm due on the bridge at nine-thirty and I'm never late."

The meal was delightful. Everyone ordered the Tafelspitz with sugar glazed egg noodles or boiled potatoes, honeyed carrots or green beans with spaetzle, and the Kaiser Schmarren. The ladies eschewed the spicy fish soup for a shrimp cocktail. All had a green salad with vinegar and oil dressing with fresh, warm Kaiser Rolls, and sorbet for dessert with demitasse and liqueurs.

At nine-twenty, the Captain excused himself, and taking Hans and Carl with him went to the bridge for the changing of the watch.

Wolfgang asked Hanna, "Are you planning on attending the dance? If so, I would be delighted to escort you."

Friedrich held out his bent arm to Sara saying, "I love to dance. Would you join me, Miss Sara?"

170

Sara took his arm and replied, "I love to dance too, but rarely have the opportunity."

Mrs. Holmesby said, "Why don't you young people go on down … I will join you later."

On the way down, Wolfgang said, "Would anyone care for a stroll on the deck? The sky is full of stars tonight."

Friedrich asked enthusiastically, "Would you enjoy that, Sara?"

"Yes, indeed I would."

The stars were bright in the clear night; Wolfgang was quite knowledgeable and pointed out the various constellations with names and stories, making the simple experience of star gazing an interesting experience.

After a half hour in the cool night air, Hanna asked Sara, "Are you getting cold?"

"Not getting – already am! I'm ready to join that lively music."

The gentlemen at once offered tailored silk arms saying, "Ladies – shall we?"

They had more fun than expected at the dance, with polkas, waltzes and conga lines. The passengers freely entered into the fun, with many a partner's shoulder tapped during the slow dances – for Hanna and Sara seemed to dance with every male on the ship. Surprisingly, most of them were good dancers, and many were also articulate.

The evening was everything young impressionable women could want. Atmosphere created by elegant young men with charming manners, interesting conversation, a clear star-filled sky, and the fun of being belles at a ball, or so it seemed, with the courtly European manners of all the gentlemen.

Hanna and Sara leaped out of bed at seven, were ready for breakfast at eight and the tour group at nine. The other girls crowded round at breakfast, wanting to hear all about their dinner with Wolfgang and Friedrich in the Captain's private dining room. They too had danced their feet off last night and had enjoyed it immensely.

The next morning, Friedrich and Wolfgang decided to join the walking tour of Bratislava. Wolfgang seemed even more knowledgeable than the docent, and Friedrich often led Sara to places not on the main tour. As long as one or two of the girls went along with them, Mrs. Holmesby allowed it.

High atop the hill overlooking the village, sat the ruins of an old castle – with manacles set into a stone wall. These manacles reputedly held King Richard the Lion Heart a prisoner after his capture while traveling home to England from the Crusades. The despicable act may have originated the phrase, 'a king's ransom'.

Hanna had worn new shoes yesterday evening for the reception, and had blistered a heel while dancing. She could not make the long uphill climb to the castle ruins, even without shoes, because of the sharp rocky pebbles. Begging off, Hanna chose a bench by the side of the disintegrated dirt road, and sat smiling at the passers-by.

Wolfgang returned shortly saying, "The castle is mostly ruins, not much to see now. Let's take a walk in the town. That's far more interesting." At the third shop, Hanna espied a pair of woven sandals, much like mules with no backs. They had her size and she bought a pair in white. The charming old village had quaint houses and tiny stores on both sides of the road – with many differing in architectural design, but made cohesive by the pleasingly assorted pastel colors. Flowering planters decorated the window sills, or flower-filled urns stood beside the doors. Some had decorative flags flying from upper windows.

Wolfgang guided her by her elbow, or gently placed the palm of his hand on the small of her back, directing her as a partner in a dance might do. She found his proprietarial gestures stimulating.

Strolling along Hanna remarked, "Do you notice that the numbers on the doors are not in any kind of sequence? How in the world do they deliver the mail?"

Wolfgang chuckled happily saying, "Only very old men can deliver the mail, for it takes a life-time to learn what number is where."

Hanna chuckled at his wit, but said, "I'm serious – it is puzzling, how do they do it?"

Wolfgang responded, "Unfortunately, so am I!"

Wherein they both laughed, tickled by the ridiculous.

"Why don't they change the numbers?"

"Because house number one was the first house built – and house number two was the second house built – although, not beside house number one, as you have observed. Over hundreds of years, the intervening spaces were built up, still using the sequential building numbers, no matter where the house was located."

"How does anyone remember that? Or how does the post office sort the mail?"

"Ah, when all the old mail carriers died, those who remembered which house was where, the Post Office changed the sorting slots to names in alphabetical order, reading: Ablund, #131, Achton, #47, Baumborg, #75, for none of the residents would agree to change the numbers on their houses."

"You are teasing me! Are you saying the people in the houses live in them in alphabetical order?"

Wolfgang could not help himself; he laughed heartily, with a feeling of glee he had long forgotten even existed. "You are much too smart to tease. I can't tell you how many times I have given this explanation and it was always accepted without question."

"Why would you have to explain these numbers many times?"

"My sister lives here; and, on occasion – so do I."

"Oh, my goodness, where?"

"Back up the hill, two doors from the shop where you bought your sandals."

"Well, none-the-less, you are still going to have to explain how the mail is delivered, and make sense of it!"

Chuckling happily, which he could not remember doing since he was a young lad; Wolfgang took her hand as he led her through a large brick archway to a wall overlooking the Danube River and the docks.

They stood admiring the view until Wolfgang replied, "I left out a part."

"But, of course you did! And a most important part too!"

"I neglected to tell you that there is a dash and another number: after Ablund #131 – there is another number 36. So, the slot labels read: Ablund #131-36; Achton is #47-93; Baumborg is #75-12. They sort incoming mail alphabetically by name; they remove the mail from the sorting slots in numerical order according to the numbers after the dash. It's not convenient, but it is do–able, and it was the only solution that could be found to keep the old house numbers."

"I think that is the oddest thing I have ever heard, but interesting. We should go back, Mrs. Holmesby will be worried."

"I don't think so."

"Why ever not?"

"Because I told her I was going to go down and carry you back to the ship, since it was my fault I danced your heels off last night."

Hanna laughed. "You did not!"

"Whatever do you mean?"

"You told her no such thing, and you did not dance my heels off, I did that! I danced with everyone, even that old man who walked with a cane asked me to dance. I never once lacked a partner."

Wolfgang felt charmed by this pert and open young woman. He had never met anyone like her. At twenty–four, he had met an incredible variety of women – not one of whom had caught his interest as Hanna did. He felt free with her. Most of his life he felt he lived in a box – a satin lined, perfumed and padded box! A most comfortable box, but never–the–less, a box, confined this way and that. The thought of the similarity hit him like a wrecking ball – very much the same as a coffin! This was his first breath of fresh air, and it was sweet beyond compare. It thrilled him as nothing else ever had. Her intelligence and lack of guile delighted him.

"I'm not saying, 'I'm sorry.' On the contrary, I'm saying, 'I have never been more pleased by someone's small misfortune'."

Hanna looked up at this extremely good looking man. Was he teasing her? She too, had felt a flutter. But how could she not feel a flutter with such delightful conversation, in such charming company. Did he really have business in Budapest … if he did, would he speak so openly of it?

"I feel things happen because they are meant to happen, even the unpleasant things often happen for a reason, by providing us with a purpose – or to move us forward when we are stuck."

Wolfgang felt thunderstruck at her words. He stood frozen immobile wondering if she was clairvoyant? Over the years, her words had become the basis for his personal philosophy – one he kept to himself and never discussed with anyone – because everyone he knew had their lives mapped out for them – from the moment of their birth, to their dying gasp. He, too, fell into that category, but he did not want that for himself. He was waiting for an opportunity to arise to change his life. He did not know exactly what he wanted … but it had to be fresh, new, unfettered and clean. He wanted his hair blowing in the breeze, not exotic wigs; he wanted comfortable clothing, not constricting uniforms; he wanted diversity, not schedules; but most of all he wanted honesty and sincerity. He craved them like a man dying of thirst craves water … to say what you mean – and to mean what you say – at all times.

"Shall we go over to the street–cart and have an ice?" Wolfgang asked.

"Oh yes, let's! We call them Italian ices in Africa."

"Why do you call them that?"

"Because it is always an Italian selling them."

"Are there many Italians in Africa?"

"No … just the ones selling ices!" and she laughed merrily.

The good feeling spread – from his nose to his toes, and bubbled up inside him.

"Oh! Here come some of the girls. Maybe they would like an ice too. Lisette! Ashley! We are having an ice, come, join us, Wolfgang is treating!"

The good feeling filled him until he found it hard to breathe, or even think. Whatever am I going to do?

The main dining room tables of *Der Mozart* seated eight. There were little side tables for four along the windows beyond the arches of the main dining/dancing hall. Mrs. Holmesby and Mrs. Raft each sat at a table with four of the girls, leaving three seats assigned to other travelers. What a lovely surprise it was when Carl, Hans and a young ensign, Gruber, sat at the table with Mrs. Raft. Wolfgang and Friedrich and a young navigator, Josep, joined Mrs. Holmesby, Hanna and Sara, at their table. They sat in the accepted social fashion, boy/girl, boy/girl at the round tables.

Julia thought to herself. It must be quite convenient knowing the Captain of the ship, personally. Only with a request from the ship's master could seating changes be accomplished so quickly. I must say, if we are going to have a few flies in the ointment, these flies will do quite nicely.

175

During dinner, Wolfgang asked Mrs. Holmesby, seated to his left, "Did any one of the girls ask you about the house numbers in Bratislava today?"

"No. Why ever would they do that?"

Hanna, seated to Wolfgang's right, interjected, "Because the numbers are all a hodge-podge. There is no order in them at all."

Mrs. Holmesby was well aware of Hanna's facility with numbers and her love of order, so she knew something unusual was afoot. "How can that be, my dear. How would they deliver the mail?"

"That's exactly what I asked."

"Did you get an answer?"

"Yes, but I had to find it among half truths."

Wolfgang smiled at the exchange. He was still basking in the glow that Hanna made earlier in the day with her forthright and cheerful common sense.

But now, all attention at the table fixed on Wolfgang, who was going to have to offer an explanation after the accusation of 'half truths'.

"I merely told Hanna that the houses were numbered as they were built, which could be anywhere along the street below the castle fortress, hence the hodge-podge numbering."

"Well," Mrs. Holmesby said, entering into the fray, "How do they deliver the mail?"

"I told her only old men who remembered where each house stood could deliver the mail. For some reason she took exception to this as an explanation."

"I should certainly hope so!" Mrs. Holmesby replied to smiles and chuckles around the table. "And did she press you for a more plausible explanation?"

"She did, and I told her the mail was sorted alphabetically."

"Did you actually believe that such an explanation would fly?"

"It has in the past."

"Please don't be offended, but are most of the people who accepted this explanation, nincompoops?"

Hilarious laughter erupted. Even Wolfgang was startled into laughing.

Hanna was the first to recover, for she knew the answer; and wondered why Wolfgang had brought up the subject. Now, he would have to dig himself out of Mrs. Holmesby's disdain.

"But, madam, it is sorted alphabetically."

"And … "

"The house number is also on the sorting slot."

"And … "

By now, people at nearby tables were listening and chuckling at this most unusual conversation, as well as the other girls, for they and Mrs. Raft had come over to join in the conversation after the burst of uncontrolled laughter.

I have met my match … twice today. It is going to be hard to live this down. Friedrich will certainly never let it lie. "After the alphabetical name and house number, there is another number, the number *one* is assigned to the first house beginning at the bottom of the street, and continues sequentially up the hill before coming back down again on the other side."

"And … "

I can't believe this is happening to me in public. I may never be able to hold my head up again at the Schönbrunn if this gets out. Wolfgang thought. "The mail is then removed from the slots according to the order of the last numbers."

The applause was spontaneous, accompanied by smiles and a lot of good-natured laughter and joking.

Again, Wolfgang thought: I will never live this down – never! It will follow me to my grave!

Mrs. Holmesby, never one to let a matter or subject go unfinished said, "Now, may I ask why the sorting numbers are not merely appended to the required number address, and the mail then sorted at the post office by those digits? Same number of slots, less work and certainly a lot less confusion."

Wolfgang, who was an honorary member of the town council which regulated and dovetailed the old with the new, was astonished.

The clear and precise thinking of Julia Holmesby, the formidable headmistress of The Croft School, had saved his face. Her concise suggestion had transformed the conversation from that of a dithering fool, into that of a man with a mission.

"I do believe, Mrs. Holmesby, that you have solved a puzzle that has plagued Bratislava for more than a century. We will be forever indebted to your erudite insight," Wolfgang said with delight.

The listeners all clapped enthusiastically, for they sensed they had been present at a small historical event.

Hanna arose, and said, "Sara and I would like to stroll on the deck to clear our minds before we accept your challenge to a game of hearts in the lounge. Would half an hour be convenient?" The men at the table had risen with Hanna and Sara; they assented, and bowed, as the young ladies left the table.

Mrs. Holmesby was surprised, thinking. Is she leaving to let him save face? Why did he bring the subject up? Was he intending to point our Hanna's cleverness, and his approach in using me backfired on him?

"If I ever have a daughter," Wolfgang said, sitting next to Julia, "I will make certain she attends The Croft School. Your young ladies are certainly a cut above the other young ladies that I have met."

"Thank you, Wolfgang. We do have exceptional young women at the school. My hope is that I will still be headmistress at that future time." Julia had married Harold when she was twenty, and was now forty-one, so if Wolfgang did not delay too long, it was a distinct possibility that she could still be there … God willing.

Walking the deck, Hanna said, "I was so embarrassed for Wolfgang. Why did he bring the subject up? Mrs. Holmesby is the most intelligent woman I have ever known and maybe the most logical too. He was defeated before he had begun."

"I don't see it that way, Hanna. I see an unusual conversation with a good bit of repartee that ended with a surprising and useful conclusion. I think everyone enjoyed the exchange, and Mrs. Holmesby was, as usual, magnificent. I'm so proud of her."

"Yes, I am proud of her too; she never falters – it's amazing. Well, are you ready to go and stomp a few nice fellows?"

"Always and ever, lead on … and into the valley to defeat the Huns, rode the Caulfield twins!" Sara paraphrased.

There were only a few readers in the lounge. The bar had closed and only room service was available. Wolfgang ordered tea and kleine-kuchen, little cakes, like cookies and found the cards. "I must warn you, I hardly ever lose at hearts," he said with a mischievous smile.

"Do you play Black Lady rules?"

"Yes, low score wins."

"Well then, it is only fair to warn you, sir, that Sara and I have the highest number of wins the Croft School has ever recorded."

Friedrich tilted his head and smirked a bit, but his eyes crinkled with humor when he said, "Well now, we'll see about that, won't we?"

The games were intense, played with concentration, finesse and a bit of noisy cheer. They had been alone in the lounge for some time when Sara glanced at her watch. "Oh, my gosh! Do you have any idea what time it is? It is almost one-thirty!" Hanna added the scores, looking up to say, "You won't believe this ... we are all tied at 204 each!"

Friedrich put his hand out for the score pad, looked at it, and said, "I've never know this to happen before – however, I'm certain it's some kind of a fluke."

"Fluke," Sara sputtered. "We were just being nice to you. We'll give you another chance to try and best us tomorrow evening – if you're up to it."

Wolfgang and Friedrich smiled ... with Wolfgang saying, "We'd be delighted!" They quietly escorted Hanna and Sara to their rooms. Their whispered *good nights* sounded like shouts in the empty corridor. The door latches sounded like klaxon bells. Quiet as mice they were, when Mrs. Holmesby said softly, "I meant early evening girls, not early morning."

The next port-of-call was a small town that had few sights, except for its ancient charm. Here the group boarded a motorcoach for a tour of the countryside, which included a vast, ancient, very musty, and incredibly ornate cathedral – inside as well as out – sitting atop a hill overlooking poor peasant houses as far as the eye could see – some not more than daub and wattle, with not a brick abode or monastery in sight. The contrast was offensive as well as oppressive. They also visited an old castle, much of it in ruins with only one wing habitable, which had a delightful park-like garden around a reflection pool.

They stopped for lunch at a market day fair, where they shopped the diverse canvas stalls. Wolfgang and Friedrich were familiar with the hand-made merchandise – the lovely arts and crafts for sale – and assisted them in dealing with the vendors. They obtained reasonable prices with their pleasant attitudes, and language fluency; so many of the tour bus passengers stayed close by to take advantage of the skillful bartering.

A smörgasbord luncheon was available on a roofed pavilion, also with canvas walls, with picnic tables nearby, where a group of local musicians played excellent music. The diners, mostly strangers to one another, enthusiastically stomped around to the country music, especially the tuba polkas. The Croft School ladies never lacked for partners. All too soon, it was time to leave to rendezvous with the river cruise ship.

Georgina and Julia walked on the deck after dinner, with Julia saying, "Another delightful day. You were right Georgina; forsaking the old tour has, so far, been simply delightful. Today's tent fair far surpassed all the other country market tours."

"Wolfgang and Friedrich certainly smoothed the way for us today. They were quite debonair, and the fair artists and artisans responded well to them. Also, I agree the diversity and quality today certainly eclipsed other market fairs we've attended."

"Yes, I thought so too. I completed my gift shopping today. Would you like to play a bit of bridge, Georgina? The sign says two more players are needed."

"Yes indeed! I'd like that."

Shortly after ten, Gruber and Josep, Hans and Carl joined the hearts players, making two tables of hearts players that evening. The skillful play drew a few watchers who were entertained by the lively interaction in the games.

The wait-staff made up a special skit to honor the players at the last dinner on the cruise, with chest ribbons reading: King of Hearts and Queen of Hearts, with golden cardboard crowns decorated with crystal clear rock candy. For the last evening, Captain Schuch ordered tea, coffee, hot chocolate and pfefferneuse served in the lounge for the players who sat around rehashing the spectacular blitzes, the sneaky passes, and the near miss runs. They exchanged addresses and promised to write.

Returning to their stateroom to pack, Sara said, "I'm going to miss Friedrich. He is good company and a lot of fun. He actually knocked on a few doors in Bratislava to introduce me to the people living there. They were delighted to see him, and were quite kind to me, wanting to serve us tea, but Friedrich declined telling them we were on a day tour from *Der Mozart*."

"Did Friedrich tell you that Wolfgang and his sister have a home in Bratislava?" Hanna asked.

"Yes, he pointed it out to me when we came down the hill from the castle ruins. It is the ancestral home of Wolfgang's brother-in-law, Gregor Schultz. Friedrich also told me that Wolfgang's parents are deceased. His mother died when he was born, and his father died not long ago. Wolfgang's father put his name forward for Service at Schönbrunn Palace before he sold the family estate in Krems. Wolfgang was glad he sold it. He prefers to live in Bratislava, or Vienna, with Elizabeth and Gregor, or in Savona, Italy with Friedrich's mother in the summer."

"I thought he grew up in that seaside village in the Captain's painting."

"He did – that is Savona – until he went to boarding school. His aunt, Friedrich's mother was married to Wolfgang's father's brother, she raised him. She lives in Savona year round. Wolfgang spent his summers in Savona during his school years. His father only came to visit."

"Since you learned so much, did Friedrich say what Wolfgang's sister and her husband do for a living?"

"Yes, they are both musicians. Gregor is first violin at the Strauss Concert Hall. Elizabeth teaches music, for prodigies. Friedrich told me Elizabeth is a prodigy too."

"My, Friedrich was a font of information about Wolfgang. Did he happen to say what they do in Service at the Schönbrunn Palace?"

"Yes, they are like docents. They escort visitors, answer questions and inform them of protocol. The Service enlistment is two years, after which they can move up, and take positions in upper levels of Service, or lower levels of government, or resign their commission. It is almost like military service without the guns."

"Wolfgang obtained the application for a position at the castle for Friedrich, but Friedrich doesn't like it as much as he thought he would; too many stuffy rules, stuffy people and stuffy and unreasonable regulations – no fun at all!"

"What would Friedrich rather do, did he say?"

"He and Wolfgang have always talked about traveling the world. He said, if they do, they would come and visit us in Africa."

Unexpectedly, Hanna felt a little thrill. "That would be nice," she said, noncommittally. "And, would you like that Sara?" Hanna asked.

"Silly girl, I would be delighted." Yes, Hanna thought, so would I.

There was no bridge game on the last evening aboard the *Der Mozart*. Everyone was packing, getting ready to disembark in Budapest in the morning. Georgina and Julia took a late stroll on deck.

"Well, it's off to bed for me. I almost hate to leave this cruise ship, it's been most delightful." Julia sighed.

Georgina kept pace saying, "Yes. It has, but soon we fly to Venice. I have always wanted to go to Venice. I like seeing all these new places. I'm so glad we're skipping Paris this year. The railway tour in Switzerland sounds far more interesting – getting off to tour a village that appeals to you, and boarding the train again later on. I'm having as much fun as the girls this year."

"I agree with you, our new itinerary is delightful. However, we didn't have two gifted pianists with us in the past, which had a great deal to do with my choices ... after I received the telegram requesting the recital in Vienna."

"You received a telegram from Vienna? You told me you had contacted them."

"Well, I did! After the minister of tourism contacted me. Wolfgang put the chain of events together for me. It seems that Louisa Marie Adolfson of Wiener-Neustadt – you remember her, she was such an elegant and charming girl – mentioned the twin girls from Africa, who were piano prodigies to her uncle, the Strauss Concert Hall Maestro, and he in turn mentioned the girls to Lady Vandercleve, who mentioned them to her sister, the Duchess, who suggested to the minister of tourism that he invite the girls to give a recital when on tour in Vienna – and he did; he sent me a telegram."

"How we are all bound together by the slim threads of chance," Georgina sighed, "or coincidence. It makes one believe in fate."

"It certainly does make one wonder, I'll agree to that."

30 ~ *Incident on Der Mozart*

"Rick, I received a telegram this evening, telling me not to deliver the packet tomorrow, but to burn it tonight," Wolfgang said. "Of course, there was no explanation. We are to return to Schönbrunn at our convenience, whatever that means, which is odd. I have to talk to Captain Schuch, and I'd like you to come with me."

"Sir, I have been directed by telegram to burn the packet. Would you authorize my going into the kitchen alone for a few minutes?"

Surprised, and a bit worried, the captain asked, "Now?"

"Yes, sir. I'm sorry for the inconvenience, but it is important."

"Of course, Wolfgang. The kitchen is closed, but I will call Greta and ask her to meet you in the hall. She has a key."

Greta waited by the hallway steps, as Wolfgang approached, smiling. He thanked her for coming out – then stumbled on the short flight of steps. With Greta's help, he righted himself – quite embarrassed. Greta walked to the kitchen door and unlocked it. Wolfgang lit the sealed packet, and dropped it into a stainless steel pot. When the packet was total cinders, he mixed the ashes with water, put the blackened slurry down the garbage disposal, and washed out the pot. The whole process took less than five minutes. Wolfgang went to the door to find Friedrich and Greta gone – with him locked in the kitchen.

He tapped on the glass window of the door, thinking they may have stepped along the corridor, but no one responded. He tapped a bit louder, but still no response. Baffled, he went to the intercom and pushed the button for the Captain.

"Captain here!"

"Captain, this is Wolfgang. I'm so sorry to bother you, but for some reason, Friedrich and Greta are gone, and I am locked in the kitchen."

"What do you mean *gone?*"

"Well, sir, I left them standing in the corridor while I went in the kitchen to burn the papers. When I went to leave they were gone, and the door is locked."

"Someone will be there in a few minutes."

Wolfgang looked around. The kitchen was a long galley, and not very large, considering the amount of food prepared here. He realized the stove was out of sight from the door because of the firewalls and exhaust system surrounding it. He could not see the door from where he had stood to burn the papers, so he had not seen Greta and Friedrich leave. A foreboding chill passed through his body. His hands began to sweat. Outrageous scenarios raced through his mind, none of which made any sense; however all of the imagined scenarios greatly disturbed him.

He heard a tapping on the glass of the kitchen door, and glanced around the firewall to see a deckhand at the door. The man rattled the knob. Wolfgang shook his head and shrugged his shoulders, for he did not have a key either. The deckhand pantomimed that Wolfgang should call the Captain and ask him to send down a key.

"Captain, this is Wolfgang again. We need someone with a key, for Greta locked the door after I went in the kitchen."

"I'm coming down."

A few minutes later Captain Schuch arrived, bringing his Security Officer, whom he asked to search the ship's common rooms, taking the deckhand with him. Captain Schuch unlocked the door and took Wolfgang to his soundproof dining room.

"Now, tell me everything," he ordered.

"There is little to tell. The Staff General asked me if I had any interest in going to Budapest on *Der Mozart*. I said, 'I'd be delighted.' He gave me a packet addressed to a man at the politburo. That is all. His only instruction was to hand the packet to the man in person. This evening, I received a telegram from the Staff General telling me to burn the packet and to return to Vienna at my convenience … which I thought was odd, but then, I thought the whole plan was odd; even so, I burned the packet."

"Nothing else?"

"No sir. Only that Greta and Friedrich, who had stayed outside in the hall while I was in the kitchen, were gone when I had finished, and I was locked inside the kitchen."

Captain Schuch sighed. "I thought you were joking when you said you were delivering a packet to the politburo – not your usual line of work."

"I was unprepared for the question, sir. I told the truth, and immediately regretted it, then tried to make it seem like a jest."

"And you succeeded, until you asked to burn the packet. But why are Greta and Friedrich gone? That truly upsets me. Friedrich is like a son to me! And Greta is a no–nonsense woman, all business she is, she wouldn't just … "

A knock on the door. Captain Schuch asked through the intercom, "Who is it?"

"We have found Greta and Friedrich," the Security Officer replied.

"Show your faces at the spyhole." As he looked through the peephole, he saw Friedrich, Greta and his Security Officer. Captain Schuch opened the door, and much to his surprise and dismay, two burly men – one tall, one short – shoved the Security Officer, Friedrich and Greta inside. Brandishing pistols, they followed them in and closed the door.

The taller of the two men said, "We want that packet."

Wolfgang said, "I have already destroyed it. I burnt it up and put the ashes in the disposal. Whatever it was, it is irretrievably gone."

"I don't believe you. The kitchen door was still locked when we got there, with these two standing outside. There was no one inside. What have you done with it?"

"I do not know why Greta locked the door after I went inside, but she did, and the papers, whatever they were, are gone, I burned them."

The taller man did not want to believe Wolfgang, but he knew the truth when he heard it. A second sense made him able to spot a lie, or a liar, a mile away.

The taller man told them all to sit on the dining table chairs, which the shorter man had arranged, with the backs a circle. They sat on the chairs with their hands behind the backs of the chairs, where the shorter man hand cuffed them: one arm to a chair rung and one arm to the next person, with the last two chairs cuffed together. He then put the key to the handcuffs on the ledge above the door, turned out the lights, and the two men left the room.

For long moments, there was silence. Wolfgang wondered what had been in the packet. Captain Schuch thanked God the boys and Greta were safe, but he worried greatly about his ship.

Greta knew she had been incredibly lucky. They had not questioned her at all, probably because she was still wearing her kitchen whites and apron. When the Captain called, she had her feet up, reading and having a drink, before taking a shower and going to bed.

Friedrich put the events together … at least he thought he had put them together, but even so, it didn't make much sense. Why would they give Wolfgang, of all people, an important or possibly secret packet to deliver? He kept the stupid thing under his mattress, for gosh sakes, playing at being a spy. That's it … who would ever suspect Wolfgang of being a courier!

After a few minutes, Captain Schuch said, "I have a beeper in my right pants pocket. It connects me to the bridge at all times, but I can't get to it with my right hand cuffed behind me to the chair. If I could get to it, I could tap an SOS on it and help would be here in a few minutes." No one thought of a way to make that happen. Suddenly, Friedrich said, "Captain! Can you reach the heat duct with your foot?"

"No, I'm about a foot short … no pun intended," but they laughed anyway, even if a bit hysterically.

"On three now, we'll all scoot towards the heat duct, one, two, three – push!" Friedrich asked, "How much closer?"

"About three inches, let's do it again on my count: one, two three – push; again, one, two three – push; again … and again. Once more … and the Captain began tapping out an SOS with the toe of his shoe against the metal duct. I'm going to find out just how good my crew really is … or not! Let's scoot one more time so I can give the duct some good hard thumps!" Every fifteen seconds, he banged three hard, three soft, three hard, while alternating feet.

In forty nine minutes, when his knees were aching beyond belief and his back was in spasm, they heard a key in the door lock. Tears of relief rolled down his face, and the Captain, pleased beyond words at their rescue, did not care who saw them.

The Security Officer searched the ship. The men were gone. A grappling hook and line remained at the stern, which answered the question of how they got on — and off — the ship.

Friedrich and Wolfgang hashed over the incident until early morning, finding no plausible explanation. Friedrich felt his earlier surmise was too far-fetched ... but if he was right, he was better off keeping the knowledge to himself. When Wolfgang stumbled on the steps and dropped the packet, Greta picked it up and handed it back to him. If Greta knew that he had seen her put a similar-looking packet in her capacious apron pocket, they could be in mortal danger. Were the papers, whatever they were, now in the wrong hands? Had the telegram been a set-up to get Wolfgang out with the papers? Were those men a part of the diversion ... or part of something else? Are we still in danger?

But why Wolfgang? Why me? Did they need someone ingenuous and naïve, someone totally unsuspecting for their ruse? Wolfgang is certainly that — and, to a degree, so am I. In my days at Schönbrunn Palace, I saw Wolfgang's marked aversion to intrigue. Had they picked him because of his lack of guile? Had they considered us expendable? If so — and Wolfy learned of their reasoning, it might compromise his self confidence, and his affable self confidence is what makes him so charming. Friedrich felt they had made the right decision in their long hours of discussion — to resign from Service — stating cause relating to the intrigue — but naming no names.

The sooner we are away from all this ... the better!

I never liked the palace, I just liked being with Wolfgang. Uncle Gregor thought it was a good place for Wolfgang to begin a career, and possibly it was — but not for Wolfgang.

There is a stigma attached to *Incomplete Service,* which we greatly resent. The incident has caused both of us to lose stature and credibility — even though we did nothing wrong. Wolfgang and I are not concerned about earning a living, but our futures in Vienna had become untenable.

However, I feel a much better destiny awaits us. We always wanted to travel together. We will go back to Savona, and make plans from there. Wolfgang will reach his majority next year, and I will reach mine in two. What is that saying about ' ... an ill wind that never blows anyone some good'?

I'm glad my father is not alive to see me leave Service under a cloud – it would have crushed him. His pride was his downfall, Wolfgang thought. It was so rigid and relentless that it made me unwilling to ever follow in his footsteps. I found the whole idea of nobility unworthy of my life. I think he knew I was just biding my time. It was providential when a wealthy Hungarian horticulturist wanted to buy the estate – I told him to sell – and reluctantly, he did.

Well, we're out of it now! Rick and I will go to Savona for the summer; take a long sail down to Monaco and Cannes – spend some money and watch some films.

I have always wanted to be free. Now that I am, I find it a bit daunting, for I've always lived with commitments and schedules. Things happen for a purpose; now I must find the reason for having attained what I have always wanted.

31 ~ Africa ~ July

Anna clung to Paula's hand, even though she was enjoying her first flight in a DC-3, nicknamed, the Tree Trimmer. The DC-3 flew well a few hundred feet above the ground, and did so when passing through mountain gaps across hidden valleys, between snowy peaks, which reached up to fourteen thousand feet or more. Its usual cruising altitude was eight thousand feet, with a ceiling altitude of less than ten thousand feet … without oxygen. The views past the broad wings of the DC-3 were magnificent and breathtaking.

Riding in a helicopter was noisy compared to the DC-3, even with the headsets, but the view straight down was thrilling. Some of the aircraft maneuvers made Anna feel air sick, but Paula told her, "If you feel air sick, just close your eyes for a bit, and it will go away."

The helicopter pilot detoured often for a closer look at the wildlife fleeing en masse to escape the noisy and fast moving shadow. It thrilled Anna to watch the majestic elephants running with trunks raised and ears flared – she could imagine their noisy trumpeting.

She saw, up close and in their natural elements, creatures that she had only seen in field guides, along with the sweeping grandeur of the vistas. The bird's eye view of the animals gave Anna a joy and happiness that she thought she would never feel again. Her mental apprehension and anxious fear waned, replaced by delight … and curiosity about what awaited her at the flight's end. Paula was right. The change will be *good for me*.

Jamie sat in the co-pilot seat, feeling happier than he had ever felt in his life. He loved his music, but flying in the helicopter totally fascinated and thrilled him. From somewhere deep inside him, came the knowledge that he had found his destiny … and it was not to teach music to snotty-nosed children, who could care less.

I will always have my music … but now, I will be free to enjoy it. I can compose, or join a small group of talented musicians who also work at other jobs. Now, my music will be my recreation. I'm going to become a helicopter pilot! I'll join the RAF program at school, or go to Officer's Candidate School – whatever I need to do to learn to fly helicopters.

The sudden joy of his decision chased away the lingering cobwebs of malaise … chased away the emptiness of indecision … chased away the hovering depression … he felt like a new person.

Paula saw the delight and joy in Jamie's face. Whatever lingering fears he still had – they had flown away in this helicopter. He looks absolutely beatific.

Anna's eyes sparkled and her cheeks had a rosy flush; the wan, pallid look and her nervous demeanor had evaporated – replaced by the thrill of a bird's eye view of magnificent Africa. It was only a beginning, yet a good beginning, for it came from inside and pushed away the bad feelings. Hold on to it, girl; keep your mind open, the best is yet to come, Paula thought.

Manutu and Sashono were sitting in the sebula, shielded from the slanting rays of the late afternoon sun when they heard the distant whump-whump-whump of the helicopter. Arising, they raised hands to shield their eyes and watched. "Do you think that helicopter is coming here?" Sashono asked his brother.

"Possibly, but it is not Tamubu, for I would have known it," Manutu replied.

"Who else do we know that would arrive in a helicopter?"

"It might be the mkebibi. But, would she come here without Tamubu?"

"Maybe it is not her, or maybe it is, and she is not alone. I guess if we want answers, we should go and greet our visitors," Sashono remarked.

When the rotors stopped, Paula alit from the aircraft. She handed Anna down, and let Jamie fend for himself. Manutu and Sashono approached smiling.

Paula greeted them in Swahili adding, "I bring you precious cargo, with troubled hearts and minds. Tamubu feels the peace of the Zuri Watu will help them."

She turned to Anna and Jamie and said, "This is Sashono, Chief of the Zuri Watu, and his twin brother, Manutu, who is the Medicine Chief. We will follow them to the village, where we will refresh ourselves from our journey before the formal introductions. For now, we just grasp forearms in greeting."

Neither Anna nor Jamie spoke Swahili, which would be an advantage for Paula, but a disadvantage for them — at least, at first. Paula had decided that she and Anna would stay in her kibanda and Jamie would stay in the visiting bachelors hut. The separation would be a good start, for they had been clinging to one another for comfort since the incident. It would be their first step in beginning to stand alone again.

Both Manutu and Sashono understood a bit of English from the years of trading at their ancestral home by the ocean, now a dig occupied by archeologists. Paula's writing lessons during her month-long stay had increased their vocabulary as well. With a bit of translating, Anna and Jamie would get along. However, that did not apply to the villagers. There they would be limited to sign language or pantomime, with the occasional Swahili word.

However, this remote village was different from other native villages. Tamubu had grown up here as the son of the Chief. He was one of them, as well as a gifted person. Paula was his wife, and the visitors were members of Tamubu's birth family. A fissure existed here in the dense racial barriers, so Jamie and Anna would find acceptance without the prejudice and mistrust so rampant — with good reason — among the other natives of Africa.

Her hope was that this special place and these special people would help Jamie and Anna regain their confidence and peace of mind; so they could move forward, happy and content in their lives, allowing the past to become the distant past.

After the evening meal, Jamie and Anna retired. Paula gave Anna some privacy, saying, "I'm going out for a walk. I won't be gone long. Do you need anything?"

"No, I'm fine. I don't know why, but I feel really sleepy. I think I will sleep well tonight."

Paula was certain that Jamie and Anna would sleep well, for she had added kimmea to their hot broth. Paula left the kibanda to talk with Manutu and Sashono. If they were going to help, they would have to know what had caused the visitors' troubles.

Manutu asked, "When did this happen?"

"Two days before we left here to go home."

"So, it has been many days, and still they are disturbed."

"Yes, a deep lassitude remains; a distinct drawing away from living life; they merely exist."

"I have seen this before, mostly in women, but occasionally in men. It is a fear of the unknown – a fear of tomorrow, or what the new day will bring. The only treatment I know is to control each day with pleasantness – until the patient reaches out willingly. It is good to do this in a controlled area with few outside influences. You were wise to bring them here."

Jamie awoke at dawn. He felt rested and eager to start the new day. He hoped Paula would be up, for he didn't want to break any rules from ignorance. He saw the chamber pot and used it, surprised to hear a soft voice say, "maji-moto, bwana." (Hot water, master.) Looking through the gaps in the door, Jamie saw a leather basin on a tripod, with steam rising – aha, hot water. He washed and shaved, and feeling a new person, strolled to Paula's hut, surprised at all the early morning activity. The villagers greeted him on the way with smiles and nods, which he returned, thinking, I should have expected this friendly atmosphere, knowing Thomas. This place is a world apart, sited on this plateau high in the mountains. It reminds me a bit of the escarpment in *King Solomon's Mines*; although I hope there are no hidden cannibalistic tribes nearby ... it was a good thing that he would never know about the Usuku Wanaume.

"Good morning, Paula. How are you this morning?"

"I'm fine, Jamie. And you?"

"I am a new man today."

"Well, that was a quick remedy. We should bottle it and sell it."

193

"I thought that's what you were doing!"

"No, we are just bottling tension relief and a good night's sleep. No new men included."

Jamie chuckled. He really liked Paula and envied Thomas a teeny bit. "How is Anna today?"

"She is still asleep. Her circadian rhythm is probably all askew from flying west and the lengthening daylight. The first night's sleep is usually when the adjustment is made."

"Can I do anything to help?"

"Hungry, are you?"

"A bit, but what makes you ask?"

"Men only offer to help when they are hungry and see a woman that isn't making food, except for Thomas."

"Just a minute ago, I envied Thomas for having found you, but now I'm beginning to think he might also need commiseration."

Paula laughed. "Thomas is the only man I have ever met who is one step ahead of me all the time. We are well-suited. Aha, here is Cenye now."

Jamie looked in the same direction as Paula to see an old woman with a pot and bowls approaching the low table in the sebula. (roofed porch)

"I've made tea and cut up a melon to go with the oatmeal." Paula grabbed hardened shells and the pot, gesturing to Jamie to grab the bowl of cut melon slices, and headed to the sebula.

Manutu said, "It is time for my morning stroll. Come with me, Mkebibi, we will talk."

"Jamie, would you stay here in case Anna wakes up while I'm gone?" Paula asked.

"Of course, I'll just sit here and read a bit," he replied.

"I have given the problem some thought," Manutu began. "I think it would be best to separate the troubled ones each day. Jamie seems in good spirits today, so I will begin with Anna when she awakens. I have decided to take her to the learning circle for there is a natural peace in that place, and it is a good place for me to look into her mind."

"I was hoping you would do that, for I agree with you; I always experience a pervasive peace when I am there."

"Let us go back. I would walk with the young man before Anna awakens."

Jamie and Manutu walked to the woods, now overgrown with grass and vines. The elephants would come soon – to eat the grass and trim the young vines from the trees, and to wallow nearby. Now, however, it was a good place to sit in the shade and enjoy the breeze; Manutu chose a fallen log and he and Jamie sat.

In English, Manutu said, "Tell me kidnap. Speak slow, please."

So, choosing simple phrases, Jamie told Manutu the story.

"It bad time for you," Manutu spoke softly. "Bad men very poor. No food for family. Make bad mistake for money. They treat you bad – not much. It way they live, very bad for all – not to do with you."

Manutu's words stunned and shocked Jamie. He could not comprehend living life that low … if indeed that was how they lived all the time. As Jamie thought back, he realized that their abductors had nothing better than Anna or I – except the freedom to move about. Nor were they tied to stakes, where they sat and slept in their own excrement, which circumstance had sent Anna over the edge. She had closed her mind to such an appalling situation, the degradation of which was emotionally unbearable for her.

"Do you think that is really true? That … 'it is the way they live' … all the time?"

"Yes, worse than wild beasts."

Tears came to Jamie's eyes. A large lump formed in his chest and he could not breathe. The horror of men, women and children living in such squalor was shocking – an incredible revelation. It devastated him, and in his weakened emotional condition, the realization was more than he could bear – he broke into sobs.

Manutu had seen his epiphany coming. He had felt his incredulous disbelief at such an appalling statement: 'it is how they live all the time.'

This is a good man, but not a worldly man. It was more than a rude awakening for Jamie; it was an emotional shock. But when he accepts that which he has just learned, he will be well; not happy, but emotionally sound. Can one ever be truly happy knowing that others suffer such terrible privations?

Jamie and Manutu arrived at the sebula to find Paula and Anna setting up a lunch of fresh fruit, dried dates, coconut and a variety of nuts, served with cold tea.

"Hi, you're just in time." Paula said. Jamie looked solemn, like he had come to a hard place and couldn't fathom it. "Are you hungry? This is my favorite lunch: fruit, nuts and coconut paste, it's like eating desert for a meal."

Jamie smiled at her enthusiasm for the simple things in life, but looking at the food on the table, he thought, I would have been overjoyed to have this lunch when I was a captive. His emotions threatened to overwhelm him, and taking a deep breath to gain control, he said, "It looks delicious!"

Jamie retired to his bachelor's quarters for a nap, after lunch. Naps are common in Africa. Almost everyone naps for an hour or so. It is a good way to let the overhead sun pass by and take its intense heat with it, for the working daylight can be as long as fifteen hours a day, depending on the proximity to the equator.

Paula, Manutu and Anna walked to the learning circle in the shade along the edge of the woods. Manutu named the birds and some of the plants and trees in Swahili saying: "Ule katibu-ndege, nyoka-kangi." (The secretary bird, a snake eater.) Paula translated into English, pointing to a black and grey bird with long legs and a raptor-like bill stalking prey in the tall grasses. "He is a very useful bird, who pounds his prey to death with his powerful feet. He also makes a frog-like croak that Thomas enjoys imitating." And so the stroll to the learning circle passed in pleasant arcadian instruction.

Manutu made a small fire and sat opposite to them. He said to Paula, "We will begin now: I will say and you will tell for I have not the English words as you do. Repeat my words: "Close your eyes and think only of the sky or the tall grasses."

Paula translated his words.

Anna did as Manutu bid. Minutes passed as she thought not of the sky, but of the tall grasses and of the unknown wildlife hiding within. She pictured the tawny lioness, totally unseen stalking her prey, hidden by the same-color grass, ... of the darting wart hog and her piglets eluding the lion ... of the fox listening for mice or rodents ... of the secretary bird hunting snakes.

Manutu said, "Clear your mind, think only of the sky."

Paula again translated his words.

Anna looked up at the pale blue sky. It seemed so far above them. I don't remember the sky ever looking so far away in England. I wonder – is it because of pollution? Is it the lack of pollution here in Africa that makes the sky seem so distant? Or is it due to global position? Would the sky in Alaska or Australia seem so far away? I don't remember the daytime sky at Dela-Aden. I spent most of my outside days in the woods. I do remember the stars in the night sky, which also seemed distant, vast and endless. Anna closed her eyes, and fell asleep, floating among the stars.

Manutu entered Anna's dreams, and spoke to her psyche through Paula.

'Life is not always a clear, blue sky; it is often overcast with problems. Sometimes, the rain does not wash the problems away.

'Unexpected events can leave a heavy sorrow in our hearts. The sorrow pulls us down and makes us its slave. Only by doing something meaningful each day can we escape the slavery of sorrow. Being productive is the only remedy that takes us away from the ravages of sorrow, and forward once again into contentment.

'As you cannot change the sky, you cannot change the past. In life, you only have today, nothing else, and each today builds on the past. If you planted seed in the past, then today could be a harvest day; or, if the seed did not grow, then today, you will have to look for something else to eat.

'Tomorrow – today will be the past. Only a fool would let a past that he cannot change ruin his today, and thereby darken his tomorrow.

'We must live each day for what it is: a new beginning. If we make the best of today, we make a better tomorrow ... and while we know not what tomorrow will bring, we will cope better with whatever it is, in knowing that we did our best today.'

Manutu then spoke to Paula, "You channeled my words to Anna?"

"Yes, I did."

"Good. She will sleep now, and feel well rested when she awakens."

Paula felt a strong desire to *roam*. I feel so lonely without Thomas. What was I thinking in coming away without him? I hope he will join us soon … or even better, I hope we can go home soon, with Anna back to her old self. Jamie feels restored; maybe that will help Anna too.

I wonder how effective Manutu's words will be for Anna. Will she even remember them? Maybe, yes; maybe, no. I will have some chats with her to encourage her to explore her feelings. Right now, she is still hiding from reality – the present as well as the past. She has to face the issues before she can heal.

Jamie told me that his miraculous change was due to an epiphany in the helicopter. Will his rejuvenation encourage Anna? Or will his focus on the future leave Anna behind, feeling even more alone, and possibly abandoned?

Oh, my, decisions, decisions! One day at a time.

Paula worked on her thesis, outlining the progress of their work to date; with a time-line defining the dates of planting and the expected results. She listed the compost recipes and any changes in the current experiments with soil media.

Anna awoke. "I don't think I have ever slept as well as I have here today and last night. It must be something in the air!" Anna said as she stretched.

"We should return now, the day is growing late," Manutu said in Swahili.

"Anna, it is time to return to the village, are you ready to go?"

"Yes. I hate to leave, I feel so free here, but maybe the feeling will go with me."

Paula thought, the feeling of this place never went with me; however, I could always remember it.'

Manutu walked back to the village in silence. Anna needed time to think now, without distractions. She would either assimilate her dreams, or cast them off. In the past, it often took days for the assimilation to become part of the psyche, and to produce a healing effect. Manutu had no experience with white women, only Paula, and she was never troubled.

Jamie was not at the sebula. Paula wondered where he had gone as she began to help Cenye with the dinner. Thomas had taught her how to make biscuits over an open fire, and it had become her job. While easy enough, it took constant vigilance to obtain the same light and fluffy result that Thomas did.

Jamie and Sashono appeared, washed and ready for dinner. Sashono always had a good appetite, for Cenye was an excellent cook.

"Where have you been, Jamie? I was looking for you."

"Sashono took me on a tour of the village, introducing me around and showing me the various cottage industries. I must say, I'm very impressed. I think the men are ingenious and clever, and the women are quite creative with their weaving and crafts. But, where do they get the iron pots, and steel spear heads, and arrow points? They have metal flensing knives, as well as hunting knives, and where do the women get the material for their dresses?"

"They go back to their ancestral lands by the ocean, and trade with the archeologists who have a dig on the site of the old village, which the Zuri Watu abandoned over a hundred years ago to escape the slave ships."

Sashono heard the exchange and said, "Mkebibi, maybe you would tell our story tonight when we sit at the fire. Tamubu told me that he had told you our history on your wilderness trek back to the sea. English is fine. Manutu and I listen better than we speak."

"I do not have the 'word-for-word' recollection of the Zuri Watu," Paula replied.

"I was expecting that – it will be a new look at an old story," Manutu smiled.

Sitting around the fire, as Paula and Tamubu had done each night in the wilderness, she began her story. The villagers came to listen. Pleased, Paula began to sprinkle her sentences with Swahili words that would help explain the story, but not diminish it for Anna and Jamie, who had already absorbed more Swahili than they realized. She abbreviated much of it, telling mostly of Ngarro's adventures in going back to their ancestral lands, hoping to trade for iron pots, hunting knives, metal flensing scrapers, fabrics and sewing needles. They took with them trade goods: handmade wooden sculptures, a child's death mask, and intricately carved teak trays, bowls and serving pieces. The archeologists were thrilled with the quality and pristine condition of the goods. So began an annual trek to the ocean to trade for goods, and to learn new ways.

Anna again slept late the next morning. Manutu went out to see his patients. Paula worked on her thesis until Sashono asked if she and Jamie would like to attend while he arbitrated a dispute between two sisters. As they walked across the village, Sashono said, "Each woman has a right, so I must decide."

"How will you do that?" Jamie asked.

"Carefully, my son, very carefully!"

As best he could, mixing Swahili with his English, he told the story.

"Their father was a talented wood carver. He made many beautiful things from many kinds of wood. When he died, he left all the handmade wooden items in his possession to his two daughters to share equally between them, which they did. But the wood carver had made only one rocking chair. He made it for his wife, now long gone. His daughters had shared the rocker when their children were infants; their daughters and granddaughters had shared it when they had babies, as well. The problem is who gets to keep the rocker in their old age, for at present, there are no women of child bearing age in either family."

When Jamie saw the rocking chair, he saw why each sister wanted to keep it. The basic chair was podocarpus, a yellowish grained hard wood. The decorative carvings were in different woods: with ebony and white birch for the elephants and zebras in the wide headpiece, framed by podocarpus. The arms were tawny yellow oak lions with red oak manes. The seat was smooth-shaped podocarpus, inlaid across the front with a pattern of ebony and ivory. The back spindles and stretchers were the striped wood of the podocarpus curved and tapered like a sitatunga's horns. The rockers, too, were solid pieces of carved striped podocarpus. The chair was an incredible work of art. And probably worth a great deal of money, especially to the archeologists working the dig.

Sashono asked the women if they had thought of any way to settle the dispute. They replied that there was no mutual accord.

Sashono said, "It would be a terrible thing to cut the chair in two ... " at which the women gasped and hastily agreed – that was unthinkable. "But the other alternative is to sell the chair, which would bring a great deal of money, and buy other rocking chairs, one for each of the sisters and their daughters."

The shock of both suggested decisions showed clearly on the faces of the sisters. Losing the beautiful hand-made chair had never even crossed their minds. Each one loved the chair, not only for its beauty, but for the memories of their father, mother and children attached to it. Selling it was beyond all comprehension, but they had asked Sashono to arbitrate.

The elder sister cried out, "Oh no, please do not do that. I give up my rights to my sister; let her have the chair to keep in her family, as long as the nursing mothers of both our families still get to use it!"

Sashono looked at the woman and asked, "Do you do this willingly?" Tears came to the woman's eyes and ran down her cheeks as she said, "I do this willingly."

Sashono looked to the younger sister, and asked, "Will you agree to the stipulations of your sister; that all the nursing mothers of both your families will be allowed to use the chair, if they desire."

The younger sister said, "I agree to the stipulations."

Then Sashono spoke, "I was called in to arbitrate, and I, too, have made a decision." The sisters glanced at one another, angst consumed them. Had their silly bickering brought on a disaster? "When the chair is not in use by a nursing mother of the family of either sister, it will reside with the younger sister, Waridi, or her eldest daughter. If either sister is deceased, her eldest daughter will inherit her rights, and so on to her eldest daughter, until a nursing mother of either sister's family again requires its use. If there is more than one nursing mother, with an infant six moons or less at the same time, they will draw lots for its use. I make my decision clear now for all future time."

Paula asked Jamie if he understood what happened. He said, "Yes, I did, and I am duly impressed, both with the selflessness of the elder sister and with the foresight of Sashono, so much like King Solomon in his wisdom. The chair is truly magnificent. Walking here, I could not fathom how a chair could warrant Sashono's attention, least of all his arbitration. I would love to own that chair myself, and would have bid for it long before it got to the archeologists."

Anna was sitting on the bed in the kibanda (hut) when Paula returned.

"So, you're awake, sleepy head. Do you feel any better?"

Anna looked up at Paula, her thoughts were in turmoil: she had a distinct feeling of dèjà vu – like she had been here before; or jamais vu – like she was seeing old things for the first time. The feelings were pervasive, persistent, confusing and contradictory.

"I feel well-rested, yet confused. I have a feeling that I should do something, but, for the life of me, I don't know what it might be; or I'm supposed to remember something – something important – but that too is eluding me; or I found out something vital, but I can't recall what it is."

Paula knew these were the suggestions that Manutu had placed in Anna's dreams. "Whenever I have feelings like that, I put them aside, and I do something that takes concentration; then, when I least expect it, my mind clears and I remember."

"Yes, that's good advice. What is on the docket for today?"

"Today is a free day. We can do whatever appeals to us."

"I'd like to go back to the learning circle and look at the sky again. I felt serene doing that. If I could grasp that serenity again, maybe I could hold on to it and make it a part of me, and if I did that, maybe the confusion would go away."

"I'm not sure Manutu is free today. I will go and see."

"I was hoping it would be just you and me. Would Manutu allow that?"

"I will go and ask him. Have you eaten yet?"

"Yes, Cenye brought me a bowl of oatmeal, a banana and a cup of tea."

"So, you had room service today! Well don't get used to it. Cenye probably wanted to clean out the pot so she could use it again!"

Anna chuckled. She was feeling better; although she did not yet feel calm or confidant, for her nerves still jumped easily. However, she'd had no bad dreams for two nights, and that, in itself, was a vast improvement.

Manutu looked askance at Paula. "Why is it, that with you, I am always stretching my parameters? It is good that Anna wants to go back to the learning circle, I'm just disappointed that she wants to go without me."

"I think it is a good sign."

"Why is that?"

"I think it shows a diminishment of fear."

"Or maybe … a lack of connection with reality."

Paula looked intensely at Manutu, "Do you really think that?"

"It is a possibility – I thought it worth mentioning. I will send three warriors with you. That should ground her in reality."

"Yes, that should indeed."

Anna did not seem affected by the presence of the warriors – it was as if she expected them to be there. With lions' dens in the boulders on the far hills, the deer and the antelope rarely grazed here. The lions hunted on the vast savanna on the other side of the hills. The valley was peaceful here, with good water and a wallow for elephants or rhinoceros, animals that were rarely prey for lions unless they were sick or wounded. However, man sometimes proved to be an excellent prey. Hence the wall of massive stones interspersed with trees around the learning circle. Also, it would never do to have a massive rhino, the self-appointed fireman of the savanna, dashing over to stomp out their little fire!

Paula and Anna sat in the shade, leaning against the boulders – no fire today. They would just talk – if Anna had something to say.

Paula thought about Thomas, and that he was probably having tea with his parents and Jon. Jon had wanted to come with them, but Sir Peter needed him to oversee the work on the new drainage system, while he was occupied supervising the tea harvest. Anna had made it easy for him when she said, 'I'd rather go alone with Jamie. It is our problem, not yours. I will make me feel worse if I take you away from your duties.'

"I had a dream yesterday," Anna spoke softly. "I remember it now. It was if an Archangel was speaking to me. I know that sounds strange, but I heard a marvelous voice, yet I did not see the speaker. I'm glad we came back here today, for now I remember his words. The voice had a soothing sound, soft, yet firm and melodious; it filled me with logic: the logic of the obvious, and the logic of reality."

Anna began to cry. Paula took her in her arms to comfort her. Anna sobbed, "I was so frightened that day. Actually, I was so terrified my wits froze. I couldn't even react. I watched Jamie put up a fight. His beating threw me into a blank state of abject fear. The conditions of our captivity were so dreadful, I blocked them out. That's when the horror began to consume me. I retreated inside my mind to hide from a reality I could not endure.

"I now see that I was weak and wrong to let those ghastly days consume me – and then to let them rule my life, even when I was safe again. I'm not saying that the terror does not linger; what I'm saying is that, I now see it for what it is – the past, and a very bad time in the past."

Paula hugged Anna close to her. "You may not believe this, but you were incredibly brave. I know the terror you felt, for natives abducted me too. They bound me up in a net, and pushed and pulled me up the mountain through dense foliage and thorn bushes. I was all alone – no one would know that I had survived the tsunami, and no one would ever know I was kidnapped ...

"Those early hours were a terrible time for me. Like you, terror froze my wits, for I had no idea what they planned to do with me. As the hours passed, I became disgusted with myself, and began to fight with my thoughts: 'you may outnumber me, but you're not going to outsmart me.'

"I know how awful abduction feels, Anna. They walked me hundreds of miles on mountain trails, while tied up. However, they did not subject me to abuse or neglect. They fed me well, and even allowed me to bathe in a pond. It was then that I began to plan, for now I knew I was a prize.

"Anna, there is no *upside* to abduction. The aftermath, however, is a different story. If the Ndezi had not abducted me, and I had not used my wits to escape – I would not have met Thomas – the most wonderful happening of my entire life!

"While your abduction was shorter in duration, it was harsher in reality. I can feel your horror of it all. But, you will forget! You will cleanse your mind. The terror will fade. Although, it will make the ordinary days of your life more meaningful, for you were tested – and you survived."

"You are so kind to me. Jon told me how he found you in the native village, all alone at the mercy of an egotistical chief. He even told me about the pre-marriage mutilation rituals you would have undergone if you had not escaped. I cannot imagine how you were able to function in such dire circumstances."

"It was a case of do or die – and I did: I got the hell out of there!"

Anna chuckled, "And you can even joke about it now!"

"It is over, like going to the dentist. I don't think about him either!"

"We both had our teeth pulled without anesthetic!" Anna said. And they laughed some more. Oh, the wonderful healing of laughter.

The next day, the four of them went to the learning circle, taking a picnic lunch. Anna found great peace and comfort there, and wanted to share it with Jamie. Manutu told them a story about the Zuri Watu life in Africa. Paula translated as Manutu spoke:

'We, of the Zuri Watu, were forced to leave our ancestral home by the sea. It was a terrible thing to have to do, but it was the only way to save our young men and women from the slave traders. The decision weighed heavily on the leaders, for they did not know what to expect in the new land. They hoped for a better life, but the future held no promises.

'It was an act of courage and daring, which isolated the Zuri Watu here in this mountain valley. At first, the isolation was good, for it made them feel safe. But, as the years passed, they encountered social problems. Rules were set-up to offset the problems of inbreeding, for we have no neighboring tribes near here. The African native is above all things, gregarious and reliant on his fellow man.

'It was as much of a trial for the Zuri Watu not to have enemies as it was not to have friends. Enemies sparked the zest for living, giving impetus to our days. Our previous leaders, especially my father Agurra, were men of

205

great vision and set up games of competition to keep our fighting skills sharp. It is these games and our rules that set us apart, like the Watusi, the Zambezi and the Pygmies, from other Africans. We do things our way, and have done so for a hundred years.

'Why am I telling you this? It is to illustrate that life itself will lead you down a path, and it is for you to follow and adapt to it. Do not expect that you have control of your lives. You can only set the rules of the game, the game being life itself.

'We think we are in control, until something unexpected happens, then we are jolted out of our complacency. No one, except the man in a coma, is free from the unexpected, so we must learn to expect snags along the way, and prepare ourselves to deal with them.

'How do you do that? You live each day to the fullest of your ability – and never slacken in your ideals or aspirations. Both of these are the cornerstones of a good life. Both will help you weather the unexpected if they are a part of you. You must strive to do your best each and every day. Then, even in adversity, you will have a chance to prevail.

'There will be things you cannot change, things you will have to accept; that too is part of life. Be kind, be understanding, be faithful and above all, be honest with yourself – and with others.

'These are the tenets of the Zuri Watu. They have served us well. We are a nation of strong people, a kind and good people. We have survived and prospered in this valley for more than a hundred years. We have kept to ourselves, but the time is coming when our young people will venture out to make new and different lives for themselves. The archeologists have offered to send us teachers, those who would bring us the knowledge of the rest of the world; those who have the reading and writing, and those who have the skills to make tools, or weave cloth.

'We move forward into the future, as we must, for it is a law of nature. Yesterday is gone, but not forgotten – for we must learn from it. If we learned well, the bad of the past will not be lived again.

'We will still make decisions, and even with the best of intentions, our decisions may not come to fruition as planned. But, if we do our best each day, we can say – tomorrow I will try again! That is the way of life!'

Paula, Anna and Jamie clapped.

Manutu felt abashed, his beliefs had carried him away.

He added: "Take the best we have to offer, and use it to find happiness."

Three days later, the helicopter, full of iron pots, came back to take them to Yaoundé. They would be at Dela–Aden by dinnertime with a different outlook on life, with restored bodies, settled minds, and a fresh attitude about tomorrow.

Paula could hardly wait! I wonder if Thomas has missed me as much as I have missed him; I've never felt so lonely. If Paula had known that Thomas was sleeping in the dog kennel with Windy, she would have felt incredibly guilty for going off on her mercy mission, and leaving him home alone.

32 ~ Dela-Aden ~ Letters

The family celebrated Hanna's and Sara's return from the continent at dinner, along with Jamie's, Anna's and Paula's return from the Zuri Watu. Thomas made the Pymtu fish recipe; Elizabeth made potatoes au gratin and beer batter sautéed squash. Paula made biscuits, and Lady Mary made a tossed salad. Dessert was a fresh fruit cup with whipped cream. They had coffee and liqueurs in the library in front of a cozy fire. In the tradition that Thomas began on his return from the wilderness, Hanna and Sara told the story of their European tour, the recital in Vienna, the Lipizzaner horses, and of again meeting Wolfgang and Friedrich on the river cruise, where they felt anything but tourists.

Lady Mary and Sir Peter were quite content. The girls were home, having had a delightful experience on their European tour. Jamie and Anna had returned from their visit to the Zuri Watu, seemingly cured of their malaise, which totally astonished and pleased them.

As Mary sat listening, she could only marvel at the diverse happenings and incredible changes in their lives in the last four months, more events and changes than in the last fourteen years. Five months ago, we were empty nesters, and now our cup runneth over.

Listening to the chatter, Mary looked at her handsome first born son, lost to her for fourteen years and returned to her a man — a wonderful man who brought with him a woman he found in the wilderness to be his wife. And a most amazing woman she is too: a gymnast, a biologist and an accomplished horseman. And Jon has found a sweet and sensitive woman too, and with courage, she will get over her bad beginning in Africa. Hanna and Sara have met young men who may come to call ... all the way from Vienna; a delightful possibility. The girls matured on their tour, they now seem more assured. Socializing has a positive effect on young women, helping them to find their niche.

Look at Peter. He looks like a Cheshire cat, sitting there with such a smug smile on his face. I'm so happy for him. He suffered terribly after Thomas was lost. I had two little girls to occupy my time, attention and thoughts, so I moved on better.

And dear, sweet Jon who suffered the most; he not only lost his brother, but he lost his best friend and companion. Loboda tried to be his friend, but he was just company. Jon tagged along after Peter whenever he could, trying to fill the void that Thomas's disappearance had left in his young life. Jon never gave up hoping that Thomas would come back to us ... to have such faith that nothing could dissuade it, no matter the years, deserved its reward in fruition.

However, it happened in such a way that Jon didn't even recognize Thomas, for both of them were intent on rescuing Paula. Thomas left a huge hole in our lives, but now that he is back, he has filled it up to overflowing.

"Mother! Did you hear me?" Jon asked his mother again.

"Did I miss something, dear?"

"I said Anna and I are going to go to England when I have the drainage work finished. Would you be willing to come to England for Boxing Day?"

"You mean you are going to live in England?"

"Right now ... yes. We are going to England, and later, we may take an ocean cruise. Hanna and Sara said they loved cruising ... you went everywhere, but only had to unpack once!"

"I see," Mary smiled ... rudely knocked off her pedestal of satisfaction.

"No, Mother, I don't believe you do," Jon smiled, and his eyes sparkled. "I have asked Anna to marry me, and she has said '*yes*'. However, she wants to talk to her parents before becoming formally engaged, so we are going to England." And, Jon thought, I feel Anna will recover better if she is away from the source of her anguish.

"Oh, Jon – Anna, I'm so happy for both of you! Of course, you must go to England to ask for her hand in marriage."

"Moth-er, we're not quite that old fashioned," Jon chuckled.

"Jon, my father will harrumph himself speechless if you do that," Anna laughed.

What more can possibly happen? Mary wondered.

★　★　★

"Mother! Moth-er!" Hanna and Sara called as they raced down to the barn! Mary came running from the tack room/office where she kept her stud books and schedules. "What is it?" she cried, feeling terror.

"We have letters!" Hanna said.

"Letters from Wolfgang and Friedrich!" Sara added.

"They are coming to Africa!" the girls said in unison.

Relief flowed through Lady Mary, as she smiled at her radiant daughters. "And when is this visit going to happen?"

"The 15th of August," again speaking in unison.

"Why that is in two weeks!" Lady Mary stated, surprised.

"Yes, isn't it just wonderful?" Sara smiled.

"You are going to like these young men, Mother; that's a promise," Hanna said.

Mary smiled happily, and said, "It is enough I think – that you like them."

Hanna, who was more reticent than Sara, said, "Every girl dreams of the perfect beau, but how many ever meet him? Wolfgang was in Service at the Schönbrunn Palace in Vienna, and committed, so while I liked him and I think he liked me, he was not free to make initial advances. But the most awful thing happened, and now he and Friedrich have resigned their Commissions at the Schönbrunn Palace, obtaining severance with honor. Wait until you read their letters!"

Sara added, "You don't have to wait, we brought them with us."

The girls and Mary trooped back to the tack room/office, a commodious room with two walls of saddle and bridle racks, and a row of blanket boxes. The door wall had a big window above Mary's desk. Lady Mary now worked here each day keeping records on the horses. She also received prospective buyers and clients here, but kept personal papers in the house.

The girls sat on the sofa, and Mary swiveled her desk chair, saying, "Do you want to tell me about these young men before I read your letters?"

"No," they chorused, and laughed, "Just read the letters."

Mary shuffled the letters, as she had always done with cards or gifts from the twins, and then chose one to open.

210

24 July 1960
Savona, Italy

My dear Sara,

    We had great excitement on Der Mozart *after you disembarked. Wolfgang and I, Captain Schuch and the sous chef were tied up and left in the dark in his dining room, after two men with guns interrogated Wolfgang. It seems they wanted the packet Wolfgang was delivering to Budapest. However Wolfgang had received a telegram ordering him to burn the packet, which he had already done.*
    Captain Schuch sent an SOS of our dilemma by kicking the ductwork with his foot. It took forty nine minutes for the Executive Officer and crew to find us, for while they immediately heard the SOS, it reverberated throughout the ship. Only by opening every door and examining every room did they finally find us.

    When Wolfgang resigned his post, I resigned with him. We went to Savona, Italy, the hillside village pictured in Captain Schuch's dining room painting. My mother is still there. We took two weeks and sailed down to Monaco and gambled a bit, before going on to Cannes for the film festival.
    We decided, while sailing, to begin our long-awaited travels with Kenya, where we would like to visit you and Hanna. It would be marvelous if we could do some touring together while we are in Africa.
    We expect to arrive in Nairobi on the 15ᵗʰ of August. We are booked in at the Mayflower Hotel for two nights. After that, our itinerary is not yet established.

    I do so look forward to seeing you again.

Yours in Friendship,

Friedrich von Hauptsborg

＊　　＊　　＊

"My goodness," Mary exclaimed! "I'm glad I didn't know about this incident sooner, I would have been beside myself."

"I know! I could hardly take in the words as I read them! Who would have ever believed it?" Sara said, sounding stunned.

"I never believed Wolfgang was a courier," Hanna said. "I thought he was joking, but I did sense an air of intrigue."

"Yes," Sara said, "Europe seemed to be full of intrigue. When we were at the reception after the recital, I had the feeling that no one was saying what they were thinking. They were saying what others expected them to say. It was disquieting."

"Well, Hanna, I do hope your letter is not quite so exciting," Mary said

24 July 1960
Savona, Italy

Dearest Hanna,

I will only say, as you have said, 'things happen for a reason.' It is hard to accept things that happen which are unpleasant, even for a good reason; but I am comforted with the thought — 'that some good comes of everything' — the good here being my freedom from a life I did not choose, and only tolerated for the good of my family name.

Friedrich and I went back to Vienna and turned in a complete report of the incident, resigned our commissions with honor, packed up and left for Savona, Italy. I had forgotten how much I love it here, for I have been away a long time. It is so peaceful — yet interesting with the harbor and the yachting.

Friedrich and I took a long sail to Cannes via Monaco to get our heads on straight again. Resignation was, after all, more stressful than we expected.

All our lives, Friedrich and I have talked about traveling about the earth as troubadours, singing for our supper in strange out-of-the-way places. It was a dream of schoolboys, then a dream of university-men, and now a distinct possibility for two young men

before they reach their majority, when they will have to settle-down to responsibility.

Our first thoughts were of going to visit you and Sara to see if your luck still holds at hearts.

I do hope you will be at home *for our arrival in Nairobi on the 15ᵗʰ of August.*

Affectionately yours,

Wolfgang von Hauptsborg

★   ★   ★

Mary felt a little flutter. She had not yet met this man, but she already liked him. She looked her daughter in the eye, and said, "You forgot to mention that Wolfgang has depth as well as charm."

Hanna smiled. "Yes, I did, didn't I? It's because his charm keeps getting in the way of everything else, not because I didn't notice it."

Mary turned to Sara, "I do think Friedrich likes excitement quite as much as you do, Sara. He sounded positively cheerful about the incident."

For the first time in her life, Sara lacked a rejoinder; but sat thinking, how does she know these things – and all from a letter?

"And it would seem these young men are brothers."

"No, mother, cousins. Their fathers were brothers," Sara replied.

"Let me finish up here, and we'll spring this surprise on your father at tea. He will be simply astonished!" Mary laughed, thinking – and that's putting it very mildly! Only a few days ago I wondered what else could possibly happen – I've got to stop tempting fate!

★   ★   ★

"Peter, are you asleep yet?"

"No, not yet."

"Do you mind if I talk?"

"It would be a first, if I did."

213

"I am quite excited about these young men visiting. I sent Julia a telegram and asked for her opinion of them. I received her reply today, and it was glowing. She is absolutely thrilled for Hanna and Sara."

"Well, we will certainly know next Monday, won't we?"

"You seem a bit off-hand about it all ... why?"

"They haven't proposed yet. They are only visiting – hoping for a free place to stay while they tour Africa."

"Peter! What an ungracious thing to say!"

"I'm a man. I know how young men think. It might have been a while ago, but through the haze of my old age, I do remember how I felt as a young man. I loved going to visit young ladies, especially when their parents were footing the bills!"

"Peter! I've never heard you be so outrageous – what is it?"

"I just got my girls back! I was hoping they'd be around for a little while."

Mary took Peter in her arms and gave him a kiss on his cheek, as she snuggled closer saying, "Your girls won't be going anywhere, at least not yet. It is just the excitement of eligible young men visiting. The young men are on holiday, and hope to share some of it with Hanna and Sara. There are no young men of proper age here in Kenya, at least none that Hanna and Sara would enjoy spending time with. While there is nothing wrong with being a farmer's son, the ones that are here have not had the education that Hanna and Sara have had, so they have little in common. These young men are different. They are traveled, educated and even sophisticated. Don't you want the best for your daughters?"

"The girls are too young!"

"They are young, yes; but not too young. They will reach a legal age in little less than a year. You will be cordial, won't you?"

"Smash it, Mary! You make me sound a frightful bore! Have you ever known me to be offensive?"

"No, dear, but I have known you to be cold and distant with visitors who come just to see the girls ... always judging them."

"Give me another kiss, snuggle with me, and I will try."

"We have so much to be thankful for, Peter, we must not be selfish."

"Mary, you do realize that these young men will probably not want to live in Africa, so you are asking a lot of me."

"I'm asking you to put the happiness of your daughters first and your happiness second – that's all. If you are gracious and it doesn't work out, you will not be to blame. If it is your fault that the young men go away, the girls will never forgive you. Is that what you want?"

"No. You're right, as usual. I promise to be on my best behavior."

33 ~ Wolfgang & Friedrich

Before Jon and Anna went back to England, Jon took Thomas to town and opened a bank account for him, saying, "If you should need money, you will have it. Who knows … you might even want to come to England to visit us!" Jon smiled.

Thomas understood Jon's deep need to share; he had always been a generous person. When I was declared legally dead in 1955, Jon inherited Woleston Hall in my stead. Now that I have refused to inherit Woleston Hall away from him, he has been doubly anxious to share. However, a bit of pocket money does have its uses, Thomas thought as Hanna and Sara piled into the Land Rover with him and Paula to go to Nairobi to meet and greet Wolfgang and Friedrich at the airport.

They planned to stay in Nairobi for two days touring before heading out to Dela-Aden, so Thomas had reserved the penthouse suite at the Mayflower Hotel. Lady Mary had said, "There is more for visitors to do and see, in and around Nairobi. It is a good place to start when getting to know Africa." And his father agreed.

Thomas left Windy at Dela-Aden with his mother. By now, the pup liked being with her almost as much as being with him, for Mary had a great way with all animals.

What Thomas would never know was that his little dog Foxy went into a deep funk when Thomas did not return home from the Arts and Science Fair in 1947. Foxy nibbled sparingly for a week, and then stopped eating or drinking at all. Lady Mary, Sir Peter and Jon were distraught by the loss of the happy little dog. It was as if he knew that Thomas was never coming back, which had added mightily to their grief. As a consequence, they never had another dog at Dela-Aden until Thomas brought Windy home from England. Mary and Peter delighted in the puppy almost as much as Thomas did.

Hanna was quiet and thoughtful on the ride to town, but Sara was a bundle of nerves and chattered away during the entire ride. Before going to the airport, they stopped at the Mayflower Hotel to off-load their luggage. Paula arranged to have dinner served in the suite, which would give them some quiet privacy, for Paula had invited Cyril Latham and his secretary, Gloria, to join them for dinner. That way the young people would not feel courtesy-bound to spend the evening with them, and could gather on the balcony, which as Paula well knew, was a simply delightful place to spend an evening with gentlemen visitors.

Also, Paula and Thomas wanted to talk to Cyril about APCO, who was now the top bidder for the kimmea. They also wanted to know how it stood with Petrides Athos and Max Smith – had warrants been issued for their arrest?

I hate this airport, Paula thought. It's just a huge cavernous building with a haphazard system of processing travelers. The traffic control personnel often split up families or groups traveling together, diverting them to different customs inspectors – not necessarily less busy ones. The unsuspecting passengers, separated without warning, then find it difficult to relocate their companions again, which produced chaos. Wolfgang and Friedrich fell into this category. Thomas and Hanna hunted on one side of the huge open space, while Paula and Sara hunted on the other.

Friedrich made the mistake of declaring presents, and was then required to fill out customs forms and pay duty. Once they found Friedrich, Sara stayed with him while Paula went back to move the Land Rover, which she had parked in a ten minute pick-up zone.

Once on the road to the Mayflower Hotel, Sara apologized, saying, "I am so sorry I didn't write to let you know that you **never** declare anything."

"What if they do a spot check?" Friedrich asked.

"Then you lie, and say they were bon voyage presents to you. If it is your property, there is no duty due, which seems silly, for visitors can give away everything they own, once they are away from customs control," Sara commented.

"And if they insist you open your *gifts* and find Brussels lace handkerchiefs, then what do you do?"

217

"Well, then you would have had to assume a foppish pose and say, in your best imitation of a dandy, "Aren't they just lovely, I think I'll wear one now!""

Everyone laughed, but Wolfgang found the mental picture of Friedrich, a man's man, doing such a thing completely hilarious.

Wolfgang thought, coming to Africa was so right to do. It almost makes me glad that devious people used me as a dupe, forcing me to resign my commission. What was it Hanna said, 'I feel that things happen because they are meant to happen, even the unpleasant things happen for a reason ... ' and I think she was right!

The laughter and merriment carried them all the way into Nairobi and the Mayflower Hotel. Paula ordered a light lunch sent up to the suite, after which they decided to nap before going on a walking tour of Nairobi. They would take a riding tour of Nairobi tomorrow, beginning with the animal park. Today, they would skip tea, and dine early at six, so Cyril and Gloria and the weary travelers would not have a late evening.

The young people took their coffee and dessert out to the balcony after dinner, while Cyril updated Thomas and Paula on the latest developments with APCO. Cyril also mentioned that a warrant was out for Petrides Athos and Max Smith, and that both had fled Africa on *The Gallant Lady*, which Athos had docked in Mombasa. "They are now out at sea, possibly headed to Greece," Cyril surmised.

"One of the squatters that abducted Jamie and Anna was apprehended when buying supplies with pound notes, which is unusual for a man in rags. The man admitted to what he had done, but otherwise, he seemed quite out of his senses and totally disoriented. He kept asking if the police were God, and begged not have his eyeballs drop out or his skin rot off, or his manhood shrivel up, or his hands and feet wither away. The man was obviously a lunatic and given over to the care of his family."

Thomas found it hard to suppress a smile. At least they had the right man.

Paula let out a sigh of relief, hoping the episode was over and finished. Hearing her sigh, Thomas thought: If Petrides Athos or Max Smith ever come back to Africa, I will go and make certain it is for the last time.

Wolfgang and Friedrich sat side by side and opposite to Hanna and Sara on the cushioned rattan chairs on the balcony. A coffee table between them held the remains of a peaches and whipped cream dessert, along with empty coffee cups.

"This balcony is simply delightful," Wolfgang said.

"Yes, and it is a special place too," Hanna replied.

"Why is that?"

"Thomas proposed to Paula here on this balcony this past April."

"Sort of an odd place for a marriage proposal," Friedrich said, "but I can see the appeal of the place. It is secluded and private with a lovely view over the gardens."

"Yes," Hanna continued. "They met in the wilderness of Cameroon in February, under the most unusual circumstances: Paula was escaping through the forest trees in order not to leave a trail for the Ndezi warriors. The Ndezi princes had abducted her from the beach where her yacht was stranded by a tsunami in a coastal tidal pool."

Both Wolfgang and Friedrich looked stunned at the idea of Paula captured, and then fleeing from her captors. Wolfgang recovered his wits first. "I should say – those do qualify as unusual circumstances; still, it was not a very long courtship."

"Not in terms of days, but a long time if you are together every hour of every day for three months – through perils, accidents and attacks by wild animals," Hanna added.

In a longer pause, the visitors digested these most startling facts, feeling utterly out of their depth. Again, it was Wolfgang who recovered first. "Yes, I know what you mean. Going through preliminary training with other cadets, we became so close that it seemed as if we had always been friends. Sharing hardships and problems serves to intensify one's feelings. I would like to hear more about their ordeal."

"When we are at Dela–Aden, we can ask Thomas to tell us the story after dinner. It is what we like to do in the evenings – listen to someone telling a story. Thomas is quite good at it!"

"I don't know why, but I can hardly keep my eyes open," Friedrich said. "Do you feel like calling it a night, Wolfy?"

"Yes, I'm sorry to say that I too am fading quickly, jet lag I suppose."

Wolfgang and Friedrich went inside to thank Paula and Thomas for the delightful evening, shaking hands with Thomas and Cyril, with heel clicks, head bows and smiles to Paula and Gloria.

The four guests left together and took the elevator down, with Cyril saying, "I do hope you enjoy your time touring in Nairobi, for there is no question that you will enjoy your time at Dela–Aden. Good night."

Walking to their room, Friedrich asked out loud, "I wonder what Cyril meant; why would he be certain that we would enjoy staying on a farm?"

"This is Africa. Who knows what they think out here? However, I'm too tired to even know what I think right now."

It rained during the night, but the sky had cleared with the sun and it would be a nice day. Paula and Thomas brought the Land Rover 'round to get off on the day's tour. Hanna and Sara had never done a local tour, and looked forward to it, mostly because of the delightful company.

They began the day with the animal park, where it is best to see the animals early in the morning. Here resided the reticulated giraffe, an albino zebra, a black rhinoceros with three horns, and a black male lion, with tawny mane and tail tip, as well as other protected specimens of the indigenous species. They toured the Nairobi streets, noting shops to visit later. They saw the brick government buildings and concrete tenements, all surrounded by the ubiquitous sea of corrugated lean-tos – home to the homeless.

After lunch and a short nap at the hotel, the six of them went out to tour Karen Blixen's coffee farm in the Ngong hills, which she lost to debt in 1931; the end of seventeen years of personal struggles in Kenya, with short-lived triumphs, to a final defeat by fire.

Karen retreated to her ancestral home Rungstedlung in Denmark, near Copenhagen, where in 1934 she wrote a book of her African experience, entitled: *Out of Africa*.

After the coffee farm, they went to the Great Rift Valley, which is so immense, mountains dot the floor of the valley like insignificant boulders. In places, miles of the valley can be viewed from the rim.

By the end of the day, Wolfgang and Friedrich were ready for a light dinner and bed.

"I thought Thomas would tell us a story tonight. Are you too tired to listen?" Hanna asked.

Thomas looked at the tired travelers and said, "It's not a long story. It's about an English Lord and a Medicine Man."

Paula asked, "Have I heard this story?'

"No, I don't think so. I just now remembered it."

"Well, I'm a bit past bedtime stories, but you've certainly aroused my curiosity," Wolfgang said. "How about you, Friedrich, want to have a go at a story?"

"Yes, what a novel idea." *'I say old chap, what did you do in Africa?'* *'Very kind of you to ask, we listened to bedtime stories.'* *'Aha, don't talk rot, what did … '* but the laughter shut him down.

'In the darkness of the deep forest amid a pile of pre-historic rocks, there lived an old medicine man. His name was Jimoba. He lived alone and had done so, since he had disagreed with the Chief on the treatment for his wife, who suffered from fits. Jimoba knew it was her diet, but the Chief declared her possessed and insane and had her locked up. Jimoba, insulted that his advice was ignored and outraged by this vicious treatment of the sick, left the village. That was long ago.

'One day, when he was gathering food for his dinner, he saw a man asleep on the ground. The man was oddly dressed, for he wore shoes with thick heels and metal buckles; his pants only came to his knees, with a coat that was short in the front and long in the back with ruffles and bows on his chest and more ruffles at his wrists. His head was bare, but nearby, was a large brimmed hat, gaily adorned with plumy feathers. The man lay on his back snoring loudly.

Jimoba did not know what to make of such a man. He watched him sleep, wondering: How did he get here? Where did he come from? Why is he all alone? Hidden in a nearby tree behind leafy vines, Jimoba watched the man until he awoke. The man got to his feet, relieved himself and then looked around.

"I say, where the blast am I? It looks like some sort of jungle!" The man spoke aloud. Jimoba did not understand the words but saw the consternation on the man's face. The man picked up his hat and began to walk away. He walked straight towards a sinking bog, so Jimoba followed him unobtrusively. When the man did not detour as he neared the bog, Jimoba picked up a fallen

221

nut, and threw it at him. It hit him on the neck. The man turned but saw nothing, although he could still feel the impact of the prickly nut husk.

'*The man was certain the missile, whatever it was, had been thrown at him, and called out, "I say, hello there, whoever you are. Can you tell me where I am?"*

Jimoba did not understand the words, but he heard the questioning tone in the man's voice. Jimoba did not know what to do.

'*The man said, "I seem to be lost ... and I don't remember how I got here ... would you please help me?"*

'*For some reason, a plea for help sounds the same in all languages.*

'*Slowly, Jimoba began to show himself. He shook his head from side to side and pointed to his mouth and ear, to say he did not understand or speak his language.*

'*The man quickly understood, and began to speak to him with pantomime. Jimoba watched the man's gestures ... he went to sleep, and woke up not knowing where he was. Jimoba beckoned to the man to follow him. He had no choice but to take him home.*

'*Jimoba shared his dinner and broth with the man. They talked using gestures, and the man told Jimoba that he had come across the sea to Africa, but when he arrived he had fallen asleep, and then woke up in the jungle.*

'*Jimoba found this story hard to believe, they were a very long way from the sea. Jimoba put an herb in the man's broth to make him sleep, and then searched him.*

'*The man had only his clothes, a round metal dial that ticked and a big white square of cloth. He had not walked here from the sea for his clothes, while a bit spattered, were in good shape, neither dirty nor torn. The dial on the round metal disc fascinated Jimoba and he sat listening to it tick. He noticed one of the arms on the dial move a bit. He heard a tinkling sound of music and suddenly, Jimoba found himself on a dock beside the sea leaning against a travel bag. Terror overcame Jimoba. What had happened? His fright was so severe that he found it hard to breathe, and gasping for breath, he fainted.*

'*The man awoke in the morning feeling well and rested, but found himself all alone. For hours, he called out for the old man, yet the old man did not return. He reached for his timepiece, the one he had acquired in a game of chance the night before the ship had docked. It was gone. Had he lost it? He remembered looking at it while on the dock. Sitting beside his carpetbag, he had taken out the timepiece, and, as he gazed at it, the watch struck the* hour of noon, and played a tune. The next thing he knew he awakened in the deep jungle. What in the world had happened?

'The man rummaged around the cave and found a store of nuts, figs, dates and a bag of powdered meat, the same powdered meat the old man had used to make the broth. He also found a bladder of water and a stack of dried twigs and sticks to keep the fire going. He placed a gourd between the rocks surrounding the fire as he had seen the old man do to heat water and made broth. He ate a few pieces of the dried fruits and some of the nuts and wondered where the old man had gone.

'Jimoba awoke from his faint, still grasping the pocket watch. He picked up the carpet bag and hid behind a steamer trunk, where he opened the carpetbag. Inside he saw clothing and personal items, lots of papers and a box he couldn't open. He cowered behind the huge trunk, terrified. He had put the watch down, but now, he picked it up again. The arms of the watch were almost together in a straight line. Jimoba picked up the carpetbag and hugged it close for comfort, wondering if he would ever see his home again, when once more, he heard the tinkling sound of music.

'Jimoba then found himself seated at his fire in his cave with the strange man asleep in his bed in the little alcove. Oh! What an awful dream, he thought. It really scared me. Looking down, he noticed the carpetbag, and scrambled away from it. It was not a dream – not a dream at all. He then realized he still held on to the round dial thing, and quickly put it down.

'Time passed, and then Jimoba began to laugh. He had traveled in time. He had gone to the man's place, as the man had come to the jungle. I have always wanted to travel in time as some other medicine men have done. Now that I have, I never want to do it again. When the stranger awakes, I will send him back to his life.

'So many days have I sat here feeling discarded and useless. Yet, I have all that I need to live well, and I am still able to help those who come to me for guidance and advice.

'What I didn't have was contentment. I longed for the past and did not appreciate the present. I now realize that I am most fortunate in the life I live, for I have my health, I have serenity, I live in peace and I have work I like to do. If a man has these things, he is truly blessed.' THE END

The applause was enthusiastic. Wolfgang and Friedrich had been spellbound, for this was their first African story, and it fascinated them – both for the telling and for the moral at the end.

"We don't have stories like that at home. Just Fairy Tales and they are full of dwarfs and witches, although some have a moral to them too," Friedrich said.

"But now, even as we thank you so much, we must go, for I don't think I can keep my eyes open another five minutes," Wolfgang added.

As he staggered to his bed, Wolfgang said to Friedrich. "I think we are going to have a very interesting time here in Africa," and was instantly asleep.

They both slept late. Jet lag is a powerful force on the body. Friedrich called up to the suite. Paula answered, "Good morning."

"This is Friedrich. Are we too late for your breakfast offer?"

"Not at all, we had a continental breakfast sent up and the croissants are still warm. Come up when you're ready," Paula replied.

Thomas and Paula had slept in a bit too. It was the first time since their return to Africa that they did not have a reason to rise early and so luxuriated in a morning together.

Hanna and Sara took advantage of the late morning to shower and wash their hair and dry it into the pageboy style they both wore. They had chosen sundresses with gauzy bolero tops, and flats; pretty enough, yet still comfortable. They heard the phone ring; then Paula knocked and said, "Your young men will be up shortly."

They started the day with a walking tour of the many shops in Nairobi featuring beautiful and often incredible native handiworks and crafts. The displays went from a miniature no bigger than a coin, to life size animals or warriors, á la the cigar store Indian of the West; from exquisite jewelry to intricately carved trays, letter boxes or multi-tiered jewelry boxes; to spoons, forks, canes – the selection was endless.

After lunch at Farah's Indian cuisine restaurant, Cyril Latham's favorite restaurant, they once again climbed into the Land Rover and headed north to Mount Kenya, about ninety miles away. Paula did the driving with Thomas navigating. The roads were mostly full of pot holes and thirty miles was top speed, but they were not in a hurry; the object of the travel was to see and enjoy the countryside.

Friedrich asked, "Where are all these natives going? The roadsides have been thick with them most of the way."

Paula replied, "I wondered the very same thing myself when I came here. No matter the day or weather, the roadsides are always full of people to-ing and fro-ing. No one has been able to answer the question to my satisfaction. I have surmised that they don't have much to do, and so are going to the roadside markets to barter, or to visit friends and relatives. Thomas told me that Africans are basically nomadic, and need to move around. Sir Peter said it is their way of life: to do something is to go somewhere. He said that in their ancestry, the men were warriors and went out to fight or hunt. The women stayed at home, flensing skins, drying meat, growing vegetables, raising children. Now, there is no meat to dry or skins to flense; the vegetables are on their own and the women and children, as you can see, are learning to travel."

Friedrich and Wolfgang asked Hanna and Sara about the rest of their European tour, and were especially interested in the railway trip in Switzerland, which sounded like a tour they would enjoy. They had gone on the trains to skiing destinations, but had not stopped in the various little towns except to change trains.

"Tell us about sailing from Savona," Hanna said. "How long did it take you to sail to Monaco and Cannes?"

Wolfgang replied, "The entire distance is less than a hundred land miles in a straight line, but we sailed into the wind to Monaco, which took three days. We anchored at night near villages. We have school friends in Monaco, so we spent some time visiting. The casinos are fun, but expensive. We then sailed to Cannes where we docked for a few days for the film festival. The sailing in the Golfo di Genova is a yachtsman's dream. In nice weather, the Mediterranean Sea is a gentle sea, and with the wind, a sailor's delight. It only took us half the time on our return trip."

"Does your family own a yacht?" Sara asked.

"Yes, my uncle by marriage is a yachtsman, although he is mostly a day sailor. He likes to go out when he has guests, or when we are at home to help with the work of sailing. The yacht is really too big for one man to handle."

"How big is it?"

"It is a forty foot ocean-going sloop, sleeping six."

"Which, of course, means nothing to me," Sara laughed.

225

Wolfgang took a vendor's price list from his pocket, turned it over and quickly sketched the yacht for Sara. "This is the hull, this is the main mast, this is the boom, these are the fore-and-aft rigged sails and this is the jib. Fully rigged, she can run before the wind at a good clip. So, as you can see with all canvas up, you can't be at the helm back here, steering the yacht, and up here raising or lowering the jib, at the same time. If my uncle goes out alone, he raises only the mains'l; she plunges a bit without a jib to lift the bow and is slower on the tack, but still manageable."

"Except for the cruise ship on the Baltic and the river cruise on the Danube, I've never been on the water. A small vessel must be exciting," Sara said. "Would you like to go sailing, Hanna?"

"I think so, though I won't really know until I try it. Have you ever been sailing, Paula?" Hanna asked.

"I was raised on the water. We sailed all summer on the Chesapeake Bay, which can be quite choppy."

"Is there anything you haven't done?" Sara asked. "You've probably even climbed mountains!" thinking her remark to be outrageous.

Paula smiled, "Yes, I've done that too."

Thomas chuckled and added: "And she can scale a sheer cliff wall like a lizard and rappel off high cliffs like walking down the stairs!" For a moment, silence reigned, and then came gales of *gotcha* laughter. "Oh Thomas, you say the oddest things," Sara chortled.

Thomas and Paula glanced at each other and joined the laughter.

Wolfgang was intrigued. While the twins thought Thomas and Paula were joking, he somehow surmised they were not. With each passing day, I feel this trip to Africa is going to change my life – in more ways than one.

Friedrich took it all in, and felt a thrill of excitement. There were unknown waters here and a prudent sailor would lower the jib.

Lady Mary made a short day of it down at the barn. She worked the horses, but left the paperwork for another day, and headed up to the house. As she fussed around the house, she thought, you'd think I was the one receiving suitors and chuckled. Even so, she could not quell the excitement of anticipation. The young men would share the second guest room on the third floor, where Thomas and Paula were ensconced. If they preferred more privacy, they could go out to the old guest house. Mary decided to go out to check on the cleaning job just in case the young men were accustomed to more solitude. Looking at the cottage with a discerning eye, Mary thought, I will have to have it painted. It is getting a bit shabby. Making a to-do list, she heard the horn of the Land Rover, and hurried back to the house.

Sir Peter heard the horn too. He mounted up and rode over to the house; tied Midnight Rider to one of the little liveried-boy stanchions along the fence, and then stood with Mary at the end of the walkway to greet the guests.

When the hubbub settled down a bit, Mary made a decision. These young men should stay in the main house. It would be good for them.

"Once your bags are inside, and you are settled, we'll have lunch here on the veranda. Sir Peter can't stay long, for he is in the middle of a harvest."

"I'll take them up and get them settled-in Mother," Hanna said. "Unless you'd rather we have lunch first so Father can get back to the tea leaves."

"It's up to you, Peter, which do you prefer?"

"Is Elizabeth ready to serve lunch?"

"Yes, I think so. We are just having tuna sandwiches with cottage cheese and corn relish, iced tea, iced coffee and brownies."

Sir Peter loved corn relish and brownies, and said, "Why don't we eat now, after I wash-up in the lav?"

Elizabeth was ready to serve and the guests were ready to eat. Paula added, "Good choice, Dad. Now we can all take a nap as well."

Peter smiled at his new daughter. She never failed to please him, no matter what she did or said. If we lose the girls to the continent, we will still have Paula and maybe Anna. I'm getting used to a full house again, and I never want it to change. Peter looked at the young men, thinking, Mary was right. These are certainly eligible young men and I think I might even get to like them.

"Have you young men ever been to Africa before?" Peter asked.

"No," they both replied in unison. Everyone chuckled.

"We should be used to people replying in unison, the twins do it all the time. We take it for granted." Mary smiled.

"Well," Peter continued, "do you young men ride?"

"Yes," they replied, again in unison, which again provoked amused chuckles, even from themselves.

"I think we will finish up picking this field by tea time. If you like, we can go out for a ride around the farm," Peter continued, unperturbed.

Looking at each other, Wolfgang and Friedrich smiled and said, once again in unison, "We'd enjoy that."

It took long minutes for the laughter to die down. Hanna could stand it no longer and said, "If you do that again, I'm going to lose my lunch from laughing so much."

Wolfgang replied, with a roguish smile, "That will never do, now will it, Friedrich?"

"No, it looks as if we must speak our minds independently."

Hanna and Sara glanced at each other. *'Do you think?'* Sara asked mentally. *'No, they were just chance phrases.'* Hanna replied.

Thomas heard their mental exchange, and he too wondered.

Once Sir Peter left for the fields, the group broke up to unpack and nap.

"Doesn't your father take a nap?" Friedrich asked Thomas, who was helping them take their luggage up to their room.

"Not in the house. Dad usually eats a picnic lunch under a tree somewhere, and nods off with Midnight Rider standing guard."

"This house is certainly not my idea of a farmhouse," Wolfgang said.

"The tea leaves have been very good to Father and Mother. They have expanded quite a bit over the years, but it never was a typical African farmhouse. Lord Edward, Mother's grandfather, built a rambling one story manor, which Mother and Father remodeled in the fifties, adding the upper floors."

"Were you were born in Africa?" Friedrich asked.

"No, we were all born in England."

"Do you have a home there too?"

"Yes, in Berkshire, near Lyford. My aunt Marga'ret, mother's sister, and her family live there now."

"Do you go to England often?" Wolfgang asked.

"Several times a year. It depends on what is happening, but usually for Boxing Day, if for nothing else. Well, here we are. I hope you will be comfortable here. If you need anything, just ask. Paula and I are across the hall. As children, this room used to be our playroom in the rainy seasons. Mother remodeled the third floor after Jon went off to Oxford."

★   ★   ★

"What do you think, Wolfy?"

"I'm not sure what to think. I wasn't expecting any of this. I was expecting farmers, not lords, knights and ladies."

"I know what you mean. Now I understand Mr. Latham's parting words. Somehow he knew we were here for a lark and knew we were going to be surprised."

"Rick, I'm here because I want to be here. It's not a lark for me. I am very interested in Hanna. I think the bug bit me in Bratislava. I haven't felt the same about anything since then. I feel grounded and purposeful, something I've never felt before. I feel joyous when I'm with Hanna. I thought you liked Sara. You said the only reason you went on the Danube cruise was because of Sara. Were those *fluff* words?"

"No, I do like Sara. She is tons of fun – she isn't all hemmed-in or vacuous like most girls. She's smart, likes the unusual, and enjoys the same kind of humor as me; but liking a person and enjoying their company is not the same as being bitten by the bug."

"Are you sure? You were quite interested in coming here."

"Yes, of course – I mean Africa and all that! I'd never been to Kenya before because I didn't know anyone here. Knowing people makes a foreign place, like Kenya, more desirable. I don't like going places where I don't know someone."

The thought struck Wolfgang – he's right; we always travel in circles where we know someone. That's why we never got off the trains in the little towns in Switzerland – we didn't know anyone there. We only planned to go to Cairo and the Pyramids because Carl Lutz's father is a consultant to the minister of antiquities there. And we are going to Morocco to visit Aunt Charlotte, Friedrich's mother's sister, before going on to the States to visit Aunt Charlotte's son, Elmer, in Colorado. He's so right! We only talked about going places where we know people! "Well, I'm quite happy to be here. It feels a bit like coming home … after you have been gone a long time, and see things from a different perspective. It just feels right to me here," Wolfy replied.

"You didn't say anything to me about being bitten by the bug. Why not?"

"I wasn't sure if it was just a passing fancy. Hanna is so different and delightful. I thought it might just be the novelty of her forthright personality and would wear off. Plus, I still had a year and more left of my commission. How could I possibly get involved with someone who lived in Africa?"

"So, you're saying it hasn't worn off?"

"Quite to the contrary. My feelings for her have grown each day we've been together. I've never been happier in my life."

"So, where does that leave me?"

"Where do you want it to leave you? Sara likes you. I know you like her, you told me so. What is your problem?"

"I'm not ready to get involved. I have a lot of wild oats to sow; I haven't even opened the bag yet!"

"It seems to me that spending time sowing oats in your own field would have a more profitable return."

"That's true; but there is so much I want to do."

"Like?"

"Travel, explore, meet people: I'm really looking forward to Colorado; to riding a horse western style and roping steers … or some such thing."

"And we are going to do those things. I want to do them too. But then, I want to come back here. I had hoped we would always be together."

Friedrich did not reply, thinking. I always wanted us to be together too. All my life, I counted on it. I always saw us together in everything, although I never thought about one of us falling in love. "I need time," Friedrich sighed. "I have only just been set free. Let's go to Colorado without ties and see what happens."

"I planned for us to finish our tour, but I have ties. I love Hanna and I think she loves me. We have time; a few weeks or months won't change what I feel."

34 ~ Dela-Aden ~ August

"We received a letter from Jon today," Lady Mary said to Peter, as she turned down the bed. It is to all of us, but I thought you might like to read it before we share it with the others."

"Good news, I hope," Peter replied.

"Actually, it is incredible news; that's why I thought you should read the letter before the others." Peter looked at Mary, but her expression was closed; no hints there.

"Well, give it here, and stand by with the smelling salts!"

"Oh Peter, it is not bad news, just astonishing news." Mary smiled.

Peter pulled the letter from the envelope, sighed and began to read:

Peach Tree Cottage ~ Swindon
August 22, 1960

Dear Mother, Father, Brother and Sisters,

It is with great pleasure, and a bit of regret, that I write this letter to you. The great pleasure is – the local Vicar married Anna and I last Saturday, August 20th, with only Anna's parents in attendance. Our bit of regret is that all of you were not with us on our special day.

Our intention now is to travel, and when we return, to have wedding festivities during our Boxing Day get-together. Julia has offered to take care of the notices and invitations.

It is my opinion that a complete change of scenery will bring Anna back to herself more rapidly. She agrees with me, and looks forward to the total diversion of world travel to heal completely

231

We are taking the Queen Elizabeth to New York, then the train to Chicago and points west; picking up a transition cruise that is leaving Alaska for Australia and New Zealand, via Hawaii. We will then cruise the Indonesian Islands to Japan, China and the China Seas, and then to the Mediterranean, before flying to London for Boxing Day.

Anna has expressed an interest in visiting Paula's family in the States, so we will need their phone number and address to contact them. We can travel to Chicago from either Philadelphia or New York. Attached is our itinerary. Cooks has done a great job, and if we make changes, they will know where we are at all times.

We know what a surprise this must be for everyone, but we know you are with us, and wish us your very best.

We send you our love,
Jon and Anna

"You were right, Mary. The letter is astonishing – I read it twice. What a surprising decision. Well, it is their lives, and they know what is best for them. I remember the ballyhoo when we said we were going to go and farm in Africa – permanently."

"When Jon and I were working together, I had the feeling that he would do whatever it took to get Anna over her bad time. Going back to England was just the first step. He doesn't blame himself, but he feels it is his responsibility to help her mend. We are truly blessed. Our boys are men to be proud of – at any time."

Mary saw tears of pride well in his eyes. She took Peter in her arms and nestled her head on his chest saying, "They just emulate their father – many sons don't do that, so it makes us both proud and thankful. Let us pray that Jon's decisions do make Anna whole again. Can you bear another letter?"

"From whom?"

"Marga'ret."

"Is she angry at Jon?"

"No, I don't think she knows Jon and Anna are married."

"Good! I couldn't take her superior attitude just this minute."

"It is just news, but interesting news."

"You usually just tell me what is happening. Why do you want me to read this particular letter?"

"Would you rather I read the letter to you?"

"Yes, do that. Her handwriting is so flowery, it is hard to read."

Mary pulled the pages from the business size envelope. Peter asked, "How many pages did she write?"

"Four."

"Whatever does she have to say that takes four pages? Am I going to be bored?'

"I don't think so."

Woleston Hall
August 22, 1960

Dear Mary, Peter, et al;

Just a note to let you know that James and I are going on the last Alaska cruise tour of the season, departing Vancouver on the 26ᵗʰ of August. We leave England on the 17ᵗʰ for Vancouver where we will tour until we fly to Fairbanks to take the McKinley Explorer south to McKinley National Park; then a wilderness coach tour to Talkeetna and Palmer, where we pick up the cruise ship for the coastal tour back to Vancouver and points south. It is too late in the season to go inland to the Yukon. This is Holland America's last Alaska cruise of the season and the ship's transition cruise to New Zealand; so we can stay on the ship to San Diego, or even go on to Hawaii, if James has the time. Wouldn't that be marvelous?

School opens on the 29ᵗʰ, with classes beginning on the 1ˢᵗ of September for both the boys and the girls, who will stay in London with Elspeth for a few days after seeing us off. Edith will stay in Ireland until the first and return to school with Lena and her father. Julia will take Edith's box to school when she comes to pick up Spice, her horse. I'm going to miss Julia and our wonderful long rides together.

Please tell Paula that I have been riding The Sultan and I have never ridden such a marvelous horse. He has tremendous abilities and loves trail riding. He is also the very first horse I have ever ridden that wants to take care of me. I began to come off one day when he shied at a stag in the middle of the trail ... only to have him jump back under me, as the stag took off. You can't imagine how happy that made me; coming off almost 17 hands of horse has got to be a hard landing. Tell Paula too, that she was right about Ding-a-Ling too. I envy the time you spend with Paula, so enjoy it!

Time has just zipped by with so much going on in the family, with Jon, Anna and Jamie back in England. George has gone camping with some of the Cricket team to celebrate winning the tourney and title. Their coach thought they needed a reward, as well as time to wind down. Since Edith is still in Ireland visiting Lena, Jamie has only Alice for company; but, that has proved to be a blessing in disguise, for Alice has become less absorbed with 'wonderful Alice' while in Jamie's company.

This summer, Harold and Julia are spending four-day weekends at the Hall with James and me, with Julia at school the other three days.

Inkpen has turned into a horticulturist's mecca for the news has rapidly spread about the initial findings, which I hear are akin to finding the Piltdown man. International experts are volunteering their time to help. Harold has found that he has an incredible talent for organization. He has compartmentalized the expert volunteer help into work groups. Each group has a specific quest and publishes their lab notes each week, so all four groups have access to all the discovery information, allowing each group to build on the other's information.

Harold arbitrates on all differences of opinion and leads his teams into the distant past with an archeologist's care and patience.

I really wrote to tell you that Jamie has recovered quite well from his abduction in Africa. Actually, he is glad for it and the things that happened afterward, for he feels he found his raison d'être in the aftermath. He wants to be a helicopter pilot and has volunteered for the RAF Officers Recruiting Program for seniors. James was a bit surprised, but pleased once the surprise wore off. Hearing about Jamie's Africa experience might have shocked Alice out of her self-absorbed mindset; the horror of his story probably made her life seem trivial. Now, they spend every day riding together. Jamie loves

*riding The Cisco Kid while Edith is away, and Alice likes riding the
Haflinger, Stevie le-la, for he is a very willing horse with incredibly
smooth gaits. I think Alice has ridden more this summer than she
has ridden in her whole life, smiles. We never know what tomorrow
will bring, do we?*

*Last, but not least, we sent Elizabeth, Albert and Betsy off on
a Baltic Cruise. They are going to disembark at Copenhagen and
visit family in Sweden at Malmö, Lund, Skanör and Kristianstad
before flying back to London. We said we would send them a
telegram when we knew when we'd be back. I'm really hoping to go
to Hawaii — Thomas and Paula so loved it there!*

*Hope all is well in your part of the world. Boxing Day can't
come soon enough, for I miss you all so much.*

My Love Always,
Marga'ret

"I think you're right, she doesn't know about Jon and Anna. Also,
I wasn't bored. However, am I right? Will Marga'ret and James be on
the same ship as Jon and Anna?" Peter asked.

"Does sound that way, doesn't it?"

"What, if anything, do you intend to do?"

"I thought of sending Jon a telegram on the ship to let him know
of the possibility, and let him take it from there. After all, he has an
agenda and relatives may not be part of it."

"That doesn't sound like our Jon! He adores his Aunt
Marga'ret."

"Yes, yes he does — that's why I'm sending the telegram. I
remember Anna saying how much she liked Marga'ret and her views
on Africa too."

"It could be great fun for all of them — meeting up like that!"
Peter remarked.

"Yes, it could; I sort of envy them the fun of it all."

Peter looked at Mary, saw her longing, and said, "You know, the
coincidence of it all might be cathartic for Anna. I just hope Marga'ret
doesn't have apoplexy when she finds out they eloped."

Mary smiled. "It is going to be a terrific shock for her – but if Marga'ret lost everything, and had nothing else, she would still have her unshakable aplomb."

Mary shared the letters at breakfast. Wolfgang and Friedrich glanced at each other several times and smiled knowingly. Paula saw the glances and wondered ... was something going on here?

Since it was a weekday, Peter left for the fields; Mary, Wolfgang and Friedrich went down to the barn; Thomas went to the garden shed; Paula went up to work on her thesis, and the girls practiced at the pianos. In the afternoon, after tea, they would all join Sir Peter to ride with him on his inspection tour. Thomas walked behind the horses with Windy; I need the exercise, he thought. I'm accustomed to walking twenty miles a day. Soon, I will start to get fat. I've already gained some weight – probably the desserts, which I love, and am unaccustomed to eating.

Paula liked helping Lady Mary with the *first training* of the colts and fillies. She often went down to the barn before going up to work on her thesis in the little Nanny's room off their bedroom, now her personal workspace, which offered her the solitude she needed.

The after tea rides also freed up Mary's busy schedule, for Wolfgang and Friedrich delighted in riding the youngsters that were ready for mounted work. Nothing pleased Mary more than having such good riders on her young horses. Before, it had taken all of her mounted time just to get the young horses ridden twice a week – and that was only in the arena.

Mary had also noticed a positive change in the attitudes of the young horses with the change to trail work. She hated to admit it, but Wolfgang and Friedrich were better riders than she ever hoped to be, and the young horses benefited from their skills.

The afternoon hours, after lunch and a nap until tea, were the hours when Hanna, Sara, Wolfgang and Friedrich played tennis doubles, or explored the forests or went sightseeing. If rainy, a game of hearts or a musical quartet filled the hours. Friedrich had brought his oboe with him and Wolfgang used Jon's violin ... they were both quite good, although not nearly as expert as Hanna or Sara; never-the-less, they enjoyed themselves.

Everyone cleaned up after the inspection ride, and dressed casually for dinner. Most often in the evenings, Thomas told stories of his growing up with the Zuri Watu. Paula once again noticed Wolfgang and Friedrich glancing at one another in a most knowing way. She closed her eyes in the wing chair beside the fireplace, pretending to doze, and *roamed* mentally. She had gained the ability in the Valley of the Sun Spirits, but avoided using it.

At first, she just heard the conversation, then softly – like a fly buzzing in the air – she heard airy phrases: ... *I told you* ... *I know* ... *satisfied?* ... *yes!* ... Paula was stunned. Wolfgang and Friedrich had psychic communications with their knowing looks. I wonder if they even know what they are doing.

Family Tree of *Wolfgang von Hauptsborg* & *Friedrich von Hauptsborg – 1ˢᵗ Cousins*

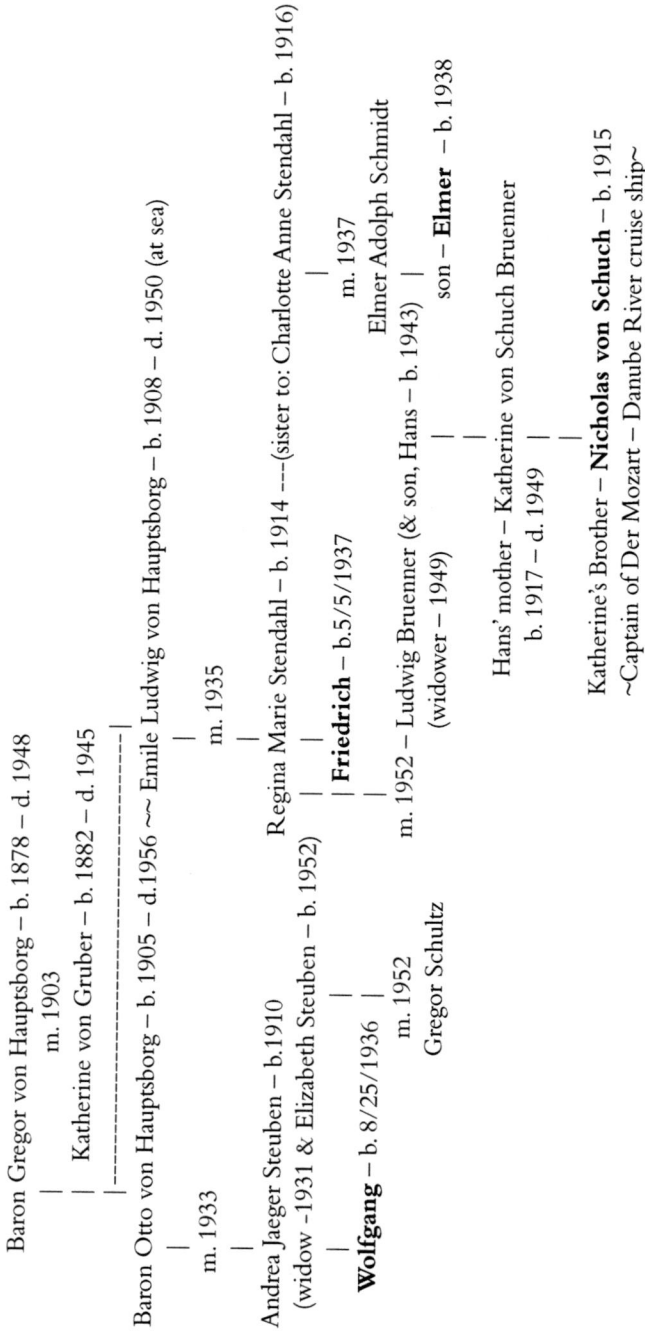

Baron Gregor von Hauptsborg – b. 1878 – d. 1948
m. 1903
Katherine von Gruber – b. 1882 – d. 1945

Baron Otto von Hauptsborg – b. 1905 – d.1956 ~ Emile Ludwig von Hauptsborg – b. 1908 – d. 1950 (at sea)

m. 1935

m. 1933

Andrea Jaeger Steuben – b.1910
(widow –1931 & Elizabeth Steuben – b. 1952)

Regina Marie Stendahl – b. 1914 ––(sister to: Charlotte Anne Stendahl – b. 1916)

m. 1937

Elmer Adolph Schmidt

Friedrich – b.5/5/1937

son – **Elmer** – b. 1938

Wolfgang – b. 8/25/1936

m. 1952
Gregor Schultz

m. 1952 – Ludwig Bruenner (& son, Hans – b. 1943)
(widower – 1949)

Hans' mother – Katherine von Schuch Bruenner
b. 1917 – d. 1949

Katherine's Brother – **Nicholas von Schuch** – b. 1915
~Captain of Der Mozart – Danube River cruise ship~

35 ~ Singular Guests

Hanna and Sara had ridden three days a week at school but had not ridden since June, and found two hours in the saddle a bit much, having sore calf muscles the next day. Since it was Saturday, the usual day for long family pleasure rides, Thomas hitched Finn to the cart to drive the girls, and to take the picnic lunch. The idea of stopping while riding and picnicking was a novel one for their Viennese guests, who had never had the luxury of riding on a thousand acres with myriad trails.

Sunday, the neighbors came for a dinner tea and a late afternoon ride, going off when they approached the lanes to home. It was a Sunday afternoon ritual, which kept the contiguous land owners in touch with one another. Next Sunday, it would be someone else's turn to host the tea.

Wolfgang said to Friedrich when they were cleaning up from riding, "I don't know what I expected when I came to Africa, but the existence of a place like Dela-Aden never even occurred to me. Did you expect any of this?"

"No, I thought we were going to be living in small thatched cottages, eating meals around a plank table and sleeping on pallets on the floor around a fire," Friedrich replied.

Wolfgang gave him a sharp glance, then smiled widely and chortled saying, "You did not!" and they both laughed.

"No, that's true, I did not, but I never imagined anything like Dela-Aden either: titled gentry, this magnificent estate, the fine horses and the upscale facilities, or the acres of tea bushes, or the vineyard and winery, nor the miles of groomed trails, the gardens, the tennis courts, the dairy, the abattoir, the sawmill, the tidy native village, the school for children, or the neighbors … who are straight out of a Wilkie Collins novel. I often feel overwhelmed."

"We are like Alice, and have been whisked to Oz," as Paula would say.

"Yes, it is a world apart … that is certain."

"Would you like to stay a bit longer?" Wolfgang asked.

"I'd like to spend the rest of my life here!"

"Seriously?"

"Seriously. However, I need to get to know Sara better. She is so ephemeral. One minute she seems interested in me, the next it's like I don't exist. It's like I've disappointed her – or I'm doing something wrong. It's very off-putting."

"I noticed that. Are you interested in her – or in Dela-Aden?"

"How do you *do* that?"

"Do what?"

"Hit the nail on the head every time?"

"I think it is because I know you as well as I know myself. Well, which is it?"

"We need to get away from this place. It is too mesmerizing and clouds the issue. I see myself happily riding and training horses every day before I write progress reports on musical prodigies in the afternoon. I just don't see Sara in that picture. Do you think she has sensed that … could it be *me* that is putting *her* off?"

"Possibly. Those fine horses are an unexpected delight and do cloud the issues."

★   ★   ★

"You are so quiet, Hanna, I'm worried. Are you okay?"

"Yes, of course I'm okay."

"Why are you so quiet? I don't think you've said more than two words all day."

"I have been thinking."

"About what?" Sara asked.

"Silly! What do you think I have been thinking about?"

"Wolfgang?"

"And Friedrich too," Hanna replied.

"Why?"

"Why! Our lives could be changing and you want to know why I'm thinking about it?" Hanna looked incredulous.

Singular Guests

"What kind of changes?"

"Oh, all sorts of things: Wolfgang and Friedrich are a bit different here in Africa, have you noticed that?"

"Yes, they are different, but I don't think they were prepared for Dela-Aden. No one ever is. It even surprises me when I return. It is a wonderful world apart."

"I do forget about the contrast," Hanna said. "Nairobi has so much squalor, and the native villages are unchanged through time. The roads are mostly potholes and the aimless to-ing and fro-ing of the natives sends a message of desperation. Then, at Dela-Aden, you find order, beauty, productivity, well-maintained buildings, self-sufficiency and happy natives. It is hard to reconcile our world within the other world of Africa."

"I am hoping they will want to stay on a bit, how about you?" Sara asked.

"I am sure they will stay on a bit, once they acclimatize to the differences. I just hope Father doesn't get put out by it all."

Sara laughed. "Yes, he is being quite nice – but it can't last!"

"He'll have them setting fence posts if they are here next week!" Hanna laughed.

"I wonder if Dad will let them sing for their suppers, since they always wanted to be troubadours."

Through their laughter, they heard a knock on the door. Hanna opened it to find Paula standing there.

"Oh, Paula! Do come in. We were just wondering how long it would be before Father puts Wolfgang and Friedrich to work setting fence posts."

"No wonder you had such a good laugh. Probably next week if they are still here." They laughed again at Paula's perspicacity.

"I came to ask a favor."

"Whatever you want," Hanna replied.

"I would like you to ask Wolfgang to tell us about himself and Friedrich – maybe in a story after dinner tonight. What do you think? Might he go for it?"

"I don't know. Ever since we met, Wolfgang has been fairly close with himself, only mentioning his sister. But it is time. He knows us, but we don't know him, or much about their families – just what

241

Friedrich told Sara in Bratislava; and nothing about their expectations," Hanna replied. "I know Dad will feel better if they open up a bit."

Lady Mary, unaware of the girl's agenda, opened the subject over coffee in the library. "I can't speak for the rest of the family, but I am simply delighted that you young men have come to visit. I know I'm being self-serving because of your riding skills, for I've never seen riders better trained in classical dressage than you two. What is your background?"

Wolfgang looked at Friedrich, who said, "You're the oldest, you go first." To which everyone chuckled.

"You must forgive Friedrich, he has been saying that phrase in one form or another all of his life – whichever way suits his purpose." Knowing smiles all around.

"I am older, but only by eight months; however that eight months did separate us by a year in school. I was born in late August, Rick was born the following May. Our fathers were brothers, both are deceased. My mother died when I was born – a sadness from which my father never fully recovered. Friedrich's mother, Aunt Regina and Uncle Emile raised me and Friedrich together. We grew up in the seaside village of Savona in Italy.

"When my grandfather died, my father and I returned to Vienna and took up residence on the estate, since father was the eldest son. The estate was self-sustaining with a few cows, pigs, chickens, geese, a buttery and all sorts of gardens. Father loved growing flowers, particularly carnations, orchids and gardenias. I did not spend much time on the estate, for I was off at boarding school. I was only home for the school holidays. I spent my summers in Savona with Aunt Regina, Uncle Emile and Friedrich. Father came to Savona for summer visits.

"Father never remarried. He spent his life growing flowers, and died of cancer. He did not suffer long. Before his death, Father had a very generous offer on the estate. Neither I nor Friedrich wanted to live in Krems. We told him to sell it, which he did, while we were still at University. Father left the disposition of the estate to the professionals, and moved back to Savona. The villa is not large, but has two wings for guests. Father took one wing, which he adapted to grow his flowers. Father died the summer after I graduated. With my permission, he had put my name forward for a commission at Schönbrunn Palace, which was accepted."

Hanna felt confused by his story, saying, "If you are an only child, how do you have a sister in Bratislava?"

"My mother was a widow when she married father. She had a daughter, who was three when they married. Elizabeth is my half sister."

"Father's younger brother Emile, married Regina two years after Father married mother, which was a year before mother died.

"Emile, my uncle – Friedrich's father, was lost in a storm out at sea while we were in Vienna. Friedrich was then thirteen. Aunt Regina later married a widower, Ludwig Bruenner who had a son Hans, who is five years Friedrich's junior. Hanna, Sara, you remember Hans from *Der Mozart*, don't you?"

"Yes, of course. Did your Aunt Regina also raise Elizabeth?" Sara asked.

"Yes. Aunt Regina cared for Elizabeth when she was home from school. Elizabeth was six when I was born and a child prodigy. She played Mozart when she was eight, and went off to a special boarding school for children with musical genius. However, she always came back to Savona in the summer, and there we became close."

"So, you are foot-loose and fancy-free," Peter said.

"Not really, sir. My sister and I share a legacy from our mother. My father put the proceeds of the estate along with my grandfather's legacy into a fund which provides scholarships for musical prodigies who have no family funding. I will begin to administer these funds with my sister next year, when I am twenty-five. I will do the financial administration; my sister will choose the scholarship recipients. Friedrich will do the initial vetting of prospective prodigies,"Wolfgang smiled. "He likes to travel."

"Where is the fund based?" Sir Peter asked.

"The fund can be administered from any place we choose. The funds themselves are in Switzerland. My sister will screen the applicants; any one of us can travel for preliminary inter-views. Since my father died, the three of us work with an investment banker, who guides our financial decisions. Father did not expect me to resign from Service ... I did not expect me to resign from Service, which has left me the opportunity to travel before I take up full-time responsibilities next year."

"I am impressed with your family's altruism for musical prodigies. With two of our own, we can appreciate the altruism of your father's decision," Peter remarked.

"It was a family decision, sir. We all agreed to it: my sister, my aunt, Rick and I, for the estate would fall to Friedrich if I died without issue."

"And do you see yourself working for the fund too, Friedrich?" Peter asked.

"Yes, sir. I will be the *inspecteur*. I will go and check on the students who are in the program. I will see that they are as committed to a musical career as we are at providing the means for them to have one. As Wolfy said, I like to travel, and will enjoy my duties. It is quite rewarding to watch the recipients mature under opportunity."

"How many students will you sponsor at any one time?" Lady Mary asked.

"Very few, I'm afraid. There may be more prodigies out there, but it is hard to find them. We send discreet letters to schools of music. Many young people have talent, but that is not the same as being a prodigy, someone that excels as did Mozart, Beethoven and Chopin, all of whom were plagued with money problems."

"Do you have anyone in the program now?" Lady Mary asked.

"Yes, we have two young men; both are presently at the Sorbonne. Elizabeth is excited about their musical genius. They are like Liszt and Chopin – good friends."

"So, when did you learn to ride?" Lady Mary asked.

Wolfgang looked at Friedrich who tossed his head and shrugged his shoulders. "We learned at school," Wolfgang replied.

"Which school was that?"

"The Spanish Riding School of Vienna."

Lady Mary, stunned, mashed her lips together to control her eyes tightening in tears as she asked, " ... but how? ... why? ... ohhhh, my!"

"There is not much to say. We didn't make the cut. At best, out of a class of eight at the most, only two might continue on ... sometimes no one continues on. Friedrich and I were in different classes, but neither one of us was chosen to continue on."

Hanna thought back to the iron discipline she had read about in the pamphlet. "Did you have to ride for two years without reins?"

Wolfgang smiled at her, "Yes, I was cut after I was given reins. It seems I did not have good hands."

"I find that hard to believe," Lady Mary stated. "I'm most impressed by your hands."

"Thank you. Even after the cut, we continued to study. We knew we would never perform, but we were determined to learn."

"How was that possible?" Sir Peter asked.

"A little known fact is that the students work hard and pay dearly to attend the Spanish Riding School. The classes are rarely full at the upper levels. So, we paid to stay until we finished at the University. We did improve, just not enough."

"Now I know why I have never seen better riders. I am just stunned at the source of your expertise," Lady Mary said, still holding back tears of joy.

Peter smiled at Mary, saying, "The young people can go on chatting, but I've had a long day today, and I expect an even longer day tomorrow. Goodnight all." Sir Peter nodded at the handsome young faces that turned to wish him 'goodnight'.

"Wait, I'll come up with you; that way I won't wake you by coming in later," Mary said, as she kissed the girls. "Goodnight, don't forget to put out the lamps."

Thomas arose saying, "It's time for me to take Windy for a walk."

"I'll go with you," Paula said, also rising.

"Well, prissy missy, you were right. Have you ever been to the Spanish Riding School in Vienna?" Thomas asked.

"No, but I've watched them in movies, and saw a special film of their training techniques at a symposium on training horses. I just knew those guys had had classical training somewhere. The young horses were spot-on–perfect with them up."

"So you said when we changed for dinner. Was Mother curious too?"

"She didn't say so, but she had to be − I mean, they were like glued to the saddles, and I never saw an aid of any kind."

"Mother must be so happy tonight!" Thomas said. "She always wanted to go to Vienna to see the Lipizzaners. To have Spanish School riders come to her must seem like an impossible dream come true. I remember when I was young, that Dad hated to leave the farm, even to go to England for Boxing Day. He never had the time for a side trip to Vienna. Mother was delighted that Hanna and Sara were going to Vienna on their tour."

"Yes, I remember her excitement when she opened an envelope from the girls and found a postcard with the Lipizzaners on it, and a circle around the place where Hanna and Sara had sat for the performance. I wonder if Mary will sleep at all tonight. What an exciting evening. I'm ready for bed. How about you?"

"Is that an invitation?" Thomas smirked.

"You will have to open the envelope to find out." Paula smiled.

★　★　★

"I thought you were coming to bed," Peter said as he looked at Mary sitting in the club chair by the window, just staring into space.

"In a few minutes, go to sleep; I'll be along directly."

Peter knew she was going to sit there until she was ice cold and then put her cold feet on his legs to warm them once she got into bed. He got up and went into his dressing room and put on the woolen knee-high socks he wore when he went hunting. Maybe with a little insulation, I won't wake up from the shock.

Mary was running the mental tape of the day's riding over and over again in her mind. Why didn't I suspect something? Even if I did, I would never have come up with the correct answer − absolutely never! The thrill of having Spanish School riders on my horses is even better than going to watch the Lipizzaners. I would never have asked for such joy. Thank you, God.

"Are you asleep," Mary whispered as she climbed into bed.

"Not yet, I'm too scared to sleep."

"Scared! Whatever are you scared of … "

"How cold are your feet?"

246

"I'm not sure, you tell me."

"Aaagh! Do you have any circulation at all?"

"Your legs feel funny … "

"Don't tell me you still have feeling in those ice cubes you call feet."

"I'm serious, Peter. Your legs feel weird."

"They are all shriveled up in fright – they may be useless tomorrow."

"I'm worried, let me take a look."

"I put on my wool hunting socks; even so, I was afraid to go to sleep."

Mary began to laugh, her mirth consumed her. Peter steadfastly refused to join in her glee; her cold feet were not at all funny to him!

★   ★   ★

"Hanna, what are you thinking?"

"Same as you, I suppose."

"Probably not; I was wondering if Wolfgang's sister, Elizabeth, was in the audience for our recital in Vienna." Sara sighed.

"Why would you wonder that?"

"It's sort of like wondering what Mozart would have thought of our performance had he been in the audience. Elizabeth would know musical genius when she hears one … or two."

"Probably, but what difference would that make?"

"None, I guess. I just can't get over this evening. Mother started the ball rolling without even knowing it. The boys clearly impressed her with their riding skills today. I'm sorry we stayed home to practice, but I needed it. I was a bit off today." Sara sighed again. "Since you were not thinking the same thing as me, what were you thinking?

"Need you ask?"

"Yes, remember, we promised not to invade each other's privacy."

"I was thinking about Wolfgang. I am falling deeply in love with him. Although, the logistics worry me. I don't want to leave Kenya, and I'm not sure he would want to live here. His résumé this evening made our togetherness a possibility. I don't want to part from you or our piano playing; I want us to always be together. Is that silly?"

"No, not silly, I feel the same way. I like Friedrich, but I don't think he likes me that way. It's off-putting for me, although I think he is a lot of fun."

"Well, we have time. Wolfgang said they plan to stay a while."

"When did he say that?"

"When I went to the lav this morning, he was taking off his boots to come in. On my way back, I heard him on the phone speaking German. He said, 'Elizabeth, we may stay here a few days longer … I'll call you before we leave … love you too, bye.'"

"That only means they are staying in Africa longer, not necessarily here."

"If you had your druthers, where would you want to stay?"

"I suppose you're right. Besides riding and tennis, there's not much else to do … except set fence posts." Once they stopped laughing, Hanna said sadly, "Yes, I guess you're right. They will probably want to move on."

Hanna thought about Wolfgang's words. He implied he could do his work from here, but what about Friedrich? How often would he be gone to check on, or interview students? Although Sara doesn't think she is in love with Rick. He does act more like a school chum, than a boyfriend.

We need to do something different … "Oh, my gosh, Sara! I've just had a great idea!"

"What? I wasn't paying attention."

"We've always wanted to go and visit the Zuri Watu. Thomas is not busy just now. It is the perfect time to go, and take Wolfgang and Friedrich with us. They would see so much more of Africa … and so would we!"

Sara sat stunned. "What a fantabulous idea! Do you think Father will let us go?"

"We will have to orchestrate it through Thomas and Paula. They will be the ones to get his permission – certainly not us! Oh, I can't wait to talk to Paula. She will know the best way to get Thomas's cooperation!"

"Thanks a lot, Hanna! Now, I'll never be able to sleep."

Hanna smiled. Nothing ever stopped Sara from sleeping – nothing! She, however, might be awake all night.

★   ★   ★

Sir Peter and Lady Mary had given up their intimate breakfasts at the table in the east window alcove of the library. Now, there were at least six of them at the table at first light. Thomas and Paula came down early, with Wolfgang and Friedrich not far behind them; and then the girls straggled in. The cold breakfast was set up when they arrived. Elizabeth would later serve eggs to order, with bacon and sausages and muffins.

Mary was now an hour later getting down to the barn, but Pompito saw to the feeding of the horses, and was busy grooming them, while Suffo and Abumi were cleaning the stalls – an on-going process. The stallions had their own barn below the lower pasture. The mares were in the barn attached to the arena with the youngsters. Mary had eight stalls for stallions or uncut youngsters, and twenty stalls for mares and horses in training. The youngsters usually sold when they were four or five years old, and their training was completed. The horses went out to pasture at night, except for the mares due to foal. The grazing field fences were six feet high, and all had electric fencing angled outwards above the top rail, to keep the carnivores out and the stallions in.

Due to the later start in the mornings, Sir Peter now had his meeting with Simmons, the overseer, while sitting under a tree eating a bag lunch.

★   ★   ★

Wolfgang and Friedrich were avid horsemen, and the pleasure of riding horses well schooled from the ground was an unexpected delight for them. Paula demonstrated the round-pen work with one of the young colts. Wolfgang and Friedrich watched; they had only worked horses on the longe lines. This was an entirely new approach and the psychology fascinated them – as did the immediate results. With three pairs of expert hands for the horses, Mary was now able to work all the young horses every other day. Friedrich was an expert at

249

driving in longe lines. He admired the Haflinger as a superior breed of cart horse and offered to work Finn in longe lines to improve his way of going.

"I think you will find him difficult," Lady Mary said. "He doesn't like men. The man I bought him from had abused him."

"What about this? You start him out. I will walk beside you and, when he is going well, I will take the reins. Then, we will see how he goes for me."

In a few minutes, Friedrich had the reins, and Finn knew it immediately. He threw his head down and lunged, for Lady Mary didn't use a check rein on the training harness. Friedrich spoke to him firmly, yet kindly: "Gemächlich Jungen … entscheiden unten … Ausstauf." It was as if he had waved a magic wand. Finn snorted, and though poised to give trouble, he settled. In two rounds, his posture relaxed: in four rounds, he carried his head with his nose straight, not poking forward, and in six rounds, his weight had moved to his rear, leaving his front legs light and airy.

The training session was not long, about twenty minutes. Once a horse does what you ask of him, and does it well – that's when you stop. Stopping is his reward for compliance.

Lady Mary had to fight tears. She pressed her lips together and went up to pat Finn and told him he was a good boy to cover up her emotions. Almost nestled into his mane, Lady Mary asked, "What did you say to him in German?"

"I said, 'easy boy' – 'settle down' – 'walk-on'."

"Why did you say it in German?"

"Haflingers are an Austrian breed; they have German in their blood. Besides, I am accustomed to speaking German when training horses. It is not the language that is important. It is the tone of your voice and the inflection that they understand. I speak *horse* best in German."

Paula, Wolfgang and Lady Mary had watched Friedrich work Finn. They knew he didn't like men at all, and expected him to show it. What they didn't expect, was the almost immediate cooperation – and then the exceptional improvement. Paula was as surprised as Lady Mary, and thought, I'm going to learn from these young men too.

★   ★   ★

Hanna and Sara finished practicing, with Hanna saying, "Let's go down to the garden shed, and talk to Thomas."

"Yes, we need to get him as our ally."

"I don't think Thomas will take sides, I think he will only do what he thinks is best."

"You're probably right, but we won't know until we ask."

Thomas and Samuel were making compost. Windy ran up to the girls, turning puppy circles around them. Thomas looked up when Windy dashed off.

"Well, hello. What brings you to my lair?"

"We wanted to see what you do down here all day," Sara replied.

"Well, there is nothing to see, unless you can see seeds sprouting in the earth."

"If the seeds are already planted, why are you making compost?" Hanna asked.

"We are making several beds using different nutrients, as Paula suggested, looking for variations in growth, since this is a first–time experiment."

"So, you are not finished planting the seed."

"No, it will take a few more days. Why do you ask?"

"We were hoping to go away next week," Hanna offered.

"Go away! Where?" Thomas asked, surprised.

"We want to go visit the Zuri Watu," Sara answered.

Thomas stopped in mid–shovel, looked at them, and asked, "Are you serious?"

"Yes," they said together.

"Don't start that – you'll frighten Samuel."

Samuel just smiled broadly. He knew about the twins speaking together. They had always done so. It fascinated the villagers.

"Why do you want to go and visit the Zuri Watu?"

"We've always wanted to see more of Africa. You speak so well of the Zuri Watu – we thought it would be a grand place to go with Wolfgang and Friedrich – as well as you, Paula and Windy."

Thomas looked at his sisters. '*Have you an ulterior motive?*'

'*Yes,*' they communed together.

251

'Would you share it with me?'

'Not in front of Samuel,' they answered.

"Samuel, Windy and I are going out for a walk with Hanna and Sara. After you get this batch of compost going, we need to start washing out the old beds."

"Yes, Bwana."

"So, now tell me what you have in mind."

"We know Wolfgang and Friedrich want to see more of Africa. We thought it would be wonderful idea for them, and us, to meet the Zuri Watu," Hanna suggested.

"And ... "

"I like Friedrich, and I think he likes me, but it doesn't go any further than that," Sara said. "I thought if we spent all our time together for a few days – or a week, we would find out if we wanted a relationship."

"Sara and I don't want to be parted. If there is a way to keep Wolfy and Rick here in Africa that would be the best of all possible worlds."

Thomas knew what they were implying; time spent together in unusual situations either brought you together, or split you apart. He'd had no intention of falling in love with Paula, but being with her every hour of every day had made him want the togetherness to go on – and on.

"Have you talked to Paula?"

"No, we were hoping you would do that."

"Why?"

"Because Paula always does what you want to do. If you want to go, she will want to go with you."

"She is busy with her writing."

"She can do that anywhere."

"Yes, I suppose she can; okay, I'll ask her. I'd like to go back too – now, before the seeds start to sprout. We have about two weeks. Will that be enough time for your experiment?" He smiled conspiratorially.

Hanna and Sara put their arms about him and hugged him saying, "We love you so much Thomas; we're so glad you're back!"

Thomas chuckled happily. He was glad he was back too, and hugged the girls close to him. If they only knew how much he had missed them, he would be their pawn, for he could refuse them nothing.

"What a day!" Paula said as she exited the bathroom. "I was transported to heaven today and I think your mother went with me."

"Why is that?" Thomas asked, smiling at his voluptuous wife.

"Oh, Thomas! Wolfgang and Friedrich are such marvelous riders and horsemen. We worked a fresh colt under saddle today, not for long, he has to get used to weight on his back; but Wolfgang just sat there mounted, not doing anything, before the colt walked off, circling the arena in both directions. On the third time around the arena, he passed left into a circle, and after several more turns around the arena, he passed right into a circle, to go around the arena. Wolfgang brought him to a halt and dismounted. The colt was letter-perfect. Your mother had tears in her eyes; even I was all choked-up. Once dismounted, the colt followed him like a puppy. It was simply fantastic … simply incredible!"

"I wish I understood what made that so marvelous, but I don't. Even so, I'm happy for you and mother. I know training the horses is important to both of you."

"Let me put it this way. Those side passes into a circle were high school movements, and this young colt has just started kindergarten."

"So the horse is a prodigy?"

"Possibly, but more plausible: the rider is a prodigy. Horses don't do anything in the classical movements that they don't do in the wild. The difference is – that they do them when asked to do so by the rider. That is the training – the horse responds to the skill of the rider. Some horses are more athletic than others due to conformation, size or shape, but all the high school movements are natural to the horse."

"I'm so happy for Mother. All her life she has wanted to go to Vienna to see the Lipizzaners; now, in a way, they have come to her. As happy as I am for the both of you, you might not be so happy when you hear my request."

"What request?"

"I was hoping to go and visit the Zuri Watu next week. We will have all the seeds planted by then, and it will be two weeks or so before we have new plants. It might be my last chance to get away for some time."

"And, what else?"

"I would like you to go with me."

"Of course, and ... "

"Hanna and Sara want to go too."

"And they want Wolfgang and Friedrich to go with them – right?"

"Right."

"Believe it or not, I don't think your mother will mind. Her training schedule is not set up to move the youngsters along so quickly. What she likes best, just now, is getting the three-year-olds out on the trails for the inspection rides. It is the one thing she can't do all by herself. So, two weeks will just be a reprieve, and if it encourages our visitors to stay with us longer, she will be thrilled."

"Why is it, that when I come to you with what I think will be a negative, you manage to turn it into a positive?"

"You see the losses – I see the gains."

"Are you hungry?" Thomas asked.

"Starved," she smiled at Thomas lasciviously, "but, what would everyone think if we didn't show up for dinner?"

"Yes, I guess it would be pretty obvious – well, can we call it an early night?"

"Is that an invitation?" She asked.

"It is, and I promise you unknown delights." Now dressed, he took Paula in his arms and held her, saying, "This pleases me. I love the idea of going to visit the Zuri Watu again. I just wish Mom and Dad could come with us too."

"I feel that they will go to visit the Zuri Watu, one day soon. Maybe, once the harvests are over. Your dad really misses Jon ... and Anna. It is good of you to help him out as you do."

"I like helping Dad. It gives us the togetherness we missed in our fourteen year gap."

"There's the dinner bell. Are you ready to go down?"

"Yes, I am quite hungry tonight." Thomas replied.

"Food won't satisfy that appetite," Paula chuckled, and opened the door.

36 ~ *The Zuri Watu* ~ *August*

"Well Rick, what do you think about that little surprise?"

"I just knew if I came to Africa, that somewhere, somehow, I was going to end up sitting on the ground in front of a fire, eating dinner with my fingers, and sleeping in a dark, smelly and bug infested hut."

"It will be something we've never done before."

"And with good reason!"

"We never belonged to the Boy Brigade or camped out, but we did climb the Alps to ski, spending a night in a tent camp. It should be better than that: no long climb, no frozen toes or fingers, and no sudden deadly crevasses."

"But, what will we do while we are there?"

"Thomas said we could hike the countryside."

"Can't we hike here in Kenya?"

"I'm looking forward to the trip. It will be different from anything I have ever done before. Have you ever gotten up in the morning and not known what to expect that day?"

"Only the days when I hiding from the headmaster at school."

"Well, I have known all my life what each new day would bring; and I want to taste the unknown. I long for the unusual and the different, if only for a week or two. I want to say, 'Yes, I willingly went into the unknown: to see, to feel and to know what doing so would be like.'"

"And if you don't yet have regrets, you might get a big dollop of those too."

"Hanna and Sara are going with us. How could you possibly think their family would expose them to harm? Are you dead-set against going? If you are, we will just have to make our apologies, and leave for Egypt."

"You would do that?"

"Yes. I wouldn't like it, in fact, I would be quite disappointed, but I don't intend to drag you where you positively don't want to go."

"Okay! Okay!! Okay!!! I'll go."

"Will you try to be cheerful?"

"Does that mean I have to smile?"

"Yes. You have to smile and laugh and be outgoing."

"I know I'm just going to hate it. It's going to be dirty and smelly and disgusting."

"I know you are fastidious, but I doubt if it is going to be anything like what you're imagining. Paula said she loved it there; that it was peaceful and beautiful. I can't imagine Paula liking dirty people."

"That's a positive thought – small, but positive."

"Who knows, there could even be other positive thoughts – and they could spoil all your negativity."

Rick suddenly laughed. "I haven't had the megrims for a long time. It must be because I like it so much here at Dela-Aden that I don't want to leave."

Wolfgang just smiled to himself, thinking: that's a step in the right direction too. Rick is always resistant to change; except for leaving Service at the Schönbrunn Palace – which he was only too glad to do.

"We are limited to one twenty four inch bag and a backpack," Paula said, as she showed the girls what and how to pack, while Thomas advised the boys. Wear a pair of stout walking shoes, and pack a pair of soft shoes or sandals; three pairs of knee socks, two sets of shorts and shirts, both long sleeve, and three sets of underwear, a warm jacket, leather gloves and pajamas; plus toiletries, a diary, a pen, a brimmed hat and handkerchiefs. Mary provided each of them with a soft wool blanket. Paula gave everyone a 3-in-1 whistle and said not to forget sunglasses, lip balm, and suntan lotion.

Thomas left to fetch penknives for them. Friedrich said, "I've packed more stuff to stay overnight with friends. Don't forget deodorant! Or bar soap or, for gosh sakes, toilet paper; a washcloth, hand towel, and a packet of tissues. Don't forget aspirin or band-aids. Do we have a first-aid kit? This is going to be a disaster!"

Since Paula had taken the DC-3 flight to Yaoundè with Jamie and Anna, which left at six in the morning, (with stops in Kisangani and Mbandaka in The Congo) three time zone changes and a two hour helicopter flight, for a total of thirteen exhausting hours, Paula suggested they take the DST, (Douglas Sleeper Transport) which left Nairobi twice a week, so they could get some sleep and not arrive at the Zuri Watu village exhausted.

Peter and Mary drove the travelers and Windy to Nairobi, where they ordered supplies while Friedrich stocked up on snack bars and toilet paper. Lady Mary had booked an early seating at the Club for dinner. The young men had brought jackets and ties, which Mary would take home with her tomorrow.

They arrived at the airport at ten for the eleven o'clock flight to Lagos, Nigeria via Yaoundé, Cameroon. Normally this was a direct flight to Lagos, but with half the berths sold for Yaoundé, the airline scheduled an interim stop. The DST arrived in Yaoundé at first light.

After a quick trip to the terminal facilities, the Land Rover jitney took them and their luggage to the helicopter pad on the far side of the airport. There, the whirlybird was fueled and ready to fly, once their gear was on board. While the driver transferred their luggage, Paula opened the basket Elizabeth had packed for them: raisin/nut scones with Bell jars of lemon tea, paper cups and napkins for a travel breakfast. She had also included a waxed paper parcel of meat scraps for Windy and a Bell jar of water for him, which Paula handed to Thomas when he returned from walking the dog.

The helicopter's lower flight path, and the godlike views of the scenery and wildlife below, thrilled Friedrich, who felt a freedom akin to soaring eagles. If the rest of the trip is as pleasant and delightful as the beginning, I'm going to have to eat a lot of humble pie, he thought. I'm having one of the best times of my life. When I think of how much I fought against it, I wonder if I really am *the stuffed shirt with a closed mind*, that Wolfy accuses me of being.

They arrived at the Zuri Watu valley as the sun rose over the rocky hills to the east of the high plateau, and shimmered across the tall golden grass, making the valley look bright and clean.

Manutu and Sashono, who were preparing for their day, again heard the whump-whump-whump of helicopter rotors, although the sound was different: heavier and deeper than before.

"It is getting busy here. A hundred years and no helicopters. In the last two moons we have had five," Sashono said out loud to no one in particular.

"It is Tamubu; I felt it earlier, but I dared not hope."

"Is that helicopter bigger, or is it my imagination? It looks huge to me."

"He has not come alone." Manutu smiled. "We are going to have visitors again."

"I like guests. I liked those young people who had problems. Maybe, when the helicopter comes back for them, it will bring some more iron pots and frying pans; then we will have a good supply."

"That is a good idea, brother. We will ask."

The helicopter shut down. The guests disembarked and Sashono greeted Tamubu, saying: "Ask the pilot if he would bring us some iron cooking pots and large iron frying pans with lids when he comes back for you."

Tamubu waved to the pilot and gave him the message. With a *thumbs-up* sign, the pilot smiled at Sashono, who nodded his head and returned the smile, signaling with his fists, by opening and closing them that he wanted twenty of each.

"Manutu," Sashono said, "Thomas has brought more good looking young people. I wonder who they are. Are the girls twins, or am I seeing double? They are certainly lovely."

Sashono and Manutu greeted Tamubu and Paula and the others in usual fashion, and led the way to the sebula. The sea of villagers parted and smiles and nods greeted the visitors; the natives were getting used to visitors from the sky.

Thomas had already explained the greeting ritual and the opportunity they would have to refresh themselves before the formal introductions, which he told them, are very important in the tribal world. You will want to state your full name, where you come from, as well as your position in life, when it is your turn. Do not omit anything of importance, he had said. Natives judge your worth by what white men call bragging.

The introductions contained a surprise when Wolfgang said, "Baron Wolfgang von Hauptsborg, formerly in Service at the Schönbrunn Palace in Vienna, Austria. My home is in Savona, Italy. Friedrich is my cousin, my father's brother's son."

It was the first time Wolfgang had mentioned his title. Tamubu translated for both Wolfgang and Friedrich, and then introduced his sisters. Even though they spoke Swahili, he told of their European tour, and the piano recital at the Schönbrunn Palace, where the girls met Wolfgang and Friedrich, who had come to Africa to visit them, and to meet the Zuri Watu.

This made Sashono and Manutu smile. They liked unusual love stories.

Tamubu and Paula helped Cenye with lunch while Sashono and Manutu took the four young people on a tour of the village. Sashono stopped often to introduce Hanna and Sara, saying in Swahili, "These lovely women are Tamubu's birth sisters, and therefore my daughters. Hanna and Sara are twins, as Manutu and I are twins, which run in families."

Manutu shared in his brother's pride, adding, "Tamubu never forgot his sisters, my nieces, remembering them in his dreams, as the little girls they were so long ago."

What Manutu and Sashono did not yet realize was that Hanna and Sara spoke Swahili. Not wanting to embarrass these kind men in their assumed oversight, the girls kept their greetings to simple hellos: 'Jambo habibi'; and 'Jambo bibi'. Wolfgang and Friedrich parroted the phrases, with gracious head nodding.

Hanna and Sara heard the obvious pride and pleasure in Sashono's voice when he introduced them; it made them feel very welcome.

'These men were Thomas's family for fourteen years; longer than we have been his family. They love him as much as we do. It is like meeting distant uncles — family you have heard about, but have never met, Hanna thought to Sara.

259

'Yes, it is quite a surprise!' Sara responded.

While Wolfgang and Friedrich did not understand Swahili, they had no doubts as to the pride and pleasure that Sashono and Manutu felt; it was so overt and sincere, that they, too, basked in their pride.

The guests leisurely explored the village, watching the natives work at making exquisite trade goods for the archeologists by the sea. After a lunch meal of fingirisha (roll-ups) they took a long nap, and spent the rest of the afternoon playing games.

The children, fascinated by the deck of cards, brought their game of stones to join the fun. This game fascinated Friedrich, for it was a game of skill, strategy and cunning, the object of which was to get five of a player's stones in a row, anywhere on the checkered cloth playing surface.

Washing up for dinner, Friedrich said, "I think I am going to like it here."

"I know what you mean, Rick. It is different — as is night from the day, but welcome in its difference," Wolfgang replied.

"I hope I never pre-judge what I don't know ever again. If I do, will you kindly remind me that a closed mind is a stupid mind?"

Wolfgang smiled. He had been wary too. He had wanted to please Hanna, and in doing so, he had pleased himself. He suddenly remembered his father saying to him: 'Orchids are flowers, but within their species, they can be as different as night to day, and yet remain a part of the genus.'

Now why did I think of my father? I have not thought about him – certainly not remembering his words – since they put his casket in the vault. Is it because I never experienced the pride a father feels for his son. The pride I felt today when Sashono spoke of Thomas? Is this an omen? Am I going to find in this alien world the honorable traits that I most admire, but rarely find in my fellow man?"

"What's taking you two so long? Dinner is almost ready. Come along now!" Thomas said outside the bachelor hut. "You don't want to appear rude, do you?"

The meal was stew. Tamubu made biscuits. Paula had cadged some white grapes from the winery for a surprise dessert. While plain, the seasonings in the stew were a palate's delight. Cenye had taken a bit of Manutu's palm wine to soak the antelope cubes, also adding a bit of wine to the pot. Even if Manutu guessed, he would say nothing, for Cenye was honoring the guests in the best way she knew how.

While the guests enjoyed Cenye's stew, Windy did not, and after a taste, walked away. Thomas soaked some of the dried meat he carried for Windy in a cup of broth, which the dog ate willingly.

The evening followed the usual ritual when guests arrived, with everyone gathering around a communal fire for a story.

Sashono asked, "Tamubu, would you tell us a story? A story about the peoples of Africa, one that will enlighten our guests."

"Do you have a story in mind that you would like to hear?"

"No, maybe a new story dealing with your travels across Africa."

Requesting a specific story was unusual. However, Tamubu smiled and began.

'In the central part of Africa live an unusual people, for they are very small. The men of this tribe are not much taller than boys, and the women are even smaller. They are Pygmies. The Pygmy legends say that their first ancestors were Adam and Eve.

'The area where they live is called the Dark Continent, because it is so inaccessible; as it is surrounded by sheer mountains, impenetrable forests and sinking bogs. The Pygmies have tanned skin, blue eyes, light hair and fine facial features, with narrow noses and thin lips. They are like no other peoples in Africa.

'Long ago, before man kept a memory of time as it passed with stories and cave drawings, the Pygmies had already lived through eons of time in Africa. They had everything they needed to live happily and well. They knew nothing of the world beyond their lands.

'One day while hunting, the Pygmy men saw a man so big, he was half again as tall as a Pygmy and wider than two boys and thicker than two women. He was sleeping on a bed of leaves in the woods. He had remnants of clothes clinging to his body. He was dirty and smelled bad. Thick matted hair covered his face; it too was dirty and smelled bad.

'The elders of the tribe came to see the man. They found him alive, but hot with fever. The men dug a pit. The women took off the giant's

clothes. The children shaved his face and head, making a fire of his clothes and hair. When the pit was finished, they lined it with elephant leaves. All together, they rolled the man into the pit, and then filled it with water. As his body heated the water, the children filled gourds and threw it away, while other children brought fresh cold water to add to the pit. They did this until the night fell, when everyone went off to sleep. The next morning the man was no longer hot with fever, but still he slept on. They covered him with elephant leaves and set the children to watch over him until he awoke. The water drained slowly from the pit. If the stranger did not wake up, he would die. Then they would enlarge the pit to bury him.

'One morning the children came to the pit and found it empty. They followed the tracks and found the man mired to his waist in a sinking bog. They went for the elders who came and hammered two sapling tree logs into the ground with rocks and then brought a sapling tree and wedged it between the logs in the ground, dropping the trunk into the bog so the man could pull himself out. He was weak, and had no strength, so everyone had to help pull on the tree to get him out of the bog.*

'They took him to a waterfall pool where he washed the bog mud off his body. They led him to their camp and fed him a bowl of stew, with a gourd of fresh water.*

'They asked the man many questions, but he only turned his head from side to side, and shrugged his shoulders. They took this to mean he did not understand them.*

'The giant soon became a problem. He ate more food than did half the tribe. The elders gathered to discuss the problem. One young boy, who listened to the debate, arose and asked to speak. This was quite unusual, but this particular boy was very clever. When given leave to speak, he said, "Why not make a bigger bow and arrows and let him hunt for his own food. We have already made a huge uumenea to cover his penis for him, so why not a bigger bow and arrows?"*

'The elders were very pleased with the lad's suggestion. By the end of the day, the men and women had fashioned a bow and arrows based on the length of his arms and his height.*

'The next day, with little fresh food in the camp, the men and the stranger went hunting. Before afternoon, the men returned to camp. The stranger had killed a duiker, enough meat to last a long time. The women had gathered nuts, tubers and edible greens. They also built a smoking shed, where the* *children smoked strips of meat using green oak leaves, and bits of bark for a smoky fire.*

'In all this time, the stranger said not a word ... in his language or theirs, which included clicks, whistles and guttural sounds as well as words.

'But the man was useful. He could lift as much as three pygmy men with one hand. He could reach fruit and nuts on lofty branches too thin to support weight. He could carry two full skins of water and two toddlers for long distances.

'One morning they found an antelope lying dead by the fire. The man was gone. They followed his spoor to a sinking bog and then it was no more. For a long time the pygmies speculated on what had happened to the man; but the question most asked, the one for which they had no answer, was — why did he leave?

'A very long time later, the Pygmies returned to camp after hunting and gathering during the day. They found a dead warthog lying by the fire pit. This was only the second time this had ever happened, and it reminded the old ones of the giant stranger, who had left them such a long time ago that the children that were then small, were now old. The others only knew the stories about him.

'Next to the warthog were many small bows and steel-tipped arrows, along with a long thick arrow with a fire-hardened tip. An old woman remembered helping to make the arrow for the strange giant when she was a child.

'The men followed the spoor of the man who had left the warthog. They found the giant with another man, a Pygmy, who spoke their language.

'This giant was young, and was not the man they had saved. When they asked why he had left the warthog, the pygmy translated his reply.

"My father was the only one of a group of explorers to survive a mapping expedition. After your help, he made it back home and became wealthy from his knowledge. On his deathbed, he asked me to come back here and return the favor with new bows and metal-tipped arrows. Now you can shoot larger game, which will feed you longer. My father died unable to thank you ... so he sent me to thank you for him.

'The translator continued: "In all the world that my father traveled, he never found a people as generous or as kind. Knowing you changed his life. Hearing him tell of your kindness throughout my life formed my character too.

263

The bows and arrows are a small payment for his life. However, the salt, cornmeal, sugar and powdered milk are my way of thanking you. For, had you not saved my father, I would not be here today."

'The elder asked the translator, "How did you find us?"

'The Pygmy translator said, "My father was a cartographer. He drew maps of places, and he drew a map for me to come back and find you, so I could give you these gifts. He made me promise not to share this map with the world. The secret path to get here will remain a secret until someone else finds his way here like my father did."

'Twenty generations later, a man would find his way through the mountains and be a guest of the Pygmy tribe, where he would find ancient steel-tipped arrows and be confounded by their presence.' ~ The End~

Thomas told the story in English, with Paula translating many of the words into Swahili. Even so, the villagers listened and understood the tale. They now knew the words, *The End*, and so began the whistling and high pitched warbles that were their form of clapping.

Sashono said, "In all my life, I have never known a better story teller than you, my son."

Still feeling the *flight* lag, the visitors were glad to toddle off to bed.

★   ★   ★

Friedrich bent over his low bed, a wooden platform covered thickly with pelts and said, "Kick me!"

Wolfgang chortled, "Whatever for?"

"For being obstinate and narrow-minded, that's why!"

"I suppose you have had a pleasant day, and are berating yourself for having resisted coming here so mightily."

"I never thought of myself as being intolerant, but I can see where the bigoted opinions of others have affected my mindset. Did you enjoy today?"

"More than many other days in my life. Different as different could be, but there was a dignity and a sense of proportion that I often found lacking elsewhere."

"Yes, that was it – dignity – but not pomposity. So glad you made me come. Good night."

Wolfgang smiled, thinking, I was prepared to tie you up and gag you, if I had to; I'm glad it wasn't necessary. "Goodnight."

★   ★   ★

Hanna and Sara were staying in Cenye's hut. Cenye preferred to sleep by the fire, which left the sleeping platform unused. It was a marriage bed, and wider than a bachelor's bed, so Hanna and Sara were comfortable.

"I think this has been the most unusual day of my life," Sara said. "I've learned more about the natives today than I have ever learned before."

"I know what you mean. Even though we have a native village at Dela-Aden, we have never been privy to their private lives, only the wedding celebrations. I can see where Thomas gets his self-confidence and strength of mind. Sashono is so kind and wise, while Manutu is forceful and inscrutable. I think Wolfgang and Friedrich are enjoying themselves. What do you think?" Hanna asked.

"I would say so – although I think they are just as confounded as we are, with shattered notions too. I would like to talk, but I'm just too tired."

★   ★   ★

"Where do you get all your stories?" Paula asked. "I was amazed at the suggestion that the Dark Continent might have been the place of the Garden of Eden. Where did that come from?"

"It came from the Pygmy Legend Keeper. These are the ancient stories, which are passed down from Legend Keeper to Legend Keeper."

"So, how do you know it?"

"The Pygmy Legend Keeper told me so when I was tending to the deep cut on her daughter's leg. I casually asked her how long they had been here, meaning the current camp, but she took it to mean their ancestry, and said, "We go back to our distant ancestors, Adam and Eve. She is the one that told me the *Giant* story too."

"Are you glad to be home again?" Paula asked.

"Home for me is where you are – this is the place of my upbringing – Dela Aden is the place of my childhood and my parents, but home for me is only with you. However, to answer your question, yes, I am pleased to be here. You know I love Sashono and Manutu dearly and always will. They made me who I am. They were interesting and exacting teachers, as you have observed, and men of honor as well."

"Yes, Manutu's wisdom is awesome, and so is his self control."

"It took me a long time to understand that control," Thomas reflected. "In the beginning, it frightened me. He was always the same, always complete, always assured, always knowing and wise.

"Sashono is a bit different in that he is reserved, yet he always sees what is right and just. Kenga and Benima are pale shadows of their father and uncle. I know that Manutu and Sashono expected me to follow one of them, most probably Manutu, but it is not to be – it is not my destiny. They understand that now, but it saddens them and it saddens me too. But life does not always go where you want it to go. Sometimes life has a purpose for you, a destiny, which you must follow."

"Yes, both of us went off our set courses, and together we are headed into the unknown."

"Life will be an adventure for us."

"What do you mean, will be – what about, has been?"

Thomas smiled as he took her into his arms saying, "Yes, that too."

★   ★   ★

Manutu said, "Brother, sit with me in my kibanda, I would speak with you."

"I hoped you would ask me. I want to talk to you too. You speak first."

"The old ways are dying. I have only Kenga for an acolyte. The young ones do not come to learn anymore. They now teach medicine in schools, although it is not the wisdom of the ages they teach. For a long time, I wished we had closer neighbors; but now, I am happy for

266

the isolation, hoping it will take longer for civilization to get here. I want us to learn, but remain the same. Can we do that?"

"I do not know. No one knows. Who knows the future? Do we even want to know the future? I am content with the present. I can only live my life, no one else's. I cannot predict the future, and I'm glad of it. I will take each day as it comes."

"You are wise. You have always been wise. I am a seeker, a questioner. How I wish I had your wisdom," Manutu sighed.

"You too are wise, but you are also curious; I am not. There is the difference."

"What do you think our guests would like to do while they are here?"

"I don't know. But whatever it is, we should not be a part of it. We are too old, and we have no zest for adventure anymore; agreed?"

"Yes, I agree!"

37 ~ Encountering Africa

The village, while busy, is quiet in the morning. People speak in whispers and go about their business silently. The morning meal of porridge, fruit and hot broth is eaten in silence, for today, their leaders have special guests, so the men linger over a second cup of broth. While the making of trade goods is not a particularly noisy job, the loquacious interaction between the workers is often marked with bursts of laughter ... and so they dallied, waiting to hear the first sounds of guests fully rested.

"Maji moto, bwana." (Hot water, sir.) Wolfgang heard the soft voice as he put the chamber pot back under his sleeping bench. Looking through the slits of the branch stems door, he saw a tripod with a leather basin and steam rising. He pulled on his safari shorts and stepped out to find a mirror on the wall of the hut over a small bench. The bench held a chamois cloth, a length of napped fabric and a disc of soap, which smelled of spice. I didn't know what to expect here, but I certainly never expected maid service. Rick is going to be so surprised.

Refreshed, alert and feeling eager for the day, Wolfy and Rick strode to the sebula where they ate the evening meal. They found Paula, Thomas, Hanna and Sara with Manutu and Sashono waiting for them.

"We hope we haven't kept you waiting," Wolfgang said, slightly abashed.

"I was quite cozy in my bed of fur skins, and I was warm too. The nights do get cold here in Africa," Friedrich added to help excuse being tardy.

Paula helped Cenye serve the porridge. The melon and bananas were already on the table with the pot of broth. "I have tea bags if anyone prefers tea," Paula offered.

"Well, what are the plans for today?" Hanna queried.

"I thought I would take you on a walk–about, so you can see the lay of the land, and the marvels of this valley plateau. Would you like that?" Thomas asked.

Sara asked, "How far do you plan to go on this walk–about?"

"Not far, about ten miles or so," Thomas replied.

"Not far? I've never walked ten miles in my life," Hanna added.

"Hmmm, well … I'll see if I can plan the walk so, if you tire, we can make it back to the village in a mile or two. Would that work for you?"

Sara sighed and asked, "What should we wear?"

"The walking shorts, knee socks, tie shoes and long-sleeved shirts that you have on are fine," Paula replied. "Don't forget sunscreen, sun glasses and a hat. Then you can help me fill the water canteens and make the lunches; bring the little backpacks I gave you."

Thomas added, "We should go soon to take advantage of the cooler morning air."

It was a glorious day. The rainy season had begun, with it raining at night. Next month, it would rain during the day too. The sky was clear and the air tasted of moisture from the heavy dew evaporating in the morning sun.

Thomas led them in the shade along a stand of woods, which stood between the village and a wide grassy clearing that ran along the length of the deep, wide river at the base of the forested mountainside to the west. "That river is full of hippos. Agurra felt the river water was the cause of village illness, so the old villages were moved to the other side of the woods about fifty years ago."

"The valley is about six miles long and more than two miles wide. The savanna here lies at about two thousand feet. The village is located near a pond, formed by spring water. "Manutu believes that our source of clean water is the reason for the good health of the villagers … and he is probably right.

"The border on the east of the Zuri Watu lands is mostly rocky hills, and the home of lion dens. A small stream runs at the base of those hills to the lake at the northern end of the valley. On the far side of the eastern hills is a vast savanna filled with deer and antelope, wildebeest, gazelles and gnu, with large areas of acacia trees for the giraffe. It is also home to elephants, zebra and rhinoceros.

"In the dry season, the African buffalo come to our valley. They like the flooded marshes near the lake. The woods beside us run the length of the valley to the lake. The hippos keep to the fast flowing river on the west. They are grass eaters and crop the grass between the river and the woods. The hippos rarely come through the woods; for fallen logs, which they are unable to cross, can easily trap them.

The rhinoceros and the elephant come through the forest north of the rocky hills on the east to graze in our valley. The deer herds don't usually come here, although sometimes we see small groups of bushbuck or reedbuck.

"Both streams run north in the valley and end in the lake, which drains into a falls through a mountain crevasse. Some of the best fishing in Africa is in that lake. Does anyone like to fish?"

Friedrich asked, "We have fished in the ocean, but not in a lake. Do you need a boat for it?"

"A boat is not necessary. The lake has a land spit made up of silt from the eons. We fish from there. It is a day's outing though. If you like, we can go fishing another day. I have fishing bones enough for all of us."

"What is a fishing bone?" Sara asked.

"It is the canon bone of a bushbuck with fishing line wound around it," Thomas said as he pulled a sample from his pack.

"Can you cast with that?" Friedrich asked.

"Yes, I attach a sinker to the line, here; and then insert this peg into the end of the bone and put cross-sticks through the holes in the peg, like this; then I swing it backhand across my chest."

"Clever, very clever." 'I say old chap, what did you do in Africa?' 'I went fishing with a bone!' 'I say, whose bone did you use?' 'I used my own jolly good bone, of course!' Friedrich had them in stitches with his parody of the upper class British accent, and facial tics and squints.

Not long after, Sara said, "What I would like is a rest."

"Me too," parroted Hanna.

"We must be wimps, but I'm with the girls," Friedrich said.

"You have a ground covering stride, Thomas. I truly believe that you are used to walking twenty miles a day," Wolfgang added.

Paula smiled thinking – or more! "There, those low rocks; that would be a good place to rest, what do you think, Thomas?"

"You wait here; I'll go scout it out." Soon, Thomas raised his hand and waved them over. He had found no traces of snakes or their land tunnels, or the sweet, sticky cocoons of poisonous spiders.

While they rested, Wolfgang asked, "How are the boundaries of the lands of the different tribes established?"

"For a long time, the boundaries floated, but as the tribes grew in numbers, and needed more food, boundaries expanded. Most of the boundaries are natural barriers, such as our mountains and the lake. In the forests, trees are marked with the sign of different tribes, or by totems placed on the trails. The savanna is usually unmarked, for the herds move constantly; but occasionally, you will see a rock with tribal signs. Most of the native villages are built in the sparse woods, where thorn bomas effectively keep out the carnivores, and where the large grass eaters have no reason to go."

They walked north. The woods thickened, and the ground became less firm. Paula knew this was the area where the river overflowed its banks in the rainy season; it was a breeding place of water snakes. "Thomas, let's walk over to that copse. I've never been there before."

"For good reason: that copse is home to a female leopard. While leopards are shy and mostly nocturnal, she might have cubs now, which could make her dangerous. We can skirt those thorn bushes and ebony trees though. The denizens there will not bother us."

"What kind of *denizens* might that be?" asked Hanna.

Thomas knit his eyebrows and scowled at his sister saying, "Weird beasts, like rabbits, shrews and cane rats, which are good eating."

"Oh, Thomas! I was serious!"

"Chuckling happily, "So was I," he replied.

"It looks like there is a path around the thorn bushes, why is that?" Sara asked.

"It is the ring the rabbits make in feeding on the grasses. They don't go very far from the safety of the thorn bushes."

271

"What do the shrews eat?" Hanna inquired.

"Ants, bugs, grasshoppers and beetles. They are the carnivores of small life."

"And the cane rats?"

"They eat roots, bark, nuts, fruits and coarse grasses."

"I don't see any nuts or fruits. Are they essential to their diets?"

"Yes. Wild blackberry vines grow among the thorn bushes with peanuts growing underground."

"Peanuts! Are you teasing me again?"

"Of course not, the cane rats love raw peanuts, which are used for bait. Some rats managed to steal the bait and buried the nuts in their holes where they sprouted."

"How do you know all this?" Wolfgang asked.

Thomas smiled at him and replied, "Manutu spent fourteen years teaching me about Africa, its denizens, its plants, its trees and the habits of each."

"Why would he do that?"

"Manutu is a Medicine Chief. His responsibility is to know about all the living things in Africa, for many plants can help heal. As his acolyte, he taught me to know Africa, and how to survive in the wilderness."

"Does being his acolyte make you a Medicine Man?" Wolfgang asked.

"Yes, it does. I love all of Africa. I never want to live elsewhere. My greatest happiness is that Paula also loves Africa, as does Windy, don't you boy?" Thomas again patted his dog.

"Do you work at being a Medicine Man?"

"On occasion ... why, are you feeling poorly?"

Wolfgang chuckled, "No, but it's nice to know there's a doctor in the house!"

Paula, Friedrich, and the girls all laughed. Thomas just looked puzzled.

Paula explained, "When someone is hurt or sick, let's say at the theatre, it is not uncommon for management to ask, 'Is there a doctor in the house?'"

Thomas, like the natives loved a pun, and delighted, laughed with them.

It was almost noon when they approached the Learning Circle. His sisters and the young men were fading. Thomas knew this was the only place that would provide safety for them while they napped; so he had asked Manutu for permission to stop here. Thomas sensed the pride that Manutu felt for his sisters, and knew their safety would concern him too. Manutu also felt that Hanna and Sara were kindred spirits and uniquely talented, as well as being Thomas's blood kin.

"This is an odd place," Hanna said. "Who made it, do you know?"

"The stones were here when the Zuri Watu arrived over a hundred years ago. No one knows why the ring of stones is here, but it has always been a special place," Thomas replied.

"Agurra – Manutu's and Sashono's father planted the aligna trees between the boulders after he buried his wife Myuma here. When Agurra died, Manutu and Sashono buried their father here with their mother.

"The circle has a very special aura. Manutu teaches his acolytes here."

Thomas's information surprised Paula. Why had Manutu said nothing? Did he fear frightening her? Are they the spirits that Manutu said dwelled in this place? Are they the spirits that come to help? The spirits that he says guide him?

Paula felt a bit breathless. Are they the spirits that took me when I first *roamed*? Are they the spirits that tried to take me away into the ethereal world? Is that what Thomas meant when he said the spirits could be jealous? Do I have something they want?

Unexpectedly, she heard: *'Yes, they want what they cannot have. They want life. Do not be frightened. They have knowledge to share with the living. We honor their memories by asking them for guidance. It is the best we can do.'*

After lunch, the girls lay down using their backpacks for pillows. The men sprawled, leaning up against the boulders, for the circle was only about fifteen feet in diameter, with the thorn bush opening about two feet wide. The circle was cool in the shade of the aligna trees, and the peace of the circle was pervasive.

Thomas slept for an hour. Normally, he only napped for fifteen minutes, or so. Windy awakened him. In two and a half months

Windy had learned not to do his business in enclosed places, except for the sandy box in his kennel, but at seven a half months his control was limited. Thomas arose and took his dog for a walk while the others slept on. It was a glorious day. The air was warm and the breeze was soft. Out in the open though, the sun was hot. We will walk back to the village in the shade of the woods. I think my sisters have had enough for one day.

I miss walking long distances, which I have not done since Paula, Jon, Kybo and I fled to Luanda in Angola to escape the mercenary. At least, nothing like I used to do with the Zuri Watu. I also feel the lack of exercise with decreased stamina. I will have to start walking longer distances at Dela-Aden. Windy will be happy for that, won't you fella? I haven't thought much about my new life. I've just gone along coping with each day. I think it's time to set some guidelines, so the good things in my former life are not lost to me.

Paula was awake when Thomas returned. She *signed* to him to move the thorn boma, for he was the only one with a spear.

"Let them sleep," she said softly. "It's so peaceful here. Let's go and sit in the shade of the woods." Walking hand-in-hand, she said, "I miss being with you."

Thomas smiled. "I miss you too, but life is different when you have company."

"I know … but company or not, I miss you when we are not together."

"A while ago," Thomas said, "I thought of all the changes in my life since I saw you hide under a laprodis plant. I don't want to lose the things that made our being together special before Dela-Aden and the kimmea."

"Oh, Thomas, I so agree with you. We must take care to see that outside influences do not change our life together. We must make a time, like in the afternoon after our lunch nap, to go for a brisk walk. We can walk in the shade of the woods trails, and note on the map the trails that need clearing. Windy would like that, wouldn't you boy?"

"I wish you would stop doing that!"

"Stop doing what?" Paula asked, surprised.

"Taking my ideas and making them your own!"

Paula laughed. "How can I stop doing that, when we think the same things?"

Thomas stopped, turned to Paula and took her in his arms. Holding her close to him, he said, "We are truly soul mates. I love you more than life. Each moment I am away from you is torture to my heart. You must promise to tell me if I ever displease you, for I would never do so knowingly."

Paula snuggled. She loved for him to hold her; it was her favorite place to be in all the world. "If I promise you, will you make me the same promise to me?"

"You could never do anything to displease me."

"Promise?" she asked.

"It's easy to make a promise that I know I will never have to keep. I promise."

★   ★   ★

Thomas asked, "Hanna, Sara, have you ever climbed a tree?"

The question was so surprising that everyone laughed. "Why would you ask such a question?" Hanna chortled, as she walked around a rock in the tall grass.

"Yes, why?" chorused the others, now curious.

"Well, in our travels today, I noticed fresh elephant mbolea."

"Manure," Paula explained.

"I think the elephants are coming to eat the tall grass here in the valley. They often do so at the start of the rainy season. Manutu and I used to climb the oak trees in this copse of woods, to wait for the elephants to come and pull the tender new shoots of vines off the trees. I think they will be here tomorrow night."

"I've never climbed a tree, and I don't think Sara has either," Hanna answered.

Thomas looked at Wolfgang and Friedrich questioningly. "I used to climb trees as a boy, but I'm a long way from being a boy," Wolfgang replied.

"Wolfy only climbed trees because I liked to climb trees," Friedrich added.

"Well, think on it. Paula and I love to hear the soft sounds the elephants make to comfort and communicate with one another. It is a sound that you never forget once you have heard it, and the sound is only heard inside the elephant herd."

Back in the village, the girls went to freshen up, while Paula went to work on her thesis. Wolfgang and Friedrich went back to their bachelor hut, washed up, and were resting before dinner when came a tapping on the door. Manutu stood there. He smiled and said, "You come, we go; bring long eyes."

Hanna, Sara and Paula waited not far away. They trooped towards the southern end of the woods, where Thomas had set up a blind, shaped like a hockey net, made out of a framework of sticks and covered with long grasses.

He motioned them to come close and to be quiet, whispering, "Over there, in that old oak tree, on a limb above a nest hole is an African wood owl. She's getting ready to fledge her chick. It is the only time when she sits on the limb that way, for she's enticing the chick to come out.

We'll move the blind out a bit, very slowly, so we can watch. You must be very quiet and not make a sound. Owls have keen hearing and even keener eyesight. The blind just looks like grass to her and grass does move. It may take an hour or more, so if you don't want to wait, Manutu will take you back to the village."

No one left. The African wood owl is about thirteen inches in height. It is a plain owl without ear tufts, with a chocolate barred breast and white edged shoulder feathers. The female lays and hatches only the one egg.

The watchers could not hear the soft reassuring garbles of the mother bird. But, every once in a while, they saw a fuzzy face with two large eyes. After several tentative appearances, the chick, now a miniature of its parent jumped to the rim of the nest hole. The mother bird flapped her wings and stretched.

Suddenly, without preamble, the young bird leapt into space … falling … then out came its wings … which stopped the fall and lifted the young bird on the breeze.

The mother owl left her perch and flew under the young bird to encourage it to seek height. The young bird's confidence grew with

276

each flap of its wings, as it followed its mother into the sky. They circled silently above the tall grass, where dipping low, the mother bird dropped out of sight. Almost immediately, she reappeared flapping her wings with a rodent in her beak. The female flew to a bare tree limb and began to eat her meal.

The youngster landed on the same limb, almost toppling forward at the sudden stop, but with quick struggling flaps of its wings the youngster managed to keep its perch. The young bird sidled over to share the meal, but the mother leapt up to a higher limb. The young owl leapt up following her. The mother owl continued the dance, leaping vertically among the limbs until she had eaten the rodent, and the youngster had cadged only a bony tail.

Long moments passed while the owls perched unmoving. Without warning, the mother bird flew silently in a deadly line over the tall grass; her fledgling chick followed her, imitating her soundless glide. The mother bird veered off, while the youngster disappeared into the tall grass.

They could see the grass tips moving oddly, but nothing more. They waited. Abruptly, as its mother had taught her chick by leaping up from limb to higher limb; the youngster leapt up out of the grass, and flapped its wings strongly to gain altitude. Up, up, the youngster went, banking steeply to come around, hitting a cross draft to fall out, but righting itself to head to the limb where its mother had alit. The youngster had a bit of a small furry beast in its beak. It offered the tidbit to its mother, who took it and gobbled it down. Long minutes later, the two owls flew off up the valley.

Paula turned to Thomas asking, "How did you know?"

"The mother owl was flapping her wings and nothing more. I knew there was not much time, and sent Manutu after everyone, while taking my blind down to cover us."

"I wish I had brought my camera," Hanna said.

"I'm glad you didn't. The noise might have stopped her from fledging the chick."

Wolfgang and Friedrich had huge smiles. Hanna asked, "Did you get a good look with the binoculars?"

"Just when the little one poked its head at the hole. After that, the naked eye gave a better picture of the events, which were quite interesting. I haven't spent much time with nature, but I'm finding it delightful. If you will show me how to climb a tree, I think I'd like to listen to the elephants rumble tomorrow night," Wolfgang added.

"Me too," Friedrich agreed. "The owl show was fascinating."

Sara said not a word. She hated heights. She didn't mind flying because she was all closed in; but she wouldn't go out on the little porch in the second floor guest room. She wouldn't look over railings either, and always walked down stairs close to the wall, or in the center if there was no wall. There was no way she was going to climb a tree. Would Hanna go without her?

That evening Manutu said he would tell a story, which he did not usually do. The villagers quickly gathered round the communal fire. Manutu was so very delighted with their guests from afar, that he had decided to honor them with a personal story.

"Many of you will know this story," he began, "some may not. It is a true story. A story of life in our village, so our guests may know us better."

'When Agurra, our father, was a young man, he suffered from a very high fever, which left him deaf. Myuma, a blind girl, had cared for him during his illness. Myuma had a natural immunity to disease, having lived in isolation with her mother, a Leper, for most of her life. Many of the sick refused to allow Myuma to touch them, and died. Of those that accepted her care, most survived, for Myuma had healing hands. When God gives us a trial, like blindness, he often gives us a superior talent or blessing to offset the tribulation. For Myuma, it was her healing hands.

'My father fell in love with this gentle caring soul. A year after he was well, they married. Two years later Sashono and I were born. Our father went to wash up in the river after the birthing, where he slipped and fell into the rain swollen stream. He could not swim and began to drown. Unseen hands helped him to shore, where he was astonished to hear the women calling out for help. He returned to his kibanda (hut) to tell Myuma the good news — he could hear again — and found her dead from extreme loss of blood. Our mother had died giving us life. Our father never remarried.

'Many came to seek Agurra's advice, with his hearing now restored. Agurra was unanimously elected to the position of chief after the old chief died — except for the dead chief's son, who thought he would inherit the *position. In our village, the man considered most worthy becomes chief — and it is not always the chief's son.*

'*My brother and I were then five years old. It was a great honor for our father, but it took his time away from us. Our father was also the medicine chief. In a short time, Agurra made an announcement: "My children need me; I am their only parent. If I am to remain both tribal chief and medicine chief, my children must go with me wherever I go. You must accept them in the councils of the elders and in the homes of the sick — unless it is a catching sickness. They will be my shadows."*

'*The council so loved Agurra that they agreed to his requests. So, at the tender age of five, Sashono and I began to learn our professions. In ten years, I too, was tending the sick, while Sashono arbitrated disputes among the young people. The villagers accepted our ministrations to honor our father, whom they greatly respected.*

'*About that time, our village was again plagued with bouts of dysentery. It weakened the strong, and often killed the weak. Father made the decision to move the village away from the river to where it is today, here by a spring and small pond.*

'*Agurra thought, and I now agree with him, that it was after the hippos came to the river, that people began to get sick. Hippos live in the water, they only come out of the rivers to feed each night, walking long distances to find grass, which is how they came to our valley — they followed the grass.*

'*It took a dry season to move the village. It was hard work. Everyone had to help, even the children. Our palisade here is not as high as it was by the river, but it keeps the carnivores out when we are sleeping, and it keeps the children safe when they are at play. Long ago, we knew there were no tribes near the valley, either for enemies or for friends. Only explorers or hunters came to our valley.*

'*Agurra made rules about the use of the pond water, which is dipped out with hardened coconut husks. The water from washing waters the gardens. All dirty water goes into the deep holes on the north side of the palisade, far from the pond. We bury plant refuse in the compost pile, and bones in the lime pit. Later, we grind them up to add to the garden soil.*

'*A low wall was built around the pond with a net placed over the top to keep out the flamingos, ducks, geese and herons. In almost forty years, we have not had one case of dysentery. Other illnesses have cleared up, and no new ones have occurred. Agurra ruled wisely and well. His legacy to us is boundless good health.*

'I tell this story to emphasize to our guests that while we live in mud and grass huts, and cook our food over open fires, we choose to do it that way. The Zuri Watu have made great strides in health and cleanliness over the other tribes in Africa and, like my father, I insist on the cleanliness that he felt produced our healthy lives.

'We do not practice ritual mutilation, nor do we allow ear, nose or lip disfigurement. As God gave us our bodies, so must we keep them to honor Him.

'We are pleased to have visitors from Europe, where they believe all of Africa to be inhabited by savages. We are not educated in the same way that Europeans are educated, but we, the Great Nations of the Zuri Watu, know how to live well, and know how to survive happily in Africa, where most white men quickly perish.

'We hope you will tell those that ask of you, what you have found here in Africa. We hope you will be honest and open in your appraisal of us.'

~ THE END ~

After long warbling and whistles and a bit of applause, Wolfgang arose and asked, "May I say a word?"

"But of course," Manutu replied.

"Will someone translate for me?"

"I will translate for you," Thomas replied.

"We want to thank the Zuri Watu for welcoming us into your village with such warmth and friendliness. I'm sorry to say, that the stories in Europe would have all Africans in the bush as cannibals." (Surprised laughter) "However, after meeting the Kikuyu in Kenya, we knew the stories were not universally true." (Delighted laughter) The pun, the native form of a joke, never escaped them without appreciation. *The pun here being ... The Kikuyu were never cannibals ... but, maybe the rest of the African tribes were.*

"It is very true what Manutu has said: ' ... in Africa most white men soon perish ... ' whereas the black man simply thrives in Europe. I say this to point out that while Europeans know Shakespeare, Euclid and the Tang Dynasty, they do not know Africa. Almost anyone can survive among a people where there is no threat to life, limb or health, which certainly does not apply to the continent of Africa. Every step a man takes here is fraught with danger: by snake, spider, animal, pestilence or carnivore. The African native has learned to live with these dangers, without obliterating them … to me that is more of a sign of education, than is the achievement of total annihilation of God's creation, for comfort's sake." (Warbling and whistling from the listeners.)

"We are pleased to be your guests. We hope we do not dishonor this privilege in any way, or through our ignorance of your customs. Asante!" (Thank you)

Again a great warbling, whistling and a smattering of applause. Thomas then added in Swahili: "So you see – not all white meat is good to eat!" The spontaneous laughter was hilarious. Even Manutu and Sashono had to laugh. The *in* humor surprised Paula, Hanna and Sara. They had never heard it before, and found it surprising.

★　★　★

In mid-afternoon of the next day, the children heard loud animal noises coming from the river. They favored the girls, who spoke their language, and came to take them to the river saying, "The hippos are mating, come, see!"

It was a fascinating scene. The water roiled in all directions and huge splashes of water flew upward as the two-ton beasts plunged and rose and plunged again. They twisted and leaped, making waves that crashed against the banks of the river. Hanna noticed a baby hippo much too close to the action. She left the jumbled boulders surrounding a huge termite mound to see if the little one was in any danger. She did not know that the bulls will often kill the calves in their mating rage. There is nothing meaner in all of African than a bull hippo when mating. He is vicious and deadly. The thrashing subsided, for the bull had gone. The calf returned to its mother, and the cow returned to the preferred shallow waters closer to the banks. Paula saw the cow's normally grey hide had long slashes of pink flesh showing – love pats from the bull?

Hanna watched the cow and calf not far from a groove in the bank of the river. The children were still atop the jumbled rocks pushing sticks and pebbles into the monolithic termite mound, an incongruous formation. Hanna heard a grunt, and turned to see what made the noise. To her horror, she saw the bull hippo half way up the wide furrow and coming towards her. Absolute terror held her immobile. The children also heard the grunt and hollered, "*Endelea! Endelea upesi!*" '*Run! Run quickly!*' Hanna stood stricken to stone by the sight of the enormous beast as it lumbered up the gully. Its eyes were red, his teeth were incredibly long in the wide open jaws and his loud grunts were terrifying.

Paula knew Hanna could not outrun the bull hippo. While huge and lumbering, they are incredibly fast on land. "**Hanna, run behind that tree trunk! NOW!**" Paula cried out.

Hanna looked where Paula pointed, saw the tree and, without looking at the hippo again, ran for the opposite side of the trunk. Instantly, Paula leapt for a tree limb, swung up and had a foot on the branch and raced to Hanna. She dropped down, hanging by her knees, above Hanna. "Hanna! Grab my wrists!" And swinging down, Paula caught Hanna's outstretched hands at the wrists. Hanna locked on. The hippo had lost sight of Hanna until he was abreast of the tree. He now turned, gaping maw open, bellowing loudly, and charged her. Paula lifted Hanna off the ground and swung her back and forth like a pendulum. At the limit of the pendulum swing, Paula let go saying, "Let go when I let go, and grab that limb!" Hanna did as she was told, landing as neatly on a limb as an acrobat sitting on a trapeze. The hippo had lost momentum in his turn, but regained it charging his trapped victim. He bellowed with rage as the object of his rage rose up out of his reach.

Long moments passed before Hanna, stunned and shaking, could ask, "How did you do that?" The children, still safe on the hill of boulders, were cheering wildly. The bull, venting his frustration, charged around before going back down the groove to find something else to attack – another male hippo probably.

When the hippos moved off, the children and Sara ran to Hanna and Paula. Chattering excitedly, they all hastened back to the village.

The children couldn't wait to tell this exciting tale to their parents and friends.

Paula gave Hanna and Sara hot broth with kimmea in her kibanda, where Paula asked the girls not to tell what happened. It would only make Thomas angry with her, for putting them in harm's way.

In no time, the girls were asleep, and slept until dinner. Since Paula had saved her life, Hanna had no option but to do as she asked. Sara, had, in the meantime, decided that she was going to climb a tree to hear the elephants. After Paula's bravery, her aversion to heights seemed silly and childish.

★   ★   ★

Paula made hot broth for the canteens, adding a bit of kimmea — just enough to relieve trepidation, if any. Hopefully, there would be no rain tonight. The sky held some stars and a rising crescent moon gave just enough light to make out shapes against the darkness.

Oak trees are not hard to climb. They have many stout limbs in all directions. The hardest thing is reaching the first limb, which, in Africa, is often far off the ground. Thomas found a tree with a large rock at the base for Sara to begin her climb. With a rope around her chest and under her arms, she was able to walk herself up the trunk while being hoisted from above. Paula went up first, demonstrating technique; Sara followed, doing as Paula did, but she was terrified. Choosing bowers in the last of the fading twilight, Sara sat on a wildebeest hide while Paula tied her to the tree trunk. Paula felt her shaking had nothing to do with temperature, and sensing her fear, took plenty of time to get her settled. With her warm jacket and a thick wool blanket, Sara would be warm. Friedrich faced Sara from an opposite perch. He had climbed with confidence, and had helped to pull Sara up. They were high enough here to avoid curious elephant trunks seeking the delicacies of the young green vines.

Thomas settled Wolfgang and Hanna in another oak tree about fifty feet away. Wolfgang had belayed the line while Thomas climbed, and both had helped Hanna walk her way up the tree trunk. "Now, that is the way to climb a tree!" she laughed.

Thomas chose a tree that formed a triangle so he could see both trees and the occupants easily. He knew Paula would soon join him.

Once settled together, two to a tree, soft conversation followed. This was the first time the girls were alone with the boys, if you could call being up a tree with someone, being alone with them. The idea was so unconventional it made them feel a bit jolly and silly. Paula shushed them, saying, "Speak only in soft whispers, sound carries at night and elephants have excellent hearing."

Paula always wore her climbing belt when outside, even when she went riding. Her father had invented it for their cliff face climbing. It was how she had escaped the Ndezi without leaving a trail. She now tossed the grapple to a tree limb and swung over to a limb below the grapple. She freed the grapple and worked her way through the tree to have a clear toss to another tree. In this way she used the grapple to swing over to sit beside Thomas.

Only Sara, tied as she was to the bole of a tree, saw Paula do this. Her surprise stopped her quivering. Her mind went blank from astonishment.

Nestled together, Thomas said, "I hear you had an exciting time today."

Paula sighed, "Who told you?"

"It is no secret, the whole village knows. The children were so excited."

"I was so spellbound by the hippos; I didn't even notice Hanna walk away."

"Yes, mating hippos are one of the most awesome sights in Africa. I have watched them myself, completely engrossed. Where were Wolfgang and Friedrich?"

"Resting up for tonight probably, I'm not really sure. The children seem quite enchanted by your sisters – being twins and speaking Swahili – they seek them out. It is not the first time. They took them away the other day to watch a goat having babies."

"Yes, I have noticed their fascination for Hanna and Sara. You do know the villagers will never again think you are just an ordinary woman. The story will become a legend, and you will always be treated with deference."

"Are you angry with me?"

"Silly puss, I'm so proud of you, my heart aches."

Paula nestled closer. "Will you hold me while I nap?"

"I will hold you until the end of time – you have only to ask."
Paula sighed; content in his love and warm in his arms, she dozed.

★   ★   ★

"I heard of your exciting day today," Wolfgang whispered to Hanna. "Africa is so unpredictable."

"I was silly and foolish to leave the safety of the boulders. I didn't know that bull hippos became so aggressive while mating that they would challenge someone on land. I had to learn the hard way. Thank goodness for Paula! She saved my life!"

"So I heard. Is it true she traveled through the trees as fast as on land?"

"It must be; I was barely behind the tree trunk before she was there with hands outstretched to me. It all happened so quickly, I have trouble remembering exactly what did happen. One minute I was on the ground with a hippo charging me, and the next I was sitting on a tree limb out of harm's way."

"I remember Thomas's story about how he met Paula, the evening we arrived at Dela-Aden. I thought he was embellishing, apparently not!"

"Thomas does not embellish or exaggerate about anything. If he says it, it is true."

"I'm pleased to be here – in this village – and in this tree with you. I'd like us to spend more time alone together. Would you like to go for walks, like we did in Bratislava?"

"I'd like that, let's plan on it." Hanna smiled.

★   ★   ★

"Sara, are you cold?" Friedrich asked.

"No, at least I don't think so."

"Then why are you shivering?"

"I'm scared to death. I hate heights. But after Paula was so brave today, I decided to come out to hear the elephants too. I think it was a mistake."

"Would you like me to come over and sit beside you?"

"Is there enough room over here for you?"

"Let's see … if you sit here with your feet resting on this limb, there will be enough room for me to sit beside you. Will that work for you?"

"You have to untie me."

"Paula tied you?"

"Yes, I asked her to – it made me feel safer."

"Do you want me to tie you again?"

"No, you'll be next to me that should be security enough."

"How long have you been afraid of heights?"

"As long as I can remember; it's mostly balconies and railings that bother me, but being in a tree with nothing under me feels just as bad – but I don't mind flying."

"Well, you seem to have stopped shaking now. Are you comfortable?"

"Yes, thank you. I think talking to you is helping too."

"Well then, I shall remain here next to you – if you like."

"Yes, I like."

"Are you feeling drowsy?"

"Yes, a bit."

"Then put your head on my shoulder, and I'll put my arm around your waist. Will that make you feel better?"

"Yes, I'd like that too. Tell me about yourself, what you want to do with your life, now that you're not at the palace anymore."

"Not tonight. We should be quiet. We can talk tomorrow."

★　★　★

"What a night! I think I'm going to sleep all day. I thought the elephants would never come. It was four o'clock in the morning when I awoke to rumbling. Sara was so scared, that I sat next to her, holding her, until she fell asleep on my shoulder. I couldn't move all night, and it's made me stiff and sore – but she smelled nice and I liked that."

"Hanna and I chatted for a bit, and then we dozed. I loved hearing the elephants rumble. What a special sound, so calming and soothing. Did you feel that too?"

"I did, and what's more, so did Sara. She was tense all night, and then when the elephants came, she finally relaxed. If we could bottle that sound, we could sell it."

"You know Friedrich, that's not a bad idea! I'll give it some thought."

★ ★ ★

"What are you going to do today, Sara?" Hanna asked.

"Sleep — aren't you tired?"

"Yes, but I'm not sleepy. I'm too excited. Wolfgang and I are going for a walk. Thomas is drawing a map of places that are safe. He says we must take warriors with us, just in case."

"That makes sense. Once outside the palisade, anything can happen."

"Did you like last night?" Sara asked.

"I loved it. You were so brave. I'm glad you went with us. Was it really awful for you?"

"In the beginning, yes. Then Friedrich put his arm around me and held me and I was fine; I even dozed."

"Did you like hearing the elephants?"

"Oh, that sound was so marvelous. I felt at peace listening to it. What a wonderful night, I will never forget it!"

Hanna gave Sara a kiss on the cheek, saying, "You have a good rest; I'll see you later."

★ ★ ★

As they walked along the edge of the woods, Hanna asked Wolfgang, "Are you enjoying your visit with the Zuri Watu?"

"Yes, very much so. I didn't know what to expect, but I never imagined it would be like it is: a kind of Utopia, a mountain Eden. Have you ever read Sir Thomas More?"

"Yes, and yes, it is utopia, but it is not regulated and austere. It is open, friendly, and interesting. At least the children are. The adults seem a bit reserved," Hanna replied.

"I think it is because they don't know what to say that would interest us. If we were out together, one on one and I spoke Swahili, I think they would be different."

"You're probably right; they worry about offending us too. They know as little about us, as we know about them!"

"The campfire stories are wonderful. What a delightful way to share the past, the present and the incidents of life. I have spent more time listening to the stories of the Zuri Watu than I ever spent listening to my father. We never got past the everyday pleasantries. I didn't know him, and he didn't know me. How rich and full their lives are here ... with strong family ties.

"It has opened a new way of life for me. I feel more at home here that I ever did at the manor ... and while I love Savona and my Aunt, she never interfered with things the way my father wanted them, which was no more than having a polite relationship with me. It was even worse for my sister. He treated her like a visiting acquaintance that had stayed too long. My father's attitude was difficult for both of us, but then we were away at school most of the time. Here, I feel as if I am family. Do you think that is silly?"

Hanna's heart went out to him. "No, not silly. I cannot imagine growing up without the love of my family. No wonder you and Friedrich are so close."

"When my father was not around, Aunt Regina treated me the same as she did Friedrich, and I love her for that, but it just wasn't the same as having a mother and a father. Listen to me going on – I'm not feeling sorry for myself, I'm just comparing situations. I like it here. I feel welcome here – as welcome as I feel at Dela-Aden. But Dela-Aden is like a dream – just too good to be true. No other place has ever pleased me so much, which is why Friedrich and I are going to finish our tour once we return to Dela-Aden.

"It was you that brought me to Africa; I want to make sure that it is you that will keep me in Africa. Am I being too forthright?"

"Stay on for a bit – before you leave to finish your tour. Make sure you want to come back for the right reasons. We don't know each other very well. I only know that I enjoy your company more than anyone else I have ever met, but I have not met many young men, and you and I have not spent much time together. Can you give it a week or so, before you go?"

"I will talk to Friedrich. Although, I don't think he is in a hurry to leave Dela-Aden either, nor am I sure of his reasons."

"We will just enjoy our time together, as friends. It is best that way. We could continue our walks together, if you like. I'll ask Thomas if that's okay."

"Yes, please do that," Wolfgang replied. "I like walking at the edge of the woods, with all the birds and their myriad sounds intermingled with those of the tree dwellers and monkeys. I like the orchestral sound of the animal calls intermingled with the birdsong."

★   ★   ★

The days settled into a pattern. The young couples took a long walk, usually in the mornings with a warrior escort. Windy began to follow Sara, so Thomas allowed her to take him on their walks, but only on a lead, so he wouldn't go off coursing after a rabbit or a fox.

Paula worked on her thesis. Thomas helped Manutu with patients or made medicines. After lunch and a nap, the young couples played Hearts, and drew a crowd of children, who brought their game of stones, and sat on the floor of the sebula to be with them.

At times, Paula and Thomas thrilled the children by playing a game of stones with them, usually allowing the children to win. It was an extremely pleasant and relaxing time.

Thomas also drew pictures of the children, and on each child's picture he wrote the child's name, which pleased them mightily.

Sashono had taken to teaching the children the alphabet as a chanted game, as in: A is for asante (thanks); B is for bwana (sir); C is for chungu (chamber pot); D is for dawamtu (medicine man): E is for Enugu (the soldier's home); F is for fingirisha (flat bread roll-ups). Paula took the chanting game a step further. She used words that began with the same letter in both languages and added them to the chant: A is for afisa – aide; B is for bwana – boss; C is for chui – cheetah; D is for derweshi – dervish; M is for mbolea – manure. The children learned quickly.

★   ★   ★

Hanna and Wolfgang walked in the shade at the edge of the woods, in front of Sara and Friedrich. Hanna said, "You told us you would begin administering the Trust your father set up when you are twenty-five. What is it that you will do?"

"Charities must keep many records when dispersing money. My sister is co-administrator of the Trust right now, but Elizabeth doesn't like bookkeeping. She is first and foremost a musician, as is her husband. We agreed to hire a Swiss Bank that specializes in Trusts. They take a small percentage based on the funds distributed each year. The arrangement has worked out so well that Elizabeth wants to continue with the Swiss Bank after I reach my majority. But, I already told you that. Could I oversee the Trust from Kenya? The answer is yes."

"Other than administering the Trust, do you have any other goals in life?"

"Six weeks ago, I thought I would be in Service at Schönbrunn Palace for another two years. I have not yet gotten used to the sudden freedom of choice – to do mostly as I please. I'm taking it one day at a time."

"But there must have been things you wanted to do when your term expired."

"Yes, Friedrich and I wanted to travel. He is anxious to go to the American West and be a cowboy."

Hanna chuckled, "Now, that is a surprise!"

"Not really, both of us love horses and the different disciplines fascinate both of us; same animal, just different ways of riding, not necessarily better or worse – just different. That was the only good thing about the manor house near Krems. Father kept a pair of Andalusian geldings as carriage horses. Gorgeous beasts and both were trained to saddle as well."

"What happened to them?"

"A neighbor bought them. They have a good home now, where they get far more attention. His wife and daughter ride and are thrilled with the lads."

"If there was one thing you could do besides travel, what would it be?"

"That's a hard question for me to answer. Not that I don't have an answer – it's just that the answer might seem self-serving. I'd rather not say – does that bother you?"

"No, not at all. I don't want to know anything you don't want to tell me."

"I talked to Friedrich. We will stay a few days after we return to Dela-Aden, before going off on our tour. We reversed our itinerary to do Egypt on our return to Africa. Rick is anxious to go to America.

His cousin, Elmer, is expecting us in September. He says the colors of the deciduous trees are spectacular in the fall. Have you been to America?"

"No. It is one of the places that is high on my list. Mother loved the redwood forests, and says they are a place out of time." Hanna paused. "Are you planning to go to California?"

"Yes, we intend to cross the country to Colorado by train and then on to California. Might I ask you a few questions?" Wolfgang smiled mischievously.

"I'm an open book, but ask away."

"Who you are and what you can do is an open book, but what you want is not yet written on the pages. Do you know what that is yet?"

"Simple things: live at Dela-Aden, play the piano, travel a bit, marry and have children. I hope Sara and I will always be together, but is a decision for fate to make. I just go on the assumption that we will be together."

"What kind of man do you want to marry?"

"That's a sneaky question. I only know the character traits he must possess: first and foremost, he must be kind and a gentleman; secondly, he must have an open mind, a sense of humor, and be intelligent; and third, he must love me with all his heart, mind and soul ... as my father loves my mother ... as Thomas loves Paula ... as my uncle James loves my aunt Marga'ret. I would rather be an old maid than settle for second-best in love from a husband."

Wolfgang smiled thinking; I might stand a good chance here. I'm besotted with this forthright, open and unpretentious creature.

"Any particular means of support appeal to you?"

"Yes. A means of support that would allow him to live at Dela-Aden. I know that sounds selfish, but I want to keep playing the piano with Sara. Right now, it is our lives, and I would be dreadfully unhappy if I was unable to play the piano with her."

"Where does the piano fit in, on your list of priorities?"

"I suppose it is number two, after finding a man who will love me completely. I never asked you, but what did you study at University besides learning to speak five languages fluently?"

"I'd rather not say."

"Good heavens, why ever not?"

"You might think I am pandering to your desires."

Hanna laughed. "And what would be so wrong with that?"

"Nothing ... however, I would not want you to think I was stacking the deck."

"I would like nothing better than for you to think you could stack the deck ... if you knew that I knew that's exactly what you were doing. So, what was your major?"

"Zoology."

"Oh, my gosh! We must keep that a secret from Mother, or she will run to the local witch to get a love potion for your tea!"

Stunned by her words, Wolfgang erupted into laughter. He laughed as never before ... and while the glee consumed him, he thought – she is the woman of my dreams. I cannot help but love her. She is my sun, my moon, my stars. She is the fresh air I always yearned for – the humorous titillation my mind craves – and the veracity needed to comfort my soul.

Wolfgang's delighted laughter was compelling, and Hanna began to laugh with him. They could not stop, and ended up falling to the ground from laughter weakness.

The native warriors laughed with them, as did Friedrich and Sara when they saw them fall to the ground writhing in mirth.

"I say, old bean, is this a private joke?" Friedrich asked.

Wolfgang could only shake his head, yes, for the laughter began to consume him again.

★　★　★

"Well, how was your walk?" Paula asked as the couples returned.

"It was a bit different," Friedrich replied.

"Oh, why's that?" Paula asked

"We just sat on the ground and laughed."

"What was so funny?"

"I don't know, Wolfgang won't tell us." Paula chuckled – was he was serious?

★　★　★

"How are you feeling today?" Hanna asked Sara.

"I feel good. I was really tired yesterday. I think my nerves just wore me out."

"You were so brave. I'm still surprised that you stayed in that tree all night."

"I'm so glad I did. Not only to hear the elephants, but to deal with my fears. Coming here has been so cathartic for me," Sara said. "I feel wiser, more content."

"So do I. I wish father could see this village and meet Manutu and Sashono. He would be so impressed with them. They have the kind of life here that he envisions for the Kikuyu at Dela-Aden, but better ... for the natives here, while shy, do not feel inferior."

"The natives here have not had to deal with English morons acting superior."

Hanna chuckled. "Don't say that in Nairobi! They'll put you in a straight jacket thinking you've gone 'round the bend."

"That's what I mean – closed minds and superior attitudes ... my way or the highway! Why are the English so arrogant?" Sara asked.

"You never heard me say this ... okay?"

"Say what?" Sara asked curious, then agreed. "Okay."

"England is a tiny country, an island. They're inbred to the teeth ... " realizing her pun, Hanna giggled. Sara caught her double meaning and laughed, saying, "You have that right!"

Hanna continued, "The only thing they have had down through the ages is their superiority, which made them seek out other places to dominate. It is a dreadful sickness, and while we were in school, I was delighted that many of the students came from foreign countries. I find the English quite boring with their closed minds and arrogance."

"But, Hanna ... we are English!" Sara said.

"I prefer to think of myself as an African."

"Never say that to Aunt Marga'ret. She will have you committed."

"See! That's what I mean, Sara! Closed minds and superior attitudes, which add up to stupidity! If they could only see what bumptious fools it makes of them."

"Where did all of this vituperation come from?" Sara asked.

"It comes from seeing the difference between the Kikuyu and the Zuri Watu. The difference between the down-trodden and the natural order."

"I think you have tunnel-vision, Hanna. Think of all the other tribes in Africa, the ones that have little English contact … the cannibals; the ones with distorted body parts; the ones who practice mutilation rituals on women. I would say the Zuri Watu are a race and men apart from most of tribal Africa, except for the Pygmies. I do not think they are the norm. I do, however, agree that most of the English treat the Kikuyu dreadfully. Father has done right by them. He has started a trend and he hopes the trend will grow. Father is English to the core, and so is Mother," Sara expounded.

"True … but they are not superior, condescending or rude."

"That is because they love Africa and can envision dignity for everyone."

"As you just said … that is because they are in Africa and do not have to deal continually with bumptious-osity."

"Well, are you ready to go? Hanna asked. It's time for our walk. I am sorry this is our last day. I loved watching the elephant herd graze from the Learning Circle. Thomas told me the sitatunga have been grazing in that boggy area between the lake and the river, for the antelope feel safer when the elephants are nearby," Hanna added.

"Maybe we can walk that way and get to see them."

"We'll ask Thomas; see what he says. However, he has expressed the opinion that it is best to stay a long distance from the elephants."

38 ~ Good-bye & Hello

"I like eating breakfast here in the library with the sun rising through the trees and washing the view with golden light. While I miss our family and guests, I feel comfortable in our old routine," Lady Mary remarked.

"Well, today we go to Nairobi to retrieve our travelers. I'm glad you decided to stay over; I hate driving those pot-holed roads at night!" Peter replied.

Mary looked at her husband, thinking. Is he getting forgetful? Or is he so parsimonious that spending the night in Nairobi had to be my idea – when it was his. Not to let him get away with it, Mary said, "I'm glad you like my idea, I reserved the penthouse suite. Since we are going to stay over, we can also get some shopping done."

Peter gasped in his coffee cup. "When did you do that?"

"At the same time, I decided to stay over in Nairobi, I suppose."

Peter gave Mary a sharp glance, but refrained from a rejoinder. Instead he changed tack, "What time is the plane due in? I forget, did you say four?"

"No, I said six. We should leave here at four. We have reservations at the Club for dinner at eight. I asked Cyril to join us, do you mind?"

"Good heavens, no. Why would I mind? I enjoy Cyril, he is good company."

"Yes, he is that. I often wonder why he never married."

"He told me it was because he was almost fifty years old when he met Paula."

Mary's turn to sputter in her teacup. "He said no such thing to you – I don't believe that!"

"As a matter of fact, you're right. He said it to Jon, and Jon told me."

"Peter, we are so blessed! Thomas is back, and such a marvelous person … bringing Paula with him, who is a true wonder. If, in all those years of suffering … if only we'd had an inkling of the future – how delightful it would be … I'm ever so grateful."

"I didn't think there could ever be a positive side to our suffering. However, you are right, Mary, we are truly blessed … oh! Look at the time; I have a lot to do today. I'll be up at two to clean up; maybe we could have tea before we go?"

"Yes. That's a good idea. It will keep us to dinner."

★   ★   ★

With repetition, they were getting the flying into Nairobi into a set pattern. They now knew what not to do … and were in and out of the terminal quickly.

"We are having dinner at the Club with Cyril," Mary told the weary travelers, "but first, we will go to the hotel to clean up and change. Since you have Windy with you Thomas, I reserved the penthouse suites. You and Paula will have the old suite with Wolfgang and Friedrich; we will take the one on the other side with Hanna and Sara," Lady Mary explained. She had heard Peter choke a bit when she said she had reserved both penthouse suites. "It will be so convenient to open a door and walk across the hall to be together. Is anyone, besides me, interested in going shopping tomorrow?"

The idea immediately delighted Hanna and Sara, with Wolfgang and Friedrich echoing their approval. They needed toiletries, new underwear and socks.

"I'm thinking of a number from one to ten," Mary said. "Each one of you must take a guess at the number." Mary had been doing this with the twins all their lives, and once again, it seemed appropriate.

The number was four, and Wolfgang chose four. "Well, Wolfgang, you get to tell us a story about your visit with the Zuri Watu."

Wolfgang had enjoyed the story-telling with the Zuri Watu. He took a few moments to compose his thoughts and then began:

'In a place forgotten by time; in an Eden surrounded by mountains, rocky hills, lion dens, a lake and a primeval forest, there is a high, wide and long plateau. Here, the people of the Zuri Watu live in good health, peace and harmony. The valley is a haven, a secret place, and for a hundred years or more,

almost unknown to outsiders. It is a place so remote and pristine that it gives the aura of a long step back in time ... a step back to our origins ... '

Wolfgang held the listeners in thrall with his vision of the world of the Zuri Watu and his observations of life in their village – he left out nothing. The usually frustrating rush hour traffic in Nairobi, where driving rules and courtesy are – *every man for himself* – went unnoticed in the telling of his tale, for he held his listeners spellbound, and no one wanted his story to end.

All too soon, he said, ' ... *it was the epiphany of my existence; the time and place where I came to know myself, and to know the path I wanted to follow in my life. The End."*

The applause and kudos of: "Well done!" "Marvelous!" "I wasn't there, but I saw it all, a delightful story!" And the comment that mattered most from Hanna who said, "You have the soul of a poet." Her eyes were shining with admiration.

★ ★ ★

Reaching the Mayflower Hotel, Sara asked, "Mom, we are really tired, would you mind if we didn't go to dinner at the club?"

Thomas asked, "Are you too tired to have Windy with you?"

"No, of course not, Windy is my pal too – aren't you, oh hairy one?" Sara replied, as she took the dog's long face in her hands and gave him a kiss.

Windy whined and wagged his tail. For some unknown reason, Windy had decided that Sara needed his protection, and he often shadowed her.

Friedrich asked, "Did you bring back our jackets and ties for dinner?"

Mary's smile vanished as she said, "Oops, I forgot about that, I should have just left them in the boot ... Peter, shall we just have dinner in the hotel?"

"I don't think so, dear. We made a reservation, and Cyril is expecting to join us there, with the Mortons. Why don't you young people just stay here for dinner? You probably want to go to bed early anyway. It was a long flight."

"Secretly delighted that Friedrich had gotten them off the hook, Thomas said to Windy, "No date for you tonight, you'll have to make do with me." Both Sara and Windy looked disappointed. Thomas relented, "Okay, a date – just until bedtime." Windy put his paws in Sara's lap and gave her a big slurping kiss. Everyone laughed for it seemed as if the dog understood every word of the exchange.

They ordered cheeseburgers, French fries and a salad for dinner, with ice cream for dessert … foods that were unknown to the Zuri Watu. "What, no one in the mood for stew?" Paula asked. Windy had his first cheeseburger and smiled and asked for more. Fortunately Paula had ordered a dozen cheeseburgers plain with pickles on the side. It was a short evening, and once they had eaten, they felt the fatigue of the long flight going east, where they had also lost three hours. They were all glad to go to bed.

Peter and Mary returned to find everyone sound asleep, even the dog.

In the morning, after breakfast, Wolfgang found Peter drinking a second cup of coffee on the balcony, and asked, "Is there a travel agency that you can recommend? Friedrich and I would like to make departure reservations, while we are out shopping today."

"Ready to go, are you? Mary will be disappointed."

"We plan to stay the week, if that is convenient for you; however, we have family expecting us, and must be going."

"What family is that?" Peter asked, thinking: I thought you were an orphan.

"Friedrich's mother has a sister, Charlotte, in Morocco. His aunt Charlotte also has a son in Aspen, Colorado; both are expecting us to visit in early September."

Wolfgang left, and Peter sympathized with him, thinking: I, too, am an only son of an only son. My mother was an only daughter of her parents, who were both only children. Mary's sister, Marga'ret, her husband and their children are my extended family now, as is John's family – Mary's older brother who had died in W.W. II. John's wife, Jane fled to the States with their three children when W.W. II hostilities began. Her departure devastated John, and Mary blamed Jane for John's death saying, 'A distracted pilot is a dead pilot.'

Jane Nelson Woleston then expected to inherit the Hall, but the legacy barred a person not a British subject, from inheriting. Neither she, nor her children, all born in the States, could inherit; and no one has heard from them – since the reading of the will. Jane even refuses to correspond. Woleston Hall then passed to Mary until Thomas reached his majority, at age twenty-five. But Thomas and the plane he was on disappeared in 1947, and Thomas was declared legally dead' in 1955, when Woleston Hall became Jon's legacy.

When Thomas returned to us, Jon wanted the Hall to revert to Thomas. But, Thomas made it very clear that he did not want to inherit property in England, so Woleston Hall still goes to Jon.

I have the dreadful feeling that Anna Louise will not want to return to Africa. She and Jon will end up living at Woleston Hall. Both Jon and Anna get on well with Marga'ret and James, and the Hall is so commodious that during leave in W.W. II, when there were twelve of us residing there – quite comfortably. We were never in one-another's way.

Look at the time! It's nine-thirty! I have dawdled half the morning away. Peter found Mary packing up. He offered her a cup of tea and asked, "Where is everyone?"

"They've all gone shopping. I offered to stay with Windy. Where were you?"

"I was on the balcony. It is lovely out there. Wolfgang said they plan to leave at the end of the week."

"Yes, I know. I'm going to miss them."

"This will surprise you, Mary, but so will I. Wolfgang's story yesterday made me want to go and visit the Zuri Watu. He made it sound like the Africa I envision for Kenya. Would you ever want to go and visit them?"

"Yes, I would. Maybe we could return from London via Yaoundé after Boxing Day. That would save two days travel time."

"I would like Thomas and Paula to go with us though, wouldn't you?"

"It would be nice, but not necessary. The Zuri Watu speak Swahili as well as Bantu. In fact, Paula said she heard very little Bantu spoken."

"I would still like them to go with us. I'd feel better that way."

"Yes, maybe the Zuri Watu would feel better too, if Thomas and Paula were with us."

"Well, I'm all packed," Mary said, "how about you? Have you cleaned out the bathroom? I told the others to leave their luggage in the hall. If you are ready to go, call down for a bell boy, so we can get the Rover loaded up."

★   ★   ★

After a late lunch, early tea at Dela-Aden, everyone napped, including Peter, who wanted to do a longer inspection ride to have time to see everything. Hanna and Sara rode out with them too, knowing their time with Wolfgang and Friedrich was drawing to a close. Thomas followed along behind with Windy, glad of the exercise.

"Do you realize this is the first time we have ever napped together here at Dela-Aden?" Mary remarked.

Peter looked at Mary, surprised. "I say Mary, what do you mean? That can't be … there must have been another time … we've just forgotten it."

"No, I don't think so. I have been mulling it over for the last half hour. You used to come up for lunch, but you never stayed to nap … 'too much to do' … you always said."

"And there was … I get tired just thinking of all there was to do … it's hard to remember how run down this place was when we arrived."

"You have accomplished miracles since 1945. Lord Edward loved Africa for the climate and the shooting, but he had no interest in improving his land grant any more than he had to – it was my grandmother that was the doer in the family. She is the one who saw Dela-Aden for the opportunity it was. However, grandfather was a bit of a stuffed shirt, who didn't like getting his hands dirty. You know, I'm glad we are well away from the snobbery of England. Here, a man stands on his deeds, and if he has a nice past and gentry for relatives, that is fine too. However, it is no longer a necessity. Why are you smiling like that, Peter?"

"I think I might get a bit of mileage out of today's peculiarity … 'How are things at the farm?' 'Fine, quite good actually. I took a nap with my wife the other day – first time in fifteen years. She asked me if I was sick.' Mary laughed at his unusual humor, thinking, you might say that to me, but you will never ever say it to anyone else!

"Peter, I do believe you are developing a sense of humor."

"Thank you, Mary. It must be the thought of napping with a beautiful woman that is making me positively jovial."

★　★　★

Once again, the days settled into a pattern: the four of them training horses in the morning while the girls practiced the piano and Thomas tended to the plants; maybe a bit of tennis, lunch, a nap and an afternoon of cards or music while Paula worked on her thesis – or they helped escort tours at the winery, until tea.

The inspection ride had changed a bit, for now they also wound through the woods to trot and canter the young horses, instead of walking only at the edges of the tea fields and vineyards. Thomas enjoyed following along with Windy. He had a ground eating stride of five miles an hour, and enjoyed the jogging to keep up with the horses trotting at eight miles an hour.

Thomas looked forward to the leisurely evenings after dinner, with games or stories or musical quartets. For Wolfgang, the walks he took with Hanna in the fading twilight were the best part of his day.

Sara and Friedrich often followed along, not for the exercise, but for the seclusion. Today was Friday, Wolfgang and Friedrich were leaving on Monday. Tomorrow was for packing up, for Sunday the neighbors were coming. Then to Nairobi for an early flight on Monday morning.

"When was the last time you saw your Aunt Charlotte?" Sara asked Friedrich.

"When I was thirteen, she and Elmer came for my father's funeral. They stayed for two weeks."

"Didn't Elmer's father come with them?"

"No. He didn't feel he could take such a long time away from his business."

"What business was that?"

"He owned a hotel in Morocco."

"What do you mean, owned; did he sell it?"

"Yes and no … he fell off a balcony and died. Aunt Charlotte sold the hotel."

"So, she is still in Morocco?"

"Yes, she has a lovely home and many friends."

"When did Elmer go to Colorado?"

"He went to the University of Colorado in Boulder for college, loved the skiing in Aspen, and decided to settle there."

"What does Elmer do now, do you know?"

"Yes, he's an assistant manager at the Hotel Jerome in Aspen."

"Well, that's convenient."

"Yes, it is. That's one of the reasons we have to go in September, after the summer tourist season – before the skiing season begins."

"I wish I were going with you. I would love to see the States and Aspen. My mother and father loved it there."

"I am looking forward to it myself," Friedrich replied.

Well, he neatly side-stepped that little opening, didn't he? I like him; he likes me, but I don't think he wants to be anything more than friends. We have a lot in common, but the spark is missing. What will be, will be; but why does that thought make me feel sad?

★　★　★

"Did you stop and see my mother on your way here from Kenya?" Elmer asked.

"Yes, and we found her living the high life. She took us to a party aboard a fabulous yacht the night we arrived and we had breakfast together the next morning. Other than that, we didn't see much of her. She had her house boy show us around town. Ahmed speaks English and made a wonderful tour guide, so we had a nice time. The bazaars are amazing!"

"What was mother doing?"

"She was having a bridge luncheon with friends, and dinner that evening with a retired Industrialist, a man she introduced to us at the party as Alfred Bates Archer. Do you know him?"

"Only the name. Mother has been seeing him off and on for a year or two. It seems he travels a lot."

"That's not surprising; his yacht, which is registered in Livorno, Italy, is impressive. It was where your mother took us for the cocktail party when we arrived. He seems like a nice man, very people oriented with a quasi-military bearing. He seems quite delighted by your mother."

"Good, Mother does better with male companionship, and it appears he is not after her money."

"Wouldn't seem that way; they act more like old friends than lovers, but I guess you didn't want to hear that."

"For mother, rapport is everything. She and Dad were the best of friends. They did everything together and had the same interests. Dad met Mother at the hotel. She was the secretary to the business manager when he bought the hotel. He kept her on because she knew what made the place tick. From a working business relationship to marriage, they shared everything until I came along and Mother became a housewife.

"When I wasn't occupying all her time, Mother started to promote the hotel. She had brochures made up and sent them to travel agents, offering them a free two day stay. The travel agents loved the place and sent them quite a lot of business. You might have seen the hotel if you were in the bazaar. It is on the corner of the square where the market begins."

"If I did, I don't remember it. Ahmed had an agenda. It seems he gets a kick-back on sales where he is the escort. He admitted it freely, hoping we would buy so he could make a bit of extra money, and his psychology worked. We brought this for you."

Elmer opened the package and found an Isfahan prayer rug, ready to hang as a wall ornament. "Why, thank you! This will remind me of home. I didn't bring any memorabilia when I came to Colorado for college. I never had extra luggage space. How did you manage it? It is a small parcel, but heavy."

"We flew first class – high baggage limits."

Elmer smiled, "So what are you doing now that allows you to fly first class?"

"I am on a scouting excursion for the Trust. You remember, I told you what Wolfgang's father did with our assets. It allows for first class flying overseas."

"Are you really scouting prodigies?"

"Yes, one in Philadelphia, and one in San Francisco."

"Did you visit the one in Philadelphia on your way here?"

303

"Yes."

"Did he pass muster?"

"It was a *she,* and it is not my job to make decisions. My job is to obtain all the required information on proposed candidates and schedule the scholarship interview with Elizabeth, Wolfgang's half – sister, who will screen the applicants. In the preliminary interviews, the parents or guardians and the person who recommended the prodigy to the Trust must be present. I take preliminary information and tape the applicants playing musical selections for Elizabeth: one of their choosing and one of Elizabeth's choosing. If the applicant is a child under ten, Elizabeth will later schedule a visit for the final interview.

"*Ruth* was recommended to the Trust by Paula's sister, Sallee Anne Thornton, who is herself a concert pianist. Paula is Thomas Caulfield's wife. Thomas is brother to the twins, Hanna and Sara whom we met in Vienna. The twins are prodigies too, but they have no financial worries, nor do they want to study music to the exclusion of everything else.

They do give a magnificent performance though, writing their own musical scores for their piano duets. They played Für Elise in different octaves with roulade flourishes, which underscored the music. Their way of playing is simply delightful. They completely entranced the Strauss musical director in Vienna with their recital encore, where they played variations on the introduction theme, and added waterfall notes, to The Blue Danube Waltz itself – only possible with two pianos. The recital was a Viennese hit."

"What is Wolfgang doing now?" Elmer asked.

"He is in the reading room writing a letter to Hanna," Rick replied.

"So, he is smitten."

"Yes, and I'm pleased for him. Hanna is a superior person. She is the breath of fresh air that Wolfgang has always longed for … and never found in Vienna."

"Do you remember our letters when we were boys?" Elmer asked.

"Yes! I just now thought of them."

"Me too, do you remember the code we made up so our mothers wouldn't know what we were writing about if they accidentally saw the letters?" Elmer asked.

"Yes, it was a simple substitution code: i was y – e was a – a was u – t was d – r was b – did I miss anything?

"No, all that seems like such a long time ago. Our two weeks together after your father's funeral were a special time for me. I'd never had a pal before then. I was attending the English school in the compound, where I was the odd man out. I hated school, and did so poorly that father finally took me aside for a heart-to-heart chat. He then advertised in America for a tutor, one willing to come out to Morocco. Nathanial Bemis was my salvation, but you were the only pal I ever had.

Bemis, as he liked us to call him, was also my friend. He was not a trained teacher, but a failed writer, or he thought he was a failed writer, simply because he could not find a publisher willing to take him on. He wrote beautiful stories set in Ireland, where his mother took him to live with her parents after his father died. When Bemis died, Mom and I went to Hawaii for his funeral. He had named me his heir and left me his manuscripts. I hope to see them published one day."

"Why was Bemis your best friend? That seems an odd relationship for a tutor and pupil. I remember that you often mentioned him in your letters."

"Bemis was a brilliant man, and his approach to learning was radical. For a week after he arrived, he asked me questions: what did I like to read? What did I know about history or geography or science or chemistry? How much math did I know and what were my interests? He then ordered a bunch of books for me to read, like Moby Dick and Jules Verne and Heyerdahl's adventures. For math, he gave me a legacy of ten thousand dollars, which I had to invest and live off the earnings; he also sent me bills to pay, with having bogus charges, which I had to refute.

But most of all, he made me write for two hours every day. I could write anything I wanted … even letters, or use one of the topics from a list he made for me. These were my English hours and he was a tough taskmaster. In four years I think I read every decent book ever written, and wrote hundreds of stories of my own. Bemis saved them all, and included them with his manuscripts legacy.

"Maybe I shouldn't tell you this, but he used your letters for writing lessons: what to do – what not to do – what was interesting – and what was not – as well as how to improve on a phrase – how to simplify – or how to embellish."

"What did he think of our code?"

"He ignored it. It simply didn't exist. He often said he would love to teach you, saying: 'I would love to teach your friend. He has great promise – what he needs is a great teacher.'"

"I didn't realize you had no other friends. Was that a problem for you when you went off to university?"

"I was worried about that, but in being my friend, as well as my teacher, Bemis gave me the skills I needed for social interaction with my peers … he would say to me: 'Let's sneak down to the kitchen and steal a few apples.' There was no reason why we couldn't just go and take whatever we wanted, but it was the interaction he was teaching me … or we would sneak out of the suite … and leave the hotel without telling anyone. On the weekends when I helped my Dad, he would say things like: 'Did you really want to tell that lady that her luggage was badly packed? Wouldn't it have been nicer to say, I'm worried about your luggage, Madam, the weight distribution might break the handle.'"

"Sounds like you had a nice life, Elmer, I'm glad."

"What about you? Didn't you have a nice life too? I always envied you having Wolfgang for a best friend."

"Yes, Wolfy and I spent a lot of time together, even though he was a year ahead of me at school. I had a few other friends, but Wolfy was my best friend. We always preferred each other for company."

"I remember Wolfy loved school, which I have to be honest, I never understood."

"He didn't love school. School was all he had, so he made the best of it."

"What about his father?"

"What about him? Wolfgang only saw him at Boxing Day and spring recess. In the summer his father came to Savona and stayed with us for a week or so. Then, he went back to Vienna. His plants needed him."

"I'm sorry to know that. I often wondered why you never mentioned Wolfgang's father, only Aunt Regina, Wolfy and Elizabeth."

"Looking back, I see that we did have a good life. I also see how awful it might have been had his Father tried to be what he wasn't, which would have filled Wolfy's life with constant heartache. His father knew that blaming him for his mother's death was irrational, but, as a baby, Wolfy was a poor substitution for his adored wife; so his father just put him out of his mind. By the time Wolfgang became a little person – his father had become set in his ways. Mother used to say to me, 'Uncle Gregor loves Wolfgang; he just doesn't know how to show it.' I think mother was wrong; I don't think he ever loved Wolfgang; I just think Uncle Gregor was never one to shrug a responsibility."

"Tell me about Kenya," Elmer said.

"Kenya was fantastic. Hanna and Sara live on this fabulous estate where their father, Sir Peter, grows tea and has a vineyard. Their mother, Lady Mary, breeds and trains horses, mostly Arabians for riding, or Sport horses for Dressage. The farm is an original land grant of a thousand acres from Lord Delamere to Lady Mary's grandfather. It is called Dela–Aden, which means: Delamere's Eden."

"What about Hanna and Sara?"

"Hanna and Sara are musical prodigies. They have been playing the piano since they were six, and now play concert duets. Their music is marvelous. They adapt everything they play to the two pianos, writing the scores themselves. They are also very nice girls, interesting, fun and quite surprising, very down–to–earth. They don't think of themselves as special."

"Do you think of them as special?"

"I sure do! Very special! Sara and I are birds of a feather. We like the same things, but as much as I like her, the bug hasn't bitten me, as it has Wolfy for Hanna."

"Will Wolfgang go back to Kenya?"

"Wild horses couldn't keep him away. Speaking of wild horses, I would love to ride cowboy style and herd some cattle or horses while I'm here. Do you know anyone that has a ranch?"

Surprised, Elmer laughed, "Why would you want to do that? It is hard, dirty work, and you'd probably get hurt! Classical riding isn't the same as cowboy riding, you know!"

"That's why I want to do it. Do you know anyone?"

"Unfortunately, I do. He's a skiing guest here who has a dude ranch down in Basalt. In September, he usually moves the horses to Grand Junction for the winter; there's good hay there, and little snow. I'll call him and see if the horses are still here."

"Thanks! That would be super!"

Wolfgang arrived, and hearing Rick's comment, asked, "What would be super?"

"Elmer went to call a friend with a dude ranch so we can ride western style."

"What do you mean, *we*?"

"Don't you want to see what it is like to ride western style?"

"It's not at the top of my list."

"Well, it's at the top of my list; it will be tons of fun, you'll see!"

Elmer returned. "Scroggins is still there. He'll be moving the horses next week, so, if you can go down tomorrow, he can accommodate you. You can use my car."

Friedrich jumped up and shouted, "YES!"

Elmer looked at Wolfy and smiled. "I do think he is pleased!"

39 ~ America ~ September

"Tell me again, how did you find out about this motor-coach tour?" Rick asked.

"Elmer told me about it. He said the tour bus stops in Aspen in the summer, going west along a northern route; but in the fall, the tour takes a southern route going east. We'd never have gotten seats if it weren't for Elmer. He said George keeps two seats open to accommodate special friends of his hosts. I thought it would be a great way for us to see some of America."

"Yes, I suppose so ... but two weeks on a tour bus? I'm going to go gaga!"

"I don't think so, Rick. I think you are going to have a good time. Elmer said the feedback from passengers stopping in Aspen has been marvelous."

"Well, at least the timing worked out well. We were able to have a nice stay in San Francisco, get our business done, go to Chinatown and Pier 39 to see all the seals, and walk the Embarcadero, which was very interesting. Remember the mime? I was sure he was just a statue ... how can anyone stand for hours in an awkward position and not even blink? And lunch – cream soup in a sour dough bread bowl! You could see Alcatraz Island when we crossed the Golden Gate Bridge going to Marin County to visit Muir Woods. I would have stayed in those woods much longer hiking all those little trails, it was so serene there – and the smell. Didn't you just love the smell of those woods?"

"Yes, I did like the smell; it was clean, fresh and fragrant," Wolfgang replied.

"What about the hairpin turns going down the mountainside, where the bus occupied both lanes getting in and out of the valley? That was scary!" Rick recollected.

"Yes, so far I have found everything about the States delightful. I thought it might be boring when I heard about all the wide open spaces, but the scenery is so magnificent that the open space is more compelling than the populated areas."

"I agree. Maybe you're right – maybe I will enjoy this bus tour."

★   ★   ★

"What were you thinking about, Rick? You had your eyes closed, but you had a smile on your face," Wolfgang asked.

"I was thinking about you and the look on your face when you sat in that western saddle. You looked positively disgusted."

"I was, but Scroggins was so friendly and accommodating, I couldn't let him know how awful the saddles were. The stirrups were so far forward that I was sitting on my butt-bone, and the swell made it impossible to sit up straight without damaging my manhood. The neck reining was okay, but holding your hand up in the air like that was truly uncomfortable.

"I'm glad we were able to watch Scoggins bring up some of the herd before we tried it. I was able to watch his body movements and interaction with his horse. Otherwise, I would have been lost. There is so little feel of the horse under you in a western saddle, and with the loopy reins of neck-reining, you have no feel of his mouth either. Riding position is adapted to fast starts by leaning forward and quick stops by leaning back and hauling back on the reins ... terrible! Over the long haul, a rider must get butt-sore. I can't imagine that the horses like it much either. However, my horse did know what to do, and soon responded to my leg aids," Wolfgang said.

"I remember how dubious Scroggins was when I told him we had never ridden western style before," Rick said. "I think he gave me a beginner horse. My horse was a little dull; however after a few turns around the corral, he perked up a bit."

"I think Scroggins considered saying no, when I asked to ride the Appaloosa mare, but changed his tactics, saying, "She's a mite stubborn, that one.""

"I like the look in her eye. She looks smart to me," I told him.

"That she is ... we call it *savvy* out here," Scroggins told me.

310

"That mare was certainly surprised when you mounted up. I saw her head come up when you sat in the saddle. Her ears turned back towards you while you just sat there. Scroggins mouth dropped open; he took his hat off, combed his hand through his hair and settled his hat on his head again ... must be a reflex action to consternation. He didn't know what you were doing, but he saw that whatever it was, the mare was thinking about it."

"When she dropped her nose and straightened her head, she walked off with a light step, and her back had come up under you. I saw Scroggins push his hat back on his head and put his hands on his waist, arms akimbo. He was stunned."

"She was a sweet mare; light on her feet, smooth as glass in the jog, and transitioned to a canter lead with light seat pressure. She was quick and willing. She likes her work. It is possible though, that she doesn't like her riders, for she is quite sensitive."

"Scroggins was sure surprised, do you remember him saying?"

"Well, I'll be a gol–darned rube! I thought you said you hadn't ridden before."

"No, we said we hadn't ridden western before."

"That mare always gives trouble. I've never seen her go so well before. How did you make her do that?"

"I talked to her with my legs and seat."

"You did what? Hey! Don't think I don't know my business just because I'm surprised."

"Of course not; the way I learned to ride, was by giving signals to the horse with my seat and legs."

"I didn't see you give that mare any signals."

"If you had, I would have been doing it wrong."

Scroggins again repositioned his hat, before saying, "Well, I guess it's safe to take you out with the herd. We need to bring the horses off the range into that big corral over there, so we can start taking shoes off for the winter. Just watch me. Do what I do. Your horses are both cutting horses; they know the drill and will do the work, if you can just stay with them."

"It was fun, wasn't it?" Rick asked.

"Yes, it was fun and would even have been pleasurable in a training saddle. That mare certainly knew more about the round-up than I did. She did all the work, and moved like a cat, leaping from side to side to cut off the bunch-quitters. I'm glad Scroggins insisted we wear chaps. Without them, I might *not* have sat there enjoying myself!"

"I loved the look on Elmer's face when we returned to the hotel. Do you remember it?"

"Yes, how could I forget it? His mouth was set in a hard annoyed line when he asked us ... "

"What did you do to Scroggins? He called me with a burr under his saddle saying, "It was a dirty trick to send me the best riders I ever saw in my life ... telling me they were beginners."

"What had you said to him to make him think that we were beginners?" Rick asked.

"I told him, I'm sending down some friends who have never ridden western."

Friedrich and Wolfgang laughed heartily. "No wonder Scroggins was so testy. He thought we were making fun of him. I hope you explained your mistake."

"I tried. I told him you were riders from the Spanish Riding School in Vienna on tour of the States and – Scroggins didn't say a word; he just hung up on me," Elmer replied.

★   ★   ★

"So, it's safe to say you are having a good time," Wolfgang said.

"Yes. It has been interesting and eye-opening – incredibly panoramic and vast. Now, if this bus tour gets a bit more interesting, I'll be suitably humble."

"What ... you didn't like the panoramic wide-screen tour of Universal Studios?"

"Of course I did. I'm sure it was better than wandering around in person. So many of the Stars welcomed us – and we saw how movies are made with all the takes and retakes, it was great!"

"Then you didn't care for the incredible vistas of the Grand Canyon; or enjoy our rafting down the Colorado River; or riding mules up those tiny narrow trails to the south rim? You thought that was dull, did you?"

"That was simply incredible ... and you know it."

"So, how is it going to get more interesting than that? I'd really like to know just what you think would make the trip more exciting and interesting."

"All right! All right!! It was a poor choice of words. But, we are heading into the desert. What could possibly be interesting in the desert?"

"Did you read the itinerary in your booklet-brochure?" Wolfgang asked.

"No. I hate travel literature. It is so boring."

"You know, you were like this as a boy. I thought you had grown up a bit. I guess I was wrong. Let me say this: the little booklet they handed out in a litter bag with tissues and hand wipes has our entire itinerary in it. It also includes where we will stay, where we will eat, where we will lodge; our departure times in the mornings, our expected arrival times, and the distance between the stops. There is a page for each day, with its itinerary, as well as a lined page to write your impressions of the day – sort of like a diary of the trip. George and Harold have gone to a lot of trouble to make this tour as delightful as possible. We are going to see a varied cross-section of this country in great comfort, with very little inconvenience. I hope you do not intend to spoil my trip by being childish," Wolfgang admonished Rick.

He's right. I'm having a great time, and yet I'm being a wet blanket. Why? What is wrong with me?

"You're right, Wolfy. I'm being a stick-in-the-mud. Sorry! I've just felt funny ever since we left Aspen. I don't know why – I just feel tired and irritable."

"Whatever it is, I hope you put it aside for the duration. It is quite annoying."

Rick found his litter bag and took out the booklet. It had a drawing on the front cover of an American Eagle aluminum bus with caricatures of George and Harold leaning out the front windows; one held a map with a big black 'X' through it, and the other one held a "Reserved" sign. He opened the cover and read:

The next two weeks will be a delight,
Morning noon and every night;
Get comfortable, relax and enjoy ~

313

Our putting on the Ritz for the hoi polloi!

Rick thumbed the pages, reading the itinerary details. "If we do everything this booklet says we are going to do – we will know more about America than we do about Vienna."

Wolfgang smiled. That was my thought too. We are so much alike; why is he feeling so negative? "I'm going to nap for a bit, Rick. Yesterday sort of wore me out."

That's it! Rick thought. That's my problem – altitude sickness. I remember I had it when we climbed the Alps to ski. I didn't enjoy myself then either, yet I love to ski. If I don't do anything super physical, I'm okay, but climbing down the gorge was work, as was the canoeing. I should feel better by tomorrow – thank goodness. I was beginning to hate myself for being such a spoil-sport. I'll have to get some Ginseng tea.

★   ★   ★

The bus made a quick tour of the Capitol in the early morning light; then a stop at Arlington Cemetery, with a run north to Paradise, Bird-in-Hand, and Intercourse in Lancaster, where they had lunch at an Amish tourist attraction that had accommodations for tour buses. The tour group had a dining room to themselves, and a most sumptuous buffet of Amish culinary delights.

Here George and Harold bid their passengers adieu and handed out cardboard-framed photos of the tour group and the shiny bus. Then a ride through an Amish farm in horse-drawn wagons, and a visit to the Amish wood-working and souvenir shop. The bus then made a bee-line for Philadelphia International Airport to disembark passengers, before going on to center city Philadelphia and the railroad at 30th Street Station to provide a connection for those who wanted to go on to New York. There, the tour ended,

Sallee Anne watched the sleek aluminum coach pull up in a bus slot. She did not know Wolfgang or Friedrich, but her mission was clear. One of the tour guides went to open the luggage bays, while the other remained by the door, helping passengers off and bidding them good-bye. In a free moment, she approached the guide and said,

314

"Would you please be so kind as to point out the von Hauptsborg gentlemen. My name is Sallee Anne Thornton, I have been sent to fetch them home."

George looked her over kindly, and replied, "They will probably get off last; they were sitting in the rear of the bus. You can't miss them."

And he was right. She would have known them as European anywhere. Their carriage of unmistakable dignity and reserve was palpable.

George spared her having to approach strangers by saying, "Wolfgang, Friedrich, I hope you had a delightful tour! But the delights are not yet ended."

Mystified, but game, for by now, they knew George liked to spring surprises on his fellow travelers, Wolfgang said, "A parting shot, George?"

George smiled and said, "I think of it more as *a parting gift of unusual quality.* May I present to you Sallee Anne Thornton … aha! I see you recognize the name. She has come to fetch you home – you lucky chaps!"

They nodded their heads knowing that pianists rarely shake hands. Sallee Anne said quickly, "Elmer asked me to waylay you here in Philadelphia. It seems your aunt, his mother, is getting married and wishes you to attend the wedding in Morocco."

George went to help them with their baggage, smiling. He loved surprises and intrigue.

Leading the way to her new Mercury Colony Park station wagon with its six foot carpeted rear deck for toting musical instruments, Sallee Anne continued, "What is your itinerary from Philadelphia? Will you have a few days to spend with us in Oxford? Paula has written to Mother about your riding skills. Mother and Father would like to take you to Fair Hill, our local seven thousand acre riding preserve, if you have time."

Of all the things that could have happened, meeting Sallee Anne and Aunt Charlotte's wedding were the most unexpected of them all. Following along, they exchanged glances and shrugged shoulders in a *why not* sort of way.

Wolfgang replied, "Except for the bus tour and interviewing Ruth and Michael, the piano prodigies, we planned to do whatever came along."

"Good! Before we head out to the country, I'd like to treat you to dinner. There's a nice little bistro that serves marvelous pasta just a few blocks away. We can leave the car here and walk there. Does that suit you?"

"I'd like nothing better than to stretch my legs just now, and I'm sure Wolfgang feels the same way. Today, except for lunch, was an all day bus day. "How did Carnegie Hall go for you?" Friedrich asked, as they headed down Market Street.

"It is always a thrill to play there. The acoustics are marvelous. I understand the interview with Ruth went well in my absence. She's a marvel, isn't she?"

For two blocks they walked against the tide heading to 30th Street Station, so conversation was limited, but turning right, the tide ceased and the restaurant, a cozy, checkered-cloth style Italian restaurant, with marvelous aromas, was at hand.

Finally, Friedrich was able to ask, "I'm dying to know; when is the wedding?"

"Hold on to your hats – it's the 8th of October."

"That's a week from tomorrow! No wonder they cast the net out for us. Do you know who else is invited?" Friedrich asked, surprised.

"Possibly ... Elmer's mother called him in Aspen, but you had already left on your cross-country tour, and Elmer didn't have a copy of the bus itinerary. However, Elmer did know the bus trip ended up here in Philadelphia, so he called Paula at Dela-Aden to get our phone number so we could flag you down."

"Why didn't he just call you directly?"

"Elmer forgot Paula's maiden name," she replied, "if he ever knew it."

"Paula called home and told me that Sir Peter and Lady Mary are going to the wedding too. It seems that the prospective groom, Alfred Bates Archer, was Peter's commanding officer in the Great War, and Peter's best man at his and Mary's wedding. Alfred asked Sir Peter to stand up for him, and invited all of Sir Peter's family too. Delighted to do so, he and Lady Mary put out the net for you. How's that for a coincidence?"

316

"So Hanna and Sara will be there too?" Wolfgang asked.

"Yes," Sallee Ann replied, "Paula and Thomas will be there, as well as Regina, Ludwig and Hans. Your aunt Charlotte called on Wednesday to tell us that she had booked six first class seats on a TWA flight to Rabat, Morocco via Shannon, Ireland, London, England and Madrid, Spain leaving on Wednesday, the fifth from Philadelphia at nine p.m., arriving Rabat at two in the afternoon on Thursday. She also said she had booked every free room in the hotel, whatever that means."

"Aunt Charlotte used to own the Hotel in Rabat, and still uses it as a place to stash visitors. I'm sure she will fill every room with family and friends. I imagine they will have the wedding at the hotel as well. It has very nice facilities, but why six seats on the TWA flight?"

"Your aunt has also invited me and my mother and father. She said it would be the perfect time for me to meet Elizabeth and Gregor, who are coming to the wedding. I think Lady Mary has written to Charlotte about meeting my parents in England, so Charlotte included them as well. Mom and Dad loved being guests at Greystone Place and Woleston Hall in England, so they were simply delighted to go.

Elmer is flying in to Philadelphia from Aspen on Monday. He said it would break up the flying for him. Mother invited him to stay with us, which he agreed to do – *to keep you both in hand*. Elmer said you two were *smoking guns* in Basalt and he has yet to *clear the air* … whatever that means."

"It was just a bit of miscommunication, but it upset Elmer's friend," Friedrich replied. "I hope Scroggins is over it by now. He's a very nice person."

"What a perfect meal, the cheese ravioli were delicious," Wolfgang said.

"Yes, they make the pasta fresh each day. It's the best I've ever eaten, anywhere. They have spumoni too. Have you ever had spumoni? Sallee Anne asked.

"Probably not, since I don't even know what it is."

"It is layers of ice cream of unusual flavors: today is Bing cherry, pistachio, rum raisin and butter brickle. They mold the ice cream flavors too. A different blend for each day, Friday's blend is my favorite."

"Sounds like something I can't possibly resist," Friedrich smiled.

*   *   *

They walked back to 30th Street Station in the last of the twilight. The pedestrian traffic was light, and street traffic flowed uncongested on Market Street.

The ride to Oxford took a bit over an hour in traffic that moved along freely. The house and drive were ablaze with light when Sallee Anne turned in the driveway. Lisa waited at the door, while Charles walked out to give them a hand with the luggage.

Introductions took place in the spacious Italian brick floored entrance hall, where Eric then helped ferry their bags up to the guest room, saying, "Come down when you're settled. Mother has coffee and liqueurs waiting in the living room."

"Did you know that Paula had a twin brother?" Friedrich asked Wolfgang.

"No, that was a surprise; we don't really know much about Paula, do we? I just took her for being a part of Africa – since she met Thomas in Africa and speaks Swahili. She never mentioned having family in the States. Well, let's go down and find out about the rest of the clan, this is getting *curiouser and curiouser*," Wolfgang sighed.

*   *   *

On the way back from the airport, Sallee Anne took Wolfgang, Friedrich and Elmer for a local tour. They did a zip-through at the University of Delaware, where Charles met them and said, "The Library and Student Union are nice facilities and you'll find the campus charming."

They walked through New Bolton Center's hospital facilities for animals – a branch of the University of Pennsylvania, where Eric was attending Vet School. Sallee Anne then drove along the Brandywine River and pointed out buildings that were standing in the Revolutionary war.

They found the Conservatory at Longwood Gardens delightful, and had a lunch of quiche and salad there, where Elmer asked, "Well, how was the bus tour?"

Wolfgang looked at Friedrich, who grinned and said, "You go first, you're the oldest."

"It was the best tour ever! Fantastic places: The Grand Canyon, Las Vegas, New Orleans, Ashville, Nashville, Mammoth Caves, Keenland in Kentucky; as well as so many incredible vistas: the Grand Canyon, the desert, the Smoky Mountains and crossing the Continental Divide. All of it was simply fabulous. George and Harold were great tour guides and had everything arranged from beginning to end. We never had to wait for anything. Their poem said, 'We're putting on the Ritz.' And they did – and I'd go again."

"That's what everyone says when the bus tour comes to Aspen, but we don't hear about the tour going east. Although, one would expect it to be great considering the diversity of the countryside," Elmer said. "I'm glad you enjoyed it."

"Is Scroggins still mad at you," Friedrich asked.

"He still pretends to be put out, but he's not really; his favorite story now is about the dudes who had never ridden western – from the Spanish Riding School in Vienna."

★   ★   ★

The Boeing 707 flight had originated in Chicago for Ireland, with stops in Philadelphia and New York, leaving right on schedule to cross the big pond – which it did not really do. The 707 went north over land to Greenland, crossing over Iceland and then Scotland before landing at Shannon Airport in Ireland. There the Boeing 707 would refuel, restock and get a new crew, while the passengers had breakfast in the terminal. The flight would then continue on to London, England; Madrid, Spain: and Rabat, Morocco.

Charles, Lisa, Sallee Anne, Wolfgang, Friedrich and Elmer followed a redcap to a small dining room to be the guests of Captain O'Daire, who made a habit of checking the passenger manifests from Philadelphia, looking for friends and acquaintances landing at Shannon. After Edith's stories of *Paula this* or *Thomas that,* during her summer visit with Lena, Captain O'Daire felt he knew Paula; and Edith's extended family were considered his friends too.

Captain O'Daire was determined to make Shannon Airport the most desired airport for all the international carriers, and he was succeeding. The modern terminal building had a dining room that could accommodate three hundred travelers, with two buffets; or travelers could order from a menu, if desired. An entire wall of glass on one side of the dining room looked out over the runways.

A delightful duty-free gift shop abutted the huge dining room, with a fine selection of linens and lace items; with hand-made wool sweaters, shawls, hats and other unusual items. An impressive array of fine Irish crystal and china took up one whole wall of the shop.

Lisa, Charles and Sallee Ann, with Wolfgang and Friedrich went together to purchase a set of four cut-glass crystal decanters, with eight matching aperitif glasses and eight small snifters, all nestled on a notched and slotted teak tray, with a selection of eight brass tags for naming the decanter's contents. The tray had a hinged lid made of formed Plexiglas to secure the contents. The tray also had a non slip rubber bottom with suction clips to secure it to a counter. The set was stunningly beautiful and certainly made for use on a yacht, which was where Charlotte and Alfred, the bride and groom, intended to spend the next six months.

Elmer brought a revolutionary stainless steel corkscrew, for a wedding gift. It always removed the cork from the bottle in one piece, by lowering the corkscrew handles. He brought a dozen with him from Aspen just to be prepared.

In London, England, there was a great shift of passengers, for many deplaned while others boarded. Charles felt a light tap on his shoulder and turned to be totally astonished, "James! What are you doing here?"

"Same as you, old chap; we are going to the wedding too." Charles and Lisa were delighted and made the introductions: "This is Elmer, son of the bride; Friedrich and Wolfgang, Elmer's cousins; Sallee Anne, our eldest daughter, who is to discuss music with Elizabeth and Gregor, Elmer's out-law cousins; while Lisa and I were invited, out of kindness, as Paula's parents." Charles grinned happily, adding, "Seeing you here James, makes me feel right at home now."

James and Marga'ret smiled back at him. They so liked Charles – he had taken the words right out of their mouths. Marga'ret had accepted the invitation at Paula's behest, when she said, "Sir Peter is Best Man and Lady Mary is counting on you and James being there." Charles and Lisa were an unexpected bonus.

★   ★   ★

Both Elizabeth and Gregor preferred aisle seats. Sallee Anne sat by the window with Elizabeth, while Elmer took the window seat next to Gregor across the aisle.

"Friedrich said you were giving a recital at Carnegie Hall, so you could not be there for the interview with Lucy. I have heard of Carnegie Hall, is it as fabulous as they say?"

"Even more so. You can hear a pin drop on the stage from any seat in the house. It makes the performing artists able to use the subtle expressions in a piece properly."

"Had you played there before?" Elizabeth asked.

"I had my debut there, so I think of it as home."

"Is music your life?"

"Yes, it is my raison d'être."

"Mine too, but I don't have the creative genius to compose symphonies, or concertos; only the ability to compose sonatas. How about you? Do you compose?"

"Not really. I like to do variations on a theme, as opposed to pure composition. I used to design clothing when I felt like expressing myself."

"Why did you stop?"

"The creative spark went away and it hasn't come back."

"When did you start to play the piano?" Elizabeth asked.

"I played when I was four and five. When I was six, I learned to read music."

"Do you play other instruments?"

"No, just keyboard instruments," Sallee Anne replied. "It takes a lot of work to keep in top form, especially playing with a symphony orchestra. I'm fortunate to have a home that allows me to spend all my time working on my performance. Mother says the house feels dead if she doesn't hear me playing. How lucky is that?"

"That's why I wanted to talk to you," Elizabeth smiled. "The Trust is taking a great deal of my time. Like you, I need to practice to keep my edge. Travel time is wasted time, especially flights to the States to test young prodigies. It is time I cannot make up. Would you consider taking a position with the Trust to help us with the testing process in the States?"

"I'd have to know exactly what was involved and how often I might be needed before I could give you an answer. Do you have a format that you follow?"

"Yes, that is the easy part. The hard part is a discerning ear. Prodigies have flair, not just competence. One test is to play a piece, about the length of the Moonlight Sonata, that they have not heard before, and then ask them to duplicate it. The other test is to play a known piece of similar length with errors in it, and ask them to play it back, hoping they will automatically correct the errors, or as one young lad asked," 'With or without the errors?'

Sallee Anne smiled and asked, "Where is that lad now?"

"At the Sorbonne – under the auspices of the Trust."

"Those are tough tests. How many pass them?"

"Just those that make it into the program, for those are the gifts of a prodigy."

"You give these tests to children?"

"Yes, based on the level of skill of the submitted piece, and the interview test pieces: one a piece they know; the other a piece they have not played before."

"How do you know they have not played the piece before?"

"That is simple. I compose the piece myself."

"Are we talking, keyboard artists only?"

Misha Heifetz once said, "If one has ears, one can hear a violin prodigy."

Sallee Anne smiled, "Yes, I suppose he is right."

"Well, give it some thought. The job pays well, and carries a bit of prestige."

"I'll do that. Regardless of my decision, I'm quite flattered that you asked me to do this for the Trust."

"And we will be extremely flattered if you accept."

40 ~ *Morocco* ~ *October*

Flowers decorated the Hotel – everywhere. Wedding guests signed their names in a guest registry, and received a white embossed envelope with their names and room number written in calligraphy. The wedding party occupied the entire penthouse floor. Each suite and the hall had fresh flower arrangements, with potted urns on the now wrought iron enclosed balconies, overlooking both the ocean and the Bazaar.

Charles, Lisa and Sallee Anne had a two bedroom suite with an ocean balcony, which overlooked the hotel terrace, the beach, and the pier. James and Marga'ret had the suite next to them. Peter, Mary, Hanna and Sara had a two bedroom suite on the ocean side, across the hall from the library, where two Steinway concert grand pianos sat nestled together in the middle of the room with their soundboard covers propped open, looking like a huge black bird on the fly.

Charlotte, the bride, had asked Hanna and Sara, Elizabeth and Gregor, and Sallee Anne to play selections after the Reception dinner, promising them a private area where they could *nimble their fingers*.

The family and wedding party occupied the entire penthouse floor.

David Thornton, Paula's uncle, was a college fraternity brother of Alfred, the groom, as was Cyril Latham. Each had manned an oar on an eight-man racing scull at the University of Pennsylvania. Ludwig Bruenner, Regina's husband and Friedrich's stepfather is Alfred's attorney in Europe, and is now soon to be his brother-in-law.

★ ★ ★

"It is so nice knowing wealthy people; I love living the way they do, even if it is only for a day or three. It's like being in the movies and living a fantasy." Lisa sighed.

"I was suitably impressed by Greystone Place; however having your own hotel at you beck and call is even more impressive. Did you happen to look at the view from the balcony?" Charles asked.

"Not yet. Is something going on?"

"You could say that, come and see."

Lisa just stared. Her mouth fell open as she looked down on the panoply below her. Canopies covered the entire dock with flowers in urns at every post. Beside the covered pier were two fabulous yachts, which took up the entire length of the pier. Lisa grabbed her opera glasses and said, *The Never End ~ Livorno, Italy.* I can't make out the name on the far yacht; the canopies are in the way"

"They will be serving tea for another hour or two. I'd like to go down and take a look at those yachts, want to come with me?" Charles asked.

"Wild horses couldn't keep me away."

★   ★   ★

Marga'ret opened the sliding door to the balcony. A luscious breeze came off the Atlantic Ocean, which fluttered the pennants atop the canopy poles. I wonder if that to-do down there is a part of the wedding celebration. Must be … I've never seen so many flower arrangements or flower urns in my life. It must be an all-day job just to water them. As Marga'ret lingered with her speculative thoughts, she heard Lisa, on the next balcony, read the name of the yacht. The groom, Alfred Bates Archer is from Livorno; so, that to-do down there is a part of the wedding celebration. She turned, crossed the room and tapped on the bathroom door lightly. "James, would you like to go down to the wharf with me? It looks like a country fair down there. I'd like to get a better look."

"Almost finished, be with you in a jiff," James replied.

He is so orderly – that must come from being an architect. I hung up my dresses, might as well put the folding stuff away too. However, I think I will change to tennis shoes, just in case someone invites us aboard one of those yachts – or are tennis shoes only required for sailboats? Better safe than sorry. "James," Marga'ret said through the door, "put on tennis shoes, in case we're asked aboard a yacht."

"What yacht?"

324

"The fabulous ones along the wharf that I want to go down and see."

★　★　★

"Don't you just love this little booklet? I wonder how many guests are enjoying this magnificent wedding. Let me read this to you, it is amazing," Marga'ret said.

"There is a picture of Alfred and Charlotte on the cover of the booklet, arms around each other smiling happily, apparently on a yacht. Inside it says:"

'Welcome to the celebration of our marriage. We are delighted you could be here to share these special days with us. The key-card attached is for your personal use only. It will give you access to services and dining while you are our guest. Please, do not share it with anyone. A schedule of events is included until check-out time on Sunday morning, October ninth at eleven, a.m. We hope you have a wonderful stay here in Rabat. Alfred and Charlotte'

"The 'Schedule of Events' reads:"

'Wednesday is a day to get settled, with tea served until five in the lobby; before the receiving line and cocktail reception in the Red Banquet Room at six; with dinner in the Blue Banquet room at eight. Immediately following dinner, Alfred and I are delighted to present Hanna and Sara Caulfield, repeating the twin piano performance from their recital at the Schönbrunn Palace in Vienna. To titillate you even more, Sallee Anne Thornton will give us an encore of her recent recital at Carnegie Hall. Our cup runneth over, for my niece Elizabeth Schultz and her husband Gregor, from the Strauss Concert Hall in Vienna, will play a piano and violin duet for us.

'Thursday is a free day to do as you please. A list of activities is at the end of this booklet. Breakfast is in the dining room until ten; lunch is in the Café from noon until two, cocktails are on board *The Never End* at six, with a buffet dinner at eight in the Blue Banquet room, with dancing until midnight.

'Friday is also a free day; breakfast is in the dining room until ten. Lunch is aboard *The Never End* at one p.m., with wedding gifts opened in the Grand Salon at two p.m. Tea is at four in the hotel;

dinner is from seven to nine in the Hotel Café. The 'stag' party begins at ten p.m. aboard *The Never End*.

'The wedding rehearsal is on the pier at five p.m., and is by invitation only; the rehearsal dinner is aboard *The Just Beginning* immediately following the rehearsal.

'**Saturday**, *our wedding* is at eleven a.m., on the pier. Admittance is by invitation only. Please bring your hand-written invitation with you. The wedding luncheon is at noon on the Seaside Terrace of the hotel, and is again, by invitation only. Alfred and I will depart on our honeymoon cruise at five p.m. on *The Just Beginning*. 'Dinner is in the Café from seven p.m. until nine p.m. for guests. The evening is free.

'**Sunday**, breakfast is in the Café from seven a.m. until ten a.m.; check-out by eleven a.m.'

'*Thank you for coming to celebrate life with us. Have a safe trip home. 'Write to us: c/o Villa Archerna, Livorno, Italy.*'

"Well, what do you think of that? I must say I'm impressed. There is a long list of things to do, not the least of which is the Bazaar, which could take days to cover. I wonder if we can talk Peter and Mary into some bridge this evening."

"I wouldn't worry about talking Peter and Mary into anything; it's me you have to worry about! I'm ready for bed now, and will never make it through the evening without a good nap."

"That's not like you, James. You're not getting sick, are you?"

"I don't think so. I just had so much work to finish before I could go off on this junket, that I'm feeling the lack of sleep. Social occasions energize you; however, they just deplete me."

"Yes, we are different that way. I know you said the Wilsons wanted changes that required new plans for the builder, but couldn't some of them have waited?"

James smiled, "That would be like shoeing only three hooves on a horse."

"I see – good analogy. But you did all four feet?"

"Yes, but the horse refused to stand."

"Does that mean you had to make more changes?"

"Clever girl! "I gave him a feedbag to distract him, or I'd still be trying to do the last foot!"

"I should think you would get exasperated with these fickle clients. How do you manage it so well?"

"I remind myself how much each *change order* is costing them. Then I manage quite well. Some of the changes are also challenging, which of course, interests me."

"Well, whatever – you do it very well. Your clients always sing your praises. How is Johnson working out for you?"

"So far, quite well; he is an excellent draftsman and is meticulous about keeping records for the Accounts Receivable. He has a liking for detail and is very organized. He will more than earn his salary if he keeps on as he is doing."

"George was put off when you hired Johnson."

"I know, but George has three years of schooling left and, he still isn't positive that he wants to be an architect. We could go under waiting for George. If George does continue and gets his degree, we will be able to expand. I have to turn many clients away, because of scheduling. My old firm is making more money off me now that I am gone than they did when I worked for them, for they usually take on the clients I can't handle immediately. I don't mind, really. I'm glad to have a reputable back-up for referrals. But, best of all, I no longer commute! I *hated* commuting! Just knowing I had to do it each day ruined my life. It was the proverbial *black cloud* in my life."

"It has made me as happy as it has made you, for now we ride together each decent morning. I can't think of a better way to start our day!"

"That's odd! I always thought of you as being quite clever – more so than me, and I can think of other *better* ways … "

"James! Maybe you are right," Marga'ret smiled. "A nap will do us both good."

★   ★   ★

"Mary, have you looked at this booklet?"

"Yes, I found it quite interesting."

"Did you see the note about Friday evening?"

"About the *stag party?*"

"Yes."

"Boys will be boys. I will have to scare up a bridge game, if I have my labeling finished."

"Did you see Cyril, today?"

"Our Cyril! Cyril Latham? Is he here?"

"Yes, I saw him when I went down to find my kit-bag. You will not believe what a coincidence this is: Cyril, Charles, and his brother David, and Alfred, the groom, all wear the same *school tie*! Cyril was even in the same Fraternity, although a few years behind, and all manned an eight-man racing scull at Penn. Now, what do you think of that?"

"Alfred went to Penn? His father was English, and his mother Italian. How did he end up there?

"He didn't make it in to Oxford, and he wanted to row, so he applied to Penn."

"I know you met Alfred in the RAF, but I always thought he went to Oxford. Sometimes, I feel it is a very small world. We have had more than our fair share of coincidences lately. They're beginning to seem normal for us."

"It's wonderful to see Alfred again, isn't it? I was so delighted to hear he was getting married again. He almost didn't make it after losing Lucinda. Two years of watching her waste away – and doctors all over the world. We sort of lost touch after she died, he wanted no reminders of the past, it was too painful for him."

"Alfred always sent a card or a note on our anniversary. He remembered the children too; until we lost Thomas, then it was just a letter now and then. I'm sure our loss reminded him of his loss, and the memory was too difficult to bear."

"Well no one can appreciate the good days as much as a person who has been through the really bad days, and there we both qualify. Where have Hanna and Sara gone? The piano playing has stopped"

"Out to the bazaar with Elmer, Wolfgang and Friedrich, to help Paula and Thomas look for a wedding present."

"I brought four cases of wine; is that enough?"

"Yes, that's quite nice. However, I also made copies of Hanna's and Sara's performances, and included a battery operated tape player with them."

"That's nice. It's very personal; I think they will enjoy our girls' music."

"I thought so too. I just have to finish labeling the cassettes."

"I wondered when you said that earlier, but I was afraid to ask ... and they both laughed.

★   ★   ★

"Charles, there's someone at the door. Can you get it? I'm not dressed yet," Lisa called out from the bedroom.

"Lisa! It's David!"

"David who?"

"What do you mean, David who? It is David Thornton, not who!" Charles and David roared at his wit, as they back-slapped one another in brotherly greeting.

"Oh my gosh, David! What are you doing here?" Lisa said, drawing her robe around her as she entered the sitting room. She hurried over and gave him a big hug.

"Alfred is an old college chum and fellow sculler. He's asked me to be a groomsman at his wedding. What about you? Why are you here?"

"We're not sure – we think we are here because of Paula and Sallee Anne."

"Is Paula here too?" David lit up with surprise.

"Yes, Paula, Thomas and Peter, who is best man, as well as Mary, Hanna and Sara. Did you look at your little booklet?" Lisa asked. "It has a guest list at the end."

"I'm still reading the *schedule of events;* I haven't gotten that far yet," David replied.

"Then, how did you know we were here?" Charles asked.

"I saw Cyril in the lobby," David said. "He told me you were here. Apparently, he *has* read the guest list," David laughed. "Now we know why he is such a good attorney – he crosses all the t's and dots all the i's."

"Is Bela with you?" Lisa inquired.

"No, she's busy with her charities. But had Bela not been at home, she would not have caught me before I left Cairo. We are interviewing for a Professor of Antiquities at Penn. I volunteered to go and do the interviews since I was heading to Athens … and then Bela called. I never thought old Alfred would marry again. This Charlotte must be a very special woman!"

"We haven't met her yet. But she looks pretty special in their photo on the cover of the little booklet. She has kind eyes and a wonderful smile," Lisa agreed.

"What room is Paula in? I must give her a call," David said.

"They might be napping; it is a tiring flight from Kenya through Cairo to Rabat. Did you come in from Cairo? You might have been on the same plane!"

"No, I came in from Athens. I did the interview in Cairo first," David replied.

"Oh, this is so exciting," Lisa said. "Let me finish dressing, then we can go down to the lobby for tea. They might be down there, and who knows *who* else?"

Charles and David smiled as they watched her go to finish dressing. Lisa was easy to please, she enjoyed everything.

★　　★　　★

Sallee Anne heard the girls practicing and took a book to the balcony. I might get a nap in before they finish, but I need to stop thinking about this fabulous wedding and the incredible guest arrangements. If I don't distract myself, I'll never nap. My new James Michener book should help – or maybe not. I might get so interested in it that I won't want to stop reading to nap.

★　　★　　★

Cyril had some papers he needed to go over for Alfred, and took them out on the balcony to read. He was quite pleased for Alfred, but he was going to miss their stag outings, especially the fishing jaunts. Seems I'm the odd-man-out now. Well, something will come along, it always does, and the next few days will be a nice change.

"Shit!" Cyril heard and looked in the direction of the mauvais mot. He saw a woman quickly grab her tissue packet, snatch out a few, and dab them over her book pages.

330

"Damn!" She said. "And this is a first edition! What damnable luck! I sure as hell hope it's not an omen of things to come!" The tall, generously shaped, silver blonde woman retreated into her room with Cyril thinking: she cusses like a man; I didn't know nice women did that!

Cyril had tucked himself into a corner that had a bit of shade from the westerly sun, so he hoped he had observed the lady's dilemma unnoticed.

Cyril went back to his papers, but the lady with the *bad mouth* kept distracting his thoughts. It's not like I've never heard a woman use bad language before ... it's just that I didn't expect to hear it here. I think I should go inside – maybe she didn't see me.

"Shit!" Sallee Anne said again, as she regained her room. Who the hell was that sitting in that corner? The Penthouse Police! I've made an absolute fool of myself. My mother always told me that my mouth would get me into trouble ... why do I feel the need to talk like a dockhand? Mother says it's a release from frustration ... and I suppose, like most mothers, she is right. If I put paper towels between the pages, and put some other books on top – maybe the lemonade won't stain, or wrinkle the pages.

Ah, the pianos have stopped. I think I'll go and practice. That always settles me. Now where did I put my music? Obviously the bride is not musically inclined, for my performance at Carnegie Hall was a concerto ... she stopped ... stunned ... no, it's not possible ... she wouldn't have hired an orchestra ... we'd have to practice together ... I really scared myself there for a moment! Sallee Anne closed the door and headed to the library. Oh, my gosh! Maybe she doesn't know that! Well, the conductor would have told her! Gotta stop scaring myself this way! I'll give myself heart problems. She took another step ... suddenly stopped ... frozen to the spot ... totally unable to move ... what if she didn't tell the conductor either? Sallee Anne's heart stopped beating, she felt dizzy and faint ...

Cyril opened his door to see her standing there, white as a sheet. He rushed over, asking, "Are you alright? Sallee Anne crumpled, and Cyril caught her. The door to his room still stood ajar. He pushed it open with his foot and carried Sallee Anne to the sofa, propping her back and head with throw pillows.

331

Cyril went to the wet bar, dumped most of the ice in the bucket into the sink, added a bit of cold water, grabbed a serviette, wet it in the ice water, wrung it out and took both to the coffee table, where he placed the cold cloth on Sallee Anne's forehead. Whatever could have happened? She looked like she had seen a ghost! I've heard about the blood draining from the head, but I've never before actually seen it happen.

Cyril stood and studied his unexpected guest, and, as an afterthought, Cyril took the cotton throw and covered her. Should he call someone? She didn't seem in distress. Her pulse was a bit low, but still normal, and the color *was* returning to her face.

Cyril took advantage of her repose to return to the hall to pick up her manila folder, which had scattered a bit when she dropped it. He pushed the music inside, noticing a name and date at the top of a selection: Sallee Anne Thornton, June 1958.

This is Paula's sister! Except for the blonde hair, they don't look at all alike. Cyril removed the cold compress, wrung it out to reapply it, when he heard a murmur.

Sallee Anne felt exhausted. She had napped, but it hadn't helped any. She hated international flights, they messed up her circadian rhythm ... other thoughts suddenly jolted her ... and her eyes flew open ...

Cyril said, "Are you feeling better? Don't move just yet. Let the blood come back. Did you have a shock?"

The Penthouse Police! Where was she? How did she get here? She did not feel good – she felt like a deflated balloon. She closed her eyes and remembered the shock of her thoughts and comforted herself with ... she wouldn't do that; this is just entertainment for the wedding guests. A full orchestra for the concerto would cost tons of money – but so does this wedding ...

Cyril was worried. "Would you like me to call someone for you? You do not look well."

"I am having some really awfly bad thoughts. They are scaring me to death!"

"Well then, you had better think of something else, before they succeed!"

A curl at the corner of her mouth; a widening of the lips; even white teeth appeared, and her eyes opened again as she smiled, "I think you are right! I must think of something else. So, who are you?"

"I am Cyril Latham, your neighbor."

"Thank you, Cyril Latham, your neighbor, for the rescue. I'm sorry to have inconvenienced you, I'll be going ... " Sallee Anne struggled to rise, but fell back as her head began to pound, and her stomach rose in protest. "Well, I might stay another minute or two ... "

"Would you like a bit of brandy?"

"You know, that might be the very thing I need just now."

Cyril poured the contents of a pony bottle into a small snifter, and handed it to her, saying, "Let me prop you up, we don't want it going down the wrong tube!"

In an almost sitting position, Sallee Anne began to feel better. The weakness faded quickly after sipping the brandy. "That's good stuff," she said, "I think it did the trick."

"Well, give it a few more minutes, there's no rush – at least I'm in no rush."

"Are you are a wedding guest too? I'm Sallee Anne Thornton, entertainment this evening."

Cyril smiled, "Hello Sallee Anne Thornton, entertainment this evening. It is nice to meet you. Do you have a shorter appellation?"

"No, today it's just Sallee Anne Thornton, entertainment this evening. However since you have resuscitated me, you can call me Sal, for short!" Her smile dazzled him.

Cyril laughed, "Sal, it is! Thank heavens!"

"What! You don't like my descriptive moniker?"

"I did not say that! It's just that I get tongue-tied easily, and didn't want to embarrass myself trying to say: I met Sallee Anne Thornton, entertainment this evening, when she fainted outside my penthouse apartment door this afternoon."

Sallee Anne laughed, asking, "Who are you? You sound like a lawyer!"

"Well! That settles that! I'm never going to resuscitate you again! You don't play fair!"

Laughter consumed Sallee Anne. "Oh, my, you must be a lawyer! I didn't mean that to sound derogatory – it's just that you were being so very precise!"

"I'm afraid the manner goes with the trade. Does it offend you?"

"Not at all. Some of us walk around with our trades stamped on our foreheads or in our speech or in our personalities. It's just an unavoidable fact of life. We are who we pretend to be, whether we like it or not."

"Well then, Cyril Latham, Esquire, your neighbor, rescuer of fainting women; I should be on my way." But then Sallee Anne had a thought and asked, "Do you have a part in the wedding performance?"

"Yes, I'm a groomsman and usher. Alfred and I went to the same university."

"Which was?"

"The University of Pennsylvania, in Philadelphia, Pennsylvania, U.S.A. Although Alfred, the groom, was a number of years ahead of me."

"Do you know my uncle, David Thornton?"

"Yes, your uncle David and I went to law school together, and roomed together, even though he was several years ahead of me, too. It was David who recommended me to Alfred, when he needed an Attorney in Africa. So, while we share the same school tie, it was business that brought Alfred and me together in later years."

"So, not only do you resuscitate well, you keep it in the family! Oh, my gosh, it just dawned on me – you must be the Cyril that Paula talks about all the time."

"Guilty, as charged."

"Cyril, would you happen to know if the bride or groom has engaged an orchestra for this evening?"

"I don't think so. A harp, and two guitars are going to play during dinner, but I think it is just you, Elizabeth and Gregor and then Hanna and Sara after dinner. There was a schedule in the back of the brochure."

Thank heavens! The brochure states that I will repeat my Carnegie Hall performance, which requires a full orchestra. That was what gave me such a gliff in the hall. You can't play with an orchestra unless you first practice with them. Each conductor adjusts himself, and therefore the orchestra, to the soloist."

"I can see why you had such a bad moment. Charlotte and Alfred have gone all out, that's for certain, and a full orchestra is not out of the question for them; however, there is only a small dais in either the blue room, where we will have dinner, with the harp and guitar trio; or the red room, which will be set up for the concert while we are at dinner. If you like, I can call Charlotte and double-check."

"Would that be too much trouble? I'm afraid the worry will devastate me until I know for certain."

"Not at all." Cyril went to the phone and said, "Please connect me to either Charlotte Schmidt, or Alfred Archer – Cyril Latham calling.

Alfred picked up his phone immediately. "Cyril, what's up?"

"I need you to clarify a point for me."

"Spit it out man, whatever it is."

"Have you engaged a full orchestra for this evening's performance?"

"Good Heavens, no! What would make you think that?"

"It says in the brochure that Miss Thornton will repeat her Carnegie Hall performance, which was a concerto with a full orchestra."

"Nah, it was just a poor choice of words. Is there a problem?"

"Not any more. Thanks Al, bye." Cyril returned to Sal, saying, "Al said, 'it was just a poor choice of words.' They are not musically lettered, concert – concerto, what's the difference?" They both laughed until their sides ached.

Through the merriment came the delightful refrains of a piano and a violin, competing with one another; with the violin saying: 'anything you can do, I can do better; I can do anything better than you!' And the piano saying: 'no, you can't' – 'no, you can't' – and the violin saying: 'yes, I can – yes I can – yes, I can!'

Elizabeth and Gregor had not played together recently. They decided to brush up on the variations for piano and violin that they had composed together so long ago.

Cyril and Sal just sat entranced. The music was divine.

★   ★   ★

Soon after arriving, Elmer, Wolfgang and Friedrich were attracted when they heard the Steinways in use. Elmer had not heard the twins play before, and their music enchanted him. Elmer took an unobtrusive seat in the library, where he could watch Sara's face as she played. Wolfgang and Friedrich soon joined him, and sat watching Hanna. Sara smiled often and nodded her head as did Hanna, and the two girls produced bliss with the pianos, stopping but once for a three note revision.

Elmer recognized the pieces, for he loved classical music, but had never heard these pieces played with such panache; or with the cascades of waterfall notes or the expressive underscores; four hands, not two and the difference was simply marvelous.

I wonder if Mother has any idea what magnificent entertainment she is providing her guests this evening. No other wedding in history has ever had such marvelous musicians regale the wedding guests … and they are all family.

When the girls finished, Elmer arose and clapped vigorously with cries of 'marvelous' – 'delightful.' He followed up saying: "It would be my pleasure to escort you ladies through the Bazaar, if you have an interest, unless you would prefer tea."

Sara immediately jumped on the invitation, saying, "I'd be delighted." Hanna smiled and said, "Yes, I'd like that too. Then I can take a short nap when we get back." Elmer turned to Wolfgang and Friedrich saying, "If you have money belts, wear them. Just keep a bit of cash in a buttoned shirt pocket. Ladies, carry nothing; if you must take something, I will carry it for you."

"Are the pick-pockets that bad?" Sara asked,

"No," Elmer replied, "they're worse!" enjoying the laughter from his wit.

As they left the hotel, Elmer offered Sara his arm, saying, "Walking closely together makes it harder for the pick-pockets too."

Wherein, Wolfgang offered his arm to Hanna. Friedrich just followed along with Paula and Thomas who walked behind, amused by Elmer's skillful maneuvering.

★   ★   ★

"Mother, it's Elmer. I was wondering who all is coming on *The Never End* for lunch today."

"Today is just family, dear: Alfred, me, you, Regina, Ludwig, Hans, Friedrich, Wolfgang, Elizabeth and Gregor."

"Would two more throw your plans out of whack?"

"Who do you have in mind?"

"I'd like you to invite Hanna and Sara, if possible. Wolfgang is stuck on Hanna, and I only have three days to get to know Sara better."

"It shouldn't be a problem, it is a buffet luncheon; I'll call the girls now. I was going to call them anyway to thank them for playing for us last evening. They were truly marvelous."

★   ★   ★

"Hanna, Sara, – Aunt Charlotte called while you were out. She wanted to thank you ever so much for a wonderful performance last evening. She also wanted to invite you to luncheon today aboard *The Never End*. Elmer will call for you at noon."

"Do you know the guest list, Mother?"

"No, but she mentioned it was a family luncheon."

"Why would she invite us to a family luncheon?"

"She said your presence was requested ... but she didn't say by whom. Are you available? You know, we are here at the pleasure of Charlotte and Alfred."

"Yes, of course we are available, and pleased to be invited."

"Well, call her and accept her invitation. Just ask the switchboard to connect you to *The Never End* and say who is calling."

★   ★   ★

"Elmer just called and asked us to escort Hanna and Sara to the family luncheon on board *The Never End* today. He was going to do it, but something has come up," Wolfgang said to Friedrich. "I didn't know Hanna and Sara were invited, did you?"

"No," Friedrich said rather sullenly.

337

Wolfgang smiled to himself. Serves him right, he should have staked a claim when he had the opportunity. Elmer has a great deal of charm. Rick's going to have a tough road ahead if he wants to make a race of it with Elmer. Although, Elmer only has three days – however, if Sara falls for Elmer, three days is enough time.

"I don't think I'll go to the luncheon."

"Giving up, are you?"

"Nothing to give up."

"If that's the case, why are you disappointing your Aunt Charlotte, your Mother, Hans and Ludwig? If you go in the bedroom, you can lean over the bed while I give you a good swift kick."

Friedrich looked at Wolfy and smiled. "That's what I need, isn't it?"

"You told me a closed mind is a stupid mind, and if you ever had one again to give you a good swift kick."

"I like Sara! I like her very much! But I've just gotten free – free from school, and free from Schönbrunn. I don't want to be tied down again so soon."

"If that's the way you feel, then you don't love her. Let her go, she's not for you if you feel that a commitment to her would be tying you down."

"But ... what about *us* doing things together?"

"There will always be an *us*, just not the *us* you had imagined. What puzzles me is that you are throwing away the present for a totally undecided future. If you had something else definite in mind, I might understand your position a bit better."

"I know ... but I've planned on us being together for so long!" Friedrich complained.

"Let nature take its course. Do what feels right for you; maybe something else is in store for you. You can't fight fate."

"But, if we are not together ... I have nothing."

"Silly boy, I don't have to live in your pocket for us to be together. We will always be close, even if we take separate paths ... just as we have always been close."

"But I don't want to go on alone; I'm only happy doing things with you. All my life I have felt that way ... and now ... when it's finally possible for us to be together most of the time, we are going to go separate ways."

"I know what you mean about our plans. However, being bosom buddies never meant that I would not fall in love, or not marry, or not have children. We will still be together, but differently; you wish for Utopia, I wish for natural order. You should live your life, doing what you want to do. Lady Mary would have you back at Dela-Aden, even if you didn't marry Sara. No one wants you to marry someone you are not in love with, and Sara deserves someone who is truly in love with her."

"I know Sara likes me, and I really like her; can't we just leave it that way for a while?"

"Certainly – but if you don't take the wind when it fills your sail, you might just find yourself in the doldrums."

★   ★   ★

I don't know why I had to come down to *The Never End* so early. I was going to listen to Hanna and Sara practice – they love the Steinways. Oh well, this is Mother's special time, and I must put her wishes first.

"Good Morning, Darling." Charlotte hugged her son. He was filling out, man style, broader shoulders, deeper chest and a bit taller too. I'm glad he is happy in Aspen; I just wish it were not so far away.

"Good to see you again, Elmer. It's been too long," Alfred added. How's it going – putting your life's experience and knowledge to work in Aspen?"

"Quite well. The Hotel Jerome is an old place with tons of charm, and quite popular, so we are usually busy. I'm glad you two decided to do this now, two weeks later and I'd never have gotten away," Elmer smiled mischievously.

"Don't you think we didn't know that? Everyone wanted to know why the short notice. It also pleased Alfred, didn't it dear."

"Yup! Get it done and over with – and move on," he winked at Elmer, conspiratorially.

"Would you like a cup of coffee, dear? I need a refill."

"No, I broke myself of the habit of drinking coffee all morning, but thanks."

"Now where is my list? Alfred, did you see my list?"

"You had it this morning on *The Just Beginning*. Did you leave it there?"

"I don't remember."

"It was in the breakfast booth with all your other papers and notes."

"Where are you going, Alfred?"

"Captain needs me topside, back in a bit."

"Elmer, would you mind going to get my list, dear. It is a five by seven yellow pad, with lots of turned back pages. I can't believe I went off without it."

"Not at all; can I peek around *The Just Beginning* while I'm there"

"Of course, but we're having the rehearsal dinner there on Friday.

Elmer arrived at the dining booth to find a large white envelope addressed to him.

"Happy Birthday, Elmer – Love, Mom and Alfred"

Inside was another envelope … from Dodd, Mead and Company, New York.

He opened the envelope and removed the letter:

Dear Elmer,

It is with great pleasure that I ask you to submit the Bemis manuscripts in your possession. The story titled: 'The Boy That Did Not', came to us from Charlotte Schmidt via Alfred Bates Archer, a member of our board of directors. We found the story delightful.

The manuscript was an original in longhand. We would prefer to see the rest of the manuscripts set in type, before submission.

Most Sincerely,

Katherine Peters, Senior Editor

Elmer sat stunned, and truly touched. Tears of joy brimmed in his eyes. Bemis had given that story to his mother about a year after he arrived to tutor me. It was about me and all the things I did not do. I think he was on the verge of despair, when he wrote it. I so hated schooling – but I loved Bemis, and in wanting to please him, he was able to turn me around. I had totally forgotten about that story. Mother showed it to me just before I went off to college. Reading his story made me realize how far I had progressed, which gave me the sand I needed to endure my freshman year.

★   ★   ★

"Cyril, David here; Peter and I are going to take the tender out for a junket down to Casablanca. Want to come?"

"Sounds like fun, but I've already made plans."

"Nothing that can't wait?"

"Nothing that I would want to wait."

"Sounds mysterious."

"Not mysterious at all – just a prior commitment."

"A woman?"

"I'm not the type to *kiss and tell*."

"We'll miss you old buddy, but have a good time!"

"I'm sure I will, thanks!"

"Peter, David here: Cyril is busy. Do you think Thomas and Paula might like to go with us, there's room for eight. I asked Charles and Lisa, James and Marga'ret, and they're coming. We have room for two more.

"I think they are going to the Bazaar, but why don't you call them."

"Peter, we're meeting on the pier at eleven. The crew is off-loading the tender now. Paula and Thomas have decided to go with us. What is Mary doing?"

"She is busy putting labels on Hanna's and Sara's performances, the date the place, their ages, the selections. It is part of her wedding present. She didn't have time to get it done before we left – notice was a bit short."

"That it was. Be on the pier at eleven, with sunglasses, sunscreen and a hat!"

★   ★   ★

Sallee Anne had agreed to meet Cyril in the Library. She loved playing the perfectly tuned piano, enjoying the depth and luscious full tones of a Steinway concert grand piano.

"I'm glad Mom and Dad went on that outing to Casablanca in *The Never End*'s tender. They so enjoy being on the water." She said to Cyril.

"Yes, your Uncle David called and asked me to join them. Is there something in particular that you would like to do now?"

"Yes, I'd like to go to the Bazaar. I put some money in my shoe."

Cyril laughed. "That's a novel place to hide money."

"Not for a female musician wearing a long sleeve silk blouse and a long black skirt. There is virtually no place else!"

"Why would you need money when you are dressed for a performance?"

"Good question. I cannot think of a single logical reason!" And she laughed gaily. "My Mother has always insisted that I have *mad-money* with me, no matter where I go."

Cyril felt even more intrigued today than he had yesterday. Sal's free and open manner was similar to Paula's, but wiser, more sophisticated, and yes, even a bit dignified, as long as she wasn't spilling something on her book. But, somehow, the knowledge that she would use unsavory expletives somehow made her more fascinating, as in still waters run deep.

"What is *mad-money?*" Cyril asked.

Sallee Anne, amused by his consternation, laughed in a titillating way. How do I say this without shocking him, she thought. Might as well see how he musters–up. "*Mad-money* is just that. When a gal is out on a date and unseemly advances are made and rebuffed, but continue to be made – a gal can get *mad* and just leave, if she has *money* for a cab, hence: *mad-money.*"

It took Cyril not a moment before he was laughing, absolutely delighted. "And you are carrying *mad-money?*"

"Always and ever – I don't leave home without it!"

They laughed so merrily that the laughter became infectious, and fed on itself.

Why am I so happy? This woman must be sixteen years my junior; she is much too young for me ... but she sparkles so, and she makes me feel alive ... all the way to my toes. What is age anyway, but a frame of mind? I've known people to be decrepit at forty. I'm going on forty-five; I will get older, of course. However, I have never felt younger! What will be, will be – and I feel boundless joy in the anticipation.

The Bazaar was fantastic and incredible. Everything under the sun was for sale: and all for *a bargain price, just for you.* Sallee Ann bought a paperweight horse made of solid brass lying on a wooden base of painted grass. It reminded her of Golden Boy back at home; it would be a good and usable souvenir.

The *Penthouse Police* has a nice sense of humor, Sallee Anne observed, even if he is a lawyer. I asked Uncle David about him at the reception last evening. I told him how he had rescued me from my first fainting spell ... which would have been terribly embarrassing except for his diplomacy and tact. Uncle David said he was fastidious: 'hates women who wear tons of make-up, girdles and clothes that are too tight. He dislikes loud and shrill voices; he especially doesn't like bossy women or women who use bad language.'

Oops, I almost measure-up: I never wear make-up, just a bit of colored lip gloss; don't own a girdle and my tightest clothing is my knee socks, or panty-hose. Why am I even thinking these things? I just met the man yesterday. True, too true, but I don't deny the attraction. I don't even know what it is ... it is just there. I like being with him ... I feel good in his company – very relaxed and comfortable. Mother will think he is too old for me – Uncle David said he was around forty-four, saying, 'There was a big difference in our ages at school, even so, we hit it off well anyway.'

★   ★   ★

I'm so glad we had time for a nap. All that sea air and wind wore me out, but what fun, Lisa thought. Charles found the tender quite interesting. The Captain of *The Never End* and David were at the controls, where they could stand or sit as they pleased. The eight passengers sat on cushioned benches, three to a side, with two on the stern around a table with deep cup holders and a wide recessed center slot holding the mixings and the ice. Pennants fluttered above the fiberglass canopy with storm windows rolled up snugly into the canopy lip.

Passenger access was from the rear, where a skiing platform, ladders and metal railings gave inexperienced sailors a handhold. The table, hinged on either side of the center well, concealed a fiberglass hatch for the engines, and fuel. Folded down, the table halves became emergency passenger seats. Emergency supplies were stowed in the wide bench, behind and under the pilot and co-pilot, who entered the craft at the dual wheels. It was a luxury jaunting or ferrying craft designed to be a life saver as well.

"Did you like the tender?" Lisa asked, already knowing the answer.

"Yes, it was delightful, and useful and efficient. But a motor yacht is not as much fun, to me, as sailing. How about you? Did you like it?"

"It was an interesting way to get to Casablanca, which was just as mysterious as it was in the movie of the same name. I love to see foreign places that I have often heard about. It is like cleaning out a closet. You find all kinds of things you didn't know were there, Lisa replied."

Charles smiled. He would never get used to Lisa's analogies. She always brought things down to simplicity, waving away the mystique with her point of view.

"It was a good group today, although Marga'ret looked a bit green," Charles said.

"She's a good egg, but I don't think she or James have spent much time on the water in small craft. You and I are used to skimming over the waves, and getting bounced around. Even so, they both held up well. Paula, as usual, was in her element."

"James was certainly fascinated by the efficient use of space. I think he now knows that tender better than the ship builder!"

"I like James," Lisa said. "He is so British … but not the stuffy, pompous type; he has a genuine interest in everything. Nothing is too small to escape his notice."

"Probably what makes him such a successful architect," Charles replied.

"Are you ready to go yet?"

"Yes! Ready and chomping at the bit; I can't wait to board *The Never End*."

★ ★ ★

"Are you having a good time?" Hanna asked Sara

"Good gosh, yes! Why would you ask such a question?"

"Elmer is showing quite a bit of interest in you. I'm sure you've noticed."

"Yes, Elmer is charming – like Wolfgang – but he is also down to earth, there is no mystique about him like there is about Wolfy. Elmer is very mature for his age; I thought he was much older. He has a marvelous sense of the ridiculous too, which you know I enjoy. His attentions are very flattering, but there is no spark. I just like him as I would anyone interesting ... his attentions have made me realize that I might be in love with Friedrich ... but that is a one-way street!"

"That's why I asked. I sensed as much. I just wondered if you were facing the facts. You and Rick do have a spark, you know; it's just that Rick is not ready for any kind of commitment. Some men are like that. I hope you don't lead Elmer on, he more than likes you, you know."

"I have been very casual with him. He asked me to go to dinner with him after the cocktail party, but I said we had already accepted an invitation to dine with Paula's parents, which we did. I'm looking forward to getting to know Charles and Lisa a bit better. Our days in England were so chaotic; we hardly said two words to each other."

"You'll probably see Elmer at the dance."

"Yes, probably; I do love to dance. Who knows, Friedrich might even ask me to dance with him." Sara laughed. "You know, Hanna, right this moment I don't give a fig about either of them. It is just too much bother! If it wouldn't cut into your fun, I'd ask you to spend the evening practicing with me on those marvelous pianos."

Hanna mentally agreed; it is a great deal of bother – I don't like feeling so unsettled. I'm very tempted to take Sara up on her suggestion that we spend the evening playing the pianos. "I could use the practice, Sara, but that would send the wrong message to

Charlotte and Alfred, they have gone all out to make these few days simply marvelous for their guests."

"Yes, I suppose so; are you ready to go, Hanna? Mom and Dad are waiting for us."

★ ★ ★

"I can see why you are drawn to Sara," Charlotte said to Elmer, "she sparkles: her eyes, her smile, and her bright conversation."

"I'm not getting much in the way of feedback from her. She treats me like a guest at a cocktail party, pleasant, but not interested."

"She is not worldly. She has just graduated from finishing school. She has yet to meet the world, although, she did have her grand tour in July, which is where she and Hanna met Wolfgang and Friedrich."

"I can see that Hanna and Wolfgang have connected, but she treats Friedrich much the same as she treats me — offhand."

"Keep at it, son. Don't get discouraged. Write to her. Ask her family to come to Aspen to ski or something. Let her stretch her wings a bit — I don't think she is ready to get serious about anyone. She needs to meet more young men so she has a basis for comparison. I admire her for her discernment." Charlotte said, encouraging him.

"I can't believe I am having this conversation with my mother, who is going to get married again tomorrow. However, if anyone knows women, it is a woman, and in that you qualify!"

"I certainly do ... and I'll thank you not to be flip!"

"Elmer, I overheard you talking to your mother," Alfred said. "She knows what she is talking about. Your Mother gave me the cold shoulder for two years, with my comings and goings. She liked me, we had good times together, but she wouldn't get serious until I told her I was going to semi-retire, and asked if she'd like to go on a long cruise together. She said, she would enjoy that, but not on *The Never End*, which was Lucinda's home.

So, I had a yacht built for her, one that she had some say in, and it changed her attitude towards me entirely. She saw that I was willing to put her first. It is what all women want from men, a commitment

346

to keep them first. So, if you show Sara that you intend to put her first and if she feels the spark, that's how it happens."

"Thanks, Alfred; I needed some manly input on this. I've had girlfriends, but none that interested me the way Sara does."

"Keep at it son, write to her like your mother said. Girls love letters. Tell her a bit about yourself, what you like and don't like and what you like to do for fun. Remember, she is a brilliant pianist, and that alone makes her exceptional. Her education makes her discerning too, but there you are her match. I do believe in *love at first sight*, but there is more true love that begins as friendship as anything else."

★   ★   ★

Wolfgang and Friedrich had a meeting Saturday evening with Elizabeth and Gregor before their late flight to Vienna, to discuss business about the Trust. They wanted to consider Sallee Anne's suggestion to streamline the interviews with applicants: that instead of making individual trips for each applicant, they make zones and visit the zones when they had three applicants in a zone. She said she would be able to work out a probable list of zones and a visit schedule if they sent her the recent demographics. Regrettably, she felt at this time, it would be best if she only acted as an advisor to the Trust.

Wolfgang said he planned on staying in Africa, and he needed to have the Trust papers set up for him to do so, by the time he was twenty-five.

Friedrich liked the idea of a specific time each month to review the progress of those already in the program. That way, he would be able to work his on-going projects around the scheduled inspection visits.

They agreed that information from board members would go to Wolfgang, and he would send out a progress letter each month, so everyone had the same information. For now, they decided on semi-annual board meetings in Savona, Italy.

★   ★   ★

Sunday morning, Peter, Mary, Hanna and Sara, with Wolfgang and Friedrich, met James and Marga'ret, Charles and Lisa, for breakfast. A last hurrah before they climbed into the jitneys to go to the airport for afternoon flights home. David Thornton and Elmer had booked a redeye flight to the States on Saturday evening. Regina, Ludwig and Hans rode with them to the airport, for a late flight to Italy.

"Wolfgang, we are so pleased that you and Friedrich have decided to return to Kenya with us. We thought you might head back to Savona," Mary said.

"There is very little in Savona for us, compared to what there is for us at Dela-Aden. Friedrich and I love horses; we will be able to do what we like best while being with people we enjoy most. We are delighted that it suits you. We intend to make ourselves useful when and where needed, especially in your training program."

Peter asked, "Does that include setting fence posts?" The laughter was spontaneous and delighted, with Hanna saying, "You were right, Sara, sufferance is over; it is time to help with the fence posts." Peter felt he was missing something and added, "Of course, I'm just joking," which produced even more laughter.

Lady Mary, always practical, added, "Beyond the jesting, Peter and I are delighted that you intend to return to Dela-Aden. We have decided to paint the inside of the guest house. That way, you will have a place of your own, with more personal room and privacy for your Trust work. We hope you will still take tea and your dinner meal with us at the big house. Helen has been asking for work. She can look after you each morning for breakfast and tend to your needs until lunch."

Hanna felt annoyed – thinking, why can't they stay in the house with us? Then she saw what her Mother saw. Distance makes the heart grow fonder, and gives one pause.

Marga'ret, never one to miss a nuance said, "I'm so glad James made accommodations over the new barn for long-term guests. That way, we have the company of enjoyable people, and they are quite comfortable, without worrying about being under foot."

★   ★   ★

Paula and Thomas were eating breakfast with Sallee Anne and Cyril in a cozy booth at the rear of the Café. Paula saw the rosy glow

348

on Sal's face and knew Sal well enough to know that she more than liked Cyril. He is a bit old for her, but love is where you find it.

Paula knew Cyril well, and his unusual jocular manner was amusing. Today, however, he was a bit glum, for the parting distressed him.

Sallee Anne spoke, "I went over my calendar last night and my bookings through December. I have a few bookings next year too, but not until April and May. So, I could return to Africa after the first of the year." Sal looked at Cyril and smiled. Cyril returned her smile asking, "Where would you like to stay when you come back?" Sallee Anne looked at Thomas and asked, "Is there room for me at Dela-Aden?"

"We have a very nice guest house at Dela-Aden; it has four bedrooms and two baths, and is currently unused. It has a small open front porch, a sitting room with fireplace, a galley kitchen and dining area, with two smallish bedrooms and a bath in the rear. There are two larger bedrooms and a bath on the second floor; however, there is no piano."

"Gloria has a piano," Cyril offered. "Her deceased husband used to play. She might like having company, if you want to stay in Nairobi."

"I'd rather be with Paula, if that is possible. Being so far away from home is bad enough, but staying with strangers would make it difficult for me. I am so used to being able to do what I please, when I please, that I wouldn't make a very good guest."

"Well, Dela-Aden has plenty of *do as you please* room, so plan on staying with us," Thomas added.

"I hope you will ask your mother and father to invite me as well, I would feel much better about coming for a lengthy stay, if you did."

"But, of course, I am the heir, but Mom and Dad are the owners – although I feel I know them well enough to say they will be delighted." Thomas smiled.

"Wolfgang and Friedrich are coming back too. It is going to be so nice having everyone at Dela-Aden," Paula added. "Sal, you are going to just love the farm."

Yes, Cyril thought, Sal will love Dela-Aden … I love Dela-Aden … we all love Dela-Aden, but unfortunately, it is not around the block … it is an hour's drive from Nairobi … and January is a long way away too.

★   ★   ★

"I'm so glad to be going home! I've done more traveling in the last four months than I have done in my entire life … or at least, it feels that way," Hanna said to Sara.

"Yes, we've certainly been gallivanting around, but it was all so glorious, don't you think?"

"That's true; there were never any dull moments. We might find our futures a bit staid in comparison, although I am never bored at Dela-Aden. I love it there, and the more I travel, the more I love it," Hanna replied.

"I know what you mean. I always wanted to go places and now that I have, I more than ever want to go home, although, the Steinway concert grands were a special treat." Sara sighed. "You and Wolfgang were thick in Morocco. He is such an elegant person, even if you didn't like Wolfgang; you'd have to admire him. Do you like that about him? It makes him seem a bit unapproachable."

"I like everything about Wolfgang; I find nothing unlikable; I just hope he likes me as much as I like him, and we do get along well. We seem to understand one another, and we enjoy many of the same things in life. Now, if only he would tell me he loves me – then I'd be walking on air."

"What do you two talk about? You always seem to be laughing at something."

"He has a marvelous sense of the ridiculous, as do I, and we both titillate one another with our observations and conversation."

"I wish it was that way with Friedrich and me. He is always nice and pleasant, but he never offers anything. I thought he might change when Elmer began monopolizing my time, but he just seemed to accept it."

"Do you like Elmer?"

"How could anyone not like Elmer? He is so urbane; always ready with a smile, and what a charming smile too; ready to satisfy your teeniest desire; and he seems to know something about everything. He loves classical music too, and is quite conversant on the subject."

"But?"

"I don't know. I've decided not to count the petals; just let them fall where they may. Did I tell you that Elmer asked me – us – to visit Aspen? They have a summer music festival there, and Elmer is on the advisory board."

"No, you didn't, but I'd like that. Mom and Dad just loved Aspen. Too bad they didn't know Elmer lived there in May when they were touring. However, that is life, isn't it? Learning today what you didn't know yesterday."

Hanna's right! I know more about men today than I did yesterday, and if logic follows, I will know more tomorrow, which tells me I don't know much at all. Her dark sky parted and the sun came shining through – and I will learn more every day! Our lives are not going to change in the near future. Hanna and I will still play the piano together, for Hanna told me that Wolfgang hopes to live in Africa – at Dela-Aden.

★   ★   ★

Wolfgang and Friedrich were still flying on their first class round trip tickets with interim stops, and so, sat apart from the others.

"What are you thinking, Wolfy? You've been unusually quiet."

"I have been thinking mostly about you. I esteem your friendship, as you well know, but your attitude to my moving on in life perplexes me. I am trying to think of a solution that will satisfy both of us."

I'm a bounder! A cad! Friedrich thought. "I had no right to rain on your parade, but I have; how can you still want me for a friend?"

"Where does it say that friends have to be perfect?"

"It's a good thing there is no such rule – I've been messing up a lot lately."

"Have you figured out why?"

"Possibly, I just need more time."

"How much time?"

"A month or so; is that too much to ask?"

"What I don't understand is: how will a month – or even a year – make a difference?"

Friedrich thought, he's right, it won't, and it hasn't. "I'm just procrastinating."

"So, why you are procrastinating?"

"How do you always know to ask the question that I don't want to answer?"

"It is because you have been this way all of your life, and I'm not that slow of a learner."

Friedrich laughed. Wolfy is right: I hate change and he knows it! "Do I do this all of the time?"

"Define 'all'!" And he smirked.

"How do you put up with me?"

"Damned if I know! But I do, and I sometimes wonder if it's worth it!"

"You just said that to bring me to *heel*. You are too loyal to abandon me. I just need to sit down and write a list of pros and cons and see which side wins."

"I have pencil and pad in my carry-on; I'll get them for you. Maybe we can get this thing settled, and put the misery of your angst out of my life."

Friedrich looked at Wolfy askance. Did he mean that? Am I making a mess of his life too? Am I that self-absorbed? His thoughts and the probable answers unsettled Rick. I have tunnel vision — all I see is me, not others. I wanted to be free of supervision, and I am. Now I'm inflicting supervision on Wolfy by restricting change in his life or our relationship. What is the matter with me? How could I do such a thing? As of today — I will embrace change, and move ever onward.

41 ~ Ever Onward

"Mary, what are you thinking? You've been sitting there for an hour? Is something wrong?"

"Peter, are you pleased with the way things have settled in the family?"

"Yes, very, although a bit saddened too. Happy that Hanna and Sara are settled, but sad, for I don't think Jon and Anna are coming back to Dela–Aden."

"I know. Jon and Anna are quite content at Woleston Hall with James and Marga'ret. Jon has found a place tutoring African Languages at Oxford, and Anna is helping her father at Inkpen, where it seems they have discovered ancient secrets or something."

"Yes, I know they are happy in their new lives, but I truly miss Jon. He was very good at working the farm. He knows as much as I do, and he needed no supervision at all. Thomas is a pale helper in comparison.

"Oh, Peter, what an awful thing to say, I'm surprised at you. That is why I've been sitting here. I was remembering … it was a year ago today that we were reunited with Thomas in Kampala."

"Oh, Mary, dearest! You know I'm no good at remembering dates. However, I should have remembered that one! My missing Jon doesn't mean I'm not overjoyed to have Thomas back … but, I'm doing to Thomas what I did to Jon, aren't I? Ignoring what I do have for what I'm missing."

"Yes, dear, you are. We have Thomas back and he is a marvelous person, different yes, but still a boundless joy!"

"You're right, Mary; I'm just feeling maudlin about Jon staying in England."

"We have nothing to feel maudlin about. Just the opposite; the last twelve months have been the best days of our lives."

"Yes, they have been exceptional … except for Jon and Anna staying in England."

"Peter, let it go; don't be selfish. Anna has her parents; Jon has Anna, the Hall, Marga'ret, James and their family, with whom he has always been close. Jon was a farmer to be with you when you so grieved for Thomas. Jon is good at anything he chooses to do, but he was a farmer to please you, to help you through a terrible time."

"I am being selfish, aren't I … ruing Jon's happiness for my loss of competent help."

Mary arose from the club chair and sat beside Peter on the bed. She took his hand and put her head on his shoulder. "You're a father. You miss your son … who has decided to live in England with his wife. That is not selfish, that is normal and understandable. I miss Jon and Anna too, but I'm pleased they are happy. It is what a parent wants for their children, a fulfilling and happy life."

Peter put his arm around Mary and gave her a hug. "You always know what to say to bring me out of my blue funks. However, I don't think you were contemplating Jon and Anna for an hour; what else were you thinking?"

"I was thinking about Dela–Aden and, of all of us living here – and of all the events of the past twelve months. More events and happenings than in our entire lives. The whirlwind began when we received the letters from Jon and Thomas, before our reunion in Kampala. While the excitement has diminished, I don't think it has ended."

"I thought everything was kind of settled now. Is there something I should know? I'm getting cold, Mary, let's get under the covers – how cold are your feet?"

"Not cold at all, feel … "

"Aaagh! Mary, I insist you put on some socks – my legs just shriveled up!"

Mary put on socks and nestled next to Peter saying: "Events took leaps and bounds after Charlotte and Alfred married in Morocco last October. Up until then everything was up in the air. "On returning to Dela–Aden, Friedrich began to seriously court Sara; his attitude changed, I think, by Elmer's interest in Sara in Morocco. Friedrich thought Sara might rebuff him after his earlier nonchalance, but Sara was secretly smitten, and glad Rick finally took up the pursuit.

"Wolfgang and Hanna were already spending every spare moment together, so planning to get married in England over the holidays was a logical progression of events.

"Thomas concluded his experiments and found the properties of the kimmea unchanged by hothouse culture. Cyril notified APCO, which set in motion all sorts of unforeseen events.

"However, the big surprise was that after Cyril set up the charitable corporation, First Aid for Africa (FAFA), he then put his office affairs in order, and left for Pennsylvania to go on tour with Sallee Anne. Paula said they rented one of those bus-like motor-homes with a driver and a spinet piano, so Sallee Anne could practice while they traveled around between her concerts. That is so like Cyril, *in for a penny — in for a pound*. So, it was no surprise that Cyril came back engaged. The surprise was that they were going to get married in England during Boxing Day when Hanna and Sara were to marry Wolfgang and Friedrich."

"Yes, that was a surprise. Thomas told me that Paula and Marga'ret were responsible for that decision; they both wanted all the family to be together to share everything," Peter added.

"And we were all together," Mary agreed. "Although I thought Cyril might balk. He wanted a quiet ceremony here in Africa, then a honeymoon cruise in New Zealand. I'm glad he realized that by getting married his way, it would be an elopement for Sallee Anne, for all the guests would be in England, except for Gloria. Cyril may be older and a bit set in his ways, but he wants to please Sallee Anne, and finally came to accept, and like, the idea of a triple wedding."

"Marga'ret certainly outdid herself during the holidays. I would have been pulling my hair out! But not Marga'ret! With her, the more the merrier; I do believe she could organize the Queen **and** the Royal Family too, without batting an eyelash!" Mary said.

Peter laughed at the thought, saying, "I agree! Three weddings in one day, a reception that filled the Hall to overflowing, houseguests in every nook and cranny, a cook that refused to let the caterers in her kitchen, so they had to set up in the summer dining hall, where

James had to pipe water and drains for the sinks. Talk about complex organization! However, Marga'ret seemed unfazed through it all."

Mary smiled. "Yes, she was, and James, who often escaped to his office to hideaway, was a brick through it all, too.

"Marga'ret wrote that it was the social event of the year. The clipping service sent her notices from Vienna, Monaco, Nairobi, Rabat and Savona: Pisa, Livorno, Florence, Rome, Aspen, and Philadelphia, as well as most of the papers in England. The county is still talking about it."

"That's quite understandable. I don't think the event will ever be topped," Peter replied. "I have heard of double weddings in a family before, but never a triple one. However, in retrospect, having the festivities in England at Boxing Day was an excellent decision ... for the logistics worked out well for everyone. Even though Jon and Anna were married in August, they were still included in the celebrations ... Marga'ret saw to that."

"Yes, she did, and did it so well. We were all together for the festivities and everyone came: Charles and Lisa, and their sons Scott, a most dashing man, and Eric, Paula's twin brother; along with David and Bela and their two boys, Dave and Chuck, as well as Alfred and Charlotte and Elmer, who is now engaged to that nice outgoing girl, Beth, whom he met on the plane returning to Aspen from Morocco; and of course, Paula and Thomas. I'm glad Samuel offered to care for Windy.

"Charlotte even remarked to me, 'I thought I was efficient at crowd control, but I don't hold a candle to Marga'ret, who has organized Christmas, New Years and the whole family married in one fell swoop!'"

"Marga'ret is amazing at organizing shin-digs, that's for sure!" Peter said, completely awed by the memory. "It was supposed to be Jon and Anna's time to shine, but they were delighted to share the limelight, for Anna said to me, ' ... we are old-marrieds now, this is a much better celebration ... for all of us.' and I think she was sincere."

"Anna is possibly the sweetest and most unassuming lass I have ever known. She is perfect for Jon, and he dotes on her," Mary added.

"But, you know, Mary, as gay and exciting as all that panoply was … I had an even better time visiting the Zuri Watu on our return trip to Africa."

"Yes, those few days were a step back in time … and yet a giant step forward. It's hard to explain … and Thomas and Paula seemed so much at home there," Mary offered.

"What was so marvelous was seeing what I envision for the Kikuyu in actual practice. The Zuri Watu are as different from the natives I have known, as it is possible to be, and still be the same race. I was so impressed with their dignity and intelligence. It made me realize that the dominance of the English here in Kenya has crushed their self esteem. Instead of improving their lives, it has degraded them. Well, we will keep moving forward … and hope it is catching!"

"When James and Marga'ret came to visit and James looked over the building sites, he told me they had a grand time together on the cruise ship to Hawaii — once he and Marga'ret recovered from the shock of seeing Jon and Anna on the ship. James said he had no intention of going on to Hawaii, but he didn't want to be a spoil-sport. He said providence was watching out for him, because Hawaii delighted him more than any other place he has ever been. Would you like to go to Hawaii?" Peter asked.

"One day, I would like to do the Alaska cruise and land tour, and then stay on the ship to Hawaii, and then go to Australia and New Zealand with it."

"Why, Mary … that would be a two-month tour!"

"I know. Wouldn't it be marvelous? Wolfgang and Friedrich could keep an eye on things here. Simmons and Hanley know what to do, and will do it, if they have someone to report to each day. Part of their diligence is our appreciation of it."

"You know, you're right! My, that is an intriguing idea … although; if we caught the transition cruise back to Alaska from New Zealand next spring, I'd still be here for the harvests. I've never been on a cruise ship; but, James did say it was the most fantastic way to travel — ever."

Mary snuggled in closer, "I like your idea, let's plan on it!"

★ ★ ★

Paula felt a bit restless. It was hard to get back into her old routine after such a fantastic time in England. Things felt a little dull here after Christmas, New Years and a triple wedding ceremony all together, with the weddings on Saturday, New Year's Eve day. Then, the combined wedding reception and New Year's Eve celebration, what a fantastic blast! On Monday, the newly-weds flew to Hawaii for a cruise of the islands, and then flew to Australia where they picked up a cruise for the west coast of Australia and New Zealand. How I longed to go with them. I know Thomas enjoys cruising … maybe we can go on one when things settle into a less hectic routine.

We've been super busy; between the charitable corporation and building the new house that James designed for Jon and Anna. We down-sized it a bit to sit on the hill above the garden shed, east of the sepele trees, so it overlooks the tea fields from the screened porches in the rear.

I'm so glad that Sir Peter likes to oversee any building process on the property. Not only does he like to do it, he has a flair for it too. All I have to do is answer their questions.

I loved being in the big house with everyone, but I wasn't getting the necessary work done on my thesis. I found myself listening to the girls' marvelous music – rather than doing my work, as I so often did with Sallee Anne at home.

Once the kimmea proved to be viable when grown in a hothouse, the money just rolled in … sudden, lavish and extreme wealth, which gave us the wherewithal to build our lovely new home. The funds Jon gave Thomas were running low from our travel expenses.

Jon declined a position on the Board of the new charitable corporation, but Wolfgang and Friedrich both accepted positions. Cyril took the job as Chairman of the Board for the charitable corporation, First Aid for Africa, (FAFA) and phased out his public law practice, keeping only the family clients. It was a big change in his life … but so was getting married. Being Chairman of the Board gave Cyril the freedom to travel with Sallee Anne to her concerts, which he enjoyed doing – wherever they were.

358

Thomas is President and CEO of the corporation and runs Operations; I am Senior Vice President and Treasurer, managing the finances with Cyril's CPA as Assistant Treasurer. Gloria is Secretary to the Corporation, and handles all correspondence. Peter and Mary control property rights and all building decisions; both are gifted with common sense and good taste, and James approves all building plans. The other nice thing is that Sir Peter no longer cries *too expensive*, when Mary has an innovative idea. We all have more money than we'll ever have projects to spend it on.

Wolfgang heads Personnel Planning, which includes training and placing personnel in the first aid stations; while Friedrich heads Logistics (supplies) and Quality Control (delivery).

A nice bonus for FAFA was that many of the native workers on Dela–Aden who had availed themselves of the opportunity to learn to read, write and do arithmetic, were able to move up to supervisory positions with FAFA ... which delighted Sir Peter, who began to build larger schools.

Cyril hashes through all the legal stuff for us, while Sallee Anne is his personal assistant, which gave us all a good chuckle. Gloria's title is Executive Secretary for FAFA, but she has her fingers in all the pies, because she has an excellent head for business. Jamie is in charge of all phases of transportation. We work well together; everyone wants to do the best job possible.

Fate took a heavy hand when it presented us with Jamie; a surprising and totally unexpected bonus. Jamie now runs the helicopter service for FAFA. He failed his physical for the RAF officers training program, because he is color blind, which no one ever suspected ... I suppose wearing a uniform of one kind or another most of his life, left him no opportunity for poor choices.

I was so proud of Thomas when he immediately offered him a job with the First Aide for Africa charitable corporation, as a helicopter pilot, and sent him to aviation school. Next month, Jamie will be up and running with a heliport, a staffed maintenance hangar for two helicopters and a nice canteen with barracks for four pilots; all built in the dead space down on the boundary road by the lime pit.

That's the change I like best … no more driving to the airport! Of course their main job will be to ferry personnel and supplies to the FAFA stations in the bush, but the helicopters will have to go to the airport to get those supplies. Paula smiled. It is an absolute wonder what one can do with a charitable corporation, unlimited funds, and a thousand acres.

Thomas has set up a school not far from the native village to teach young men and women first aid. The young people promise to give two years to a first aid station somewhere in the bush in exchange for the training. Thomas is hoping they will like the work and will stay on with an increased salary. He has more applicants than he expected, and we are now looking for more qualified teachers.

All the children of the workers have gone to school and some parents had paid for their children to go to school in Nairobi for higher education. It is these young people who have heard of the opportunity to work for the charitable corporation and those still living at Dela-Aden who have presented themselves to Thomas, asking if they could qualify. Sir Peter was over the moon when he heard of their response … a vindication and affirmation of his long years of going against the flow.

Sir Peter spends an hour or two after the inspection ride each day helping to enroll the applicants. I help out at lunch time. I reserve the mornings for work on my thesis. I hope to be finished by next spring. Our afternoon inspection ride has become even important, because we now discuss the FAFA happenings of the day

★   ★   ★

"Peter, come walk with me in the gardens, we haven't done that in a long time."

"It's certainly the perfect evening for a stroll."

"Peter, from here you can see the guest cottage. It has a marvelous view, don't you think?"

"Yes, I imagine that is why they built it there. I did some deed research when I planned to build the winery. That old guest house was the original farmhouse on the Land Grant, did I tell you that?"

"No. I thought the manor that my grandfather built was the Land Grant house."

"No, there was a previous owner. The first owner of the Land Grant built the guest house, and like some others, he was unable to meet the requirements stipulated to keep the Land Grant, and so lost it to your grandfather."

"I can't imagine that you didn't tell me this before."

"I'm sure I meant to, but building the winery fully occupied me at the time; I guess I forgot. The Land Grant cottage had a summer kitchen building at the rear with a walkway to the house. When the kitchen burned down, your grandfather built the manor house, and the farmhouse became a guest cottage."

"Does that mean the building has historic significance?"

"For Dela-Aden it does. It was the qualifying structure for the original land grant."

"It is providential that you brought the subject up this evening. I was thinking of razing the guest house and building a nice modern bungalow on that site for us."

"Why would you do that?" Peter asked, stunned. "We have a perfectly lovely home."

"I was thinking we would give the manor house to Hanna and Sara, allowing the girls to take over as chatelaines, and have a nice, smaller place for ourselves."

"You know, Mary; I actually like that idea, but we need to pick another site for the new house. What would you think of building it in the manner of the winery, stucco over building block, with tile floors and roof?"

"I see that you been giving the idea some thought too."

"A bit; the young married couples will quickly outgrow the guest cottage, if they haven't already. Wolfgang and Friedrich need proper offices, and the girls won't have to commute to practice."

"My, you have given the idea more than casual thought. Do you have an alternate site in mind?"

"What about building on the east lawn — west of the sepele tree line? That is a five acre tract; you could even put in the swimming pool you have talked about. We would then be between Thomas and the girls, and still have the land grant building as a guest house."

"Peter, those are marvelous ideas. Have you been thinking about this for very long?"

"Yes, I guess I have. Those young men now have a full plate: managing their own Trust, training horses and working positions on the FAFA Board. They need proper offices, and once the children start arriving, the guest house will become impossible for them ... if it isn't already too cramped. I want them to be happy here. I want them to feel as much a part of this family as Thomas and Paula do. I don't want them to ever regret being here."

"And to think, you were once worried that they were here for a free ride ... "

"I hope all my misgivings turn out so well," Peter smiled, a bit abashed.

"Those young men are different from you, dear. They have had niches carved out for them their entire lives, which they did not want, and from which they have escaped to a life they chose. I don't think they will ever want to leave Dela-Aden. Our cup runneth over, we are truly blessed. I think they are more than satisfied with being here. However, you are right. They do need more space and the manor house will provide it for them.

"Now that the kimmea has proven viable when grown in hothouses, and the charitable corporation is organized, with Thomas recruiting more staff to teach courses for the first-aid clinics, we are all quite involved," Mary said. "I'm glad we changed our wills so that Thomas inherits Dela-Aden, for Jon will inherit Woleston Hall when he is twenty-five. The codicil which provides a home here for Hanna and Sara was a good idea too. Adding a codicil to accommodate the FAFA Charitable Trust was a good idea too, for it protects the girls both ways.

"Yes, the Trust was certainly a big change for all of us; more so for Cyril who accepted the job as Chairman of the Board, which required him to phase out his public law practice in Nairobi. Although moving out to Dela-Aden pleased Sallee Anne to no end. It was a good idea to assign them the twenty acres out by the gate as a wedding present, for use in their lifetimes. It is convenient to the highway and still close to us," Peter added.

"Yes," Mary agreed. "Sallee Anne so liked Thomas and Paula's house that they built the same house using James's drawings, with a small change to accommodate a concert grand piano! I was very pleased when Sallee Anne built a little two bedroom cottage adjoining the main house for Gloria, who is a truly loyal person; she deserved that kindness."

"Yes, Gloria has worked for Cyril since she finished business school … what eight years? She is so intelligent that Cyril seeks her opinions. While their cottage is close to the airfield, I was surprised that Gloria offered her spare bedroom to Jamie.

I thought Jamie would want to stay in the barracks with the other pilots, and I was right. He needs to keep an eye on everything just now, to keep a firm hold on the reins of his new steed … letting him know who is boss.

"Sallee Anne has a passion for design and it was evident in her revisions of the floor plans," Peter added. "She built the rain water cisterns of concrete with a pond in the center of the flower gardens to take the overflow, with a water pressure fountain spraying the flowers. The matching one-storey buildings slightly above ground level on either side of the main house – one for garages, and one for Gloria's house – make it very elegant looking."

"Talent and good taste just ooze from that gal," Mary agreed.

★   ★   ★

"I'm sorry," Hanna said to Sara. "I can't focus today. I'm still excited by the surprise Mother sprang on us this morning when we came up to practice."

"I know! Wait until our fellows hear about it! However, it makes eminent good sense. We will need the space eventually, and they will be more comfortable all on one floor. Dad has fallen in love with the southwest style of the winery and wants to replicate it in a house. He's all excited about putting hot water pipes from the fireplace under the tiled floors for heat in all the rooms, not just for the hot water tank. They will have the same lovely view from there as we do from the verandah on the manor house. It is one of the prettiest spots at Dela-Aden with its view of the pastures, the tea fields and the grapevines with the winery in the distance," Sara said.

"Wolfgang and Friedrich will be stunned!" Hanna added. "I know they are feeling a bit cramped in the guest house … although I love cozy, and it is that."

"I think the guest house worked out very well for us," Sara added. "The men both use the second bedroom on each floor as an office, and we each had our private bedrooms and baths on different floors, which gave us all plenty of privacy. However, you are right, everything else is done in the small living room/dining area. It's a good thing we all get on well together. You and Wolfy can have the master suite, Rick and I will take the guest room suite. He can use the upstairs library as an office, unless they decide to share the downstairs office."

"I feel like the Blue Danube today, how about you?" Hanna asked.

"Yes! That's what we need … the gay and free Blue Danube Waltz!"

★   ★   ★

"You're off your game today, Wolfy. I've beat you straight sets, and I do believe that's a first for me."

"I can't concentrate! I'm too stunned … aren't you?"

"Yes, completely – but not as stunned as you are, for I can still play tennis."

"Rick, let's take a breather in the shade, okay?"

"Sure. A winner always feels magnanimous."

"Rick, are you happy here?"

"More than you can know, and it's all because you made me make up my mind. Once I took the bull by the horns, I felt unimaginably free. It was my indecision that was making a slave of me. I've never ever felt so free – yet never been so tied down. Does that make sense to you?"

"In a way, although I don't feel tied down, I feel committed – as I did when I was at the Spanish Riding School – and as then, I'm gaining by leaps and bounds from my efforts."

"Yes, that's a good way to express it. Sara is such a minx she keeps me on my toes, and I'm more involved with life now than ever before. Each day is a novelty of some kind or other – like I'm on some kind of perennial Easter egg hunt."

364

"What a year it has been, too! A year ago we were arriving for a visit," Wolfgang said, "and in a year, we are nearly the masters of all we survey? I feel the need to do something to *pay my dues* for my good fortune in life, but I haven't a clue. Do you have any ideas?"

"What about a music school for the children at Dela-Aden? The natives have a great sense of music; we might even find some unknown talent among them."

"Rick! Sometimes, you are positively brilliant. Let's see what Sir Peter and Lady Mary have to say about your idea."

★   ★   ★

"Gregor, did you read this letter from Wolfgang?"

"Yes, extremely interesting isn't it?"

"I'm stunned. He says they have found a child prodigy in the native village on Dela-Aden. His name is Joshua. He is nine years old, writes and speaks English and Swahili, knows his sums and plays the ocarina with all the finesse of a flute. He can duplicate any song that he hears, but he cannot read music. They are taking the boy under their wings and want to start a music school at Dela-Aden. For now, Hanna and Sara and Sallee Anne are taking turns teaching, but they say they need a permanent teacher."

"They want to have the next Board Meeting at Dela-Aden in August. What do you think of that?" Gregor asked.

"I'd love to visit Dela-Aden, and see a bit more of Africa. August is a good time for me to get away – how about you?" Elizabeth asked.

"I'm glad you finally want to visit Dela-Aden and see a bit more of Africa. It's what I have wanted to do since we were in Morocco."

"Greg! You are a hopeless romantic … and I love you for it!"

★   ★   ★

"Charles, read this letter from Sallee Anne!"

"What does she say?

"Read it, you will be so amazed."

"You were right, I'm amazed and delighted. I'll put the yacht in dry dock early, unless Eric wants to use it. That way we will have a nice fall competition season. How is Eric's friend, Patty working out? Have you asked Eric if he could stay here and take care of the horses, yet?"

"First, Patty is working out fine. She now brings her sister, Bernie, with her to keep her company when conditioning the horses for us. Both are delighted to have horses to ride in return for keeping to my schedule, and Patty keeps a good daily log. And, yes, Eric would stay to look after the horses. The student rooms at New Bolton are small. He likes being here by himself; it is only the commute he doesn't like, especially if he's called for emergencies."

"I'm glad they chose early August. That way, I won't miss any of the faculty meetings – which is always a bad way to start a school year."

"They expect their house to be finished at the end of July."

"Does it have to be finished? We could stay in the guest house, now that the girls have moved up to the big house. Didn't you say Peter and Mary built a bungalow next to Paula and Thomas? The guest house might be better anyway; closer to the activities of the farm."

"I'll drop Sallee Anne a line. I agree; it will put too much pressure on her to get the house ready for company, especially if there are any construction delays. I don't think Elizabeth and Gregor will mind sharing with us, do you?"

"Why don't you call, or send a telegram? I still need to make plans. By the by, what do you think of this fellow, Cyril?" Charles asked.

"He is charming. It wasn't what I wanted for Sallee Anne, but you never know where you will find love, and Sallee Ann is very much in love. I was saddened when she told me they had decided not to have children. They like their lives as they are, traveling around the world for concerts. It's probably the right decision for them."

"What do you think of the charitable corporation Thomas and Paula have set up?" Charles asked.

"It's a stupendous thing! I'm so impressed. Paula said they have more money than they can ever spend – can you imagine that?" Lisa replied.

"No, I can't," and Charles laughed, "but I like thinking about it. You know, I can't wait to go to Africa … just tell Sallee Anne we can only come at the end of July, before school starts."

"I'll do just that. I can't wait to see Dela-Aden – half of our children are in Africa!"

★   ★   ★

"Cyril, why are you smiling like a Cheshire cat?"

"Am I? It's not surprising, but it is plausible. I was thinking how happy I am. I was marveling at all the changes in my life – which I never imagined, even in my most outrageous thoughts. Are you not a bit overwhelmed?"

"I am completely confounded, but not overwhelmed, just overawed, with a teeny bit of happiness tossed in for good measure!"

"Why just a 'teeny bit of happiness'?"

"Because the *overwhelmed* and *overawed* don't leave much room for anything else – even gross happiness."

"Come over here and sit beside me; I like having you close."

"I can't see you if I sit beside you."

"My intention entirely. Then I can continue to smile like a Cheshire cat, and get away with it!"

"We don't have much time. Mary and Peter have invited us to a family dinner for *news*, but she gave me no hint at all as to what it might be. Do you know?"

"No! Now that I'm a neighbor, I seem to know nothing of what is going on. I suppose that is how one treats a neighbor – I don't know for certain – I've never been a neighbor before … although, now that I think on it, you might say I was once a neighbor in …

"Stop! Just Stop!"

"What? Is something wrong?"

"No, but we just don't have the time for you to do a treatise on being a neighbor! We have to go and get changed … " Sallee Anne laughed.

"Of course, I know that! I don't want to waste my time doing a treatise when I could be doing something far nicer!"

★   ★   ★

"Thomas, did I tell you that Marga'ret and James are coming for a visit in July? Mom and Dad are coming, and so are Elizabeth and Gregor. It's going to be so wonderful to have them here. I wish Jon and Anna were coming too. Although, in his last letter, Jon said Anna was finally healing – that she doesn't have bad dreams anymore. I think it was his way of saying they are not coming back to Africa."

"We must be thankful that we will see them each year at Boxing Day. Jon loves Africa, but he loves Anna more, we must accept that." Thomas said softly.

"I've had an idea," Paula said. "Why don't we make those in the family that have been helping us with advice and expertise, members of the FAFA board? That way FAFA can pay their travel expenses to Africa, or Livorno, for board meetings."

"We ought to run that by Cyril at dinner, but I think it is a positively grand idea."

"And we could pay them an honorarium too. It would be nice to share our good fortune with our families, especially those who have advised us so well. FAFA has more money than Croesus. Would you mind spreading it around?"

"It's the only thing worthwhile doing with money – spreading it around – we'll see what Cyril thinks."

Paula snuggled in tight with Thomas, and said, "Would you like a surprise?"

"What kind of a surprise? We interviewed three new teachers this morning and I'm desperate for a nap. I'm not cut out for all this business stuff, it wears me down."

"The surprise can wait – maybe another three, maybe four months, I suppose; then I won't be able to keep it a surprise any longer."

"It's just that I'm so … what did you say? Did you say what I think you said?"

"I think I did say what you thought I said, but I'm not sure, of what I said that you thought I said, or what you thought when I said it." Paula laughed.

Thomas chuckled too, and held her close as he laid his hand gently over her tummy, saying, "When do you expect the baby to arrive?"

368

"Nine months from our first anniversary should be about right. Not to burst your bubble of happiness, I still want to go to the States to birth the baby and I want to leave after we go to Woleston Hall for Boxing Day. I know that is longer than you will want to be gone, but I don't want to fly after the beginning of my last trimester."

"I will go with you whenever you want to go. I agreed to that before we were married, and I will abide by my agreement. Dad and Mom can look after things while we are gone."

"It will be a nice vacation for us. We can hire a coach and driver like Cyril and Sallee Anne did and tour the southern states to avoid the nasty, cold winter weather of January and February in Pennsylvania until the last two weeks."

"Umm-hum," Thomas replied automatically, completely lost in the rapturous thoughts of becoming a father.

★　　★　　★

How can things get any better? Jamie thought. Mom, Dad, Edith, Alice and George are coming in July. By then we will have things ship shape here to go to the airport to pick them up. I wonder if they will be worried with me as the pilot. I told them I was top man in aviation school, and my instructors said I had a knack for flying helicopters that they didn't often see. It was like riding a horse – I never had to learn to do that either, it just came naturally to me. Of course, like flying there were all the fine points to absorb. I am so happy here at Dela-Aden. I have work I love, and in the evenings, we often get together and play two pianos, two violins, oboe, and now the lad, Joshua, joins us with his ocarina. Hanna and Sara have adapted some classical pieces for us, although Joshua does not yet read music.

Sallee Anne is planning on all of us going to the Aspen Summer Music Festival next year. I'd really like that! I like teaching the lad Joshua too. He is simply marvelous. Anything I can play, he can duplicate. He doesn't yet see the point in reading music, he still thinks it is silly; ' … why bother to write the notes down when you can just hear them and remember them?' He had to think about it when I told him there was music he would never hear, but if he learned to read the notes, he would be able to play it. That seemed to get his attention.

What a year this has been ... from our awful abduction to being rejected by the RAF, to sitting my exams early so I could start flight school in the new year ... to having my own helicopters, pilots, and heliport. A year that started out badly has ended up being simply fantastic!

Well, family dinner tonight. Better go and get cleaned up. It will be nice to see Gloria again. She's not family, thank goodness, but she's an important part of the charitable corporation, which is a family trust. Sallee Anne and Cyril seem to be taking good care of her; still, she is living all alone. Maybe I should have taken her up on her offer of the second bedroom, but I feel I need to be in the barracks with the men until we get used to one another and a proper routine. When I see her tonight, I think I'll ask her over to dinner, to show her the place. Yes! That's what I'll do. We'll have a cook-out. The fellows will enjoy that too. Maybe I'll ask Thomas and Paula too, have another girl around, yes that would be proper and Thomas can see how well we have organized everything. With a mission in mind, Jamie rushed off to get ready for dinner.

★   ★   ★

"Mary, are you content with the house? Did things turn out as you expected?"

"It is even better than I expected, dear. The hot water pipes under the floors are a delight. Even my cold feet like the warmth. I love living on one floor; the layout that James designed for us makes it feel like several small houses attached to one another. And the generator for electric lights is simply delightful. It was a good idea to put a two thousand gallon petrol tank in a concrete bunker to serve the generators of the four houses as long as we were building one for the heliport. I was surprised when Hanna and Sara said they did not want electric lights in the manor house ... that they liked it the way it is. I do agree with them about the ambiance of those Victorian Era oil lamps. They only installed electricity in the kitchen and baths.

"Are you still looking forward to our transition cruise from Alaska?" Peter asked.

"Yes, of course, I'm sorry it didn't work out time-wise for you to do the spring transition cruise, as you had planned. You will still see the grape harvest though. Why do you ask? Is it because you think I will hate to leave my delightful new house."

"It used to be you hated to leave the horses."

"I know, but with Wolfgang and Friedrich here, the horses will be kept in training, so I have nothing to worry about. The progress of the young horses is positively exciting. Did I tell you we now have more buyers for young horses, than we have horses to sell? I was thinking of adding another Andalusian mare. The most popular horses are the Andalusian/Arabian geldings. I know of an Andalusian mare that drops only colts, but she is expensive."

"There was a time when that was a considering factor, which now no longer exists. Is there another reason you are hesitant?"

"The mare is flighty. Sometimes her progeny are flighty too. Friedrich says that a flighty mare is a scared mare, and he feels proper training will rid her of the problem. He and Wolfgang are going to look at her next week, after we are gone."

"Well, I must be getting old, for I haven't looked forward to anything as much as I do this cruise – since I was getting my first car" ... he looked at Mary and quickly added ... "or since I was getting my first wife!"

"Better zip it up, Pete, before you get yourself into some real trouble!"

They laughed, and laughed, and laughed some more. Life was good!

★   ★   ★

The twelve of them enjoyed the first family meal under the new chatelaines' supervision and finished coffee and dessert in the dining room, before retiring to the Library for an after-dinner liqueur.

Peter stood up saying, "We are gathered here this evening to share some delightful news, and to express our wishes for the order of things while we are away. First, the order of things: Cyril will manage the estate in our absence, as he is the one with the most business acumen. Cyril and Thomas must agree on all changes. We don't want to find ourselves disenfranchised when we come home. Hearty laughter greeted this remark, for Peter rarely made jokes.

Mary has left Wolfgang and Friedrich in charge of the horses, however, Paula must agree to any changes, so Mary will not come home to find Diablo-Airé or Midnight Rider sold and Lipizzaners in their stalls. Again, hearty laughter, with a few knowing smirks.

"We are looking forward to our first extended vacation and cruise. We know all is in good hands here. We are pleased that each family is happy in their circumstances at Dela-Aden. We are delighted to tell you that Thomas and Paula expect their first child next March ... which will make us grandparents! Instead of feeling older, Mary and I feel positively young."

Sir Peter paused for the delight, and well-wishes, before saying, "Each new day takes us into the future ... that is life ... however, a glimpse today of the joy of tomorrow, makes us content with today, as we move *ever onward*."

~THE END~

Living in Africa – Reference Lists

Main Characters:

Caulfield, Paula Thornton	b. 1935/m. Thomas Caulfield 5/17/60-Oxford, PA
Caulfield, Thomas Peter	b. 1937/lost 1947-1960/legally dead 1955/a.k.a. Tamubu (Sweet Gift) Medicine Man-Artist

Family Characters:

Caulfield, Jonathan	b.1939 (Jon)-Oxford 1958/African Languages
Caulfield, Hanna & Sara	b.1942-twins-younger sisters of Thomas & Jon
Caulfield, Lady Mary	Mother: nee-Woleston/Dela-Aden/Kenya, Africa
Caulfield, Sir Peter	Father: m. Mary 1933/Dela-Aden-Kenya, Africa
Sotheby, Aunt Marga'ret	Lady Mary's sister-Woleston Hall-Lyford, England
Sotheby, Uncle James	Marga'ret's husband/Horseman-Architect
Sotheby, James	b.1939 (Jamie)-music, polo/helicopter pilot
Sotheby, George	b.1941/sports enthusiast/Athlete
Sotheby, Alice	b.1943/self-preoccupied-Croft School
Sotheby, Edith	b.1945/Horseman-Sports-Croft School
Woleston, Jane Nelson	American wife of John Woleston-dec'd 1943 Brother to Lady Mary & Marga'ret

Other Characters:

Ahmed	House boy in Morocco – Wedding
Albert (Reilly)	Butler & Chauffeur at Woleston Hall
APCO	Asher Pharmaceutical Company
Archer, Alfred Bates	Groom in Morocco wedding-m. Regina Schmidt
Andrews	Former head gardener-Woleston Hall
Athos, Petrides	Owner: *Gallant Lady* - Unscrupulous tycoon
Bemis, Nathaniel	Elmer Schmidt's tutor – Writer
Betsy (McBurke)	Kitchen maid – Woleston Hall, England
Bradley, Phil & Evelyn	Dela-Aden neighbor-sister of Dr. Matthews
Brompton	Retired butler at Woleston Hall
Cleary, Mrs.	Retired Housekeeper at Woleston Hall

Other Characters – Continued:

Dela Aden-Barn	Pompito: Head lad/Suffo & Abumi: Stable boys
Elizabeth (Reilly)	Cook at Woleston Hall/husband, Albert
Evans, Cmdr. Ethan	Pilot/Wife-Rita/Son, Sean/Flew Edith to Ireland
George & Harold	Tour bus hosts – U.S.A. –Wolfgang & Friedrich
Greystone, Lord Edward	Diplomatic Service-India, twenty years to 1950
Greystone, Lady Elspeth	nee Sommes-1st cousin-Lady Mary & Marga'ret
Holmesby, Anna Louise	b.1942 Swindon, Eng./Croft School/Jon's Love
Holmesby, Harold	Horticulturist/m. Julia - father of Anna Louise
Holmesby, Julia	Principal-Croft School/Mother-Anna Louise
Julian	Sallee Anne's boyfriend-killed in auto accident
Kurt	Schönbrunn Palace pageboy
Latham, Esq., Cyril	Nairobi Attorney for Dela-Aden/Gloria, Sec'y
Lena (O'Daire)	b.1945 (Helena)-Irish classmate-Edith Sotheby
Lucinda	Alfred Bates' first wife-died of cancer
Lewiston, Phil & Kate	a.k.a. Kate Matthews-Paula's Advisor at Penn
Mabel (Brown)	Housemaid at Woleston Hall
Matthews, Dr. Kate	a.k.a. Mrs. Phillip Lewiston-Paula's advisor
Mortons	Neighbors at Dela-Aden
O'Connor, Jack	Stable Mgr. Woleston Hall
O'Daire, Captain Liam	Lena's father/Manager-Shannon Airport, Ireland
Patty & Bernie	Exercise riders for Lisa & Charles Thornton
Phillips, Mr.	Bloodhounds for search at Dela-Aden
Prodigies:	Ruth-PA-piano/Michael-CA-violin/Joshua-
Ocarina	
Raft, Georgina	Asst. Principal – The Croft School
Raft, Robert	Georgina's husband-Marlborough-Berkshire, Eng.
Rice, Mrs.	Music Teacher – The Croft School
Schmidt, Elmer	Son of Regina/Friedrich's cousin/girlfriend-Beth
Schultz, Gregor	Wolfgang's brother-in-law/ half sister-Elizabeth
Scroggins	Dude Ranch owner-Basalt, Colorado
Smith, Max	Henchman for Petrides Athos-Tycoon
Springer, Hank DVM	Vet/Windy-Afghan hound pup /Florence, Sec'y
Suzie (Brown)	Housemaid – Woleston Hall
Tilly (Murphy)	Laundress – Woleston Hall (Matilda)
Tomison	New head gardener – Woleston Hall
Victoria (Sims)	Housekeeper – Woleston Hall
Von Hauptsborg, Friedrich	Vienna/1st cousin to Wolfgang /Violin
Von Hauptsborg, Wolfgang	Baron/Vienna/1st cousin to Friedrich/Oboe
Wainwright, Esq.	Edmund/Caulfield atty – Woleston Hall Estate

Native Characters:

Abumi	Barn boy at Dela-Aden
Aku	Zuri Watu boy
Benima	Manutu's 1ˢᵗ son-follow Sashono as Chief
Cenye	Woman helper to Chief Sashono
Kenga	Manutu's 2ⁿᵈ son- works as Medicine Man
Loufa	Zuri Watu pregnant woman
Minba & Sombutu	Kidnap Jamie & Ann Lou for Petrides Athos
Ngarro	Zuri Watu emissary to Archaeologists by sea
Pompito	Head boy at Dela-Aden barn
Mohboa	Manutu's wife-mother of Benima & Kenga
Samuel	Retired field hand-cares for kimmea plants
Simmons, Mr.	Estate Manager at Dela-Aden
Sombutu & Minba	Squatters/kidnapped Jamie & Anna Louise
Sufo	Barn boy at Dela-Aden
Usuku Wanaume	Cannibalistic tribe of cave dwarfs
Waridi	Rose – name of death mask child

Places:

The Croft School	Bath, Somerset, Eng./School for girls 14-20
Bedercroft Estate	Bath, Somerset – The Croft School since 1948
Greystone Place	London, England/Lavish home – India décor
Woleston Hall	Clarke Lane/The Cotswolds-Lyford, Berkshire
Walberry Hill	Cliff-top overlook and picnic spot- England

Other Names:

Diablo-Aire	Lady Mary's Arabian stallion
Foxy	Fox terrier dog of Thomas's & Jon's childhood
Midnight Rider	Sir Peter's Saddlebred mare
Spice	Julia Holmesby's Thoroughbred mare
Sunshine	Paula's Arabian-Saddlebred Palomino mare
	Gift from Lady Mary & Sir Peter
The Cisco Kid	Edith's Arabian-Saddlebred Piebald gelding
The Sultan	Unruly horse-Woleston Hall-retrained by Paula
Windy	'Son of the Wind'-Thomas' Afghan hound puppy
Rolls Royce	1934 Silver Ghost- legacy to James Sotheby from Rebecca Alice Clarke Cecil

Glossary:

Afisa	Aide
Akufaa	Fitting or apt
Boxing Day	Christmas – England
Bromby	Brombies – Australian wild horses
Bwana	Sir
De-rigueur	The rule- necessary - required to do
E.C.T.R.A.	Eastern Competitive Riding Assn. – U.S.A.
FAFA	First Aid For Africa – Charitable Corporation
Fingirisha	Lunch roll-ups
Golfo di Genova	Gulf of Geneva
Haya	Okay
Herufi	Alphabet
Jamais-vu	A feeling of seeing something for the first time
Jambo habibi	Hello, Mr. (husband)
Jambo bibi	Hello, Mrs. (wife)
Kibanda	Hut/Abode (native)
Kizimu-akili	Spirit Walker – Spirit Talker
Kujua-akili	Transcendentalist
Majicho	*Sharp Eyes* – nickname for Afghan hound pup
Maji-moto	Hot water
Mauvais mot	Spoken bad word
Megrims	Feeling out-of-sorts/depressed
Mkebibi	Lady wife
Mtu Mpya	Neophyte
Mti	Tree
Mwana	Mistress
Ndugu	Brother
Petit farine	Small meal
Pfefferneuse	German anise cookie balls
Pumba	Testicles
Sous chef	Soup chef - second in command- kitchen
Staajabu	Be amazed
Raison d'etre	Reason to be
Sebula	Open roofed porch – gazebo
Sisimizi	Black ant
Spaetzel	Hungarian noodle garnish for vegetables
Uumenea	Penis cover (Pygmy)
Vipande	Sandwiches
Walinka	Knob-end throwing club

CPSIA information can be obtained at www.ICGtesting.com
Printed in the USA
BVOW072036300112

281758BV00002B/1/P